URBAN LEGENDS

URBAN LEGENDS

666 ABSOLUTELY TRUE STORIES THAT HAPPENED TO A FRIEND . . . OF A FRIEND . . . OF A FRIEND

BY
THOMAS J. CRAUGHWELL

Black Dog & Leventhal
Paperbacks

Published by
Black Dog and Leventhal Publishers, Inc.
151 West 19th St.
New York, NY 10011

Cover design by Edward O'Dowd
Interior design by Filip Zawodnik
Cover photographs courtesy of Getty Images and Picturequest

Manufactured in the United States

ISBN-13: 978-1-57912-466-3

h g f e

Library of Congress Cataloging-in-Publication Data
is on file at Black Dog & Leventhal Publishers, Inc.

ACKNOWLEDGMENTS

Usually when I write a book I wind up spending most of my time in libraries. The best place to find urban legends, however, is not in a reference room but in e-mail from family and friends.

I am especially grateful to my sister Karen Jeffreys and her fellow "Teamsters" at the firm of Cole, Schotz, Meisel, Forman and Leonard, and my brother-in-law John Varda, who is always willing to help me make a buck. Dave Feeney, Jim Feeney, Christine Feeney, Kevin Donovan, Teresa Gibbons, Candis LaPrade, and Rob and Sandra Sesink-Clee supplied what turned out to be some of my favorite stories in this collection. Msgr. Richard R. Soseman proved to be an especially rich source for urban legends. My thanks to them all.

Finally I would like to recognize two tireless cheerleaders for my urban legend books: Sean Donovan and Megan Charlton. May they never encounter alligators in a sewer, nor have an insect crawl into their ears and eat its way to their brains.

Contents

Introduction

*There may be some Americans who don't know the name of the
vice president of the United States, but virtually every American
knows that the sewers of New York are full of alligators, that the
cute little Chihuahua a tourist picked up in Mexico was really
a rat, and that a foolish woman tried to dry her poodle in a
microwave oven.*

*These stories are known as urban legends, or urban myths,
or modern folklore. Like all folklore, they are passed by word
of mouth, or—in today's world—e-mail. Urban legends are
ultimately ubiquitous. Everybody knows at least a few.*

*My personal favorite is "The Stolen Kidney." In this
story, a business traveler ventures into some barely developed
Third World country and is seduced by a local lovely. Said
seductress then drugs the businessman and cuts out a kidney
to sell on the black market. This is one of the classic urban
legends. Professional folklorists define a pure urban legend by
three qualifying factors: It is a story of unknown origin, it is*

demonstrably untrue and it uses either humor or something fairly gruesome to teach a lesson about what happens to people who disregard the taboos of Judeo-Christian civilization. Thus, according to the hard-hearted code of classic urban legends the businessman who opted for a one-night stand with some floozy deserved to lose his kidney. And let that be a lesson to you!

A common theme in these tales is the fear that some frightening or dangerous foreign element will invade the human body. New homeowners find a cask of excellent brandy in the cellar and never suspect that the barrel holds a corpse. While a woman sleeps, a pregnant female insect crawls into her ear and lays its larvae inside the victim's skull. A girl checks the coin slot at a pay phone and is stabbed by an HIV-infected needle. In urban legends, the most innocent action is fraught with peril. Many urban legends have this distinctly dark cast to them. Fear, paranoia, envy, suspicion of the unfamiliar—all the baser elements of human nature—find an outlet in urban legends.

Adolescents and college students seem to have a preference for gruesome urban legends. For example, "The Psycho Upstairs" or "Mass Murder on Campus." Favorites tend to be horrible stories of young lovers who look for a secluded spot where they can do a little necking and find a grisly death instead. The plots of these horror legends are something out of Edgar Allen Poe, but the tellers invariably try to make them convincing by supplying details of

time and place that their audience will recognize, relate, and react more strongly to.

Of course, it's not all mayhem on campus. College-based urban legends also celebrate the clever student ("He Should Have Been More Specific") and the unexpected windfall ("The Suicide Rule"), and take satisfaction in seeing wise guys and cheaters get their dues ("Late for Finals" and "I Like It Better Each Time").

Urban legends feed our fantasies as well as our fears. One of the most enduring themes of these stories is luck-changing encounters with celebrities. A good Samaritan stops to help a limo that's broken down on rainy night, and has his mortgage paid in full by Donald Trump.

Like all folklore, urban legends change over time. A classic example of the evolution of an urban legend is the story of the black man on the elevator who is mistaken for a mugger. In its earliest known version, the man turns out to be Reggie Jackson. Jan Harold Brunvand, the acknowledged guru of urban legends, has collected variants in which the "mugger" is Jesse Jackson or Michael Jackson. Other versions are linked to the increasing popularity of a black performer, such as Eddie Murphy or Lionel Richie. There is even a bizarre variant in which the "threatening" black man turns out to be Lionel Hampton, the 80-something jazz musician. This story is still told today, but with Mike Tyson in the starring role.

It would be a mistake to adopt the stance of a purist and regard alternate versions as corruptions of classic urban legends. In fact, variants are an essential component of folklore. After all, these stories aren't memorized verbatim like the Pledge of Allegiance or the Our Father. Urban legends are fluid, and tellers adapt them to reflect their own era, their own preferences, even their own fears or prejudices. The legend known as "The Enormous Bouffant" dates back to a time when the eponymous hair style was very popular. Now that the bouffant has gone out of style, it's not uncommon to hear the story told with the substitution of a middle-aged woman with no fashion sense, or a young man with unruly hair, or even a Rastafarian with dreadlocks. Variants keep urban legends alive, and keep folklore scholars in business.

So enjoy the legends, customize as needed, and be sure to savor them with a grain of salt.

THE CURSED MUMMY
AND OTHER
SUPERNATURAL ENCOUNTERS

The Cursed Mummy

In the late 1890s a party of four well-to-do young English gentlemen made an extended tour of archaeological excavations in Egypt. One evening in the bar of their hotel in Luxor, they met an antiquities dealer who engaged them in a lively conversation about archaeology and some of the artifacts he had acquired over the years.

"In fact," said the dealer, "I've just purchased an exquisite sarcophagus that contains the intact mummy of a princess of the Thirteenth Dynasty. It is the crown jewel of my collection. Would you like to see it?"

The young gentlemen said they were very eager to see the sarcophagus. "Please come to my warehouse tomorrow morning about nine," the dealer said.

At exactly nine o'clock the next morning, the dealer met the four travelers on the narrow street outside his warehouse. "Good morning!" he said as he shook each man's hand. "You're very punctual." Then, drawing a key from his pocket, he unlocked the warehouse door and threw it open. "Please come in," the dealer said.

The dealer led the young men through a labyrinth of wooden crates to a room at the rear of the building. Inside, standing upright in the middle of the small room, was the princess's sarcophagus. It was eight feet tall and inlaid with gold and semiprecious stones. On the lid was a portrait of the princess herself, her face serene and lovely, and her eyes wide open as if she were still alive.

"It's superb," one of the young men said.

"I think so, too," said the dealer.

For the next hour, the five men examined the sarcophagus closely. The dealer read the inscriptions for them and even opened the lid so his visitors could examine the mummy of the princess.

Then one of the Englishmen cleared his throat and said, "Would you . . . have you . . . considered selling the sarcophagus?"

The dealer seemed taken aback by the suggestion. But now all four of the young men pressed him to sell them the treasure. After some negotiation, the men settled on a price of ten thousand pounds sterling. They each wrote the dealer a check for £2,500 and asked him to have the sarcophagus packed up and sent to their hotel that evening as they were planning to begin their journey home to England the next day.

"Before we conclude our arrangement," the dealer said, "I should warn you that the mummy is said to be cursed. If you are having second thoughts, I will tear up the checks now without any hard feelings."

The gentlemen smiled, and one said, "Thank you. But none of us is superstitious."

Late in the day, the packing crate containing the sarcophagus arrived at the hotel. As three of the gentlemen met in the bar for drinks before dinner, they saw the fourth member of their party walking out toward the desert. They waited for him all that evening and looked for him the next morning. At last they went to the British consulate to report their friend missing. They notified the Luxor police, but a thorough investigation turned up no trace of the missing Englishman. He was never seen again.

From that moment, trouble seemed to haunt the young travelers. One was shot accidentally in the right arm as his servant packed

his hunting rifles. Although a surgeon from the British embassy in Cairo came to Luxor to treat the young man, the wound became gangrenous and the arm had to be amputated.

The third man in the foursome found on his return home that bad investments had destroyed his family's fortune.

The fourth man was struck down by an illness which no doctor in England could diagnose or cure.

Remembering the dealer's warning of a curse, the surviving travelers put the sarcophagus up for sale. They found a buyer almost immediately, a London businessman with a passion for Egyptian antiquities.

But no sooner had the sarcophagus been installed in the businessman's home than the curse struck again. His wife and two of his children were severely injured when their carriage overturned. Then the family's house caught fire, destroying every Egyptian artifact in their collection—except the sarcophagus.

Some days later, the *Times* reported that the British Museum had received a superb sarcophagus from an anonymous donor. As two workmen unloaded the sarcophagus in the museum courtyard, one of the men slipped and broke his leg. The other dropped dead two days later.

Now the princess's curse fell upon the British Museum. Night watchmen heard the sound of frantic hammering and sobbing from the coffin. Other artifacts displayed in the same gallery as the sarcophagus were hurled about by some unseen hand. A guard who witnessed the uncanny events died of fright. A charwoman who scoffed at the curse and flicked her dustcloth at the mummy's face lost her only child to a deadly case of measles.

By now, the newspapers had heard of the strange occurrences surrounding the princess's sarcophagus. A photographer who took a picture of the sarcophagus for his newspaper found when he developed the film that the serene image of the princess was replaced by a grotesque, horrifying face. The photographer hurried home, locked himself in his room and shot himself in the head.

The museum's curators ordered the sarcophagus to be kept in storage in the basement. Within days the foreman who had supervised the move was found dead at his desk.

A private collector with an interest in the occult purchased the sarcophagus from the British Museum and then invited the renowned spiritualist Madame Helena Blavatsky to perform an exorcism. After spending a few moments in the princess's presence, however, Madame Blavatsky hurried out of the room, saying, "No one can overcome such evil."

For 12 years, the sarcophagus passed from one owner to the next, leaving behind a trail of disasters and tragedies. Then an American archaeologist purchased the sarcophagus. The curse did not frighten him; he attributed all the misfortunes of the previous owners to the quirks of circumstance. In early April 1912, he arranged for the sarcophagus to be shipped to America and booked a stateroom for himself aboard the same ship—a luxurious new cruise ship of the White Star line that was making its maiden voyage to New York.

The name of the ship transporting the sarcophagus was *Titanic*.

The Bloody Rain

It was almost noon on a hot day in the beginning of July 1863. For a little over six hours, the slaves had been working in the tobacco fields of the Chandler farm in Tennessee. Mr. Chandler was entertaining a neighbor, Mr. Peyton, on the verandah when several field hands came running up to the house in panic. As they grew closer, Chandler and Peyton could see splotches of what looked like blood on the men's skin and clothes.

At first, the men were too worked up and out of breath to tell a coherent story. But finally one of them blurted out, "It's raining flesh and blood in the tobacco fields!"

The field hands described how a large red cloud had mysteriously appeared over them and covered the field with a gory rain. Although they were skeptical, Chandler and Peyton followed the slaves back to the field and waded into the tall rows of tobacco plants. To their amazement, they saw the tobacco leaves covered with dark red stains. Scattered on the ground were small whitish and grayish fragments that resembled fresh meat.

"It could be a hoax," Peyton said. "But just to be sure, let's collect some samples and take them over to the university in Nashville for analysis."

Chandler sent one of the field hands back to the house for two large cloth sacks. In one they put a few dozen stained tobacco leaves. In the other they put several handfuls of the fleshlike scraps. As they carried the bags of the samples out of the field, both men tried to ignore the putrid smell rising from the bag of fragments.

At the house, they washed up, then mounted their horses and rode to Nashville.

The laboratory of Nashville's Central University's science department was housed in a handsome stone building on Rutledge Hill. Chandler and Peyton found the chairman of the science department, Professor Jackson, told him their story and produced the two sacks.

"That's a wild story, gentlemen," Professor Jackson said.

"We don't believe it rained flesh and blood in my tobacco field," Chandler said, "but I would be obliged if you would analyze these samples for me."

"It will take a few hours to run the tests," Professor Jackson said. "Come back tomorrow and I will give you the results then."

"If it's all the same to you, Professor," Peyton said, "we'll wait."

A few hours later, a student found Chandler and Peyton walking about the campus and invited them to join Professor Jackson in his office. They found the professor standing beside his desk, looking uneasy.

"Well, gentlemen, I confess that I am perplexed by the results of my analysis," he said.

Chandler and Peyton kept silent, so Professor Jackson continued.

"The red stains on the tobacco leaves are most certainly blood." Professor Jackson paused for a moment before speaking again. "And those fragments are human flesh."

On the ride home, the two men discussed the professor's analysis.

"I still say it's a hoax," Chandler said.

"If I were a superstitious man," Peyton said, "I'd say this rain was a bad omen."

Before long, Peyton's instincts proved to be correct. The next day, both Chandler and Peyton received telegrams announcing that their sons had been killed at Gettysburg.

Variations: Tennessee folklore also tells of a mysterious inky darkness that descended on western Tennessee one day. A legend set in Memphis describes another odd rainstorm in which hundreds of snakes fell from the sky.

The Dying Man

One weekday morning on the North Side of Chicago, as Father Muller was removing his vestments after Mass, a woman appeared in the sacristy.

"Father, could you bring the last sacraments to my son," she said. "I know he will not live through the day. He lives at 1136 West Wellington."

"I'll go now," said the priest. "Wait here while I get the Host and the holy oil."

But when Father Muller returned to the sacristy, the woman was gone.

Nonetheless, he went out to his car and drove to the address the woman had given him. He found a parking spot near the house, walked up the front steps and rang the doorbell.

A healthy-looking young man in his late twenties answered.

"Can I help you Father?" he asked.

"I've come to give Last Rites," said the priest.

"You've got the wrong house, Father," the man said. "No one here is sick."

"A woman came to me only half an hour ago, gave me this address and told me a young man here was dying," Father Muller said.

"Father, I'm the only one who lives here, and I'm as healthy as a horse." But as the young man spoke, Father Muller looked over the man's shoulder and saw a photograph on the wall.

"That's the woman who came to see me," he said, pointing to the portrait.

The young man grew pale. "Why don't you come inside, Father."

Together they walked over to the photograph. "I'm certain this is the woman who asked me to bring the sacraments to this house. She said her son would not live to see another day."

"Father," said the young man, trembling now, "this is my mother. She's been dead for five years."

The two men were speechless for a moment. Then the young man said, "Father, maybe you should hear my confession and give me Communion after all."

A few hours after Father Muller had given him the last sacraments, the young man dropped dead of a massive heart attack.

The Devil's Tower

From Route 9 in northern New Jersey, one can see a tall Gothic stone tower. It is all that remains of a grand manor house that was torn down decades ago. Over the years the estate has been divided into lots, so today the decrepit tower rises incongruously at the end of a cul de sac lined with fine new houses.

Residents in the area call the relic the Devil's Tower.

Soon after the mansion was torn down, while the estate was still deserted, the tower caught the attention of a strange cult that mixed druid lore with Satanism. At the solstices and equinoxes, the members gathered at the tower for bloody rites. Children wandering around the empty estate often came across the gory remains of cats and goats.

The holiest day of the year for this cult was Samhain, the day we call Halloween. The druids had believed that on the night of Samhain, the barriers between earth and hell were removed and demons and the souls of the damned walked among the living.

"They are hungry for blood," the cult's leader told his band of followers. "And we will feed them."

In the days before Halloween, members of the cult began to visit the local high school, looking for a suitable victim. They wanted a girl—tall, clear skin, beautiful. Then they spotted Laura, the high school's homecoming queen.

On the afternoon of Halloween, several of the cult members drove to the high school in a black truck. They watched Laura leave the school with several friends. Driving very slowly, the cult

followed the girls at a distance. One by one, Laura's friends went down side streets to their own homes. When Laura was alone, the driver accelerated and pulled the truck onto the sidewalk in front of her, blocking her way. Before the girl knew what was happening, three men grabbed her and threw her into the back of the truck. They gagged her and tied her hands and feet while the driver turned the truck toward Devil's Tower.

That night, at midnight, when all the trick-or-treaters were safe in their beds, while the police went door to door through the town looking for anyone who had seen Laura, as Laura's frantic parents waited for some scrap of hopeful news, the cult gathered in the tower. They laid Laura on a cold stone slab, cut out her heart and splashed the walls of the tower chamber with her blood.

The next morning, when the police finally came to the tower, they found Laura's body. But the cult had vanished and were never seen in the area again.

Since that day, anyone who comes to the Devil's Tower on Halloween night will see a frightening apparition. At midnight, out of the mist emerges the ghostly form of a beautiful girl, dressed in a blood-soaked gown and screaming for someone to save her.

Variations: Some versions of the story say that if you walk backwards around the tower six times at midnight, the devil will appear.

The Light in the Church Tower

On a warm summer night in July 1921, a young couple walking along Pavonia Avenue in Jersey City, New Jersey, saw two pale lights in the bell tower of St. Joseph's Church.

"Look," said the woman. "There are lights on in the tower."

Her boyfriend glanced up. "Maybe it's a signal for Paul Revere," he said.

"Don't make jokes," the woman said. "They're eerie. They look like cat's eyes."

Soon more people along the avenue stopped to stare at the strange lights. As the crowd grew larger, one of the parish priests came out of the rectory.

"What's going on here?" he asked.

"See for yourself, Father," answered a man in the crowd as he pointed up to the tower.

"It's nothing," the priest said. "Someone's left the lights on in the tower. I'll go turn them off myself."

But by the time the priest got to the top of the tower, the two lights had disappeared.

Night after night, the "cat's eyes" appeared in St. Joseph's Tower. The sexton of the church decided he would get to the bottom of the mystery. He posted guards at the foot of the tower stairs. But they saw no one enter or leave. He removed all the light bulbs from the fixtures in the tower. But the cat's eyes still appeared. He scattered flour on the floor of the bell chamber. But whoever or whatever had been in the tower left no footprints.

The pale glimmering cat's eyes appeared for nine nights, and on the ninth night, the eyes showed a bloody red streak.

Standing among a crowd of spectators on the sidewalk, the church sexton said, "That's it. I'm going to the belfry."

The next morning, the church sexton was found sitting in the choir loft, dead. The cat's eyes disappeared and were never seen again.

The Prophetic Videotape

A newlywed couple went to San Francisco for their honeymoon. They filled up their days sightseeing and shopping, and every night they enjoyed long, leisurely dinners in the city's best restaurants. But after a week of nonstop activity, the couple were exhausted.

"Let's stay in tonight," the wife suggested. "The suite has a VCR, and there's a video store around the corner. We can have room service bring something up."

"Sounds good to me," the husband said. "I'll go get a movie. Do you have anything in mind?"

"Get something romantic," the wife said. "Rent that Demi Moore–Patrick Swayze movie."

"You mean *Ghost*?"

"Yeah," the wife said. "I'd like to see *Ghost*."

After dinner in their room, the couple stretched out on the bed to watch the video. The movie ended. The credits had finished rolling. But the husband couldn't find the remote to rewind the tape. Suddenly, Patrick Swayze appeared on the screen.

He looked straight at the woman on the bed and said, "Call your mother."

Then the screen went blank.

"That was weird," said the husband.

"Yeah." After a moment the wife said, "Maybe I should call home."

"What are you going to say? 'Hi Mom! Patrick Swayze said I should give you a call?'"

"Okay. It's weird. But I have a funny feeling about this."

"Forget about it," the husband said. "It's just some strange trailer."

"I guess," the wife said.

The husband rewound the tape while the wife put the tray of dinner dishes outside the door of the suite.

The next morning, while the wife was getting dressed, the phone rang.

The husband called from the bedroom, "Honey! Your brother wants to talk to you."

The wife picked up the phone. "Eddie? Is everything okay?"

"I'm sorry to do this to you," her brother said. "But you've got to come home. Mom died last night."

Variations: In a variant of this legend the movie is Always *and the star who speaks to the woman is Richard Dreyfus. When the husband takes the video back to the store, he tells the staff about the strange "trailer." They check the tape the man rented as well as every other copy of* Always *in the store, but none of them have the eerie message from Richard Dreyfus.*

Three Men and a Ghost

Studio executives deny this story completely. They insist the scene in question was filmed on a set in Toronto, not in a New York City apartment.

The 1987 movie *Three Men and a Baby* was filmed in various locations in New York City. One scene involving Ted Danson and Celeste Holm takes place inside a New York apartment. Behind the actors is a window, and in the window, standing behind a sheer curtain, is the indistinct figure of a little boy. Strangely enough, no one spotted the mysterious figure when the movie was playing in the theaters, but thousands have seen it on videotape.

The little boy is wearing jeans and a T-shirt. He is absolutely motionless. And leaning against the wall beside him is a rifle. At no time in the scene do Danson and Holm interact with the boy. They do not even seem aware that he is in the room with them. Nor does the little boy appear at any other point in the movie.

The cast and crew of *Three Men and a Baby* were mystified when they were shown the image on the videotape. And since the apartment was vacant when they rented it for the movie, they did not know who to turn to for a solution.

Finally, it was the superintendent of the building who solved the mystery. Not long before the movie was filmed there, he said, a little boy living in the apartment had accidentally shot and killed himself with his father's hunting rifle. His distraught parents could not bear to live in the place where their son had died, so they moved out of the apartment.

"I saw the parents yesterday," the super said. "They came by to see me. They had just rented *Three Men and a Baby*." Then he paused. "That's their little boy in the movie."

Mass Murder on Campus

One Halloween afternoon, Geraldo Rivera brought a renowned psychic onto his talk show. In the course of the interview, Rivera asked his guest, "Most of your predictions are for the distant future. Do you see anything we should be concerned about today?"

The psychic concentrated and then she said, "There's a university in the Midwest. It's a Big Ten school. I see a statue of Abraham Lincoln on a hill. There is a large lake at the foot of the hill. The school's name begins with 'W.' And I see red."

"Wisconsin," Rivera said. "Wisconsin's colors are red and white."

"No," said the psychic, "not the red of school colors. I see the red of blood. There's a murderer loose on the Wisconsin campus at Madison. And before the night is over, 12 students will be dead."

In Madison, the psychic's prediction caused a panic. Students who had planned to join the huge outdoor Halloween celebration on State Street that evening now ran for their cars and got out of town as fast as they could drive. Other students barricaded themselves in their dorms. Sponsors of the State Street Beer Bash announced that the party was off. But one of the fraternities refused to be intimidated. Halloween in Madison was one of the biggest events of the year, and the brothers were not going to miss it

because some psychic had predicted mayhem on campus. The guys let it be known that the party in their frat house was still on.

By nine o'clock, about 40 fearless partiers were doing shots in the frat house's cellar bar overlooking Lake Mendota. It was a small turn-out by Madison standards, but the hardy few were determined to have a good time anyway.

As the night wore on, one by one, the guests slipped off to find empty beds and sofas where they could pass out. By three in the morning, a dozen partiers remained in the cellar bar. The last one awake was the frat's president. He unlocked the sliding glass doors and stepped out onto the lakefront terrace. He was pretty drunk and he thought a little fresh air would clear his head. Then, after a few moments, he went back into the house, collapsed in a ratty recliner and fell asleep.

Late the next morning, one of the hungover brothers woke up in his room. The house was freezing. He stumbled downstairs to see if the heater's pilot light had gone out in the night. In the cellar bar he found the sliding doors to the lakefront terrace wide open. Twelve bloody corpses were scattered around the room.

Variations: Virtually every college has a version of this legend and tailors the details to fit the school. In its original form, Jeanne Dixon, the renowned psychic of the 1960s, predicts the murders.

The Phone in the Crypt

A wealthy man named James Ball had a morbid fear of being buried alive. When he had his mausoleum constructed in Boston's Mount Auburn Cemetery, he arranged for a telephone to be installed in his crypt.

In time, Mr. Ball died. His widow, accompanied by a great crowd of relatives, friends and business associates, followed Mr. Ball's body to the grand limestone tomb.

After the funeral, Mrs. Ball gave a lunch for the mourners at the Ball mansion. By sundown, the last guests had gone home and Mrs. Ball was alone.

Just after dark, the phone rang.

A maid passing outside the sitting room heard Mrs. Ball say, "Hello?" Then she heard a blood-curdling scream. The maid rushed into the room and found Mrs. Ball sitting upright in a chair, clutching the telephone, a look of horror frozen on her face. The maid took the phone from Mrs. Ball's hand and put the receiver to her own ear. The line was dead, and so was Mrs. Ball.

An autopsy concluded that Mrs. Ball had died of a massive coronary. But the identity of the caller remained a mystery.

On the day of the funeral, the same crowd of mourners gathered and once again followed a body to the Ball mausoleum. When the crypt was unsealed, the crowd saw that the lid of Mr. Ball's casket was open. And the telephone was off the hook.

The Graveyard Wager

Variations on this story have been in circulation since the Middle Ages.
Five girls had gathered at a friend's house for a slumber party.
Behind the house was the town graveyard. Jessica, the girl hosting
the sleepover, had a clear view of the cemetery from her bedroom
window.

"Could you see Old Man McCluskey's funeral yesterday from
up here?" one of the girls asked her hostess.

"Yeah," Jessica said. "It was pretty boring. But things got a lot
more interesting after everybody went home."

"What do you mean?" her friend asked.

"I think they buried Old Man McCluskey alive."

Erin, the most outspoken of Jessica's friends, made a face.
"That's really stupid," she said.

"No. Seriously," Jessica said. "I've been watching the grave. And
the dirt keeps moving around. Like something underground is
trying to get out."

"The ground's probably just settling," Erin said.

"No," Jessica insisted. "I think Old Man McCluskey was really
buried alive."

"I still say you're goofy," Erin told her friend.

"Well, if you don't believe me," Jessica said, "I dare you to go
out to the grave right now and—" She looked around the room; her
skis caught her eye. "And drive this ski pole into the grave."

"Yeah!" one of the other girls cried. "He'll probably grab it and
make you pull him up!"

"That's so stupid," Erin said. "What will that prove?"

"I think you're chicken," Jessica said.

All the other girls joined in, crying, "Chicken! Chicken!" and "Dare! Dare!"

"All right!" Erin said at last. "I'll do it."

"We'll turn off the light so we can see you," Jessica said.

Erin put on her shoes, grabbed the ski pole and slipped out the back door of the house. From the window, her friends saw her climb over the fence and then she was swallowed up in the darkness of the graveyard.

They waited. Minutes went by. Then an hour. Then another hour. The girls waited all night for their friend to come back. In the morning they ran to the parents' room.

"Erin's gone! Old Man McCluskey killed her!"

The parents got up, dressed quickly and everyone ran out the back of the house to the graveyard. There, on the freshly dug grave of Old Man McCluskey, lay the body of their friend, facedown in the dirt. She had driven the ski pole through the bottom of her nightgown and pinned herself to the grave. The ground around her was churned up from her desperate efforts to pull herself free from the ski pole.

The thought that Old Man McCluskey had caught her had frightened poor Erin to death.

Variations: Alternate versions of the legend feature a drunk who drives a stake through the hem of his overcoat, a braggart soldier who plunges his sword through his long cloak or a person who hammers a nail into a wooden cross and pins himself to the grave marker.

Bloody Mary

Mary Worth is said to have lived in Massachusetts in the 17th century. Her face was hideously disfigured by dark red scars. Children in the village called her "Bloody Mary," and followed her through the streets chanting her name over and over.

During one of the colony's witch scares, Mary was accused of being in league with the Devil and was hanged. One night, not long after Mary's execution, a group of children decided to play at conjuring. They set up a mirror against the wall and sat in a semicircle around it. Then they all began to chant, "Bloody Mary, Bloody Mary." When they had chanted the name for the 99th time, Mary appeared in the mirror. Her face was more hideous than ever. Her hands had turned into claws. She reached through the looking glass to tear the children's faces.

Shrieking and screaming, the terrified children tumbled out of the room.

Although Bloody Mary disappeared that day, her spirit remains, waiting for someone to call her name.

Variations: In some places children chant, "I do believe in Mary Worth." In other parts of the United States the spirit's name is Mary Whales, Mary Johnson or Mary Lou. Some folklorists believe there is a connection between the Bloody Mary legend and the Chicano legend of La Llorona, a weeping ghost who wanders forever searching for her children whom she murdered.

The Jersey Devil

People in southern New Jersey have been scaring each other with stories of the Jersey Devil since 1735.

A teenage girl in southern New Jersey was left alone for the weekend while her parents went to the casinos in Atlantic City. On Saturday night, a terrible storm swept into the area. A heavy rain pounded on the roof. The wind rattled every window. And a bolt of lightning knocked out the power in three counties.

All alone in a dark house lit only by candles, the girl was very frightened. But she had her dog with her—a big golden retriever. He wasn't exactly a killer, but at least he was comforting.

When she was ready to go to sleep, the girl took the dog into her room with her and had him lay down beside her bed. Every time thunder crashed over the house, she awoke and reached down her hand. "You still here, Boo?" The dog would lick her hand and the girl was reassured that she was not alone.

Eventually she fell into a deep sleep. At about six in the morning, something dripping in the bathroom woke her. She climbed out of bed and went down the hall. There was her dog, hanging by its neck from the shower head. Scrawled on the mirror in blood was the message, "The Jersey Devil can lick hands, too."

Variations: Dozens of grisly stories are told about the Jersey Devil. He is said to have caught a babysitter one night and hacked off her arms and legs. When he sees young lovers parked in remote spots, he lures the boyfriend out of the car, kills him and suspends the body over

the roof. Other legends claim that he climbs into the back seat of a car and murders the driver with a razor-sharp pruning hook.

Mothman

The Mothman stories first appeared around Point Pleasant, West Virginia in 1966.

The Mothman is a manlike creature with a 10-foot wingspan and huge red eyes. He was a worker who was severely injured in an accident at a chemical plant in West Virginia. Instead of dying from his injuries, he mutated into a giant moth. He haunts remote country roads, especially dead ends where lovers go to park.

Most kids around Point Pleasant know better than to stray into Mothman territory. But there are always a few skeptics.

One such kid, a high school football star, scoffed at the Mothman stories and drove his girlfriend to a secluded spot off a county road. Just as the guy started to make his move, his girlfriend saw a large shadow pass over the car.

"It's him," she screamed. "Let's get out of here."

"It was probably just a hawk. Take it easy."

He kissed her, and she relaxed a bit. But then there was a thump on the roof of the car.

"Please. Pleeeeze. Let's go."

"Why? Because some dead branch fell out of a tree? Come on. We finally have some time to ourselves."

The guy put his arms around his girlfriend. Then there were scratching sounds on the roof of the car.

The girl began to scream.

"Okay. Okay. Calm down. I'll go take a look. But you're going to feel dumb when I show you it's just branches again."

"No! Don't go outside. Just drive me home. I want to go home. Right now."

"I'll be back in a minute. Lock the doors if it makes you feel better."

As the girl locked the car doors, she heard one final thump on the car roof, as if something heavy had been dropped on it. And then nothing.

A minute passed. Then several more. The guy did not return, and it was deathly quiet outside the car. The girl was on the verge of panic. She didn't have the keys to drive away and she didn't have the courage to get out of the car herself. She didn't know what to do. So she leaned on the car horn.

Out on the county road, a state trooper heard the horn and followed the sound of it down the dead end where he saw the car.

The trooper came up to the car on the passenger side and motioned to the girl to roll down the window. Before she could say anything he told her, "Miss, you need to stay in the car until I can get some help."

But the girl would not stay inside. When she stepped out, she saw her boyfriend sprawled atop the roof of the car. Someone, something, had ripped open his chest and eaten his heart.

Variations: Gruesome accidents in chemical plants have produced a host of bloodthirsty monsters, including the Green Man of central

Pennsylvania, Hyrum the Ax Murderer in the mountains of Utah and the Lizard Man of South Carolina.

The Well to Hell

Newspapers in Finland were the first to report this story as an actual event. From there, it has spread around the world.

Engineers working on the Kola Peninsula in Siberia were drilling a well, searching for oil or natural gas. In addition, they found rare geological formations and even gold. Eager to discover what else the well would yield, they kept drilling.

After more than a year, the well was about 1,800 miles deep. Then one day, the drill bit suddenly began to rotate wildly. The geologists and engineers felt a blast of searing heat gush out of the hole and thought they heard faint sounds emanating from the well.

They raised the drill and lowered temperature gauges to measure the heat at the bottom of the hole. It registered over 2,000 degrees Fahrenheit.

"We've penetrated to the molten center of the earth," one geologist said.

"But that doesn't account for the sounds," one of his colleagues said.

So they lowered highly sensitive microphones down the hole. Up from the well came the sounds of agonizing screams.

"We haven't penetrated the earth's core," the geologist said. "We've entered the gates of Hell."

Variations: An alternate version sets the story at an Alaskan oil rig where 13 workers were killed when the devil came roaring out of Hell.

The Image in the Glass

An elderly woman had been bedridden for many years. Her only pleasure was looking out the window beside her bed. Her neighbors grew accustomed to seeing her sitting up amid her pillows, a shawl around her shoulders and her lacy nightcap on her head, watching the activity in the street.

One evening, there was a tremendous thunderstorm. The elderly invalid saw a lightning bolt strike a tall pine tree beside her window and shatter it to splinters. The woman must have felt the shock of the bolt, for she fell into a coma.

She lingered through the night and passed away quietly the next day without ever regaining consciousness.

The woman's nurses asked her friends to come and prepare the body for burial. When they entered the bedroom and approached the bed, they were astonished to see a clear image of the old woman in the windowpane. It was a perfect likeness of her—just like a photograph. She was propped up among her pillows in her shawl and cap, looking intently out the window, just as she had for years.

Variations: In some versions of this legend, the image in the glass is the portrait of a prisoner who spent many years in a cell, staring out his window. In another version, the image is the portrait of someone

who was murdered in that room. And in some accounts of the legend, the image is a miraculous portrait of Jesus or Mary.

The Dead Body in the Car

On a dark night in December 1941, a couple were driving along a country road in Indiana when they saw a hitchhiker. He was a middle-aged man dressed in a trench coat and wearing a fedora. As the car came closer, the hitchhiker pushed his hat back on his head; the headlights lit up his handsome face.

"Should we pick him up?" the husband asked.

"He looks very nice," said his wife.

The husband stopped the car and rolled down his window. "Where are you going?"

"Fort Wayne," said the hitchhiker.

"That's on our way," the husband said. "We can drop you off."

As the hitchhiker climbed into the back seat he said, "Thanks for the lift. Where are you folks heading?"

"We're going to stay with my sister in South Bend for a few days," the wife said. "She's been scared to death since the attack on Pearl Harbor."

The three travelers made small talk until they arrived at the outskirts of Fort Wayne. "You can drop me off anywhere along this road," the hitchhiker said.

Once he was out of the car he said, "Thanks again. Look, I have no money, I can't pay you anything for your kindness. But I can answer any question you care to ask me."

The husband shot a mischievous look at his wife. "Any question at all, huh? Okay, sport. Tell us when the war is going to end."

"The war will end in August 1945," said the hitchhiker.

"August 1945," the husband repeated. "You're sure about that."

"As sure as I am that you will have a dead body in your car before you reach South Bend." Then the hitchhiker turned and vanished into the night.

"Did he say we would have a corpse in the car tonight?" the wife said.

"He's a loon," said the husband. "Don't pay any attention."

Several miles later, the couple saw an accident up ahead.

"Jeez, what a night," said the husband.

"Pull over! Pull over!" the wife said. "Somebody might be hurt."

"My God," said the husband. "It's an ambulance." Before he could stop the car, a paramedic ran up shouting, "I have a patient here. He's severely injured. You have to get us to the nearest hospital."

As they placed the injured man in the back seat, the paramedic said, "I'll direct you. Drive as fast as you can."

As they pulled up to the hospital, a half-dozen nurses, orderlies and doctors hurried out the door with a gurney to receive the patient. The husband and wife followed them all inside.

It was only a matter of minutes before the ambulance paramedic and an attending physician joined the couple in the waiting room. "It was good of you to try to help," said the doctor. "But I'm afraid he died on the way here."

The Ghost Pilot

A commercial airplane pilot with 30 years' experience was flying a 747 from Chicago to Los Angeles. One of the flight attendants on board was his daughter.

During the course of the flight, the plane suffered one problem after another. The pilot did everything he could to compensate for the mechanical failures. His daughter, in the meantime, tried to keep the passengers calm.

Finally, she had a spare moment and slipped into the cockpit. "Daddy, tell me what's going to happen," she said.

"It's serious," her father answered. "We can't get to any airport. I'll have to make an emergency landing in one of those fields down there."

"We're all going to die, aren't we," the daughter said.

Her father looked her straight in the eye. "I promise I will never let anything bad happen to you."

His daughter went back and prepared her passengers for the landing.

As they descended, the pilot could barely keep control of the aircraft. Then the landing gear failed. The 747 hit the ground hard. One of the wings broke off and the plane swung around wildly before it came to rest.

Among the passengers there were a few lacerations, plenty of bruises and one or two broken bones. But everyone was alive. It was a different story in the pilot's cockpit. In the impact the pilot's neck had been broken. He was dead.

The daughter was grief-stricken. But she was also proud of her father for having saved the lives of more than 200 people.

Several years later, the daughter was preparing a plane for takeoff. As she stepped into the galley she saw her father's ghost. "Get off this plane. There's trouble with the engines. If the ground crew doesn't correct the problem, this plane will crash."

Frightened, the woman hurried off the plane, found the foreman of the mechanics and convinced him to inspect the engines one last time. The foreman found a fault in the engine that would have caused the plane to explode on takeoff.

The young woman's father had kept his promise: He had saved her life again.

The Phantom's Warning

On a cold wet night in the 1920s, a man named Hugh Hamblen walked along a mountain road. He was heading for the hospital where his son had been taken after the police pulled him out of a wrecked car.

The road was slick with rain and heavy fog made it impossible to see more than a few feet ahead. Yet time and again cars flew past Hamblen at high speeds, impervious to the bad road conditions and the bad weather.

At a turn in the road Hamblen saw another car barreling along. As it came closer, Hamblen froze—it was skidding sideways. It was not going to make the turn.

The car hit Hamblen and tossed his body against the guardrail.

By the time the ambulance arrived, Hamblen was near death. His ribcage was shattered and both of his lungs were punctured.

He lingered for two days at the hospital before finally succumbing to his injuries.

Since then, on stormy, foggy nights, drivers have seen Hugh Hamblen standing along the side of the mountain road, signaling them to slow down.

Taking Laurie Home

A young man home from college for the weekend went to a dance at a church hall. While he was standing around the refreshment table, talking with his friends from high school, he saw a young woman standing at the threshold, watching the dancers. She was beautiful. Her blonde hair fell over her shoulders. She wore a white dress that must have come from a vintage clothing store.

"Who's that?" he asked his friends.

They turned, looked and shrugged their shoulders. They had never seen her before.

"I'll catch up with you guys later," the college boy said. He headed over to the vision standing in the doorway.

"Hi! My name's Tony. Do you want to dance?"

The girl smiled slightly and nodded her head.

Tony took her hand and led her onto the dance floor.

"Your hands are cold," he said.

"I'm cold all the time these days," the woman answered.

"Excuse me for asking, but I don't know your name," Tony said.

"It's Laurie," she answered.

"Are you new in town? I grew up here, and I've never seen you around before tonight."

"My place is outside town," Laurie said.

Laurie was not much of a talker, but Tony was smitten with her nonetheless. At about eleven o'clock, Laurie said she had to go home.

"I'll drive you," Tony said.

As they walked across the parking lot to Tony's car, Laurie shivered and said, "I'm so cold."

"Here," Tony said. "Take my jacket." He draped it over Laurie's shoulders and held the car door open for her.

Laurie directed him to a farmhouse about 10 miles outside of town. She would not let Tony walk her to the door, and stood at the curb until she saw him drive away. But a few minutes later, Tony realized that Laurie still had his jacket. He went back to the house and knocked on the door. An elderly man answered.

"Good evening," he said. "I just dropped Laurie off, but I forgot to get my jacket back from her."

The elderly man sighed. "It happens every year."

"Sorry?"

"Laurie died 20 years ago on this very night. Every year she comes back and spends a few hours among the living. I don't know where your jacket is."

Tony could hardly believe what he had heard. But some strange force seemed to draw him to the cemetery. With a flashlight, he wandered among the graves. At last he found Laurie's. His jacket was neatly folded and lying on top of her headstone.

Variations: A ghostly apparition who tries to return home is one of the most prolific of all legends. Among the variants are stories of a bride who waits for her dead lover, a Woman in Black who was cruel to her slaves and spends eternity haunting her old plantation and a little girl who died in a theater fire and waits in the balcony for her parents to come and take her home.

THE SCUBA DIVER
IN THE FOREST FIRE
AND OTHER STRANGE DEATHS

The Scuba Diver in the Forest Fire

For days, brushfires ravaged the dry hills of southern California. When the fires were out, firefighters found the body of a diver in full scuba gear in the middle of the charred wasteland.

They turned the body over to forensic investigators, but the conclusions of the autopsy were mystifying.

"The diver did not burn to death," the chief of forensics said. "He drowned."

"You're saying he drowned in the middle of a brushfire? How is that possible?" the fire chief asked.

"We gave this some thought," the chief of forensics said. "You called in firefighting helicopters that haul water out of the ocean and dump it on the fire, right?"

"Right."

"Once the scoop is full, it seals itself automatically, right?"

"Yeah. So?"

"We figure one of the helicopters must have scooped this guy up when he was scuba diving in the ocean. He ran out of oxygen during the flight. With no way to get out of the scoop, he drowned. The helicopter got to the site and dumped its load of water, and the diver went down with it."

Variations: Versions of this legend have cropped up from southern California to the south of France. Sometimes he is a scuba diver, while in other versions he is a snorkeler. In some accounts the body of the diver is discovered caught in the branches of a charred tree.

The Flying Chevy

At the bottom of a sheer cliff in the middle of the desert, two officers of the Arizona Highway Patrol came upon a vehicle shattered beyond recognition. About 100 feet up the cliff face they spotted large chunks of metal embedded in the rock wall.

"Looks like a small aircraft," one of the cops said.

"Look again," said his partner. "It's got four wheels. This was a car."

"Okay. But where's the driver?"

There was no trace of a body. And searching the area, they found no sign that someone had walked away from the wreck (not that anyone could have survived the crash).

First the cops radioed for a wrecking company to come and collect the debris. Then they notified a forensics lab.

A week later the chief of forensics sat down with the two highway patrol officers who had found the wreck.

"We found parts of a Chevy Impala," he said, "and parts of a solid-fuel rocket identical to the type the military uses to give their aircraft an extra boost at takeoff."

"You're kidding," the first cop said.

"Not in the least. In fact, by studying the wreckage and visiting the site, we were able to piece together the rest of the story.

"It appears that the driver took his car out to the desert, to a long, straight stretch of road. It was probably there that he attached the rocket to his car. We found the spot where the driver fired up the rocket—the asphalt showed signs of having melted. This was about

three miles from the scene of the crash.

"A solid-fuel rocket achieves its maximum thrust in five seconds—which means the Chevy was traveling at 350 miles per hour. Not surprisingly, the driver tried to reduce his speed. We know this because we found traces of the destroyed brakes and the four blown tires half a mile from the crash site.

"Then there are no more signs of the car on the road. We surmise that at this stage the Chevy was airborne. Seconds later, it hit the cliff, approximately a hundred feet above the ground. That accounts for the parts of the vehicle you saw embedded in the rock above the wreckage. The rest of the shattered vehicle fell to the ground."

"And the driver?" the first cop asked.

"We recovered some fragments of bone and hair."

"That's all?" said the second cop.

"There were also bits of fingernail embedded in a piece of debris which we believe was part of the steering wheel."

The Airborne Lawn Chair

A truck driver who had always wanted to learn to fly but could never get around to taking lessons came up with a unique alternative. An inveterate tinkerer who was always working on some odd invention in his garage, he was certain that his ingenious flying machine would get him into the record books.

One Saturday morning his neighbors saw him anchoring his favorite lawn chair to the ground. Then he went into the garage and

came out carrying 50 deflated weather balloons and rolling a large tank of helium. He called to his neighbors, "You guys want to give me a hand here?"

As the neighbors collected in his yard, the truck driver assigned them jobs. "You fill the balloons. You tie them off. You secure them to the lawn chair."

"Mike, what are you doing?" one of the neighbors asked.

"I am going to pilot the first flying lawn chair," he answered.

"You're out of your mind."

"Nope. I've figured the whole thing out. These weather balloons are strong. I should have no trouble getting off the ground. And my own weight will keep me from flying too high. It should be a nice, graceful flight over town. I can't wait to see the looks on people's faces as I drift over their houses."

"So how do you get down?" the neighbor asked.

Mike rummaged in a large backpack strapped to the back of the lawn chair and pulled out a pellet gun. "When I'm ready to make my descent, I'll shoot out the balloons one by one and make a perfect landing.

"In case anything goes wrong, I've got this." He reached into the backpack again and pulled out a parachute. "Plus I've got my cell phone. I'll be okay. And I'll make history."

By this time, the neighbors had finished tying the weather balloons to the lawn chair. Mike took his seat, strapped himself in with leather belts, and said, "See you all later!"

Then he cut the moorings that anchored the lawn chair to the ground.

Mike had been right: the weather balloons were strong. He and

his chair shot up a few thousand feet into the air at a surprising speed. He was terrified. First he vomited over the side of the chair. Then he got out his pellet gun and shot out a few of the balloons to slow his ascent.

As planned, the flying lawn chair began to lose altitude. Then Mike lost his grip on the pellet gun.

He fumbled with his cell phone and dropped that, too. He was still about 100 feet in the air—not high enough to use the parachute, but far too high to jump. And aside from waving and yelling to people as he drifted over their yards, he had no way to call for help.

A stiff breeze came up and began to push Mike and his lawn chair farther and farther away from home.

Soon he was outside the town, in open country. No houses, no businesses and not even much traffic on the roads. That was worrying, but not nearly as worrying as the high-voltage power lines that were stretched across the path of the flying lawn chair.

With his hands trembling, the frantic "pilot" tried to untie some of the balloons. But his neighbors had followed his directions and secured the balloons tightly to the chair, and Mike hadn't thought of bringing a knife to cut the cords.

A few seconds later, the driver of a passing car saw the flying lawn chair, propelled by the wind, move swiftly toward the power lines that ran alongside the highway. He saw the man in the chair lean back and extend his legs, as if that would enable him to veer away from the wires. Then there was a sharp sound of crackling electricity, followed by a roar as the helium balloons exploded into flames. In his rearview mirror, the driver saw the burning lawn chair crash to the ground.

The Deadly Log Flume

A new amusement park had opened in Florida on the edge of the Everglades. During the hot Florida summer, the most popular ride was the log flume.

Half a dozen high school kids came to the park one blistering day in August. They waited in line for the flume for over an hour, and finally their turn came to climb aboard the ride.

"I can't wait to get soaked," one guy said to his girlfriend. "I'm burning up."

His girlfriend said, "My mom says if you put your wrists in cool water, it lowers your body temperature."

"It's worth a shot," the guy said.

As the ride started to move, he plunged his arms into the water. "This feels great," he said.

A moment later he yanked his arms out of the water, yelling, "Something bit me!"

His friends saw small puncture wounds all over his arms. They yelled to the flume operator, "Somebody's hurt! Let us off!" But their car was too far along. It had to go through the first circuit of the ride.

The car flew around the track, then slowed and began to climb the chute that was the climax of the ride. The kid said to his girlfriend, "My arms feel like they're on fire." Then he fell unconscious.

As the car went over the crest of the chute, his girlfriend began to shriek.

By the time the car came to a stop, the boy's arms were swollen and discolored. He was barely breathing.

The park's emergency medical team rushed him to a local hospital, but the boy died on the way. An emergency room doctor took the kids into his office. "I don't understand this. Your friend died of snake bites. It was my understanding that you kids were at an amusement park."

Meanwhile, the management of the amusement park had shut down the log flume. They drained all the water from the ride. In the canal just past the ride's starting point, the park's safety inspectors discovered a large nest of poisonous water snakes.

Snake Lake

After several days of heavy rains, Alabama's Guntersville Lake overflowed, covering fenceposts and tree stumps that under normal conditions were many yards from the water's edge. On the first sunny day after the rainstorms, a group of college kids decided to spend the day waterskiing on the lake.

At first, the kid piloting the speedboat was careful to stay clear of the shallow water. But by the end of the afternoon, the skiers had become more and more daring. Finally, in what was supposed to be the last run of the day, the boat's driver made a wide turn and the skier swung into the shallow end of the lake, barely missing a shattered tree stump that jutted above the lake's surface. Something below the surface snagged one ski and the skier tumbled into the water. When he came up, he found himself ensnared in a tangle of

barbed wire. He thrashed around in the water trying to get himself free. He shouted to his friends for help and cursed as the wire spikes pricked his skin.

Then the occasional pinpricks became sharp, agonizing stings as dozens of poisonous water snakes sank their fangs into the skier's flesh. By the time the boat filled with the skier's friends got to him, he was screaming in pain and terror. The water was churning with the frenzy of the snakes and the skier's frantic efforts to escape. Worse still, his friends were too frightened by the mass of snakes to reach into the water and haul him to safety in the boat.

He died in the water, while his frightened friends watched helplessly.

Variations: Another version tells of a boy who jumps into a pond and lands amid a mass of water snakes. Before he dies, he manages to warn his friends not to come near the water. The most grisly variant of this story involves small children who play in a sandpit filled with snakes.

The Giant Catfish

Something was clogging one of the channels that released water from the bottom of the dam at the Tuttle Creek Reservoir in Arkansas. The foreman of the dam's maintenance crew hired a team of three divers to see what the problem might be.

They had only been gone a few moments when two of the divers almost exploded out of the water, sputtering and gasping for air, trying desperately to climb out of the water.

"What's wrong?" shouted the foreman. "What's happened? Where's the third guy?"

The two divers talked at once and made no sense.

"Huge!"

"It's the size of a truck!"

"It bit him in half!"

"What are you telling me?" the foreman said.

Shaking uncontrollably, almost crying from fear, one of the divers said, "There's a huge fish down there. An enormous catfish. The size of a car. It's at the bottom of the dam, blocking the channel. It must be eating everything the current carries its way."

"And it just ate Harry," the other diver said.

"You're out of your minds," the foreman said.

"No. The fish bit him in half. He's dead."

"Bull—" the foreman began. But as he looked over the railing, he saw a dark reddish stain on the water. And then a human leg bobbed up to the surface.

Variations: Almost every dam and lock in the United States has a story of a giant fish that devours swimmers or maintenance men. There are even tales of marine monsters lurking near oil rigs off the coast of Texas and swimming amid the wreckage of the USS Arizona in Pearl Harbor.

The Bug in the Ear

The origins of this very popular story have been traced back to England about the year 1000.

While a woman was sleeping on the beach in California, a tiny earwig climbed into her ear and burrowed forward. Several days later, the woman went to her doctor complaining of a terrible earache.

After peering into her ear, the doctor sat back. "I can't see anything," he said. "Let's see what an X-ray can tell us."

When the film came back, the doctor sat down with his patient and her husband in his office.

"Now I want you to stay calm. An earwig is burrowing through your ear canal. We can't get to it. The only thing we can do is to wait a couple of weeks until it makes its way clear through your skull. It will climb out of your other ear and you'll be fine."

Of course, when the woman heard this news, she was not fine. She became hysterical. It took her husband and three nurses to hold her down just so the doctor could give her a tranquilizer.

"We'll hospitalize her and keep her heavily medicated for the

next couple of weeks," the doctor said to the husband. "That should help her get through this."

Sure enough, about two weeks later, the earwig crawled out of the woman's ear. The husband was at his wife's bedside when the tiny creature appeared. He grabbed it and put it in an empty water bottle. The next day, the couple, with the earwig in the bottle, sat down with the doctor for a final examination.

"Let's get another set of X-rays," the doctor said.

It took a little longer for the film to return this time. When the X-rays finally arrived, the woman, her husband and the doctor all assembled in the office once more.

"I'm afraid I have to modify my diagnosis," the doctor said. "I've examined the earwig and the X-rays." He took a deep breath. "This was a female. It must have been pregnant when it crawled into your ear canal. It's laid its eggs in your skull. When the eggs hatch, the young earwigs will devour your brain."

Variations: It is thought that the name "earwig" gave rise to the belief that these insects liked to crawl into human ears. The idea that the bug ate its way through the head and out the ear on the other side, or laid its eggs inside the skull, is a later embellishment that was dramatized in the 1970's television series, Rod Serling's Night Gallery.

The Good Luck Tee

A devoted golfer moved to a new town in Connecticut. Once they got to know him, his neighbors nominated him for membership in the local country club, which was famous for its especially challenging golf course.

One evening, a neighbor dropped by the newcomer's house. "You're in," he said. "You can start playing first thing tomorrow morning if you like."

The new member was the first one at the links the next day. He was thrilled by the beauty of the course. The grass was thick, lush and free of any kind of weed. He had never seen a golf course so magnificently tended.

After he teed off, he picked up the tee and put it in his mouth. At every hole, he used this tee. "I always do this for luck," he told the other members. "This will be my new good luck charm."

He played 18 holes of golf the first day. The next day he returned for another 18 holes, once again using his lucky tee. As he walked happily from hole to hole, he chewed and sucked on the lucky tee, as if he were ingesting its good luck.

On the third day, the golfer wasn't feeling well, but he couldn't keep away from the links. He played badly, and he felt worse. Yet he struggled from hole to hole, the lucky tee stuck between his clenched teeth.

At the 13th hole, the golfer dropped dead.

An autopsy showed that he had died of poisoning. A follow-up lab report on the lucky tee found that it carried a lethal amount of

pesticide—the type the country club's groundskeeper used to kill weeds.

Variation: In another version of the story, the golfer is a military man who dies, not from a lethal dose of pesticide, but from a severe allergic reaction to a supposedly harmless weedkiller that has been spread on the golf course. The legend ends with the golfer's widow winning a $20 million lawsuit against the manufacturer of the weedkiller.

The Ancestral Boots

An old Texas rancher was rounding up stray cattle when a rattlesnake reared up and bit him through his boot. He had nothing he could use to treat himself, so he applied a tourniquet, climbed on his horse and headed for home.

Through the kitchen window, the rancher's wife saw him coming. Even from a distance he looked strange. His head was bowed and the reins were slack in his hands. A few minutes later, the horse and rider arrived in the front yard, but the old rancher did not climb down off his horse. When his wife and the hired hands got to him, they found that he was dead in the saddle.

"Imagine him having a heart attack and not even falling off his horse," said the rancher's son.

The morning after the funeral, as the son was getting dressed, his mother came into his room. "These are Daddy's boots," she said. "I thought maybe you'd like to wear them."

The son took them and put them on his feet. They pinched a little, but he didn't say anything about it to his mother. He didn't want to hurt her feelings. Besides, they'd probably stretch after he'd worn them for a couple of days.

At the end of the day, the son came riding into the yard of the ranch, slumped over his horse. Like his father, it appeared that he had had a massive heart attack out on the range.

The morning after the son's funeral, the old rancher's wife came into her eldest grandson's room. Her face was pale and drawn. "Your Grandpa wore these boots for twenty years," she told the young man. "Your Daddy only got a chance to wear them for one day. Do you want them?"

The grandson said yes, and put them on. The boots were too tight, but he couldn't complain about it to his grandmother after all she'd been through.

At the end of the day, the grandson came riding into the yard of the ranch, slumped over his horse, as dead as his father and his grandfather.

A few days later, the grandmother called her youngest grandson to her. On the floor beside her were the boots. She was weeping. "Your Grandpa always said these boots were good luck. I'm beginning to think they've cursed us. Take them out and burn them for me."

The boy picked up the boots, and as he did, he saw something sticking out just above the heel. He carried the boots out to the tool shed, took a pair of pliers and pulled at the object embedded in the boot. He expected it to be a thorn. Instead, out came a rattlesnake fang still filled with venom.

Variation: In a modern version of this story a rancher runs over a rattlesnake with his truck. Some of the snake's fangs are embedded in one of the tires, so the rancher drives to his mechanic's shop to have them pulled. The careless mechanic is scratched by the fangs and dies.

No News but Bad News

One of the earliest printed versions of this grim legend appeared in 1879 in McGuffey's Fifth Eclectic Reader.

After being away on business for several weeks, a well-to-do man began the journey home. As he neared his farm, he met his steward on the road.

"So, steward, what's new at home?" he asked.

"Sir, I'm afraid your dog has died," the steward replied.

"How could that happen? He was barely two years old."

"He gorged himself on burnt horseflesh, sir."

"Where did he find burnt horseflesh?"

"Sir, I'm sorry to say that all the horses died when the barn burned down."

"How did the barn burn down?"

"A spark from the house blew onto the barn roof. We were so busy trying to save the house we didn't notice that the barn had caught fire until it was too late."

"My house burned down?" the man asked in horror.

"Yes sir. One of the candles set around your wife's coffin was placed too close to the window curtains. The curtains caught fire, then the whole house went up in flames."

"My wife is dead? Did you say my wife is dead?"

"She died of a seizure, sir. After your eldest daughter ran off with the hired man."

The man groaned and covered his face with his hands. When he regained his composure, he said, "My wife is dead. My daughter's run off. My house is gone. The barn is gone. My horses and even my dog are dead. Where am I to live with the other three children?"

The steward cleared his throat.

"I wouldn't worry about that, sir. They all perished in the house fire."

The Elaborate Suicide Attempt

After his business failed and his wife left, a man decided to kill himself, but he wanted to be sure that he wouldn't botch the operation. After some thought, he decided that hanging would be the best method. He found a tree with a stout limb reaching out over the edge of a cliff 50 feet above the sea and chose this spot for his suicide.

Although he was eager to leave this world, he did not want to feel any pain. So he collected a few dozen sleeping pills.

Of course, sleeping pills don't work immediately, and the man had read terrible stories of people who had taken half an hour to die at the end of a rope. He decided to shoot himself, too—just to be on the safe side.

On the day he decided would be his last, the man took the rope, the sleeping pills and the gun to the cliff. He swallowed the sleeping

pills. He tied the rope to the branch and slipped the noose around his neck. He put the gun to his head and as he stepped off the edge of the cliff, he fired.

But the sudden drop threw off the man's aim. The bullet missed him completely and cut through the rope instead. The man plunged into the sea where he swallowed so much seawater that he vomited up the sleeping pills.

He swam ashore and resolved not to attempt suicide again.

The Funny Smell

This legend was dramatized in the 1995 movie Four Rooms.
A couple went to Las Vegas for a few days of vacation. Once they were in their hotel room, they detected a peculiar smell.

"I'll call the desk and get a different room," the husband said.

"No," the wife said. "I don't want to change rooms. I like the view from here. Just call housekeeping. They'll take care of the problem."

While the couple went down to the casino, a maid inspected the room, but she could not find the source of the odor. She sprayed air freshener in the room and left.

When the couple returned to their room, the smell was no better. They called housekeeping again and went out for dinner. Another maid came to the room. She searched for any spills or food that might have been left lying around. When she found nothing, she sprayed the room with air freshener and left.

Late that night the couple came back and found that their room

still stank. This time they decided to search the room themselves.

"It's strongest near the bed," the wife said.

"Maybe somebody wet the mattress," said the husband.

They stripped the blankets and sheets off the bed, and lifted up the mattress. There, in the platform that served as the frame of the bed, they found the decomposing corpse of a prostitute.

Shrink-to-Fit Jeans

On a Saturday night in the late 1970s, a sophomore at a New Hampshire college put on a pair of new jeans and went to a party at a frat house. By midnight, he was profoundly drunk. On a trip to the bathroom, the bathtub looked so cool and inviting that he climbed in and promptly passed out.

The next drunk to use the bathroom thought this was comical. From the bathroom door he yelled, "Hey! You gotta see this!"

A handful of partiers crowded in around the tub.

"He must be really wasted."

"Next time, remind me to sleep it off in his bathtub."

Then the only girl in the group said, "You know, it's a shame he didn't think to fill the tub first."

Everyone looked at her as if she were out of her mind.

"Seriously. If you wear new jeans and soak in them in the bathtub, they shrink to the shape of your body. They look really good."

One of the guys said, "Then let's do this guy a favor and shrink his jeans for him!" He plugged the drain and turned on the water.

With the type of seriousness only drunks can summon up, the little group stood and watched as the tub filled. When the water was chest high, they turned off the taps.

"He's going to be so grateful in the morning," the girl said as everyone filed out.

About noon the next day, one of the frat brothers staggered out of bed into the bathroom. The frat's houseguest was still in the tub.

"C'mon. Wake up!" he shouted.

But the kid in the tub didn't move.

"Let's go. Time to get up." He splashed some water in the drunk's face, but still he got no response.

"Look, you gotta sleep it off somewhere else. People want to use the shower." He shook the guy; the body was deathly cold.

"Oh shit!" he exclaimed.

The frat brother called 911. Minutes later, a crew of paramedics with their paraphernalia crowded into the bathroom.

"He's dead, isn't he," the frat president said.

"Yes he is," one of the paramedics said. "Who put him in a bathtub filled with water?"

"One of the girls who was here last night said it would make his jeans shrink to fit his body."

"Yeah, it did that," the paramedic said. "The jeans shrank so well they cut off his circulation. It killed him."

Variations: In an alternate version of this legend, a young woman dies when she purposely soaks in a bathtub filled with water so her jeans will be as tight as possible. Another variant claims that the

woman does not die, but is mortified when the police and ambulance crew have to cut her out of her too-tight jeans.

The Cask of Excellent Brandy

The roots of this legend go back to an historical event: In 1805, the British Navy packed Lord Nelson's body in a cask of rum to preserve it and shipped it back to England for a state funeral.

In London, a young couple bought an old house that had once served as a tavern. There was an old wine cellar in the basement, filled with empty casks. The barrels were too large to fit through the cellar door, so the husband and wife broke them up and carried out the pieces. When the cellar was almost empty, the husband found a last cask hidden in the corner.

"This cask is still full," the husband said.

"You get a tap," the wife said. "I'll get a couple of glasses. Maybe the wine or whatever is still good."

To their delight, the couple discovered that the cask held excellent brandy.

"I've never tasted anything like this," the husband said.

"It must have aged down here for a hundred years," the wife said. "What else could account for this incredible flavor?"

For years, the couple celebrated every holiday and every important family occasion with a decanter of their prize brandy. They served it to their friends at the conclusion of all their dinner parties. The fame of the brandy spread, until an editor of a British

food and wine magazine asked if the couple would agree to be the subject of an article.

The magazine sent a connoisseur of brandy and cognac to the couple's house. They took him down to the old wine cellar and poured him a glass of their brandy directly from the cask.

The connoisseur held the glass under his nose and inhaled. "The bouquet is remarkable," he said. Then he took a small sip and rolled it around on his tongue. "Wonderful. Wonderful! My friends, this is a unique 18th-century brandy. I have never tasted its like. If I were to advance a supposition, I would suggest that this brandy was distilled at a long-vanished French vineyard. Perhaps one destroyed during the Revolution. May I have another glass?"

The couple could not have been more pleased, although after the article was published, they were besieged by "connoisseurs" eager to sample their remarkable brandy.

Finally, after giving them many years of pleasure, the cask ran dry.

"Let's save the cover of the cask and the tap as a memento," the wife said.

The husband agreed that it was a fine idea. Together they went down to the cellar to break up their prize cask.

They swung their mallets together and loosened the cover. The husband set his mallet down, grabbed the cover and wrenched it free.

A moment later, out spilled a skeleton, still wearing scraps of 18th-century garb.

Gloomy Sunday

In 1933, a new song, "Gloomy Sunday," debuted on radio stations in Hungary.

> *Sunday is gloomy, my hours are slumberless.*
> *Dearest, the shadows I live with are numberless.*
> *Little white flowers will never awaken you,*
> *Not where the black coach of sorrow has taken you.*
> *Angels have no thought of ever returning you.*
> *Would they be angry if I thought of joining you?*

It was rumored that the songwriter's girlfriend had committed suicide; this melancholy ballad was his attempt to express his grief. The song was so popular that it spread to America, where Billie Holiday sang it in nightclubs. But just as the song was becoming an international hit, radio stations in Europe were instructed to stop playing the song.

Since the debut of "Gloomy Sunday," government officials had noticed a sharp increase in suicides. Often family members and friends of the victims found suicide notes that made reference to "Gloomy Sunday" or quoted some of its lyrics. The situation was particularly bad if the song was played on a rainy Sunday: The next morning, the morgues of major European cities would be filled with corpses.

One by one, the nations of Europe banned the song. The United States joined the "Gloomy Sunday" ban when government

officials saw a rise in the American suicide rate.

Meanwhile, the composer of "Gloomy Sunday" was in desperate straits. Royalties from his hit song dried up. No one would publish any of his new music. And the possibility that his song had been instrumental in the deaths of hundreds of people on two continents tormented him constantly.

The composer slipped into a deep depression. He stopped writing. He would not leave his apartment. He refused to see his friends. The only person with whom he had any contact was the delivery boy from the grocer.

One day, when the delivery boy came to the composer's apartment with his bags of groceries, he heard the composer playing the piano. He recognized the song at once—it was "Gloomy Sunday." He stood in the hallway for a few minutes, listening. The song came to an end. There was a pause. And then a gunshot rang out in the apartment.

Dying to Get into the Movies

During the making of the 1926 version of *Ben-Hur*, several scenes were filmed in Italy. The movie's famous sea battle between Roman soldiers and pirates was shot at the seaport of Livorno. The director needed hundreds of extras, so he hired local residents to play these parts. The only requirement was that they had to be able to swim.

The scene would be magnificent. Several Roman galleys had been built for the battle and were anchored offshore. The extras

were outfitted in replicas of Roman armor, including heavy metal breastplates and helmets. The cameramen and the director were on modern boats anchored on the perimeter of the Roman ships.

The director shouted, "Action!" and the battle began.

Everything was going perfectly. The costumed residents of Livorno put their hearts into the fight. The special effects people had arranged for a few fires to break out on the Roman galleys to create even more excitement. But on one of the galleys, the fire got out of control and began to spread through the entire ship.

Frightened extras jumped into the sea to escape the flames.

"This is great!" the director said.

"No it's not!" said his assistant. "Look out there! Some of the extras are having trouble swimming. Stop the filming so we can pull them out of the water!"

One of the cameramen looked at the director.

"Keep the cameras rolling!" the director commanded.

"But they're drowning!" the assistant said.

"I can get more extras for ten dollars a head. But this scene is costing me a hundred grand!" As several of the extras sank beneath the waves, the director yelled to the cameramen, "Keep the damn cameras rolling!"

The Lethal Hospital Room

The nursing staff of the intensive care unit in a hospital in Johannesburg dreaded Friday mornings. Week after week, whoever was placed in Room 713 would be found dead first thing on Friday.

The hospital administrators launched an extensive investigation of the room, from the air-conditioning ducts to the single electrical outlet that powered the life-support system. But the investigators found no sign of airborne viruses, no trace of faulty wiring, no indication of power surges. Nothing. In fact, one investigator commented on the cleanliness of Room 713. "They don't just clean the floors," he said, "they polish them."

If the investigators were baffled, the staff of the intensive care unit was uneasy. What was going on in Room 713?

In the absence of any rational explanation for the strange deaths, the nurses decided among themselves that they would no longer assign patients to Room 713. But one day intensive care became so crowded with new patients the staff had no choice. Someone would have to go to Room 713.

Early on Thursday evening, the senior nurse of the night shift assembled her staff. "Tonight, we're all going to take a one-hour shift in Room 713. I've worked out a schedule. No nurse leaves that room for any reason. If the experts can't figure out what's going on, then we'll solve this mystery ourselves."

Hour after hour, all night long, the nurses took their turns sitting with the patient in Room 713. By nine in the evening, all the visitors had gone home. By midnight, even the most restless patients

were asleep. The only sound in Room 713 was the gentle hum and hiss of the life-support system.

The last shift in the room ended at six. It was Friday morning, and the patient in Room 713 was alive. The nurse who had had the last watch of the night stood, yawned, stretched. She wished "Good morning" to the cleaning lady who was rolling her floor polisher into Room 713.

As the nurse headed to the lounge for a cup of coffee, the cleaning lady reached down to the room's only electrical outlet. She unplugged the cord that ran to the life-support system and plugged in her floor polisher. The whir of the polisher drowned out any other sounds in the room. The cleaning lady did not hear the patient convulse in his bed. Why should she? She had never heard any of the others.

The Embarrassed Family

The 91-year-old patriarch of a large family in Taiwan was dying. His eight children, their spouses and all the grandchildren assembled at the family home in order to be present when the old man passed into eternity.

A day or two after the clan had assembled, the patriarch took his last breath. The mother of the family, who had been calm throughout the crisis, broke into hysterical weeping. She grabbed her husband's body and tried to lift him. She tore at her hair and scratched her face. It took all four of her daughters to physically

restrain their grief-stricken mother and lead her from the death chamber back to her own room.

All night long, the widow howled and shrieked until, an hour or so before dawn, emotional exhaustion overcame her grief and she fell asleep.

Her children were distraught. Her grandchildren were terrified. So the eldest son called a family conference while their mother slept. "I have never seen Mother like this," he said.

"I don't think anyone has ever seen Mother like this," said his eldest sister.

"Nor should anyone," the eldest son said. "That's why I think we should go to the herbalist and get a sedative so Mother will be able to control her emotions at the funeral."

The suggestion made good sense to everyone. No one wanted the embarrassment of seeing their mother carry on in this manner at their father's funeral.

The next day, the eldest daughter went to the herbalist's store. The herbalist was an old friend of the family. He sympathized with the daughter over the loss of her father, and seemed genuinely shocked to hear that her mother had lost control of her emotions.

"This will calm your dear mother," he said as he handed a small bottle to the woman. "It's a strong sedative, but if you put five drops in a pot of tea that will dilute it. After she drinks one cup, she will be herself again. Calm, but alert. Remember—five drops. No more."

The daughter thanked the herbalist and hurried back to her parents' house.

The next morning was the day of the funeral. The house was in confusion as more and more relatives and friends arrived to pay

their last respects. The eldest daughter was determined to prepare her mother's tea herself, but she endured constant interruptions. Newly arrived mourners asked to see her. Her children seemed unusually demanding. Her husband couldn't find his best shoes.

At last, she had a moment to herself. She took out the small bottle from the herbalist and put five drops in her mother's teapot as the herbalist had instructed. But given her mother's condition, it really didn't seem to be enough. So she added three more drops to the tea. She was about to screw the cap back on the bottle when she heard her mother begin to weep hysterically once more. "Well," she thought, "a couple more drops can't hurt."

Finally, with ten drops of the sedative in the tea, the daughter carried the teapot and a small porcelain cup to her mother's room.

Her mother was wrapped in a dressing gown, sobbing in a chair beside the window.

"Good morning, Mother. Did you get any rest last night?" the daughter asked.

The grief-stricken woman did not say a word; she just gestured to her daughter to leave the tea on a table beside the bed.

The daughter kissed her mother on the forehead and left.

Two hours later, the entire family was ready for the funeral, but the mother had not come out of her room yet.

Her daughter went up to get her. She stood at the door and knocked. There was no answer. She called softly, "Mother?" There was no response. She called more loudly, but her mother still did not come to the door.

At last, the daughter opened the door. Sitting in a chair beside

the window was her mother, cold and dead. On the bedside table was the teapot, completely empty. The old woman had drunk every drop of the overdosed tea.

The Enormous Bouffant

The bouffant was the most popular hairstyle in the mid-1960s. Some girls prided themselves on their ability to tease their hair and stiffen it with hairspray into a very high bouffant. One woman at a college in Mississippi had a bouffant that was almost two feet high.

To keep it intact, she slept sitting upright in bed and wrapped it in plastic before she stepped into the shower. Her hair was washed only once a month when she went to the beauty salon.

One warm spring day, just after she had returned from an appointment with her stylist, the girl decided to take a walk in her college's botanical garden. As she passed under a flowering dogwood tree, her bouffant caught a spiderweb hanging from the branches. The woman never noticed.

Three weeks later, while she was sitting in class, she felt something warm and wet trickling down her forehead. She touched it with a tissue. It was blood.

She excused herself from class and was on her way to the college's clinic when she collapsed. A passersby hurried to her assistance, but the woman was unconscious. By the time the paramedics arrived, a pool of blood had collected around the woman's head and her bouffant was matted with blood.

A physician and two nurses met the ambulance at the emergency room entrance.

"What have you got?" the doctor asked.

"It's a head wound. But we can't find the source."

"Let's get her into Trauma One. And cut off that hair!"

With the first snip of the scissors, a massive nest of spiders spilled out of the bouffant. It was pandemonium in the trauma room as the spiders leapt onto the doctors and nurses, swarmed over the woman's body and scurried across the floor.

Later, after the orderlies and hospital maintenance crew had the spider infestation under control, the trauma crew returned to examine the corpse. They cut off the rest of the bouffant and scraped away the spiders' nest. Underneath it was a hole the size of a dime where the spiders had eaten through the woman's skull and into her brain.

Variations: In some versions, the young woman becomes mysteriously ill and it takes the doctors some time to determine the cause of her malady. Once the bouffant went out of style, the subject of the story became a middle-aged woman with no fashion sense. In some versions, the protagonist is a young man with long unkempt hair.

Demon Alley

Off Route 23 in northern New Jersey is a road where no car or truck has gone for many years. The asphalt is crumbling and potholed. Weeds and tall grass grow from cracks in the pavement. Every other tree along the abandoned road bears a No Trespassing sign. People who live in the area call this road Demon Alley.

At the end of the road are a few dozen wooden houses. All the doors are padlocked. All the windows are boarded up. It's obvious that the houses have been empty for years, yet the buildings are pristine. No one has spray-painted graffiti on the walls. No one has pried the boards off the windows or broken the padlocks on any of the doors. No one would dare break into any building on Demon Alley.

 In the 1920s this was a growing neighborhood. Then a stranger moved into one of the houses, and odd things began to happen. Pets disappeared. If a little girl left her doll outside, she would find it later with its head missing. The incidents were beginning to make the residents uneasy. Then the newcomer suggested that they hold a neighborhood meeting to discuss the problem. Since his house was the largest on the street, he invited everyone to meet there the next evening. "Bring the entire family," he said. "There's plenty of room. We'll turn it into a party."

The next day, after sundown, every man, woman and child walked over to their neighbor's house. Once everyone was inside, their host locked the front door. Suddenly, men and women in heavy black hooded robes burst into the room. They wielded large knives,

meat cleavers and axes. Within minutes, they had massacred all of the helpless residents.

It was a local police officer cruising through the neighborhood who first suspected that something was wrong. At six in the evening, not a single light was on in any of the houses. When backup arrived, the cops began investigating the houses, one by one. Everything was orderly and tidy in every house on the street. There was no sign of violence anywhere—until they came at last to the largest house on the street. The drapes had been drawn; they could not see in the windows. All the doors were locked, so the police had to break into the house. In the large front parlor, they found the bodies of the dead—hacked, disfigured and dismembered.

The identity of the newcomer and his followers remains a mystery. They vanished the night of the massacre. Police investigators speculated that the murders had been committed by a Satanic cult, but no one was ever arrested or charged with the crime.

The Gunslinger

An obnoxious little man from Newark moved out to Tombstone, Arizona. Surrounded by traces of the Old West, he began to fancy himself a gunslinger. He bought a six-gun and drove out to the desert to teach himself how to shoot.

Day after day he returned to the desert to practice. His favorite targets were giant saguaro cacti. He imagined that they were desperadoes and he was John Wayne. There was one saguaro in particular he liked to use for target practice. It was massive: 15 feet

high and 4 feet around at the base, with two huge arms that made the cactus look like it was surrendering to the Newark cowboy. After a couple of months of taking potshots at this cactus, it was chewed up by bullet holes. But the marksman never gave a thought to the damage he was inflicting on the cactus.

One day, as usual, he drove out to the desert to indulge in his favorite fantasy of saving the life of Cameron Diaz from a 15-foot-tall outlaw. He blasted away at his saguaro. When he stopped to reload, it seemed to him that the saguaro swayed slightly. Curious, he walked over and saw that the base of the cactus was soft and spongy—almost rotted through. It wouldn't take much to make this giant fall over.

As he contemplated the loss of his favorite adversary, a new gunslinger appeared in the desert. This one came from East St. Louis and he, too, saw himself as a hero of the Old West. But while the Newark cowboy favored a six-gun, this character had bought a shotgun. He saw the giant saguaro cactus, but not the small man who was standing behind it. He took careful aim, pulled the trigger and caught the saguaro in the middle.

It wobbled for a moment, then lurched backward.

The man with the shotgun heard a high-pitched "No!" as the saguaro fell. When he ran over he found the gunslinger from Newark, crushed beneath the giant cactus.

Skin-So-Tight

A woman who had been overweight all her life resolved one New Year's Eve that she would lose 100 pounds by the next New Year's Eve. Her friends thought that was too ambitious a goal, but the woman was determined. She checked herself into a weight-loss spa and began a six-month regimen of exercise and carefully prepared low-fat meals. By the end of the six months, she had lost 50 pounds. The woman was jubilant, but it was not enough. She had set 100 pounds as her goal.

She left the spa, returned to New York City and hired a chef to ensure that she ate properly and a personal trainer to design an effective exercise program for her. In the remaining six months she succeeded in shedding another 50 pounds. But when she looked in the mirror, the woman was not pleased by what she saw. After being overweight for so many years, her skin was stretched and flabby. So she sought out the best plastic surgeon in New York.

"Tightening the skin to your new body is a simple procedure," the surgeon assured her. "You'll be pleased with the results."

After surgery the woman was indeed delighted by what she saw. Her skin clung to her new lean and firm body as if she had exercised all her life.

But even thin people experience setbacks. The woman's boyfriend left her for a 20-year-old underwear model. She made risky investments and lost a fortune, which forced her to sell her home in the Hamptons.

In her depression she turned to the one thing that had always

consoled her. Food. For several weeks it seemed that she did
nothing but eat. The woman's skin stretched itself to the limit,
trying to accommodate the new weight, but the plastic surgery had
left no place for these fresh deposits of fat to go. One night, as she
was working on her third pint of Heath Bar Crunch ice cream, the
woman exploded.

When she failed to appear at her office for several days,
concerned friends went to her apartment. They convinced the
building's doorman to open the apartment for them. They found
the woman's ruptured body in the kitchen, where the walls and floor
were splattered with bits of Heath Bar Crunch.

Naked at His Own Surprise Party and Other Erotic Accidents

Naked at His Own Surprise Party

An executive at IBM turned 40, and all day long members of his staff and his colleagues dropped by to wish him a happy birthday. His assistant, a beautiful 25-year-old woman, came into his office last. "I'd like to buy you lunch today," she said. "Something special. Just the two of us at that romantic little French bistro on 55th Street."

The executive agreed, of course. At noon, he and his assistant slipped out of the office and headed for the restaurant. She ordered champagne, and they lingered over their meal for more than two hours.

As the waiter served them coffee and dessert, the assistant said, "Did you know that I live on this block?"

"I had no idea. That's very convenient—for getting to work, I mean."

"Yes, it is convenient," the assistant said. "In fact, why don't we get the check and then drop by my place for a drink."

A few minutes later, they were in the assistant's apartment. As she fixed the drinks, she spilled club soda on her skirt. "I'd better change," she said. "You wait here, and when I get back we'll have an afternoon you'll always remember."

Thinking he was about to get lucky, the executive stripped off all his clothes. But no sooner had he stretched out naked on the couch than he heard a loud cry of "Surprise! Happy Birthday!"

The bedroom door burst open, and there were his wife, his kids and all of his colleagues from the office.

Variations: A husband organizes a surprise party for his wife. To get her out of the house, he takes her to a restaurant for a romantic dinner. When they return home, the wife goes upstairs to get ready for a night of lovemaking, while the husband smuggles the guests into the living room. A few minutes later, the wife, now stark naked, throws open the living room door and cries, "Come and get it!"

She's Having a Baby

A mother and father returned home early from a night out and found their 15-year-old daughter and her boyfriend naked, making love on the living room floor.

In a rage, the father dragged the boy outside, while the mother sat her daughter down on the couch for a talk.

"I'm not going to lecture you," the mother began. "Instead, I want to talk to you about taking precautions."

"Oh Mom. I know all about this stuff. I've been real careful. In fact, I've been using your birth control pills."

The mother was silent for a moment. "Honey, why would you make up a story like that? None of my birth control pills have been missing. I think we better make an appointment with the doctor in the morning."

The girl sighed heavily. "I'm not making up a story. I *have* been using your birth control pills. You haven't noticed because I've been replacing the ones I took with aspirin."

The next morning, the mother made an appointment with her doctor. He told her she was pregnant.

The Stuck Couple

Two policemen were cruising the block when they heard the long blare of a car horn. Following the sound to its source, they found a man and a woman trapped inside a brand-new Ferrari, completely naked in the missionary position. In the tiny confines of the car, the man had thrown his back out and they had been unable to free themselves from their loving embrace.

Unfortunately, the policemen couldn't untangle the couple either.

"Look folks," said one police officer. "We're going to get an ambulance out here and a wrecking crew."

"Oh no!" cried the woman.

"Do it!" the man said. "Do anything you can to get us out of here."

Once the wrecking crew arrived, they saw only one way to free the lovers. They sawed the roof off the Ferrari. Then the paramedics lifted the man out of the car and onto a stretcher.

Before they left for the hospital, one of the paramedics came up to the woman and said, "Don't worry ma'am. It's just a slipped disc."

"I don't care about him!" she exclaimed. "What I'm worried about is how I'm going to explain to my husband what happened to his car!"

Variations: In one telling of the story, the lovers decide to go at it while parked outside the woman's house. Another bizarre version insists

that if a woman is startled while making love, her muscles cramp, making it impossible for the man to withdraw.

The Surprise Lover

Two high school sweethearts from Long Beach Island on the Jersey shore pitched a small tent behind some sand dunes so that they could spend the night together.

About an hour later, two police officers spotted the tent on the beach. The first cop lifted the flap, looked inside and said, "You kids are in big trouble."

"Please officer," said the boy, "give us a break."

"Kid," said the cop, "fornicating in public is a serious offense in this town."

That's when the girl spoke up. "Maybe we can come to an understanding, officer. If I make love to you and your partner, will you let us go?"

"No!" cried the boy.

"Sure!" said the cop.

"Eddie," said the girl, "this way our parents will never know. Now step outside."

Poor Eddie couldn't stand it, so he ran down the beach while the first officer entered the tent.

After a time, the officer crawled out. "Your turn," he said to his partner.

The second cop turned on his flashlight and crawled into the tent.

"Oh no!" he cried.

The girl shrieked, "Daddy!"

Variation: In another version, a father visits his daughter at her college. Back at his hotel, he feels restive and calls an escort service to send someone over to spend the night with him. The prostitute who comes to his hotel room is his own daughter.

The Unseemly Stain

A young woman's parents were going away for the weekend, so she invited her fiancé over. "We have the whole weekend," she told him. "We'll make love in every room in the house."

On Friday night, they started their marathon in the living room—on the parents' brand new white couch. When they got up the next morning, they discovered an unseemly stain on the white upholstery.

"Don't worry," the fiancé said. "I'll get some furniture cleaner. The stain will come right out."

But furniture cleaner didn't work. Neither did the more abrasive stain removers. Not even straight bleach eliminated the stain.

"We're screwed," the guy said.

"Not necessarily," the woman said. "All we have to do is put the blame on somebody else. Get your car keys."

On Sunday afternoon, when the parents returned home, the couple met them at the front door with a welcome-home gift—an adorable golden retriever puppy.

A Night with Batman

A woman on a business trip was sitting in a hotel bar in Dallas when she was approached by a very handsome man. Usually she rebuffed strangers, but this guy was too good to resist. She let him buy her a drink, and then another. And then another. After a couple of hours of conversation, the man invited the woman upstairs to his hotel room.

Once they were alone, the man asked her, "Are you playful?"

"I'm ready for anything," the woman said.

So the man undressed her and laid her down on the bed. From the nightstand drawer he pulled out four white silk ropes and tied the woman's wrists and ankles to the bedposts.

"I'll be back in a moment," he said, and went into the bathroom.

A few minutes later, he bounded back into the room dressed in a Batman costume, crying, "Don't worry, miss! I'll save you!"

After striking a heroic pose, the man leapt onto the dresser. But he lost his footing, slipped, hit his head and knocked himself cold.

The woman tugged at the silk ropes, but she couldn't get free. She waited for half an hour, but still "Batman" did not regain consciousness. Desperate, humiliated and cold, she began to scream for help.

Guests in the adjoining room heard her frantic cries and called the front desk. Within minutes, hotel security, the hotel manager and a small crowd of guests from nearby rooms burst through the door.

"I'm getting real tired of this," said the hotel security officer as he untied the woman. "Tell your friend Batman that the next time he comes to Dallas, I'd like him to stay at a different hotel."

*Variations: The most common alternate version of this story
features a married couple. The husband ties his wife to the bed,
puts on a Superman costume and knocks himself unconscious while
leaping from tall furniture in a single bound. In another variant,
the victim is a traveling businessman and the would-be superhero
is a transvestite.*

The Costume Party

A married couple was invited to their friends' annual Halloween
costume party. The husband announced that he would go as Zorro,
but the wife insisted upon keeping her costume a secret. On the day
of the party, the wife fell ill. "You go anyway," she told her husband.
"I'll be fine here."

Reluctantly, the husband put on his Zorro costume and went off
to the party.

A couple of hours later, the woman felt much better, so she
decided she would go to the party after all. And since her husband
did not know that she was coming dressed as a French maid, it
would give her an opportunity to see how her husband acted when
she was not around.

The party was in full swing when the wife arrived. The wife
spotted Zorro right away—he was dancing with a buxom milkmaid.
Then he had a couple of drinks with a sexy female vampire.
Afterwards, he returned to the dance floor with a leggy blonde
dressed in a parochial schoolgirl uniform.

When the dance was over, the wife decided to test her

husband's fidelity. She sidled up to Zorro and said, "Could you get a lady a drink?"

After a little chatter at the bar, they headed out to the dance floor. She whispered in his ear, "I don't suppose they have any empty bedrooms around here."

"I know they do," Zorro said. "Let's go."

Hand-in-hand, they hurried upstairs and slipped into an empty bedroom. "Keep the lights off and your mask on," the wife said.

"Anything you say," Zorro answered.

After they made love, the woman kissed her masked lover and wished him goodnight. Then she hurried home, hid her costume in the back of the closet and climbed into bed.

About an hour later, her husband returned.

"How was the party?" she asked.

"Not so great," the husband replied. "I really don't have much fun without you."

"You're so sweet. So what did you do all this time? It's after one in the morning. That's a long time to be miserable at a party."

"Oh, I spent the night in the hot tub. One of the guests came to the party without a costume, so I loaned him my Zorro outfit. He told me he had a terrific time tonight."

The Unzipped Fly

A woman came home from the grocery store and saw her husband working under the car. She was in a playful mood, so as she passed she reached down, unzipped his fly and fondled him for a moment. Then she went into the house.

There was her husband, sprawled on the couch in front of the television, watching a football game.

"What are you doing here?" she exclaimed.

The husband looked confused. "I'm watching the game."

"Then who's that under the car?"

"That's Neal. Our mechanic."

"Oh no. You're not going to believe what I just did. I thought it was you, so I pulled down his zipper and played with him a little. If you get my drift."

"Neal's gonna love this," said the husband. "Come on, I'll go with you and help explain."

They found Neal, still under the car, out cold. When the lady of the house had unzipped him, he was so startled that he tried to sit up and knocked himself out on the muffler.

The Erotic Video Scam

A scam artist placed small ads in Australian newspapers and magazines advertising a series of erotic videos at very reasonable prices. Soon the orders began to pour in. In an average week, the scam artist was depositing $10,000 in checks from his buyers.

But none of the customers ever received any videos. Instead, they got an apologetic letter from the company saying that it was unable to fulfill their order. "We are deeply sorry for any disappointment," the letter read, "and we are pleased to enclose a refund."

Printed in large black type across the top of the refund checks was the company name: "Bestiality and Other Perversions Video."

Few of the customers could bring themselves to present the check to their banks. The scam artist made off with over $200,000.

Artificially Endowed

Inspired by the movie *Saturday Night Fever*, a kid from the Bensonhurst neighborhood in Brooklyn started hanging out at discos. After a few nights at the clubs, he realized that women were less interested in men who were good dancers (he happened to be pretty good on the dance floor) than with men whose tight pants revealed an entirely different kind of endowment.

So the following Saturday he put on a tight pair of black polyester pants, and then squeezed a thick 8-inch-long plastic tube

into the crotch. It pressed uncomfortably against the inside of his thigh. In fact, it hurt. But when he looked in the full-length mirror he smiled at what he saw. Tonight he would be irresistible.

The kid was a big hit with the women at the disco. His only problem was which one he would go home with that night. Then around midnight, while he was on the dance floor, he felt lightheaded and couldn't keep his balance. The lights and the crowd began to whirl around him. A moment later, he collapsed.

When the kid woke up in the emergency room, he was wearing a hospital gown. A nurse stood beside his bed. In her hand was the 8-inch plastic tube.

"What happened?" the kid asked. "What's wrong with me?"

"It's your plastic friend here," the nurse said. "It pressed up against the arteries in your crotch and cut off the circulation. That's why you passed out."

She tossed the tube into his lap. "You can go home now. You'll be fine. But just a little advice: next time, stuff your pants with tissues."

The Turkey Neck

On New Year's Day in Scotland, a newly married man went out drinking with two of his buddies. By the time the pub closed, they were all staggering drunk, but the young husband was in worse shape than his two friends.

His friends carried him home, fished his house keys out of his

pocket and carried him into the parlor where they laid him down on the carpet.

"I'm feeling a bit hungry," said one. "How about you?"

"A snack would be good right about now," said the other. "Let's go into the kitchen and see if we can find the remains of the missus's New Year's turkey."

They hauled the leftover turkey out of the fridge and carved themselves generous slices. When they were ready to go, the first friend said, "I have an idea."

He took the turkey neck into the parlor where the man of the house was still passed out on the carpet. The friend unzipped the husband's fly and let the turkey neck dangle out. Snorting with suppressed laughter, the two drunks slipped out of the house as quietly as they could.

Very early the next morning, the wife woke up. When she realized she was in bed alone, she put on her robe and went downstairs. There was her husband, asleep on the carpet. Crouched between his legs was the family's cat, eating what the wife took to be her husband's penis. "No!" she screamed. At which point the cat took fright, seized the turkey neck and ran. The woman fainted from the shock, but the commotion woke her husband, who found his fly open, his wife collapsed at the foot of the stairs and his cat running around with a turkey neck.

Variation: An alternate version is also told in Scotland, in which the drunk's friends take him home and the wife makes a bed for him on the sofa. Before they leave, the two pals unzip their friend's fly and

slip in the turkey neck—all unbeknownst to the wife. During the
night, she goes down to see how her husband is faring and finds the
cat chewing on the turkey neck. She faints from the shock and breaks
her arm.

The Honeymooners

A newlywed couple spent their honeymoon at a theme hotel that
featured giant round beds, mirrored walls, large whirlpool baths and
complimentary champagne. It was tacky, but the couple got into the
spirit of the place and had some of the best sex of their lives.

Their first anniversary rolled around and they decided to go
back to the hotel for a romantic weekend.

When they checked into their suite, they found that everything
was exactly as they had remembered it—with one exception. Now
there was a large screen TV with a VCR and a library of adult
videos.

"What do you say we uncork this champagne and watch a
video?" said the husband.

"Fine with me," said the wife. "You pick something while
I change."

"They've got a movie called *The Honeymooners*," the husband
called to his wife.

"Sounds perfect," she answered from the bathroom.

A moment later, the wife emerged from the bathroom in a lacy
red-and-black teddy. The husband had stripped down to his red silk

boxers. He popped in the video, and the couple settled back into a mountain of pillows covered in red velour.

"Look," said the husband, "the set looks just like this room."

"And the guy is wearing a leather jockstrap, just like the one I gave you for our honeymoon," said the wife.

As the camera moved in for a close up, the wife let out a shrill scream. "That *is* you. And that's *me* on the bed!"

Caught in the Pumpkin Patch

Police in Westchester County, New York, arrested a 27-year-old man in a pumpkin patch at 11:38 pm on a Saturday toward the end of October. The charges were lewd and lascivious behavior, public indecency and driving while intoxicated.

In court, the man said that he had gone out to a bar for a few beers and some company. Getting the beers was no trouble. But finding a woman who would go home with him wasn't nearly as easy.

"About eleven-thirty, I was pretty frustrated, so I decided to go home," the man testified. "I was feeling the need real bad when I passed this pumpkin patch. It occurred to me that pumpkins are nice and soft inside. So I pulled over. There was nobody around for miles. Or at least I thought nobody was around.

"I picked out a nice pumpkin, cut a hole in it with my pocket knife and let nature follow its course."

The arresting officer testified that when she approached the man she said, "'Excuse me sir, but do you realize you are screwing a

pumpkin?' Then he answered, 'A pumpkin! Damn, is it midnight already?'"

He was found guilty on all charges.

Walking the Dog

Every evening after dinner, a husband took his Labrador retriever on a four-mile walk. One day he came down with a bad case of the flu, so it fell to his wife to walk the dog.

After supper, she clipped on the dog's leash, and they headed out the door. She wanted to go to a large open lot at the end of the street, but the dog tugged at the leash and all but dragged her around the block to a house on the corner. The dog pulled the poor woman up the stairs and began scratching furiously at the door.

The wife scolded the dog and was trying to pull it away when she heard a sweet female voice inside the house call, "You're a little early today, darling! Just one minute."

The next moment, the door swung wide open and there stood a pretty young woman in a sexy negligee holding a large bone in her hand. "This should keep the dog happy while we're—Uh-oh."

The Bad Bachelorette

The friends of a future bride arranged a raucous bachelorette party for her, including live entertainment provided by a male stripper, a handsome black bodybuilder.

By the time he arrived, the bride had had one drink too many. After the show, she took the stripper by the hand and led him to a bedroom for a private performance.

The stripper left a couple of hours later, and the bride woke up the next morning with no memory of the night's events. Her friends had already decided among themselves to keep the story a secret, so the wedding went on as planned.

When the newlyweds returned from their honeymoon, the wife discovered that she was pregnant. The happy couple waited eagerly for their first child. Nine months later, the woman went into labor. The husband was at her side in the delivery room. "Here we go," said the doctor. "It's a . . ." And then he stopped.

"What's the matter, Doc?" said the husband. "Can't you tell if it's a boy or a girl?"

Without a word, the doctor held up a healthy little mixed-race boy.

Variations: In another version of the story, the woman gives birth to twins: one white, one black. In some retellings of the legend, the husband storms out of the delivery room and files for divorce.

The Clogged Toilet

The toilet in a couple's master bedroom kept backing up. The husband tried the plunger and poured drain opener down by the quart, but nothing worked. Finally, he called a plumber.

In a matter of minutes, the plumber found the obstruction. He pulled up a mass of condoms—dozens of them—that had lodged in the line.

"Look mister," the plumber said, "I'm really happy for you that you've got such an active love life. But just toss these babies in the garbage and you won't clog up your toilet anymore. Okay?"

The husband was quiet for a moment. He didn't use condoms. But he wasn't going to tell the plumber that. "Right. Thanks for the advice."

After the plumber left, the husband confronted his wife with the wad of condoms. "Anybody I know?" he asked.

"No. You don't know him. He's the landscaper. He shows up after you've left for work."

The next day, the husband left for work at the usual time. But instead of going to the office, he hid in the woods across the street from his house. He had his shotgun with him. Around ten o'clock, the landscaper pulled his truck into the driveway. As he stepped out of the cab, the husband fired.

The landscaper fell to the ground with his backside full of birdshot. The wife hurried from the house. "You idiot!" she screamed. "My boyfriend is on vacation. This guy is just covering for him!"

The Baby Train

The census bureau in Canberra, Australia, was surprised to learn that in a little oceanfront town north of Sydney the birthrate was three times the national average. One employee at the bureau was so intrigued that he made a special trip to the town to learn more about it.

When he arrived he saw kids everywhere. All the schools were jammed. The maternity section was the largest wing of the local hospital. Every park and playground was swarming with kids.

Aside from the extraordinary number of children, the town seemed like any other place in Australia. Nor could the census bureau employee detect anything special about the adults. So he stopped by the town hall to see if he could learn anything there.

The mayor welcomed him into his office.

"Mayor, I couldn't help noticing all the children around here."

"Yes, we are especially blessed with little ones. My wife and I have eight, you know."

"Congratulations," the census bureau employee replied. "If you could throw any light on your town's high birthrate, the census bureau would appreciate it."

"It's very simple. It has to do with the *Kyogle Mail*."

"That's a train, isn't it?" the visitor from Canberra said.

"Absolutely."

"A train is the reason your town's birthrate is three times the national average?"

"Yes. Let me explain. The railway line makes an S-curve through our town. When the train crosses the town line, about four-

thirty every morning, it blows its whistle which wakes up everybody in the place. Two miles later, when it's on its way out of town, it blows the whistle again. Well, it's too early to get up, but hardly worth falling back to sleep. So to fill the time before the alarm clock goes off"

Variations: Many places claim that an early morning train gives their town or region an unusually high birthrate—from the campus of Michigan State University to small towns in rural Utah.

The Stylist Makes a Mistake

An unkempt man walked into a styling salon in a shopping mall about half an hour before closing and asked for a haircut. The man looked strange, and the stylist was hesitant because she was working alone and there were no other customers around. But in the end she agreed to give him a haircut.

She pinned the sheet around his neck and had just picked up her comb and scissors when she noticed the man's hand moving up and down in his lap beneath the sheet. Thinking he was a sexual deviant with a hair fetish, she hit him with a large bottle of shampoo and knocked the man out cold. Then she called the mall's security department.

When security arrived, the man was still unconscious and the stylist was standing over him, holding her shampoo bottle. When the police removed the sheet, they saw the man's hands in his lap, holding a handkerchief and a pair of eyeglasses.

Variations: In English versions of this legend, the hairdresser knocks the man out with a hairdryer. There is another English version in which the stylist grabs a large hair brush and hits the lump under the sheet, breaking the man's glasses.

"Go for It, Mr. Gorsky"

As astronaut Neil Armstrong took his first step on the moon, he uttered those immortal words, "One small step for man, one giant leap for mankind." A moment later, mission control heard Armstrong say, "Go for it, Mr. Gorsky."

Nobody at NASA had any idea what Armstrong was talking about. At first some thought that it was a private message to a fellow astronaut, but there was no one named Gorsky in the American or in the Soviet space program. Once he was back on earth, Armstrong brushed off all inquiries saying it must have been a jumbled transmission.

Twenty-six years later, Armstrong and a friend from NASA were having dinner together. As they reminisced about the old days, the friend asked Armstrong, "So what was that 'Go for it, Mr. Gorsky' remark all about?"

Armstrong sighed and said, "Well, he's passed on now, so I suppose I can tell you the story. Years ago, when I was in high school, I was playing baseball with my brother. He hit a foul ball that flew over the fence and into our neighbors' bushes. Our neighbors were the Gorskys. It was summer and all the windows were open.

So when I went into the bushes to get the ball, I heard Mrs. Gorsky say, 'You want to know when I'll give you oral sex? I'll tell you when. I'll give you oral sex when the kid next door walks on the moon!' "

THE STOLEN KIDNEY
AND OTHER MEDICAL MISHAPS

The Stolen Kidney

A business traveler from New York was sitting in the bar of his hotel in Rio de Janeiro when two well-dressed men took the seats beside him. While the two men waited for their drinks, they struck up a conversation with the American. They introduced themselves as executives at the Bank of Brazil. Soon, all three were deep in discussion about international trade. After a couple of drinks at the bar, the three men had dinner together in the restaurant. Then they returned to the bar for a few more drinks.

Some hours later, the American traveler awoke in the bathtub of his hotel room, naked and submerged up to his neck in ice. Scrawled in large letters on the wall facing him was the message, "Don't move. Just call 911." On a small table beside the bathtub was a telephone.

When the 911 operator picked up the man said, "I don't know what's happened to me. My back hurts. I'm in a bathtub filled with ice and there's this message that I must not move until I've called 911. But I don't know what the emergency might be."

"Sir," the operator said, "it is important that you remain calm. I've received calls like this before. Now, reach behind you carefully. Can you feel a tube in your lower back?"

The man did as he was instructed.

"Yes. There's a tube back there. What does it mean?"

"Sir, please keep still. I've already traced your call and sent an ambulance to your hotel. They'll be there soon."

In a few minutes, the man heard the door to his room open.

"I'm in the bathroom," he cried.

A team of paramedics, hotel security and the hotel manager filled the room. They lifted him carefully onto a gurney and rushed him to the nearest emergency room.

"What's wrong with me?" the man asked.

"The doctors at the hospital must examine you first," the paramedics told him.

In the emergency room, a doctor performed a quick examination. "It's as we suspected," he said. "Sir, I am afraid that whoever you were with this evening drugged you and harvested one of your kidneys while you were unconscious."

"One of my kidneys is gone?!"

"Yes sir," the doctor replied. "But you are fortunate. I have seen cases where the thieves took both."

Variations: In some tellings of this legend, the unsuspecting donor is seduced by a beautiful stranger who takes him back to her hotel room where, after making love, the victim is drugged and a surgical SWAT team harvests his kidney. The version told in Central and South America is even more gruesome: Babies are kidnapped and murdered for their organs.

The Unsuspecting Donor

Mike, a salesman from Philadelphia, was driving one Monday night in winter when his car hit a patch of black ice and slammed sideways into a tree. When the paramedics arrived, they found him unconscious and his right leg severed just below the knee. They packed the limb in ice and rushed Mike and his leg to the hospital, but the damage to his knee was too extensive for the doctors to reattach the leg. He would have to be fitted with a prosthetic device.

Mike took the bad news well—he had lost a leg, but at least he was still alive. And he was eager to begin physical therapy so he could become accustomed to his prosthetic leg.

Two weeks later, at a therapy session, Mike met a guy named Ray who worked construction. Ray's right foot had been crushed in an accident on the job and the doctors had been forced to amputate.

"But I was lucky," Ray told Mike, "because the hospital found a donor and the doctor attached that foot to my leg. I've got some feeling back already and I can even bend a couple of my toes. The only trouble is my left foot is a size eight, while my new foot is a size ten. Learning how to walk again is tough enough without having feet that don't match."

Mike was quiet for a minute.

"When did they give you your new foot?" Mike asked.

"Two weeks ago. On a Monday night."

"And the docs said that a donor came in that evening?"

"Right."

"Does your new foot have a mole on the big toe?"

"Yeah, it does. Hey, why all the questions?"

"Because," said Mike, "that's my foot you're wearing."

The Stomach Pump Luncheon

Although this story appears in John Berendt's recent bestseller Midnight in the Garden of Good and Evil, *the origins of the legend go back at least to the 1940s.*

During the week between Christmas and New Year's, a prominent Los Angeles socialite hosted a holiday luncheon. For the fish course she served generous portions of a delicious salmon mousse.

While the maid served the salad, the hostess went into the kitchen to see how the rest of the meal was coming along. She found her cat on the kitchen counter, gobbling up the remainder of the salmon mousse. The hostess grabbed the cat, opened the back door and tossed it outside. Then she returned to her guests.

The rest of the meal went off without a hitch, and the hostess knew that her party was a triumph. But while her guests were lingering over their coffee and dessert, the maid approached and whispered in the hostess's ear, "Ma'am, could I speak with you for a moment, please? There's been a bit of trouble."

The hostess excused herself and went into the kitchen with the maid. There, lying on the kitchen floor, was the hostess's cat. It was dead.

"I found him this way by the curb," the maid said. "I don't know what happened."

"Oh no!" said the hostess. "I caught him eating the salmon mousse. He must have died of ptomaine! What will I tell my guests?"

She rushed back to the dining room, where she made an announcement. "My dear friends, I regret to say that it has just come to my attention that the salmon mousse was a bit off. As a precaution, it would be best if we all went to the Mercy Hospital emergency room."

At the hospital, the emergency room doctors insisted that the hostess and her guests have their stomachs pumped. It was a horrible ordeal for everyone.

That evening, the hostess was in her sitting room, trying to recover from the humiliation of having nearly poisoned all of her friends. The doorbell rang and rather than wait for the maid, she answered it herself. A neighbor from down the street stood on the doorstep.

"Dorothy," he said, "my conscience has been bothering me all day. So don't say a word, just hear me out. This afternoon, about lunchtime, I hit your cat with my car. I couldn't bring myself to tell you, so I just left its body by the curb. Can you forgive me?"

The Backwards, Bare-Bottomed Skier

A young woman went with several friends for a ski weekend in Aspen. Although she was still fairly inexperienced, her friends talked her into joining them on one of the more challenging slopes.

There was a long line at the chairlift and while she waited the woman felt the need to use the ladies' room. "Don't worry," one of her friends told her. "There are probably restrooms at the top."

It was another 20 minutes before the young woman finally got a chair and the long ride, especially in subfreezing weather, only added to her discomfort. By the time the chair arrived at the top of the slope, the need was urgent. And then she discovered that there were no restrooms.

"I'll have to go in the woods," she told her friends. "Keep your fingers crossed that nobody sees me."

She found some rhododendron bushes that looked like they would give her cover. With a sigh of relief, the young woman scrambled behind the bushes. She was just about done when she felt herself beginning to slide. She grabbed a branch, but it snapped in her hand. Suddenly she was skiing swiftly down the hill, backwards, with her ski pants around her ankles and her bare bottom completely exposed. She shot down the slope in a straight line, picking up momentum, until she crashed into a pylon.

The ski patrol arrived a few minutes later, pulled up her pants, put a splint on her broken arm and rushed her to a hospital emergency room.

As she was resting in bed, waiting for her friends to come and

pick her up, a hospital orderly wheeled another bed into the room. It was a young man with a broken leg.

To pass the time she asked, "Did you break that on the slopes?"

"Oh yeah," he answered. "And in the damnedest way possible. I had just started my run, when out of the bushes comes this woman skiing backwards, with her pants around her ankles. I couldn't take my eyes off her. That's when I skied right into a tree. So what happened to you?"

The woman hesitated for a moment. "I slipped climbing out of the bathtub."

Variations: This story varies only in its setting. It is usually set in Vail or Aspen, but many people have heard it from "a friend of a friend" who "really saw it" while skiing in Pennsylvania or Canada. In Sweden this story was reported on the evening news as an actual event.

The Infected Needle in the Pay Phone

A young woman stopped to use a pay phone in New York City's East Village. When she completed her call, she stuck her index finger into the coin return slot to check if a previous caller had left some change behind. But instead of finding a coin, she felt a sharp pain in her finger.

She yanked her finger out. It was bleeding. She looked inside the coin return and saw a hypodermic needle jammed inside. "Damn New Yorkers," she said. "I hate this town."

She wiped off the blood with a tissue and went about her business.

A couple of weeks later, the young woman felt ill and went to her doctor. As part of the examination, her doctor drew some blood and sent it to the lab. "I'll call you with the results tomorrow," he said.

First thing the next morning, the young woman got a call from her doctor asking her to come by his office so they could review the test results.

He invited her into his private office and closed the door. As he sat down in the chair beside her, he said, "I'll have to ask you some personal questions. Do you practice safe sex?"

"Of course. Why do you ask?"

"Have you ever been an intravenous drug user?"

"No! Never! What are you saying?"

"Just one last question. Have you used a pay phone lately?"

"Yes. A couple of weeks ago. I remember because someone had put a needle in the coin slot and I pricked my finger on it when I checked for change."

The doctor was silent for a moment.

"We've learned recently that some drug users are disposing of their used needles in pay phones. Most likely their motive is revenge for becoming infected with hepatitis or some other disease."

"Are you telling me that needle gave me hepatitis?"

"No," the doctor said. "I'm afraid that needle infected you with HIV."

Variations: In a popular alternate version of this legend, the victim feels a pinprick when he or she takes a seat in a movie theater.

Another less common variant has the victim being pricked in a crowded place, such as on a bus or a subway.

The Oozing Brain

The invention of slice-and-bake cookie dough gave birth to this legend. A woman in Baltimore belonged to a volunteer organization that ran errands for invalids and the elderly. During an August heatwave, she received a call from an elderly woman who needed someone to do a little grocery shopping for her. The elderly woman read off her shopping list and then gave her address. It was a rundown part of the inner city, but the volunteer couldn't refuse the poor woman.

The volunteer drove to the supermarket, picked up everything the elderly woman had asked for and then headed for the rough part of town. It was as bad as she suspected: burnt-out buildings, vacant lots strewn with garbage, groups of hoodlums gathered on every corner. The volunteer was so frightened that she locked her doors and rolled up all the windows. Her car was not air-conditioned and within minutes it was a sweltering oven.

Then the woman heard a loud "Pop!" and felt something oozing down the back of her neck.

"My God!" she cried. "I've been shot!"

Somehow, she regained her composure and drove to a nearby hospital. Through superhuman effort, she even walked into the emergency room where she told the nurses at the desk that she had been shot in the head. Immediately, a team of doctors and nurses put her on an operating table and rolled her into an examining room.

"Where's the wound?" one doctor said. "I can't see any blood."

"Look at the back of my head!" the woman cried. "Can't you see my brains oozing out?"

Carefully, the doctor turned the woman's head. He touched the wet, white mass that clung to her hair.

"Ma'am," the doctor said, "this isn't your brain. It's slice-and-bake cookie dough."

The Menopausal Party Girl

A mother in the throes of menopause decided to visit her daughter in San Francisco. After a couple of days, the mother was so cranky and physically uncomfortable that the daughter implored her to visit her gynecologist. Under the best of circumstances, the mother did not like going to a gynecologist, let alone a strange one in a strange city. But her daughter assured her that this one was considerate and kind and had a charming sense of humor. At last the mother agreed to go.

On the morning of her appointment, the mother was very nervous. She took a bath. Then she took a shower. She used deodorant from head to toe and even borrowed her daughter's vaginal spray. Ready at last, she called a cab to take her to the doctor's office.

The gynecologist was everything her daughter said he would be. Thoughtful, gentle and very sweet. But when he began his examination, he said, "Well, it looks like we've got a party girl here!"

"What did you say to me?"

"I said that you must be quite the party girl." Then the gynecologist smirked and winked at the woman.

Completely humiliated, the woman did not utter another word for the remainder of the examination. When it was over, she dressed quickly and hurried out of the office.

That night the daughter came home from work and found her mother in tears.

"What happened? What did the doctor tell you?"

"He took one look down there and he called me a party girl," the mother wailed.

"He said what?!"

"He said I was a party girl. I've never been so humiliated in my life."

"I don't understand. It's not like him at all. Let's take a deep breath and go over this slowly. What did you do before you left the house for your appointment?"

"Well, I was extremely careful about hygiene. I took a bath and a shower—just to be on the safe side. I used plenty of deodorant. And I borrowed your vaginal spray."

"Mother, I don't have any vaginal spray."

"Of course you do. I'll show you."

Together, they walked to the bathroom where the mother pulled the spray bottle from the cupboard beneath the sink.

"Oh Mom!" the daughter cried. "That's not vaginal spray. That's the gold glitter hairspray I used last year at Halloween."

The Contaminated Tampon

Several years ago a new tampon was introduced on the market. It was attractively packaged and reasonably priced, so many women tried the new product. But over time, many of the women who used the new tampon noticed that their periods were heavier than they had been before. Some women sent letters urging a consumer advocacy group to investigate the product.

In their labs, the advocacy group found that the tampon included asbestos. Asbestos induces bleeding. Naturally, if a woman's flow is heavier, she will have buy more tampons.

The advocacy group published their results in a woman's magazine, and the manufacturer was forced to take their tampons off the market.

AIDS Mary

A woman from Seattle named Mary decided to escape the rainy winter months and spend a few weeks in Aruba. Her travel agent booked her a suite in a deluxe resort hotel on a gorgeous private beach. Thirty minutes after she checked in, Mary was lounging on the beach enjoying the attentions of a very handsome cabana boy.

The cabana boy set up a large beach umbrella for her, brought her fresh towels and refreshing drinks from the bar and even rubbed sunscreen on her back and shoulders. Mary relished the luxury of having a personal attendant.

Then one evening, as she was about to go to bed, there was a knock at her door. It was the cabana boy with a bottle of Dom Perignon and a bowl of strawberries. Mary invited him in and they spent the night together. In fact, they spent every night of Mary's vacation together.

On the morning of her departure, Mary almost wept at the thought of leaving her handsome young lover. After they had said their good-byes, a woman from the front desk took Mary aside.

"Excuse my intrusion, miss," she said. "But have you been intimate with that man?"

"How dare you stick your nose in my business! Where's the hotel manager?" Mary exclaimed.

"I know I have offended you, miss. Do whatever you must. But take my advice as well: When you return home, go to your doctor and have a blood test. That boy has AIDS and he does not care if he infects anyone else."

Mary was shocked and terrified. Back in Seattle, her doctor gave her the bad news: She was indeed infected with HIV.

Mary spent days locked in her apartment weeping. But then she became angry. Since the boy in Aruba was doing all he could to infect unsuspecting women, she would seduce every man she could.

That night Mary went to a hotel bar and picked up a businessman. The next morning, when the man woke up, he found that Mary was gone. But in the bathroom, scrawled across the mirror in blood-red lipstick was the message, "Welcome to the world of AIDS!"

Variations: One version of the story presents AIDS Mary as especially vindictive: She dates each of her victims for at least a month to increase her chance of infecting them with HIV. In some tellings, Mary is a prostitute who is retaliating for her mistreatment at the hands of men. Another variant is about AIDS John, a bisexual American soldier who infects both men and women.

The Orgasmic Side-Effect

A clinical psychiatrist in Canada discovered an unusual side effect to a new antidepressant drug.

One day, a male patient who was taking the antidepressant called.

"Doc, this stuff is great!" he said. "I want to stay on it for life."

The psychiatrist said that if his depression was in complete remission, then they should suspend the treatment.

"No way, Doc," said the patient. "Since I've started taking these little pills, every time I yawn I have an incredible orgasm. Of course, it's a little embarrassing ejaculating in the office or on the train. But I'm willing to put up with the inconvenience—this is the best antidepressant I've ever had!"

The Hairball

In the middle of math class, a fourth-grade girl clutched her stomach, let out a sharp scream and fell to the floor. By the time her teacher reached her, the child was dead.

The rest of the students became hysterical. The principal closed the school for the rest of the day and called the parents, the police and an emergency medical team.

"I don't know what happened," the teacher said, sobbing. "She was working quietly on the math problems I had assigned, and chewing on the ends of her braids like she always did when she was concentrating hard. Then she cried out and fell out of her chair."

The police and the medical team held a brief conference together and then announced to the parents, "We're awfully sorry to do this to you folks. But we'll have to perform an autopsy."

The next day, the parents met with the county coroner. "I understand your daughter was in the habit of chewing on her braids whenever she was doing her schoolwork."

"That's right," the father said. "All her teachers said the harder she was working, the harder she'd chew on her braids. It was so sweet."

The coroner shuffled some papers on his desk top and cleared his throat several times.

"We found that your daughter died of a large obstruction in her intestine. You see, she wasn't merely chewing on her hair. She was eating it. It formed a hairball in her stomach. And it was the hairball that killed her."

Variation: The most common variant of this legend is of a barber who keels over at work one day. An autopsy reveals that he was suffocated by an enormous hairball in his esophagus, the result of years of breathing in his clients' hair.

The Lost and Found False Teeth

Three men, all of them about 65, went deep-sea fishing off the coast of South Africa. They hadn't been out long when one of the three became violently seasick. Worse, as he vomited over the side he lost his set of false teeth.

Nauseous, angry and depressed, the frustrated fisherman went off by himself into the ship's cabin.

Not long afterwards, one of the fishermen hooked a swordfish. They called to their friend to come out and share the excitement of the catch, but he wasn't interested.

"Let's try to cheer him up a bit," the guy who caught the fish said. With that, he removed his own set of false teeth and put them in the swordfish's mouth. Then he called to his friend, "Charlie! Come here! You'll never believe it. This fish has got your teeth in its mouth!"

Charlie hurried out of the cabin. He opened the swordfish's mouth and pulled out the false teeth. "It's a miracle!" he said. "What are the chances of you boys catching the fish that swallowed my teeth?"

But as he inspected the set more closely, Charlie lost his

enthusiasm. "I knew it was too good to be true," he said. "These teeth aren't mine."

And before his friends could say another word, Charlie tossed the false teeth over the side.

Sedating Rover

A veterinarian in a small Texas town hired a recent graduate from a veterinary college who was pleasant and eager, but had no experience with a practice. One day, while the vet had gone home to lunch, a man came in with an ancient, wheezing old mutt.

"I'm taking the whole family on a vacation to California," the man explained. "And it would be easier on Rover if you could put him to sleep."

The young vet-in-training scratched old Rover behind the ears, lifted him up on the examination table and gave him a lethal injection. In a few moments, Rover closed his eyes and passed quietly into eternity.

"Could you give me a hand getting the pooch in the back seat?" Rover's owner said.

As the young vet and the man wrestled Rover into the car, the man said, "Thanks for your help, Doc. Lord knows I love this dog. My kids are just nuts about him. But it's a long drive to California and as your boss can tell you, Rover really can't travel that far anymore without being sedated. See you when we come back!"

The young vet never said a word, just stood there and waved as

the man drove off.

"If I'm lucky," he said to himself, "the family will think Rover passed away peacefully during the drive."

THE MURDERER IN
THE BACKSEAT
AND OTHER LEGENDS OF THE ROAD

The Murderer in the Backseat

A newspaper in Phoenix reported this legend as if it were a true story.
A woman walked out of a shopping mall near Phoenix, Arizona,
and across the parking lot to her car. She was aware that a man
was walking a few steps behind her, but she was not especially
concerned: It was the middle of the afternoon and the lot was filled
with people. She got to her car, climbed in, locked the doors and
pulled out of the parking space. By coincidence, the man who had
followed her was parked right next to her.

She drove to the exit. The man's car was directly behind her.
She turned onto the highway. The man made the same turn. She
accelerated, but the man kept up with her. In fact, now he was
drawing closer, almost riding her rear bumper. And he began to
flash his high beams.

Frightened now, she got off at an exit for downtown Phoenix.
The man stayed with her. She sped through the city streets, running
red lights in her panic. But she could not shake her pursuer.

So she headed toward the home of her brother-in-law, a police
officer. Blaring her car horn, she pulled into the driveway. Her
brother-in-law hurried out of his house.

"There's a man following me!" she cried. "All the way from the
mall! There he is now!"

The stranger pulled his car into the driveway. The cop ran over
shouting, "Phoenix Police! Get out of the car! What the hell do you
think you're doing?"

As the stranger stepped out of his car, the cop wrestled him to

the ground. "Take it easy, officer," he said. "I was just trying to warn the lady about the guy in the backseat of her car."

The cop stood up, pushed his sister-in-law away from the car and threw open the back door. There, huddled behind the driver's seat, was a man with a big hunting knife clutched in his hand.

Variation: In another version of the story, the woman pulls into a gas station late at night. When she hands over her credit card for payment, the attendant tells her that there is something wrong and convinces her to come into the office with him. He makes a phone call; moments later the police arrive and pull the would-be killer from the backseat.

The Hairy-Armed Hitchhiker

The earliest version of this legend dates from England, 1834.
A woman went to the supermarket late one rainy evening in the middle of the week. By the time she finished shopping, the store was about to close and the parking lot was almost empty. As she pushed her cart across the lot, a tall, heavy woman approached her.

"I'm so embarrassed," the strange woman said. "I came here to buy a few things, but once I got to the checkout counter, I found that I didn't have any money with me. Then I got outside just in time to see the tow truck taking away my car. It's been repossessed. I haven't been able to make the payments since I lost my job. Now it's raining and I don't have an umbrella and my apartment is five miles from here. This is so humiliating. Could you give me a ride home?"

The shopper hesitated for a moment. The stranger was definitely odd. Her clothes didn't fit very well, and her voice was harsh. But it was cold and the rain was coming down hard now.

"Yes. I can drive you home. It's no trouble at all."

The woman put her groceries in the trunk, then she and the stranger climbed into the car. As the stranger reached up for the seat belt, the sleeve of her coat slipped down. The woman saw a thick, hairy wrist. Like a man's.

Now she was frightened. What could she do to get this person out of her car?

They drove for a mile or two when she had an idea.

"Oh damn!" she said.

"Is something wrong?" the stranger asked.

"I think both of my tail-lights are out."

"Well, we aren't far from my place now. You can always take the car to the mechanic tomorrow."

"You don't understand. This happened once before and I was rear-ended. I spent three weeks in the hospital. I can't go through that again. Could you do me a favor? I'll pull over and you get out and see if at least one of the tail-lights is working. I'd feel so much better."

"Yeah. Sure," the stranger said.

So the woman pulled her car to the curb. "You're sweet to do this for me," she said.

Once the stranger had climbed out of the car, the woman hit the gas and sped away. She drove straight to the police station where she filed a report. "Now let's go outside and inspect your car," a police officer said.

Pointing to a large handbag on the front seat, the cop asked, "Is that yours, ma'am?"

"No. That's hers. Or his. It must have been left behind when I got her . . . him . . . to step out of the car."

"Let's see what we have here," the cop said. Pulling on a pair of latex gloves, he opened the bag. And drew out a large, sharp hatchet.

Variation: In the earliest printed version of this legend, a gentleman in a rig stops to give a lone woman a ride. Once he notices "her" hairy forearms, the hitchhiker runs off, leaving behind an overnight bag. Inside the gentleman finds a pair of loaded pistols.

The Headless Biker

On a road outside Newcastle, England, a man on a motorcycle drew up beside a large truck loaded with thin sheets of steel. Before the biker could pass the truck, the top sheet came loose, slid off the truck bed and neatly decapitated him.

Convulsively, the corpse tightened its grip on the hand throttle. The bike accelerated until it was even with the cab of the truck.

Glancing out his window, the truck driver saw the headless corpse riding a motorcycle. The horror of the sight gave him a heart attack. As the driver slumped over the wheel, the impact of his body turned the steering wheel slightly. The truck swerved to the right— and straight into a small crowd of people waiting for a bus, killing them instantly.

Variation: The most common alternate version of this story is of a beautiful collie who loves to ride in the family car with its head out the window. One day, a truck passes a little too closely to the car and the poor dog is decapitated.

The Snake in Her Jeans

On a warm summer's day in San Francisco, a woman headed out to her car to go shopping. As she backed her car out of the garage, she remembered that she had left her wallet in the house. Leaving the car door wide open, she went back inside. Five minutes later, with her wallet tucked in her purse, the woman pulled out of the driveway and headed for the city.

As she drove across the Golden Gate Bridge, she felt something tickling her ankle. She glanced down and saw a snake disappear up the leg of her jeans.

Screaming and kicking, she barely managed to pull her car to the side of the road. She leapt out of her car, shaking and slapping her leg until she fell to the ground shrieking.

A passing driver saw her and thought she was having an epileptic seizure. The woman was flailing about on the ground so wildly that the man was afraid she might hurt herself. He pulled over to help, but he was not a doctor and had no idea what to do. So he tried to hold her down.

Another driver saw what he took to be a woman struggling violently with an attacker on the side of the road. "I can't believe he's assaulting her in broad daylight!" he said to himself. He pulled

over and grabbed the tire iron from his trunk. He took a good swing, caught the man along the side of his face and broke his jaw.

As the good Samaritan collapsed on the pavement, the woman's cries became even more hysterical. "It's not him!" she said. "It's the snake!"

The man with the tire iron was certain he had misunderstood the woman. But as he glanced down, he saw a small garter snake slither out from the leg of the woman's jeans.

Variations: In other versions of this legend, the woman is traveling with her pet mouse/gerbil/hamster in her lap. At some point during the drive, the little critter slips down to the floor of the car and climbs up the leg of the woman's pants.

"Pig!"

A man who was always self-conscious about his weight was speeding on a country road in Oregon one fine spring morning. At a fork in the road the driver bore to the left without reducing his speed. There was a farmer walking along the shoulder of the road. He looked up as the car approached and shouted at the driver, "Pig!"

The driver hung out the window of his car and shouted back, "You're not so great-looking yourself!"

Then he drew his head back into the car and returned his gaze to the road. As he rounded the next bend, he saw an enormous sow sunning herself in the middle of the road, only a couple of yards

ahead of him.

The driver hit the brakes and tried to swerve around the animal. But the pig was too close and the car was moving too fast. All the driver heard was a squeal of terror and the brakes' screech as he plowed right into the pig.

The Flat Tire and the Madman

Late one night, a woman driving alone got a flat tire outside a hospital for the mentally unstable near Pendleton, Oregon. She was irritated that she would be delayed getting home, and it was unnerving to be on a dark road alone late at night. But she knew how to change a flat; she could be on her way in 15 minutes.

She popped the trunk and took out the tire iron, the jack and the spare tire. She pried off the hubcap, removed the five lug nuts, and placed them inside the hubcap so she wouldn't lose them. As she reached for the jack, she heard a rustling sound in the bushes beside the fence. Looking over the rear fender of her car, she could see the dark, silent figure of a man pressed against the fence, watching her.

She tried to remain calm and keep her mind on her task. Her hands trembled slightly as she removed the flat tire and put on the spare. A high fence topped by coils of razor wire stood between her and the hospital patient who watched her, but she was still ill at ease. In her nervousness she kicked the hubcap. The woman's heart sank as she heard the lug nuts scatter into the tall grass along the side of the road. Frightened and frustrated, she began to cry.

"Don't cry," said the figure at the fence. "Don't cry. You can still fix the tire."

The woman stifled her sobs for a moment and listened.

"Take one lug nut from each of the other three tires. That will keep the spare on until you get home, or find a gas station."

The woman was still afraid, but she did as the stranger suggested. When the job was done, she managed to stammer out a "thank you."

"You're welcome," said the figure at the fence. As she drove away, the woman glanced back at the spot where the stranger had stood. But he had vanished.

The Severed Fingers

Versions of this legend date back to 16th-century France.
In the 1960s a college senior took his girlfriend to a drive-in movie in his new Volkswagen Beetle. Four loud, obnoxious guys in a beat-up Plymouth Valiant pulled into the space next to the young lovers. The guys hauled a case of beer out of the trunk, wedged it into the back seat of their car and settled back to watch the movie.

As the movie progressed, the four louts became drunker and drunker. They started a running commentary, in the foulest language, on the storyline of the movie and speculated on the sex lives of the actors.

The boy in the Volkswagen was getting angry. "I'll be right back," he told his girlfriend. Before she could stop him, he got out of his car and walked around to the drunks' car.

"You guys want to keep it down?" he said.

The loudmouths answered with a barrage of obscenities. The boyfriend answered in kind. As all four guys reached for the door handles, he realized that maybe a confrontation with a carload of drunks was not such a bright idea. He rushed back to the Volkswagen, rolled up the windows and locked the doors.

"We've got to go," he said to his girlfriend.

"I told you to leave them alone," she said, annoyed.

But no sooner had the ignition turned over than the four drunks surrounded the car. Three of them lifted the back of the car off the ground. Without any traction, the rear wheels spun helplessly in the air. The boyfriend kept gunning the engine.

"What are you doing?" his girlfriend screamed.

"They can't hold it up forever," the boyfriend said.

He was right. After a few minutes the exhaust fumes, combined with the weight of the car, became too much for the drunks. They dropped their load and the Volkswagen sped away.

"Did you hear a scream?" the girlfriend asked.

"No. And who cares if we did," he replied.

Back home, the boy inspected the rear of his Volkswagen for any sign of damage. As he rested his hand on the rear bumper, he felt something wet. Shining the flashlight at the spot, he first saw blood. Then he saw, wedged between the bumper and the trunk, three severed fingers.

Variations: The earliest printed version of this legend dates from a book published in France in 1579. A robber stops a horseman on a deserted road. To keep his victim from escaping, the highwayman

wraps the horse's bridle around his fingers. Suddenly the rider uses his spurs and the horse bolts down the road, taking several of the bandit's fingers with him.

The Collision

One rainy evening in Germany, two trucks, coming from opposite directions, were speeding along a back road near Bonn. They both hit a slick stretch of road at the same time and plowed head-on into each other.

When the ambulance crew arrived they found that both drivers were dead. Meanwhile, the wrecking crew discovered that the impact of the collision had been so great that the trucks could not be pried apart. The trucks were towed to the junkyard as a single vehicle.

For the first day or so the wrecked trucks were a popular curiosity at the junkyard. Mechanics, used-car dealers and members of the highway patrol dropped by to inspect them. By the third day, however, the visitors were complaining of a foul smell.

"Something dead is in there," one of the highway cops told the foreman of the yard. "You better get it out before it becomes a health hazard."

"The ambulance pulled the bodies of the drivers from the wreck," the foreman answered. "What else could be in there?"

"The only way to find out," the cop told him, "is to pry those trucks apart."

The yard crew hooked up four huge tow trucks. To the screeching sound of tearing metal, the two wrecks were finally

wrenched apart. From between them spilled a completely flattened Volkswagen Beetle—and the decomposing remains of the car's four passengers.

Trapped by Their Seat Belts

This story made the rounds in Wisconsin when the state legislature passed a mandatory seat belt law in 1987.

A stretch limo pulled up in front of a house in Dickeyville, Wisconsin, to carry five bridesmaids to church for a friend's wedding.

"Now promise me you'll all wear your seat belts," said the mother of one of the bridesmaids.

Her daughter rolled her eyes and sighed heavily, but the other young women all promised. The mother watched as the bridesmaids buckled themselves in, and then the limo driver pulled away from the curb and headed toward the church.

The driver paused at a stop sign and was halfway through the intersection when he heard the blare of a horn. He turned his head toward the direction of the sound, and saw an oil truck barreling down the street, headed straight for them. Before the driver could react, the out-of-control oil tanker smashed into the limo. The tanker ruptured from the impact and the oil burst into flames.

The limo driver was dead, but his five passengers were still alive and conscious. One of the bridesmaids threw open the car door and reached for the button of her seat belt. It would not release.

"I can't get out! I can't get out!" she screamed.

Nor could any of her friends.

They tugged frantically at their seat belts and begged for help from the crowd of bystanders who rushed to the scene of the accident. But the burning oil kept any would-be rescuers at bay. The five trapped bridesmaids were still pleading for help and tugging furiously at their seat belts when the flames reached the limo's gas tank. The limo exploded in an enormous fireball, taking its "safely" belted-in passengers with it.

The Lost Car

A road construction crew was widening the highway to Miette Hot Springs in Alberta, Canada. One day, as they shoved rocks and boulders over the side of a deep ravine, they heard the clang of stone striking metal. Curious, the crew scrambled down the slope and began chopping through the underbrush.

Beneath the tangle of vines and bushes they found a car with license plates from 1950. Inside, still sitting upright and staring straight ahead, were the skeletons of the car's four passengers.

The wallets and handbags of the passengers were still intact. From these, police investigators established that these four people were a family that had vanished without a trace decades before. Their fate had been an unsolved mystery, until a road crew pushed some rocks off the edge of the ravine.

Variation: The original version of this legend dates to 16th-century Scandinavia. A hunter shoots an arrow at a pheasant and

misses, but hears the clang of his arrow striking metal. With his hatchet, the hunter chops his way through the undergrowth. There, hidden beneath a thick canopy of centuries-old trees, he finds an abandoned stone church. Inside he discovers an entire congregation of skeletons scattered across the floor of the church and the skeleton of a priest at the altar.

When the Black Death was sweeping across Scandinavia, the hunter's region of Norway had been especially hard hit. Whole villages had been wiped out. These villagers had gathered in their church with their priest, hoping they would be spared. But the plague found them, and here they remained unseen and forgotten, until by chance the hunter's arrow struck their church bell.

The DWI

One day after work, a man joined his friends for a drink at a bar in downtown San Diego. One drink became several, and although he was in no condition to be on the road, the drunk insisted he would drive himself home. His friends were not in much better shape, so they did not argue with him.

He wasn't on the road long before he was pulled over by a state trooper.

While the cop and the drunk were going through the standard license-and-registration procedure, a fender bender occurred a few hundred yards down the road.

"Just stay where you are," the cop instructed the drunk. "I've got to check out this accident. Then I'll be back and we'll finish up

our business."

But after 15 minutes of waiting, the man got impatient. "The hell with it," he said, as he climbed into the car, drove home and locked the car in the garage.

Even in his sorry condition, the drunk knew he would be in serious trouble if the police found him.

"If the cops call," the man told his wife, "just tell them I was at home all night. I had a couple of drinks here and then went straight to bed. Promise you'll cover for me."

Reluctantly, the wife promised.

The next morning, two cops came to the door. One of them was the state trooper who had pulled the drunk over the night before.

"That's the guy who ran off last night," the trooper said to his fellow officer.

The man and his wife swore that the police had the wrong man.

"Folks, there's a simple way to settle this," said the other officer. "Would you mind opening your garage door?"

"What for?" the man asked.

"Sir, it will take just one quick look inside for us to determine if we've made a mistake."

So the husband and wife led the police to the garage. The wife punched in the security code and the door lifted. Inside the garage was a state trooper's car, its red and blue lights still flashing.

The Helpful Car-Stripper

A rash of car strippings in New York City inspired this legend.
One night before Christmas, as a man was driving home from a
shopping mall, his car broke down on the Long Island Expressway
on the outskirts of Queens. Cursing, he pulled over to the shoulder
of the highway, climbed out of the car and popped open the hood.
A moment later, another car pulled up behind him.

"Mind if I give you a hand?" the stranger asked.

"That'd be great," said the stranded motorist. "Thanks."

But rather than inspect the engine with the motorist, the good
Samaritan walked to the back of the car. Like an expert, he jimmied
open the trunk where he saw bags of merchandise from the
motorist's holiday shopping spree.

So he yelled to the driver, "Here's the deal, buddy. You keep
everything you can get out of the front, but the back of the car is
mine."

The Microwave by the Side of the Road

*This story originated in England when speed detectors were first
introduced along the highways.*
A woman was driving near Norwich when she spotted a large
microwave oven abandoned by the side of the road. She suspected
the microwave was probably not in working order, but she pulled
over anyway. Her husband was an electrician and he might be able

to repair it. The woman stowed the microwave in the back seat and headed home.

She was so proud of her find that she didn't notice she was exceeding the speed limit—until she heard the siren of a police car behind her.

Leaning in the window, the cop said, "You were traveling pretty fast, ma'am—" Then he saw the microwave in the back seat. "Where'd you get that, ma'am?"

"The microwave? I found it abandoned by the side of the road."

"Please step out of the car. You're under arrest for theft of government property."

As the officer led her toward the police car the woman protested. "Since when is a microwave government property?"

"That's no microwave, ma'am," the police officer replied. "That device checks motorists' speed. Into the back seat now. And mind your head."

Playing Chicken

A group of friends liked to take their motorcycles out at night and tear up and down back roads with their headlights off. One night they went to an access road that led to a quarry. One biker was having an especially good time. He had a new Harley that was outdistancing all of his friends' bikes.

At one point he shot away from the rest of the group and raced down the long dark road. At the quarry gates he stopped and turned

his bike around. A long way back he could see two headlights.

"They've gone chicken," he thought. "They've switched on their lights."

He gunned his engine and tore back down the road, intending to dart between his two friends.

The headlights were blinding, but he increased his speed. He aimed dead center between the two headlights—and ran straight into the grille of a gravel truck.

Variation: An alternate version of this legend tells of a high school boy who likes to play chicken with oncoming cars. He sees a single headlight coming toward him, assumes it is a motorcycle and decides to give the biker a real scare. The kid goes barreling down the road—and straight into the grille of a truck with one blown headlight.

The Unrepentant Driver

At Christmastime, a man was circling a shopping mall parking lot looking for a place to park his Cadillac. He tried to squeeze into a space that was too small and wound up making a large dent in the fender of a Ford Escort.

The culprit's first impulse was to drive away. But the parking lot was filled with people, and a small crowd had stopped to observe what he would do next.

With a contrite expression on his face, he climbed out of his car, wrote something on a piece of paper and slipped it under the

windshield. Then he got back into his Cadillac and drove away.

When the owner of the Escort got back to his car, he saw the dent first and then the scrap of paper on his windshield. He opened the note and read: "The people watching me think I'm leaving the name of my insurance company to cover the damage to your car. But I'm not."

Theft Takes a Holiday

During the week between Christmas and New Year's Day, a businessman was making the long drive from Seattle to Spokane. He was bored, so when he saw a hitchhiker along the side of the road, he pulled over and offered him a ride. As soon as the guy climbed into the car, the businessman regretted his decision. The hitchhiker was shabbily dressed, his hair was greasy and unwashed and he smelled bad.

When another hitchhiker appeared along the side of the road—a clean-cut, nicely dressed young man—the businessman pulled over again and offered the kid a ride. Now he relaxed. He figured the scruffy hitchhiker wouldn't try anything with two men in the car.

They hadn't traveled far before the kid pulled a pistol out of his backpack and ordered the driver to pull off the highway and drive down a dirt road.

"Give me the keys," he said. "Now get out of the car. Both of you."

He backed the driver and the scruffy hitchhiker away from the

car. Waving the gun back and forth, he demanded their wallets and their watches. Suddenly, the scruffy hitchhiker lunged at the kid and knocked him cold with a single powerful blow to the head. He took the gun and went through the kid's pockets.

"Only forty bucks," the scruffy hitchhiker said. "From the way he was waving around that gun, I knew he was an amateur. But it's better than nothing. Here. You take a twenty," and he handed a $20 bill to the driver.

"What are you going to do now?" the driver said.

"Don't worry. I ain't gonna rob you," the scruffy hitchhiker said. "I don't work during the holidays."

The Sympathetic Car Thief

A man from Cape Town, South Africa, bought a new Porsche for his wife as a birthday present. As he was driving it home from the car dealer, it occurred to him that a big bouquet of flowers in the front seat might be a nice touch.

While the generous husband was in the florist's shop, a car thief spotted the spanking new Porsche. In a matter of minutes, he forced the lock, hot-wired the car and drove off. Soon afterwards, the husband stepped out of the shop with a large bunch of flowers and found the Porsche gone.

His first thought was to call the police, but then he recalled that he had had a car phone installed in the Porsche. He went back inside the florist shop, borrowed their phone and dialed the car

phone's number. The thief picked up.

"Look," the husband said, "that car is a gift for my wife. It's her 30th birthday. While you were taking the Porsche, I was buying her flowers. Couldn't you be a sport and just leave the car in front of my house? My address is on the sales slip inside the glovebox. I promise I won't press charges."

"I'll give it some thought," the thief said. Then he hung up.

The florist asked if the husband wanted to call the police.

"No. I'll go home first and see what happens. You never know."

A little while later, a cab brought the husband home. There, sitting in front of his house, was the Porsche. With a big bouquet of flowers in the front seat.

The Bargain Corvette

This story made the rounds in the 1970s when "tiny" sports cars became popular on the American market.

In 1977 a woman whose son was killed in Vietnam called a used car dealer and offered to sell him the old car her son left behind.

"All I want is five hundred dollars for it," the woman said.

The dealer was sure that she was selling some jalopy, but he wanted to be kind to a grieving mother. "I'll tell you what," he said. "I'll come out to look the car over after lunch. Then let's see what kind of arrangement we can come to."

Early in the afternoon, the dealer arrived at the woman's house. She led him out to the garage and removed a tarp, revealing a gorgeous red 1967 Corvette sitting on wooden blocks, all the motor

fluids drained from the engine.

"Ma'am, this is one beauty of a car. Why are you asking only five hundred? Don't you know you could get . . . a few hundred more for a car like this?"

"I don't see how anyone would pay more than five hundred dollars," the woman said. "The car's ten years old. And besides, it's so small."

The Adulterymobile

The owner of a small corporation in Munich was fined the equivalent of $300 for speeding on the Autobahn. She called the traffic police to dispute the penalty.

"The BMW cited in the summons is an office car," the executive said. "Any of a dozen of my employees could have been driving it. You have to prove that I was the one behind the wheel."

A few days later, a package arrived from the police. In it were radar trap photos. The pictures showed the executive at the wheel of the BMW—while a man nibbled her ear and fondled her naked breasts. The man was not her husband.

The police got their money. And the executive's husband got a divorce.

The Zombie in the Flatbed

On a dreary day outside Alexandra Township in South Africa, a driver for a coffin manufacturer stopped to give an old man a ride. The old fellow climbed into the flatbed of the truck. Suddenly the sky opened and sheets of rain came down. To get out of the wet, the old man climbed into a coffin.

While it was still raining, the driver saw another man, obviously very drunk, staggering along the side of the road. The driver stopped and offered him a lift. The drunk climbed into the flatbed and sat down among the coffins. When the rain stopped, the elderly man in the coffin raised the lid and began to climb out. Shrieking with terror, the drunk dove off the back of the truck.

The poor frightened man broke both his arms in the fall. When an ambulance crew found him, he insisted that he had jumped off a moving truck to escape a zombie.

"You're okay now," one of the paramedics said. "We'll get those broken bones patched up, and then you can rest up at the hospital."

Then, turning to another paramedic, he whispered, "Radio the psych ward that we've got a delivery for them."

"R" Is for Race

For his 17th birthday, a kid in southern California received a new Camaro from his parents. That night, he picked up his girlfriend and they went out cruising.

At a stoplight in Malibu, they came alongside a Ford Mustang driven by a guy about the same age as the birthday boy. The drivers gunned their engines and exchanged a few insults. Then they decided to race.

The light turned green, and with a roar of dueling engines, the Mustang and the Camaro took off. After a few hundred yards, the Mustang pulled ahead.

"We're losing," the girlfriend complained.

"Don't worry. I've got a special gear."

"What are you talking about? There's no special gear—"

But before the girlfriend could finish, the kid shifted up. The transmission emitted a sickening grinding sound before the car spun out of control and slammed into a tree. Miraculously, neither the driver nor his girlfriend were hurt.

"You moron!" the girlfriend shrieked. "What did you do?"

"Nothing," her indignant boyfriend answered. "All I did was put it in 'race.'"

"Race! There's no gear for race, you idiot!"

"Oh yeah? Then what does the *R* stand for?"

The Phantom Speeder

A highway patrol officer near the Texas–Mexico border had a favorite speed trap on a dark country road. Late one night, his radar went off. It read "150," but the cop saw no car. He radioed another patrol car, but they saw no traffic on the road at all. So he dismissed the reading as a glitch.

The next day at the station, before he went on his shift, he checked his radar gun and found that it was working properly. After dark, he returned to his favorite spot. Sometime after two in the morning, the radar gun went off, this time reading "157." But again, the officer saw no car. He radioed another patrol car in the area.

"You boys seen any speeding vehicles? I just clocked something at 157."

"We ain't seen nothing," said the other cop. "Are your phantom speeders out on the road again?"

A few minutes later, the cop with the "faulty" speed gun was called to the scene of an accident about ten miles down the road. Wrapped around a tree was a matte black Corvette. Its windows were tinted dark like a limousine and its lights were out.

Inside were two men, both dead. The driver was wearing night-vision goggles. In the trunk the police found three briefcases packed with cocaine.

"Boys," said the cop, "I think we just found my phantom speeders."

The Gas Thief

A college boy driving cross-country one summer ran out of gas on a dark stretch of road outside Bloomington, Indiana. It was after midnight. There were no gas stations in sight and no traffic on the road, so he pulled his empty gas can and a length of hose from his trunk and started walking. An hour later, he still hadn't found a gas station. Finally, he came upon a campground filled with RVs.

By now it was nearly two in the morning. Everyone in the campground was sound asleep. "I hate to do it," the kid said to himself, "but I'll have to siphon some gas from one of these RVs."

He crept up to the closest RV and tried to find the gas tank. By running his fingers over the bottom of the RV he found a cap. He twisted it off, slipped the hose into the tank and began to suck.

As soon as the liquid filled his mouth, the kid vomited violently. Retching uncontrollably, still holding his gas can and the hose, he staggered out of the campground and into the night.

The next morning the father confronted his family in the RV. "Okay. Who left the cap off the septic tank last night?"

The Amateur on the Roof

A married couple in suburban New Jersey had a leaky roof. "Call a roofer," the wife said, "and ask him to come over and give you an estimate."

"Roofers cost a fortune," the husband said. "And they'll leave with the job half-finished. I can do it myself."

"I think you're out of your mind," said the wife. "But do what you want."

On Saturday morning, the husband climbed out the attic window and onto the roof. It was much higher than it looked from the ground, and the pitch of the roof was steeper than he had imagined. He climbed back in and wondered what he could rig to make himself feel more secure while he repaired the leak.

Then he had an idea.

From the basement he brought up a very long clothesline. He anchored one end of the rope to the attic window frame and tossed the other end over the peak of the roof. Then he went downstairs and out to the yard, where he tied the clothesline to the bumper of his car. Back at the attic window, he wrapped the other end of rope around his waist, tied it securely and climbed out on the roof to begin the repair job.

About 15 minutes later, his wife left the house. She never noticed the rope tied to the car's bumper. But as she drove away, she thought she heard something behind her go "splat."

The Fly and the Biker

A motorcyclist in rural Minnesota refused to wear a helmet. He loved the feel of the wind in his face and hair as he raced down the highway, and he wasn't going to give up that sensation.

His family and friends tried to talk sense into him. The highway patrol cops gave him one ticket after another. Even his fellow bikers urged him to wear a helmet. But he could not be persuaded.

"I've been riding for 15 years," he would say. "I've got great reflexes and I've never had an accident. So forget about helmets."

One hot summer day he was on his bike, speeding along his favorite stretch of road in the back woods of Minnesota. The road was empty. No cops were in sight. So he decided to take his Harley to the limit. At 150 miles per hour, something hit his eye. He lost control and flew off the bike into a ditch, where a passing motorist found him a few hours later. He was dead.

At the hospital the doctors sat down with the biker's distraught family. "It wasn't the crash that killed him. He was dead before he was thrown from the bike."

"Was it a heart attack, then?" the father asked.

"No. In fact, it was a freak accident. A fly killed him. You see, your son was traveling at such high speed that when he hit a fly, it pierced right through his cornea and into his brain.

"The sad thing is," the doctor continued, "this tragedy could have been avoided if he had been wearing a helmet."

LATE FOR FINALS
AND OTHER TALES FROM COLLEGE

Late for Finals

Three students at Marquette University in Milwaukee blew off the entire weekend before final exams and indulged in heavy-duty partying. About noon on Monday, the boys woke up in their dorm room. They were all suffering from bad hangovers. Worse, they realized that their chemistry final had ended an hour ago.

"We're gonna fail! We're all gonna fail!" one of the three party boys said.

"Don't panic," said one of his friends. "All we need is a solid story to explain our absence."

A couple of hours later, they found their chemistry teacher in his office and explained that they had gone to Chicago for the weekend.

"On Sunday night, while we were driving home, we got a flat tire out in the middle of nowhere," one kid explained. "We didn't have a spare. The state police found us about an hour later, but by then it was two in the morning and no service station was open to replace the flat. So we had to spend the night in a motel. Then, the next morning, we had to have the car towed to a service station to get a new tire. We raced back to the school, but we didn't arrive in time for the final. Couldn't we please have an extension?"

"Yes, you can have an extension," the professor said. "Come here again tomorrow morning at ten. Of course, it will have to be a different exam than the one I gave the rest of the class today."

The next morning, the three happy students arrived at the professor's office for the exam. He handed each student a test booklet and sent them into separate rooms. The first question,

worth 5 points, asked about molarity and solutions.

The second question, worth 95 points, read: "Which tire went flat?"

The Definition of Courage

A philosophy professor at Georgetown University was notorious for his brutal final examination questions. As the end of the semester approached, students in his ancient Greek philosophy class were studying furiously to prepare for the exam.

On the day of the final, the professor walked into the room and surveyed the room of nervous students. Without a word of introduction, he passed out the exam. There was only one question: "Define courage."

Every student in the examination room began to write furiously. Except one. He jotted something down, walked to the front of the room, handed his test to the professor and left.

The professor looked at the exam. Under the question "Define courage," the student had written, "This is."

The professor gave him an A.

Variations: The difficult final exam question is a staple among academic urban legends. In some legends, the question is long-winded and complex, generally beginning, "State succinctly whether or not you support the proposition that . . ." and ending with, "Support your answer with reasons." The student writes, "Yes. Because you do." The professor gives him an A. Another version, popular in divinity

schools, tells of an elderly professor who for decades has asked the same question on his final exam: "List in chronological order the kings of Judah." Then one year he changes the question to: "List the major and minor prophets." One student tries to dodge the new question by writing, "Far be it from me to say which of those august personages was major and which was minor. Instead, permit me to name the kings of Judah."

"I Like It Better Each Time"

An English professor at Brown University was a notoriously tough grader. Few students in his class received anything higher than a D. But one bright kid labored for weeks on a ten-page paper about Shakespeare's *Measure for Measure*. When the professor returned the term papers, the student was thrilled to see that he had received a B minus. He took the paper back to his room and hung it on the wall over his bed.

The next year the student joined a fraternity and he brought his prize paper with him. One Saturday night he held an auction and sold the paper to the highest bidder.

The frat brother who submitted it got a B. The next semester, another member of the frat bought the paper, turned it in and got a B plus. The semester after that, the scenario was repeated and this time the owner got an A.

Beneath the last grade the professor wrote this comment: "I've read this paper four times now, and I like it better each time. P.S.: I've notified the Dean—all four of you will be expelled."

The Midnight Scream

For years, UCLA had a traditional "dead period," a solid week of silence on campus during finals week so students could study undisturbed. But in the 1960s a new tradition was born: the Midnight Scream. At the stroke of midnight on an appointed day, every student on campus would go outside or lean out their windows and scream for five minutes straight. It was supposed to be a great stress release.

At midnight on the day of the Scream, a young woman was racing down the back stairs of her dorm to join the shrieking crowd outside when she was grabbed from behind and dragged to the bottom of the stairwell. She screamed for help as she tried to fight off her attacker, but no one heard her in the commotion of the Midnight Scream. The next morning, her roommates found her battered corpse in the basement of their dorm.

Since then, UCLA has outlawed the Midnight Scream and many other colleges, which once had the custom, have followed suit.

A Matter of Taste

A college in Rochester, New York, offered a class known as "Bonehead Biology." It was a concession to students who had no other chance of passing the college's science requirement.

One day, the professor was lecturing on the human reproductive system. "One of the major components of male ejaculate, or sperm," he said, "is fructose. Fructose, you will recall, is a complex sugar."

A woman sitting in the front row of the lecture hall was perplexed, so she raised her hand.

"You have a question?" the professor said.

"I'm confused," the woman said. "If sperm is mostly sugar, then why does it taste so salty?"

Variation: In another version the biology instructor says that on average, a human male ejaculates only one teaspoon of sperm. The dimwitted student asks, "Then why does it make such a big mess?"

The Suicide Rule

The 1998 movie, Dead Man on Campus, *was inspired by this legend.* As any college dorm resident can tell you, the easiest way to get a 4.0 for the semester is to have your roommate die. Murder, suicide, accidental death or a fatal illness all qualify, but the requirements vary from school to school.

Some schools insist that you must be present at the time of death. Surviving roommates who have not personally witnessed the death only get a 3.5 for the semester.

In other schools, the death must occur in the dorm room. In this case, the survivors can choose between a 4.0 for the semester, or first pick in the next dorm room lottery.

Some schools have rather stringent requirements. For example, the death must occur in the last six weeks of the semester.

Students who murder their roommates do not qualify for the automatic 4.0.

Variations: Students in some schools believe that the death of a parent or a sibling also qualifies for a 4.0. A related legend tells of a final exam in which a student killed himself. To console the other students in the room, the school gave them all an A for that exam.

Cakes and Ale

During a history final at England's ancient Cambridge University, the proctor saw a student raise his hand.

"Yes?" said the proctor.

"Sir, please bring me cakes and ale," the student said.

All the other students in the room stopped writing.

"Is this a joke?" the proctor asked.

"No sir. I request and require you to bring me cakes and ale."

"I will do no such thing. Continue with your examination."

"I am afraid, sir, that you must bring me cakes and ale," the student said. "The university's book of laws stipulates as much."

"I've never heard of such a thing," the proctor objected.

"Happily, I have a copy of the book with me," said the student. "You do read Latin, don't you?"

The student produced an ancient book and showed the relevant clause to the proctor. It read, "A student sitting for an examination may request and require the proctor to bring him cakes and ale."

"Very well," said the proctor. "I shall be back in a moment."

Twenty minutes later, the proctor returned with a serving tray. On it was a pitcher of ale, a glass and a small cake on a plate. "Here we are. May I borrow that book while you complete your exam?"

The student handed it over. The proctor returned to his desk at the front of the room and sat reading until the exam was over. Two hours later, the student brought his exam book up to the proctor.

"Thanks for the cakes and ale!"

"Just a moment," said the proctor. "I'm afraid you've violated one of the ancient laws of the university."

"What are you talking about?"

"Look here. It says very clearly, 'A student sitting for an examination who fails to wear his ceremonial sword shall be fined one pound.' You can pay the fine to me."

Variations: The setting for this story is always either Cambridge or Oxford. In other versions the student requests a glass of port or a jug of wine. Later, the proctor fines the student for failing to wear shoes with silver buckles, a tabard or a starched ruff collar.

The Letter Home

This urban legend has been circulating since the 1960s.
Dear Mom and Dad,
I can't believe it's been three months since I went off to college, and I can't believe it's taken me this long to write to you. But I have been VERY busy.

Now, before you read any further. I want you to sit down. Are you sitting? Okay. Here goes.

First of all, I am fine now. The doctors say the concussion I got when I dived out of the window during the dorm fire is healing

nicely. Things were touch-and-go during those two weeks I spent in the hospital, but my eyesight is almost completely normal now, and I hardly ever get migraine headaches anymore.

Nobody died in the dorm fire, because Jimmy Ray, the night clerk at a 7-Eleven, saw the flames and called the fire department. He called the ambulance for me, too. He came to see me every day in the hospital.

When I got out, Jimmy Ray invited me to live with him (since my dorm room was totally destroyed). It's a basement apartment, and he has it fixed up like a dungeon with chains and cages. And because almost everything I brought with me to school was burned up, Jimmy Ray bought me a lot of new clothes. He says I look great in black leather.

I've never met anyone like Jimmy Ray. He's so interesting, you'd never suspect he dropped out of school in the sixth grade. I have fallen in love with him and we have decided to get married. The wedding will be very soon, since the baby is due in seven months or so.

I was afraid we'd have to wait, because when we went for the blood test the lab found that Jimmy Ray had some kind of infection. But he says it's cleared up now.

I know you will welcome Jimmy Ray into the family. I just wish his family could be at the wedding, but his mother ran off with a door-to-door Bible salesman when Jimmy Ray was still a baby and it doesn't look like his daddy will make parole in time for the ceremony. Our society is so intolerant of repeat offenders.

Now that I have brought you up to date, I want to reassure you. There was no dorm fire. I did not suffer a concussion. I am not

engaged. I am not pregnant. I don't even have a boyfriend. I am, however, getting a D in biology, an F in French, and I will have to repeat English Composition. I just wanted you to see that as bad as my first semester in college has been, it could have been a lot worse!

Your loving daughter,

Jenny

Variations: Other versions of this letter have a racist tone: the boyfriend is black or Latino. More recent editions of the letter include the suggestion that the daughter is involved in a lesbian relationship or has contracted AIDS.

The Obligatory Waiting Period

Virtually all college students believe that their school has a policy known as the "obligatory waiting period," which specifies how long students must remain in the classroom before leaving if the instructor fails to appear. In some schools the waiting time is based on the academic rank of the instructor.

Teaching Assistants: 5 minutes.

Visiting lecturers and nontenured faculty: 10 minutes.

Tenured faculty: 15 minutes.

If His Hat Is There, Then He's There

A math professor at MIT got to class early. As he placed his hat on his desk, he remembered that he had left some papers in his office.

But on the way back to the classroom, the chairman of the department stopped him and talked to him at length about new office assignments for tenured faculty. By the time the professor returned, it was fifteen minutes into the class period and the students were gone.

The next day, as the bell rang to announce the beginning of class, the professor strode to the podium. "You had no excuse for leaving class," he said.

"But professor," one of the students said, "you were not there. We waited the full 15 minutes."

"Nonsense. Didn't you see my hat on the desk? If my hat was there, it meant I was there." Then he proceeded with the day's lecture.

The next day when the professor arrived at class, he found the room empty. But on each desk was a hat.

He Should Have Been More Specific

The professor of an introductory English literature course at Duke University announced that the upcoming final examination would be an open-book test. "You can use whatever you can carry into the classroom," he said.

A week later, on the day of the exam, one student entered the classroom carrying a doctoral candidate in English literature.

The Off-Color Professor

This story dates from the early 1970s when the rise of the feminist movement on college campuses inspired many urban legends.
An anatomy professor at the University of Wisconsin often enlivened his lectures with suggestive anecdotes. A group of women from his class came to his office one day to complain.

"We've had enough of your snide, leering, adolescent humor," the spokesperson said. "The next time you say anything even remotely off-color, we will walk out of the room."

The professor listened in silence. Then he said, "As you wish, ladies."

For several weeks the professor was the model of decorum. Then one day he began his lecture saying, "As you know, France is suffering from a sudden shortage of prostitutes."

Before he could say another word, a dozen women in the room rose and headed for the door.

"Ladies," said the professor, "why the rush? The next plane for Paris doesn't leave until ten this evening."

The Surprise Visitors

Two college kids who were notorious for playing practical jokes on each other roomed together at Villanova. One Saturday afternoon, one of the guys came back to the room after his run. He stripped off his sweaty clothes, grabbed a towel and headed down the hall to the shower.

A few minutes later, there was a knock at the door. It was the runner's girlfriend with her parents. They had dropped by for a surprise visit to see their daughter and meet her boyfriend. The roommate closed the door and asked them to take a seat. "He just stepped out. He'll be back soon."

Meanwhile, the runner came padding down the hall from the shower. Outside his room, he dropped his towel and kicked open the door. With his penis in his right hand, he burst into the room shouting, "My enormous heat-seeking moisture missile lays waste to everything in its path!"

Football Is for the Birds

A student at the University of Nebraska did not make the cut for the football team. When he asked why, the coach was brutally honest. "You're too short, you're slow and you can't catch the ball."

Angry and humiliated, the student went back to his dorm and plotted his revenge.

He got a campus job for the summer, then called his parents and told them he would be spending the vacation on campus.

The next day, he put on a black-and-white striped shirt, took a large bag of birdseed and headed over to the football field. He blew a whistle, then stepped onto the field and scattered birdseed for the next half hour. Every day, rain or shine, all summer long, he would put on his black-and-white striped shirt, blow his whistle and scatter birdseed across the football field.

When Nebraska played its first home game the student was sitting in the stands. As the national anthem ended, the referee stepped onto the field and blew his whistle. Immediately, hundreds of birds flew out of the sky and landed on the field, waiting for their daily ration of birdseed.

Short Takes 1

• A wealthy ice cream manufacturer made a generous bequest to Harvard with one string attached: Ice cream had to be served at every lunch and dinner.

• The parents of a Swarthmore College student who drowned donated a swimming pool to the school with the stipulation that all students be required to pass a swimming test to graduate.

• The mother of a Harvard student who drowned on the *Titanic* donated a new library building to the school with the stipulation that all students be required to pass a swimming test to graduate.

• Carnegie-Mellon University has the second highest workload and the second highest suicide rate of all American universities.

• As a prank, the registrar at Yale filled an entire class with students whose last names were also the names of animals, such as Byrd, Fox, Lyon, Finch and Lamb.

• A Harvard professor gave a final exam with only one question on it: "Why?" Students who answered "Why not?" got an A. "Because" got a B. Everyone else flunked.

• Henry Kissinger, Class of 1950, was the last Harvard student to graduate with straight As.

• The University of Utah library is sinking because the architect who designed the building failed to allow for the weight of the books.

• When *Playboy* magazine ranked the top ten party schools, the University of Wisconsin did not appear on the list. The editors explained, "We don't rank professionals with amateurs."

• A shrewd student financed his college education by asking everyone he met for a penny. He got enough to cover all his expenses and go away for Spring Break every year. When he graduated, he had $28,000 in the bank.

Aliens in Roswell, New Mexico, and Other Close Encounters

Aliens in Roswell, New Mexico

In July 1947 residents of Roswell, New Mexico, saw something odd streak across the sky and crash outside town. The first witnesses to arrive on the scene were two sheep ranchers who swore that they found the wreckage of some type of strange aircraft. The ranchers said fragments of the aircraft bore symbols or letters unlike anything they had ever seen.

Meanwhile, the mortuary officer at the Army base nearby called a Roswell funeral home and asked the director if he could procure some small airtight caskets. Then the Army officer asked for advice on how to preserve bodies without contaminating the tissue. The funeral director drove out to the base to see if he could help. When he arrived he saw large pieces of metal inscribed with odd markings sticking out from the back of a military ambulance. Then he went inside to say hello to a nurse he knew on the base. When the guards spotted the funeral director, they forced him to leave.

The next day the nurse came to the funeral director's office. "You know those little caskets you brought over yesterday?" she said. "They're for spacemen."

"What are you talking about?" the funeral director asked.

"A flying saucer crashed outside town and the Army retrieved these bodies. I saw them," the nurse said. "This is what they look like." She pulled a prescription pad from her pocket and drew pictures of small, thin men with elongated heads.

Not long afterwards the nurse was transferred to a base in England. She has never been heard from since.

After sending out an intelligence officer to examine the crash site, the base commander issued a press release on July 8, 1947, stating that the wreckage of a crashed flying saucer had been recovered near Roswell. The following day, an Army spokesman retracted the story and said that the wreckage had in fact been a weather balloon.

But the residents of Roswell who were at the site still maintain that they can tell the difference between five pounds of balsa wood and conventional aluminum foil and the otherworldly debris that was strewn across their fields.

Aliens Among Us

Only a few months after the recovery of alien bodies and the debris from their spacecraft at Roswell in 1947, President Harry S. Truman created MJ-12, a top-secret organization to collect intelligence on UFOs.

In 1954 President Dwight D. Eisenhower expanded the mandate of MJ-12 by founding the clandestine Jason Society, a hand-picked group of scholars charged with evaluating data about UFOs and contact with alien life forms. Members of the secret society have included Allen Dulles, director of the CIA; Dr. Zbigniew Brzezinski, president of the Trilateral Commission from 1973 to 1976; and Dr. Henry Kissinger, the mastermind of America's foreign policy.

MJ-12 is funded by profits from the drug trade (MJ-12

members insist the drug trade is simply a tool to eliminate the weaker members of society). The power of MJ-12 has grown to the extent that it manipulates the CIA and the FBI; early in its history it monitored individuals through the mail and the telephone, and today it uses the latest computer technology to accomplish the same task.

Through a project code-named SIGMA, MJ-12 first made contact with aliens. MJ-12's PLATO project established diplomatic relations with several alien civilizations and even secured formal treaties with them. Special operatives known as Men in Black are responsible for the security of all aliens and alien spacecraft currently on earth.

The Real Men in Black

The Men in Black (commonly known as MIBs) have one job: to intimidate anyone who has seen a UFO and prevent them from talking about their experience.

As their name suggests, MIBs always wear a black suit, a thin black tie and an immaculate white dress shirt. Their voices are monotone. Their faces betray no emotion. They usually travel in vintage black Cadillacs, in mint condition. This was how the MIBs looked when they appeared at the door of a man in Toledo, Ohio, named Shepherd.

Three days earlier, Mr. Shepherd had been driving home when he came around a bend and saw a large, strange metallic object

blocking the road. He hit the brakes, but could not stop in time and collided with the object. But at the moment of impact, it disappeared.

Shepherd called the police who inspected the scene with him. The front of Shepherd's car was damaged from the collision, and there were skid marks from his tires on the road. But there was no sign of the other vehicle. The police filed an accident report and Shepherd filed a claim with his insurance company. It seemed that the strange incident would be forgotten.

But Shepherd could not forget what happened. He returned to the scene of the accident, and this time he found a piece of metal unlike any kind of metal he had ever seen before. He sent it to a metallurgical lab for analysis.

Three days later, at 11 PM, two MIBs appeared at Shepherd's door. Over their shoulders, Shepherd could see their car—a black 1953 Cadillac. They asked Shepherd a few questions, and then they asked him for the piece of metal he'd found at the accident site.

"I don't have it anymore," Shepherd said. "I've sent it to a lab for analysis."

"If you want your wife to stay healthy," one of the MIBs said, "then you better not mention that fragment to anyone."

Shepherd was stunned—by the threat and by the MIBs knowledge of his find. Only his wife and the lab knew about the fragment. Still, he took the threat seriously. The first thing the next morning, Shepherd called the lab and asked them to return the fragment. The technician he spoke to said they had no such fragment, never had such a fragment and that no one in the lab had ever had any contact with Mr. Shepherd.

Variations: Some legends tell of a doctor who was acting as a consultant in an alien abduction case who was visited by MIBs. To demonstrate their power and convince him to withdraw from the investigation, they made a coin dematerialize. Others claim that a Canadian man who saw a UFO was visited by MIBs who warned him not to talk about his experience if he valued the life of his wife and children.

Abducted by Aliens

One morning, a woman from Alabama awoke from a terrifying dream. Over breakfast, she described it to her mother and brother. She had seen herself in a circular room in some type of spaceship. She was lying on a table, naked and powerless. Standing around her were small white creatures with large black eyes who were performing medical procedures on her that she did not understand.

The woman's family dismissed it as a nightmare, but after the dream became more frequent and more intense, they suggested that she see a psychiatrist who specialized in hypnotic regression. Under hypnosis, the woman recalled that she had been abducted by aliens several times. And the abductions have continued.

She has found strange marks on her body, including signs that she had been stuck with sharp instruments. She often hears odd beeping sounds, similar to Morse code. Furthermore, after she has an "abduction dream," she suffers from soreness in her ovaries that lasts for several weeks.

The woman believes that she is being monitored by her

abductors. Her telephone emits strange sounds that phone company repairmen cannot explain nor correct. Her home security system shuts down spontaneously—again, repair crews have never been able to locate the source of the problem. Sometimes, the woman's house reverberates with unearthly sounds.

The psychiatrist was disturbed by what his patient revealed under hypnosis, so he ran a battery of psychological tests to determine if she had any delusional tendencies. The test results showed that the woman was normal; in fact, they indicated that she was less likely than most people to indulge in daydreams or fantasies.

Variations: Many alien abduction stories begin with the subject recalling how he or she passed easily and painlessly through solid matter such as the roof of their home or car, and floated up to an awaiting spacecraft. The aliens that abduct the humans are described as short creatures of whitish, grayish or bluish hue. Once the human is aboard the spacecraft, an alien the abductees generally refer to as "the doctor" takes over. Assisted by others, the doctor performs intricate procedures on the abductee. The medical procedures include forcing the abductee to swallow a strange liquid; drawing the brain from the skull and examining it; implanting small objects within various parts of the body; and drawing samples of blood, tissue, marrow and bodily fluids. Many male abductees say a device was placed over their testicles and penis for the collection of semen, while female abductees describe a similar device that collected their ova.

Aliens Collect Blood Samples

Two men who worked at a casino in Buenos Aires, Argentina, were driving home at the end of their shift when they saw two metallic disks that resembled upside-down soup bowls hovering over an empty lot.

At the same time, the car's electrical system failed. Then the engine died. The next thing the two men knew, a beam of unearthly light emerged from the disks and struck the car. A door panel opened in one of the disks, and three small bald-headed creatures came gliding on the beam of light toward the car.

The creatures communicated with the two men telepathically. The two men understood the creatures to say that they had come to study Earth civilization and to collect blood samples of its various life forms. Then the men lost consciousness. When they came to, they saw a dazzling flash of light as the disks soared into the sky.

The men were about to dismiss the entire experience as a hallucination when they noticed pain in their index fingers. They each looked and saw traces of blood around a large puncture wound.

Mutilated Cattle

In 1973 a Kansas cattle rancher discovered a dozen of his cows dead and grotesquely mutilated. All the blood had been drained from their bodies. Their hearts, lungs, kidneys and reproductive organs had been surgically removed. Perhaps strangest of all, scavengers such as coyotes and buzzards had not touched the corpses.

The rancher called the local police, who notified the FBI. An investigation of the site found unusually high radiation levels around the dead cattle. The evidence of clamp marks on the animals' rear legs suggested that the cattle had been taken someplace where they had been suspended by their hind legs and mutilated before their bodies were dumped back in the pasture.

Some ranchers thought a crazy hippie cult or devil worshippers were to blame. But as the wave of cattle mutilations spread across the West, other evidence began to emerge. Witnesses saw UFOs or strange unmarked black helicopters hovering over herds.

Since that first incident, 10,000 head of cattle have been mutilated. To this day, no one knows who has been carving up the cows or their motivations.

Variation: One theory holds that "mad cow disease" was brought to Earth by aliens. After vivisecting cattle, they learned how best to infect the cows and, in turn, humans.

Crop Circles

In the 1970s outside the town of Warminster in England, a farmer awoke one morning to find that portions of his wheat crop had been flattened into perfect circles of various sizes. When he examined the damage, the farmer found that the stalks of wheat were only bent, not broken. In fact, the wheat continued to grow in the swirling circular pattern until harvest.

Soon crop circles began to appear in fields in Canada, the United States, Hungary, Russia, Australia and Japan. As the phenomenon spread around the globe, the patterns in the fields became more geometrically complex: rings, lines, squares and triangles also appeared.

In 1991 two men admitted to creating some 250 crop circles. But the circles these two hoaxers made had always been suspect—they lacked the precision and intricacy that were the hallmarks of this phenomenon.

Although no one knows exactly how these crop circles were created, several farmers observed bright disks of light hovering over their crops in the night. When the farmers inspected their fields, they found crop circles in the precise spot where the light had been the night before.

Variations: Whoever—or whatever—makes crop circles seems to prefer fields of corn, although the circles have also been found in fields of barley and oats. Sometimes the stalks are woven together. In other versions, the bottom stalks swirl in one direction while the stalks

on top swirl in another direction. There have also been reports of multiple layers swirling in different directions. Electronic equipment is said to malfunction inside crop circles and magnets lose their magnetism.

Bar Codes and the Mark of the Beast

Top-level government researchers have been laboring for years to create a microchip that would be encoded with an individual's complete personal and medical history. To display this information, all one would have to do is pass a scanner over the chip.

But this research also has a sinister side. A lethal virus would be programmed into the chip. Since the implant would emit a signal that could be monitored through a cellular system or even by satellite, governments could eliminate criminals, the chronically ill, the disabled, dissidents or other "undesirables" by causing the chip to melt within the person's body, thus releasing the deadly virus.

Once the chip was developed, everyone on the planet would be required to have it implanted under their skin. Anyone who refused the implant would be exiled from society, denied employment and all civil rights and liberties.

Some biblical scholars have interpreted the development of the implant as the fulfillment of the apocalyptic prophecy of "the mark of the Beast"—the mark of those who reject God in the last days of the world and are subsequently damned for eternity.

The Battle of Los Angeles

On a moonless night in February 1942, just eight weeks after the attack on Pearl Harbor, a young Los Angeles woman who had volunteered as an air raid warden looked out her living room window and saw a massive aircraft that gave off a golden-orange light hovering above the city. Los Angeles was observing blackout regulations every night, so the craft appeared in the sky with wonderful clarity.

"I imagined it was some type of superweapon belonging to the Japanese," the woman recalled later. "And I should have been afraid of it. But it was so beautiful suspended in the night sky."

The next thing the air raid warden saw were Army fighter planes attacking the object. They flew in beautiful formation, fired at the craft and then swerved away. Wave after wave of fighters fired everything they had, but they made no impact on the object. As the planes fell back, the artillery batteries on the ground opened fire.

For half an hour, the guns blasted the object with high-explosive shells. Hundreds of eyewitnesses—by now the entire city was watching the battle—claimed they saw at least a dozen direct hits, but the craft showed no signs of damage. Nor did it return fire.

Suddenly, the golden-orange light began to pulse in slow, rhythmic waves. Then the mysterious aircraft disappeared.

Fighting a UFO in Korea

One night during the Korean War in 1951, as an American infantry battalion bombarded an abandoned village, the soldiers saw a strange object that emitted an orange light descend the mountain and head into the village. It seemed impervious to artillery fire. For the next hour, the men watched in amazement as the glowing thing glided unscathed amid the inferno.

Then the object moved out of the village and approached the American batteries in the hills. Suddenly the light changed from orange to blue-green. And instead of a steady glow, it began to pulse. One of the men received permission from his commander to fire on the object. He took an M-1 rifle and fired off several rounds of armor-piercing bullets. The sharpshooter was surprised to hear the sound of a bullet piercing metal. The object may have been untroubled by artillery, but rifle fire was apparently another story.

Suddenly, the object went wild. It moved erratically from side to side and its lights flickered. Then it attacked.

Powerful rays of brilliant light shot out of the object, sweeping across the troops like a searchlight. Officers ordered the men to fall back to their bunkers. For the next half hour, the object hovered over the bunkers, discharging wave upon wave of dazzling light. Then it vanished.

When the attack was over, the men felt burning, tingling sensations throughout their bodies. By dawn, they were all suffering from dysentery and were so weak that the entire company had to be evacuated by ambulance. At the field hospital, doctors found that all

of the men had unusually high white blood cell counts. Within three days, every member of the company was dead.

Alien Antiwar Activists

In March 1967, the commander of an Inter-Continental Ballistic Missile (ICBM) site in Montana received a call from a security guard, who said that he and several other guards had seen UFOs above the military installation. The commander was skeptical, but told the guards to call him again if the situation changed. Five minutes later, the commander's phone rang again. It was the same guard.

"Sir! There's a disk-shaped aircraft emitting a red glow hovering above our front gate."

A moment later, the commander's second phone rang. An officer in the missile launch bunker reported, "Sir! The missiles are shutting themselves down. They've gone from Alert to No-Go status. We can't determine the cause of the failure."

Twenty miles away, the commander of another missile site found that his ICBMs were also shutting themselves down. Since there was no command in the launch bunker that could turn off the weapon systems, the commander was mystified.

For three hours the missiles were out of commission. Then, just as suddenly as they had shut down, the ICBMs came back on line. No repair work had been done on the system. An investigation found no broken cables or damaged hardware. Even the contractors

from Boeing and Sylvania who had built the system could not determine what happened to the missiles. In fact, when the Boeing and Sylvania teams tried to duplicate the shutdown, they failed.

UFO watchers have offered possible reasons for the mysterious event. Some say the extraterrestrials who visited the missile sites may have come to urge humankind to abandon its weapons of mass destruction. Others insist that the aliens wanted to demonstrate how feeble our technology is compared to their own—perhaps as a warning that an alien invasion is imminent.

The Australian Fireball

In October 1994, a family in western Australia had gathered on their patio for a barbecue when they saw a large ball of fire hurtling directly overhead.

"Everyone into the house!" the mother cried. "Now!"

Meanwhile the father called the local police station. "Jack! Look outside. A jet airliner is on fire and about to crash!"

The two cops ran out to the street just in time to see the fireball pass over the police station. By now the entire town of 4,000 people was outdoors watching the phenomenon.

Observing it straight on, the police thought the front appeared to be a dense mass of reddish orange flames. Residents who saw the fireball from the side said it trailed yellowish white flames. The family of barbecuers, now back on their patio and looking at the fireball as it passed right above them, described flames swirling

inward and disappearing into a kind of vortex or black hole. From their perspective, this was more a ring of fire than a fireball.

For seven minutes or so, the inhabitants of this small town watched the fireball rocket across the sky. Then with a flash of bright blue flame, it accelerated. In an instant, the fireball was gone.

The Hiker and the Humanoids

This report appeared in the early 1970s.

An Australian hiker was camping near Warragamba Dam in New South Wales, about 110 miles from Sydney. One night, just as he was getting ready to turn in, he heard a loud humming sound. He took his flashlight and walked into the bush to find the source of the noise.

He had only walked a few hundred feet when he saw a brilliant white light up ahead. He turned off the flashlight and edged forward on his hands and knees. Between the trees he saw a large clearing. In the center was a strange egg-shaped structure that was giving off the bright light. Scurrying around it were half a dozen humanoid creatures.

After an hour or so, the creatures entered the egg. Suddenly the humming sound ceased and the egg vanished.

UFO Escorts

A United Airlines DC-3 was flying from Salt Lake City to Seattle when the copilot flashed the landing lights. When the captain asked him what he was doing, the copilot answered, "Don't you see it? There's an aircraft off our bow."

The captain looked and saw a strange disk-shaped craft. Suddenly, four more flying disks came into view. He called the flight attendant on the intercom. "Look out of the cabin windows. Tell me what you see out there."

The flight attendant came back on the intercom. "What are those things? And don't tell me we're being followed by flying saucers."

The captain radioed the nearest station on the ground and asked if they were picking anything up on radar. The reply came back, "Negative. The skies around you are clear."

The captain, his copilot and the stewardess observed the five disks for another 15 minutes. Then the disks disappeared.

The Great Martian Face

In the 1970s, when *Viking* spacecraft sent photographs of Mars back to Earth, one picture showed a formation that resembled a human face in an area now known as Cydonia. The two eyes, the broad nose and the mouth of the face can be seen clearly. In addition, all around the face are mounds that bear a striking resemblance to pyramids found in Egypt and Mesoamerica.

The initial reaction to the Cydonia face was that it was a kind of extraterrestrial Rorschach test, the Martian equivalent of the Man in the Moon. But in the decades since the first *Viking* photos of the face arrived on Earth, some scientists have re-evaluated their initial conclusions.

• The face does not resemble a face because of the play of light and shadow. There are actual three-dimensional contours to the structure.

• Military software designed to detect man-made objects—even if they are camouflaged—register the face as a structure built by living beings.

• Mounds are rare on the Martian surface, but they are numerous in the Cydonia region. There is also a regular pattern to them that cannot simply be dismissed as chance.

• Finally, the face appears at a significant location on Mars—its equator.

The Cydonia face is too far away to be seen by viewers on Earth. In fact, the face cannot be detected even with the most powerful telescopes. This has led researchers to believe that the face was meant to be seen from some other point in the solar system—presumably the home planet of the face's builders.

Ancient Peru: First in Flight

In the late 1960s and early 1970s a researcher named Erich von Daniken argued that either the Inca or the pre-Inca civilization of ancient Peru had the technology to build and pilot aircraft. Von Daniken came to this conclusion during an archaeological dig when he found a miniature "airplane" in an ancient Peruvian grave.

Skeptics dismissed von Daniken's discovery and insisted that the figurine was really some type of mythical insect. But two German engineers decided to test von Daniken's theory. They built an aircraft with a propeller according to the model found in the Peruvian tomb. Then, with witnesses and a video camera on hand to record the event, the two engineers launched their airplane.

It flew!

Ancient Egyptian Flying Machines

What technology did the ancient Egyptians use to build the pyramids at Giza? How could they have lifted those immense blocks of stone? Such questions have perplexed historians and archaeologists for centuries.

In the early 1970s some theorists advanced the idea that extraterrestrial visitors assisted the Egyptians in their massive building projects.

The notion has been dismissed by almost everyone in the academic community. But in the early 1990s, an Egyptologist made an astonishing find in the ancient Egyptian city of Abydos. In an ancient temple, she found carvings of strange flying machines—including one that bears a strong resemblance to a helicopter—a craft that would have been ideal in lifting the blocks of stone that built the pyramids.

The Barrel of Bricks
and Other Working Day Weirdness

The Barrel of Bricks

This classic legend has been made into the Irish ballad "Why Paddy Won't Be in to Work Today."

A bricklayer was working alone on the roof of a new six-story building. When the job was done, he had quite a few bricks left over. Rather than carry the bricks down by hand, he decided to put them all in an empty barrel he had with him on the roof and lower the barrel using a pulley the construction crew had attached to the side of the building.

The bricklayer tied a heavy rope around the barrel and dropped the loose end of the rope over the side of the building. Then he went down and secured that end of the rope at ground level. Back up on the roof, the man swung the barrel out and began to load the bricks. When the barrel was full, the bricklayer descended again and untied the rope from its moorings intending to lower the barrel of bricks slowly to the ground. But the bricklayer had made one miscalculation. The barrel full of bricks weighed a little over 300 pounds, while the bricklayer tipped the scales at 195.

When he untied the rope, he was jerked swiftly into the air. In his surprise and fright, he didn't think to let go of the rope. At the third floor the bricklayer and the barrel of bricks collided, breaking the man's collarbone and fracturing his skull.

As the barrel of bricks plummeted, the bricklayer kept ascending and did not stop until he had driven the fingers of his right hand two-knuckles deep into the pulley.

At the same moment, the barrel of bricks hit the pavement with

such impact that the bottom fell out. Now it was the bricklayer who outweighed the empty barrel. As he began to drop, the barrel flew upward. Once again they collided at the third floor. This time the bricklayer came away with a broken ankle.

When he hit the pile of bricks on the ground, the bricklayer finally let go of the rope. And he looked up just in time to see the empty barrel hurtling back down at him.

"Are You Gay?"

A USAir employee named David Gay took advantage of his company's "Employees Fly Free" program for a flight to Hawaii. When Mr. Gay made his way to his seat, he found it occupied by a paying passenger. Rather than make a fuss, he took an empty seat further back in the plane.

Meanwhile, another USAir plane, also flying to Hawaii, was experiencing mechanical difficulties. The passengers from this flight were being redirected to other airlines and a few were coming aboard Mr. Gay's plane. As a result, the flight attendants were instructed to review their passenger list and "bump" anyone who was holding a free ticket.

Armed with her passenger list, a flight attendant approached the seat assigned to Mr. Gay and asked the man, "Are you Gay?"

The man was silent for a moment. Then he said, "Yes. What of it?"

"I'm sorry. You'll have to get off the plane."

A few rows back, Mr. Gay overheard this conversation. He stood

up and said, "You've got the wrong man. I'm Gay."

Then a third man stood up and yelled, "Hell, I'm gay, too. They can't kick us all off!"

The Gullible Tourist

Lake Louise, near Banff, Alberta, is a remarkably deep shade of blue. The color is so striking that it almost seems artificial.

On the shore of the lake is a five-star hotel, the Chateau Lake Louise. One day an American guest at the hotel came down to the beach and approached the lifeguard. "I've never seen anything so beautiful," she said. "What makes the lake so blue?"

The lifeguard thought he would have a little fun with the lady, so he said, "It's the paint they use. Every year, on September 22, we drain the lake and paint the bottom a vivid shade of blue. It takes weeks of hard work, but I think it's worth the effort, don't you?"

The American woman was astonished and didn't question the lifeguard's story. That night, the lifeguard had a laugh about his tall tale with his friends. The American woman left a couple days later and the lifeguard forgot all about the incident.

Two months later, on September 21, the same American woman approached the lifeguard on the beach. "Well, as you can see, I've come back," she said.

"Ma'am?"

"For the painting of the lake bottom, of course. And I've brought lots of film to record the event."

The Greedy Dealer

A dealer at a blackjack table in Atlantic City was bored with his job and unhappy about his pay. The owner of the casino believed that at least a third of a dealer's income should come from tips from the players, and he paid his employees accordingly.

The blackjack dealer hated pandering to the players who came to his table, but he didn't know what else he could do to supplement his income. Then one afternoon, when things were a little slow, he took a silver dollar from the stack in front of him and dropped it down his pants leg and into his cowboy boot.

It worked beautifully. Nobody noticed. The dealer knew he was on to something. At the end of his shift, he walked out of the casino with $20 in his boots.

It was easy. In fact, it was too easy, and the dealer got greedy. He spent an entire shift slipping coins into his boots. When it was time to leave, he was carrying $200 in silver.

But the dealer hadn't counted on the weight of all those coins. He'd barely gotten three steps away from his table when he tripped—and all the silver dollars spilled out of his boots, scattering across the casino floor.

Unbleached Salmon

An entrepreneur in Alaska wanted to start up a canned salmon business. Since he was low on cash, he looked for ways to cut his expenses. A commercial fisherman told him that white salmon was considerably cheaper than pink salmon.

The entrepreneur bought several tons of white salmon and went into business. He was very happy, but his marketing manager was not.

"We took the white salmon to focus groups," he told the entrepreneur. "Consumers are turned off by the stuff. They're too used to pink salmon. What are we going to do?"

"Give me a day or two to think about this," the entrepreneur said.

Two days later, the entrepreneur came back to his marketing manager. "I have the solution. Start an ad campaign that says, 'Guaranteed not to turn pink in the can.'"

"That won't work," the marketing manager said.

"Humor me. Try it and see."

In fact, the campaign was an enormous success. The white salmon business took off, while canneries that sold pink salmon saw their sales plummet.

For several months, the white salmon entrepreneur was a very happy man. Then one day he was in a supermarket and he saw his competitor's canned pink salmon. A large banner across the label read: "Guaranteed: No bleach used in processing!"

The Last Kiss

This is one of the rare urban legends that originated in New Zealand.
A newly married man named Nelson had a job at a quarry as part
of a team that worked the rock crusher. One day, a couple of weeks
after his wedding, he slipped as he was stepping over the conveyor
belt and was dragged into the machine. His friends managed to turn
the machine off, but it didn't look good for Nelson.

The medic assessed the situation, gave Nelson some painkillers
and then took the foreman aside.

"Here's what we've got. He's been chewed up from the waist
down. Even if we get him to the hospital alive, he'll be dead in a
couple of hours. But if we turn the machine back on, it will all be
over in a couple of seconds. What do you want to do?"

"I can't make that kind of decision," the foreman said. "I'll have
to ask Nelson."

Nelson chose the quick way out. "But get my wife down here
first. I want one last kiss before I go."

The foreman himself brought Nelson's wife to the quarry. The
team went behind the stone crusher so the couple could have a few
final minutes of privacy. At last, they saw Nelson's wife run from the
quarry, sobbing.

"We're clear," the foreman said. Then, with his voice choked
with emotion, he gave the order, "Start her up!"

*Variation: The American version of this story is identical in all the
details except one: In the U.S. telling, the man is trapped beneath a
steamroller.*

The Frustrated Bookkeeper

*This story dates to 19th-century England. W. Somerset Maugham
used it as the basis of his short story "The Verger."*

A 17-year-old boy from the country traveled to London to seek his
fortune, but he had no luck finding honest work. He was desperate
when he wandered into London's red light district. Seeing no
alternative, he walked up to a bordello, knocked on the door and
asked for a job.

"I have work for you," the madam said. "I need a bookkeeper."

The boy was heartbroken. "I can't take the job," he said. "I can't
read or write."

"That's a shame. But take these at least. You look hungry." And
the madam handed the boy half a dozen apples.

Back on the street, the boy noticed that one of his shoelaces had
come untied. He put the apples down on a wooden crate and knelt
to tie his shoe. Suddenly he heard a man's voice say, "How much for
the apples, boy?"

The boy was startled, but he thought fast. "Two pennies apiece,
sir."

The man bought all six apples. With his 12 pennies, the boy
ran to a fruit wholesaler at Covent Garden where he bought more
apples. Soon, he parlayed his street-corner fruit stand into a
grocery store and from there he became the owner of a string of
markets. Forty years later a British newspaper acknowledged his
entrepreneurial skills by naming him Man of the Year. A journalist
interviewed the country boy-turned-tycoon. "Well, sir, what did you

think when you read the announcement that you were Man of the Year?"

"The truth is, I can't read. Or write."

The journalist was stunned. "And yet you've built a retail empire. Was that your goal from the beginning?"

"Actually no," said the tycoon. "What I really wanted was the bookkeeping job in a whorehouse."

Variations: European folklore is filled with stories of young men plucked from obscurity by chance. The most common story tells of military recruiting officers who see a muscular young man plowing a field—without a horse. They sign him up for the army of the king/ emperor/tsar, and the boy becomes a military hero. In an American version, Minnesota football coach Don Spears saw Bronko Nagurski plowing a field and asked for directions. Nagurski picked up the plow with one hand and pointed the way. Spears, of course, immediately signed up Nagurski for his team.

The Standard Bedbug Letter

This story has been circulating in Canada and the United States since the 1880s.

An elderly woman traveling by train from Buffalo to Pittsburgh was horrified to discover a bedbug in her berth. When she arrived home, she wrote a strongly worded letter of complaint to the president of the railroad.

To her delight she received a reply, two pages long, just a few

days later. On the first page, the president offered an abject apology and assured her that he would attend to this breach of sanitation personally.

The elderly woman was very pleased with the president's letter and turned to the second page. It was a handwritten note that read, "Send this cranky old bitch the standard bedbug letter."

Traveling Companions

The CEO of a Canadian airline that specialized in business travel was concerned that his company was not doing enough for its female travelers. To gauge how the airline served women business passengers, the CEO inaugurated a new company policy that encouraged employees to take their wives on all of their business trips. Furthermore, the human resources department kept a file of all employees who traveled with their wives.

Three months into the new program, the airline sent the wives a detailed questionnaire about their flight experiences. When the responses had been tabulated, it was found that 90 percent of the wives had answered something along the lines of, "What business trips? My husband never took me on any of his business trips."

Variations: In an alternate version of this story, American Airlines distributes 200 blank airline tickets to their employees so wives can accompany their husbands on business flights. A follow-up of the program finds that none of the women whose names appeared on the 200 tickets were wives of the business travelers.

The Unexpected Bequest

A botanist traveled to Honduras to study rare tropical plants. One day, while driving along a dusty road, he passed a cemetery where a very poorly attended funeral was in progress. Only a priest and another man in a black suit stood beside the grave. But atop the casket was a large arrangement of extremely rare orchids. The botanist pulled into the cemetery and joined the priest and the lone mourner.

When the prayers were concluded, the mourner took the botanist aside and asked him if he would join him in the cemetery's office for a moment.

Once they were inside, the man introduced himself. "I am the late Señor Ortiz's attorney. My client was very wealthy, but he was a difficult man to get along with. He made an stipulation in his will that if anyone other than the priest and myself attended his funeral, that person should receive a bequest of a $100,000 dollars."

The botanist was stunned. He didn't know what to say.

"If you come with me to my office in the city, I can write you a check. I know this must come as a shock. So is there anything I can get you now?" said the attorney.

"Yes," said the botanist. "Can I have that bouquet of orchids?"

Variation: In the most common alternate version of this legend, two men stop at an inn. Both make love to the hostess that night. One tells her that he was flattered that such a lovely woman took an interest in him, while the other proves to be a lout. A year later, a lawyer

contacts the grateful lover to inform him that the innkeeper has died and left her considerable fortune to him.

The Leopard in the Luggage

A sheep farmer in the Transvaal of South Africa was having a terrible time. A leopard was killing his sheep. Every night the farmer set out new and ever more ingenious traps, but the leopard eluded them all. Finally, he called in a professional trapper. The trapper knew that the farmer was desperate, and he charged an exorbitant sum. Still, the sheep farmer saw no alternative.

The next morning, the farmer went out to his pasture and there was the leopard, caught in the trap. He ran to the house for his tranquilizer gun, shot the leopard and then got out his knife to slit its throat.

But as he stood over the animal he thought about its rarity and beauty. He couldn't bring himself to kill it, so he resolved to take it to a wildlife preserve instead.

The only trouble with this noble thought was that the farmer had no cage to transport a wild leopard. In fact, the only container he had around his place that was big enough for the animal was a large steamer trunk. It would have to do.

He wrestled the unconscious beast into the trunk, punched some air holes in it, locked it and then tied it with heavy rope. Somehow, he managed to get the trunk into the back of his truck.

When the job was done, he rewarded himself with a pint of cold beer. Then he set off on the long drive to the wildlife preserve.

An hour later, the sheep farmer felt the call of nature and pulled over to the side of the road to relieve himself. As he stepped out of the truck, he heard the leopard yawn. It wouldn't be long before the animal was fully awake. The sheep farmer scurried into the bushes to complete his business. A few minutes later, he stepped out of the brush just in time to see another truck pulling away—with his trunk in the back.

The farmer was furious and was about to give chase when he recalled what was inside the trunk. He imagined what would happen to the thieves when they opened the trunk. So, with a contented smile on his face, the farmer turned his truck around and drove home.

The New Ambassador

The ambassador from a newly independent nation in Eastern Europe traveled to Paris for an international conference. It was the first time his country would be counted among the nations of Europe, and the ambassador was intent upon making a good impression. Consequently, he arrived in Paris a few days early and purchased several beautifully tailored suits and a fine wool overcoat.

On the day of the conference, he entered the Palais de Luxembourg to find that he alone had come wearing an overcoat. Nervous and self-conscious, the ambassador looked around for a place where he could check his coat. Standing beside the door to the anteroom, he saw a distinguished-looking gentleman in a black suit.

The relieved ambassador walked over and handed the man his coat, but the man would not take it.

"Why will you not take my coat?" the ambassador demanded.

"Because I am not a valet," the man replied indignantly. "I am the Prime Minister of France."

The Chatty Employee

The CEO of a large corporation in Kansas City was convinced that every time he walked along the corridors of his headquarters, more employees were chatting than working. He decided to take drastic measures to correct this failing.

The CEO called a company-wide meeting in the auditorium and announced that he would no longer tolerate idle chatter during work hours. Then he waved a stack of checks over his head and said, "I have checks here, all of them made out to *Cash* in the amount of two thousand dollars. That will be your severance pay if I find any of you talking when you should be working."

Then the CEO dismissed his employees. After lunch, he made a tour of his headquarters. Every office was silent and all of the employees were quietly doing their work. Except one. In the human resources department, he found a man chatting away to the vice president of personnel.

"Didn't I say I would get rid of anyone I found talking? Now take your two thousand dollars and get out of here!"

The man looked stunned at first, but he accepted the check and left the office without a word.

"Some fools don't know what's good for them," the CEO said. Then, turning to the vice president, he said, "By the way, who was that guy?"

"He was a job applicant," the vice president said quietly.

The Unexpected Escort

A newly divorced woman from a wealthy town in Connecticut was going to a posh charity ball. She wanted to make an impression on her friends, so she called an escort service and insisted upon speaking to the manager.

"This is an extremely important engagement for me and I want the best you have," she said. "He must be over six feet tall, very handsome and between thirty and thirty-five years old."

"We have several men who fit that description," the manager said.

"And there's one more thing," the woman said. "He mustn't be Jewish."

"I promise you," the manager said. "The escort I send you will not be Jewish."

A week later, on the evening of the charity ball, the woman opened her front door. There stood a tall, devastatingly handsome black man.

"Good evening," he said. "I'm from the escort service."

The woman stammered, "No. There must be some mistake."

"That's not possible, ma'am. Mr. Shapiro never makes a mistake."

Awake at His Own Wake

A funeral director in New Jersey received a call informing him that an elderly man had died quietly in his bed. The director sent his newest assistant out to collect the body. "And remember," the director said, "when you get back here, lean on the corpse's stomach to let all the air out."

Two days later, the family filed into the funeral home for the wake. The body was laid out in a handsome casket with banks of flowers all around. The funeral director was certain the family would be pleased. He himself escorted the widow forward so she could inspect her husband.

They had just arrived at the casket when the body began to tremble. Then it sat bolt upright in the casket. The family members screamed, while the widow shrieked and fell into a dead faint on the floor.

A few minutes later, the widow came to on the couch in the funeral director's private study. "He's alive!" she screamed. "Cosmo's alive!"

"No, no," the funeral director said. "You're husband's not alive. He was just suffering from a little gas."

Give the Guy a Hand

Whenever surgeons at a Long Island hospital had to perform an amputation, they always called upon two new interns to get rid of the severed limb. The interns were getting pretty tired of the job, so one day when they were assigned the disposal of a man's left arm, one of the interns had an idea.

He took a shirt from his locker, tore off its left sleeve and put it on the severed arm. Then he sutured a $20 bill to the hand.

"Let's go for a ride," he said to his friend.

They drove off toward New York City. When they got to the first tollbooth, the driver held out the severed arm with the $20 bill attached to it. As the tollbooth clerk held out his hand for the money, the intern let go of the arm and said, "Keep the whole thing. It's yours."

Then he hit the gas.

ELVIS'S MOTORCYCLE
AND OTHER CELEBRITY RUMORS

Elvis's Motorcycle

A man went to an outdoor flea market near his home in Indiana and found a beat-up vintage Harley-Davidson motorcycle. After some spirited negotiation with the seller, he got the price down to $600 and took the motorcycle home.

The next day, the new owner went to a Harley dealer and requested the parts he would need to restore the bike. He and the dealer started talking, and the dealer mentioned that he collected vintage Harleys.

"Do you collect?" the dealer asked.

"Nope. But when I saw this bike, I felt that I had to buy it."

"You don't say. What's so special about this Harley?"

"The color's strange. It's a funny shade of blue. In fact, the first time I saw it, the Elvis song, 'Blue Suede Shoes' popped into my head."

The dealer was silent for a moment. Then he said, "Blue is a pretty unusual color for a Harley. I'd like to see this bike."

"I could bring it by this afternoon."

"I'll be here."

After lunch, the man returned with his blue Harley. The dealer looked the bike over closely. His hand seemed to tremble a little when he placed it on the seat cushion.

"I've got to tell you. This is one rare Harley. I could offer you . . . oh, let's say . . . $75,000."

The Harley's owner took a deep breath. "Well, I'm kinda attached to this bike. But since you're a collector, let's say $125,000."

"That would be fair if the bike were in mint condition. But it's a little beat up. The best I could do is $100,000."

For appearances' sake, the owner hesitated before he said, "You've got a deal."

That night, inside his locked garage, the dealer removed the bike's seat and held it up to a light. Engraved on the underside was the inscription he knew would be there: "To Elvis, from James Dean."

The dealer sold the Harley at an auction for $4 million.

Variations: A motorcycle enthusiast finds the beat-up bike in a barn at an estate sale. In an effort to track down parts for it, he calls the Harley-Davidson customer service number and gives them the bike's serial number. His call is transferred to a vice president of the corporation, who tells the collector that the company will give him a quarter of a million dollars for the bike. In another version, the bike was a gift to Elvis from his wife, Priscilla.

James Dean's Car

James Dean died on September 30, 1955, when his new Porsche Spyder crashed head-on into another car. After the accident, a secondhand car dealer purchased the wrecked Porsche. He planned to put it on display and charge admission. But when a flatbed truck delivered the car to the dealer's lot, it rolled off and broke a mechanic's legs. Spooked, the dealer decided to strip the Porsche and sell it for parts.

A Beverly Hills doctor bought the Dean engine and had it installed in his Porsche. The doctor was killed in a crash the first time he took his car out.

Another physician in southern California bought the Dean transmission. He was killed when the transmission locked in fifth gear, and the Porsche hurled itself through a guardrail and into a ravine.

A New Yorker bought two of the Dean tires. The first time he took his Porsche out on the road, both of the tires blew out at the same time. The car flipped over, crushing the driver.

An auto museum in Salinas, California, purchased the body of the Dean car. But as it was being transported there, the driver of the truck lost control of his vehicle, skidded off the highway and was killed.

No one knows what became of all of these cursed auto parts. One story claims that they were collected again, crushed and buried in a landfill near the Mexican border.

Elvis Lives!

The Elvis faithful claim to have spotted their King everywhere from rooms that are off-limits to tourists at Graceland to the K-Mart in Kalamazoo, Michigan. And they've collected the data that proves Elvis is still alive.

• Two days before his alleged death, Elvis telephoned a friend named Foster to tell her he would cancel his upcoming tour. Miss

Foster was surprised and asked if Elvis was ill. "I'm fine," he said. "In fact, I feel better now than I have in a long time. My troubles will soon be over. But remember this: Don't believe anything you read about me over the next few days." Then Elvis hung up.

• Two hours after Elvis's death was announced to the public, a man who bore a striking resemblance to the King showed up at the Memphis airport and purchased a plane ticket to Buenos Aires. The traveler paid cash and gave his name as "John Burrows," the alias Elvis always used when he was on tour.

• Elvis's full name is Elvis Aron Presley. He and his family were always sticklers for the unconventional spelling of his middle name. Yet his gravestone bears the incorrect spelling, "Aaron."

• Toward the end of his life, one of the King's favorite books was the spiritual autobiography of a Hindu yogi who urged his followers to relinquish wealth and fame and find peace in obscurity. Did Elvis abandon stardom to find spiritual serenity in the out-of-the-way town of Kalamazoo?

Paul Is Dead

One of the great legends of the late 1960s was the rumor that Paul McCartney was dead. Believers found clues in the Beatles's album covers and in the songs.

• The cover of *Abbey Road* was interpreted as a kind of funeral procession. John, dressed all in white, represents the minister; Ringo, in a dark suit, is the undertaker; George, in a denim work shirt, is the gravedigger; and Paul, in a suit but barefoot (because, supposedly, that is how they bury bodies in England) is the corpse.

• The *Abbey Road* album cover shot shows a car parked on the street. Its license plate reads "28 IF," meaning Paul would be 28 if he were still alive.

• If the *Sgt. Pepper's Lonely Hearts Club Band* album is held to a mirror, the characters on the drum in front of Paul read "HE DIE."

• On Paul's Sgt. Pepper uniform is an arm patch with the initials OPD, for "Officially Pronounced Dead."

• At the end of "Strawberry Fields Forever," John can be heard saying, "I buried Paul."

• Play "Revolution 9" backwards and the phrase "number nine, number nine" becomes "Turn me on, dead man."

Tupac Lives!

Fans of gangsta rapper Tupac Shakur have uncovered a host of clues and inconsistencies to prove that Tupac faked his death.

• Tupac always wore a bulletproof vest. It is inconceivable that he would have gone to so public an event as the Mike Tyson fight without protection.

• Not long before the shooting, Tupac told interviewers that he wanted to step out of the limelight. "But the only way I could pull it off," he said, "is if people think I'm dead."

• Tupac's funeral was canceled for unknown reasons.

• The cover of *The 7 Day Theory* album shows Tupac crucified and bleeding from five bullet wounds. Is this a clue that he is planning a resurrection?

• The only witness to the shooting, Yafeu Fula (Kadafi of the Outlawz), was gunned down in an apartment building hallway in East Orange, New Jersey, not long after Tupac was shot. Was he about to blow Tupac's cover?

• "R U Still Down" was released under the name "2Pac." Does this mean Tupac is back?

Saving Richard Nixon

In the late 1970s, after his resignation from the presidency, Richard Nixon retired to his beachfront home in San Clemente, California. The house was on one of the hottest surfing spots in southern California. But the land was private property, and the former president would not give the public access to it.

One day Nixon went swimming alone. The riptide caught him, and he began to call frantically for help. Two surfers who were illegally on the beach heard his cries. They swam out on their boards and rescued the former president.

Once he was safely on the beach, Nixon said, "Boys, you've saved my life. Whatever you want, if it's in my power to give, you can have it."

One of the surfers said, "Open the beach to the public."

"Done," said Nixon. Then turning to the other surfer he asked, "Now what would you like?"

The other surfer said, "Can I have a burial plot in Arlington National Cemetery?"

"Yes, I could arrange that," said the former president. "But why do you want such a thing?"

"Because," the surfer said, "when my dad finds out I saved the life of Richard Nixon, he's going to kill me."

Two Legends from Johnny Carson's Tonight Show

One of the most famous legends from the 1960s involves an appearance by golfer Arnold Palmer on Johnny Carson's *Tonight Show*.

During the interview, Carson asked Palmer if he had any superstitions or rituals he performed before a tournament.

"Yes," said Palmer. "The night before a tournament, my wife kisses each of my balls."

Carson said, "That will make your putter stutter."

In another *Tonight Show* legend, Burt Reynolds mentions that he has just won a massive judgment against AT&T. Part of the settlement is unlimited free phone calls. So the generous star reads off his calling card number and invites all of his fans to reach out and touch someone at AT&T's expense.

Variations: The most common variation on the putter legend is that it was Mrs. Palmer who was being interviewed by Carson. Lately, the legend has been updated so that Palmer is being interviewed by Jay Leno. The details of the calling card legend are remarkably consistent, only the name of the celebrity changes—to Steve McQueen, Paul Newman or Sammy Davis, Jr.

Michael Jackson's Telephone Number

When Michael Jackson's megahit album *Thriller* premiered in December 1984, the first seven digits of the product number in the bar code were rumored to be the Gloved One's phone number.

A spokesman for Epic Records in Los Angeles denied the rumor that one could reach Jackson by dialing the code numbers. But people tried anyway—as the stylists at a hair salon in Bellevue, Washington, know. They were getting an average of 50 calls a day for Jackson.

The Bozo No-No

Bozo the Clown was a popular kids' TV show in the late 1950s and early 1960s. The program was filmed live, with children who had written in for tickets joining Bozo on stage and playing a variety of games.

One day, the contest was a race carrying an egg in a spoon. When one little boy dropped his egg halfway across the stage, he said, "Shit!"

Bozo hurried over, put his hand on the little guy's shoulder, and said in his most cheerful voice, "That's a Bozo no-no!"

To which the kid replied, "Ram it, clownie!"

The Anxious Tourists

Two elderly ladies who had never traveled out of their home state, Iowa, decided they needed a little excitement in their lives. So they asked a travel agent to arrange a week in New York City.

When they landed at La Guardia Airport, two flight attendants walked them to the baggage claim area. "Now be careful in the city," one of the attendants said. "Always hold on tightly to your handbag."

"And avoid the subway," said the other attendant. "Cabs are more expensive, but they are the safest way to get around town."

The limo driver who took the ladies to their hotel in Midtown had some advice, too. "If you do run into trouble, just do what the man says and you won't get hurt."

Naturally, all of this advice made the two out-of-towners a little apprehensive. But after a day or two of sightseeing without any unpleasant incidents, the ladies decided that New York City was not such a frightening place after all.

Their travel agent had made dinner reservations for them at the Rainbow Room in Rockefeller Center. Feeling bolder, the ladies decided to walk the four blocks from their hotel to the restaurant. But after a block or two, they became uneasy. A very tall, broad-shouldered black man with a rottweiler was following them. "Let's walk a little faster," said one of the ladies. "Once we're on the elevator, he can't follow us."

So the two friends picked up their pace, hurried through the revolving doors and scurried across the lobby to the bank

of elevators that would take them up to the Rainbow Room. As the elevator doors opened, they could hear the man and the dog entering the lobby.

"Hurry! Push the close button!" one of the women said to the other.

But as the doors began to shut, two strong hands reached in and pried them apart. The man and the dog got on the elevator. He hit the button for the penthouse.

There was no place for the ladies to go. They backed into a corner of the elevator car, clutching their handbags and looking nervously at the rottweiler that sniffed at their feet.

Suddenly the man said, "Sit, Lady!"

Both women plopped down on the floor.

At that moment, the elevator came to a stop and the doors opened onto the lobby of the Rainbow Room. The man with the dog called to the hostess, "Could you help these ladies to their feet and escort them to their table."

"We were so frightened," one of the ladies confided to the hostess. "He shouted, 'Sit lady!' and we did just what he said."

"Oh, ma'am. The gentleman wasn't talking to you," the hostess replied. "He was just giving a command to his dog. His dog's name is Lady."

"But how do you know all this?" the other lady asked.

"The gentleman lives in the penthouse. We see him and his dog all the time. Didn't you recognize him? That was Michael Jordan."

Variations: Over the years, the black celebrity the ladies fail to recognize has changed, depending on who is most prominent at the

moment. Earlier versions of this legend feature Reggie Jackson, Eddie Murphy and Mike Tyson.

A Good Samaritan Gets His Reward

Late on a cold, rainy night in November, a factory worker was driving home along I-95 in Connecticut when he saw a well-dressed man standing beside a limo on the shoulder of the road. The man was trying to flag down passing traffic, but no one stopped. So the factory worker pulled over.

"What's the problem?" he asked as the driver of the limo ran up to his car.

"The ignition's dead," the limo driver said. "And so is our cell phone. Could you give me a lift to a service station so I can get a tow?"

"Sure. Hop in. There's a station about five minutes from here."

The factory worker took the driver to the station, waited while he arranged for roadside service, drove him back to the limo and waited again until the guys from the service station arrived.

"You've been great," the driver said. "My boss would like to thank you."

The limo door opened and a tall man in a cashmere coat stepped out onto the rainy highway. "I'm Donald Trump. My wife and I want to express our appreciation. You've gone to a lot of trouble on our behalf. Is there something I can do for you?"

For a moment, the factory worker was stunned to meet one of the wealthiest men in America, but he recovered quickly. "Sure," he

said. "There's one thing. Send my wife flowers. My wife would love to get flowers from Donald Trump."

"My pleasure," said the Donald. "Just write your wife's name and address here." He handed the man a leatherbound notepad and a gold pen.

Then they shook hands, and everyone continued on their way.

The next morning, while the factory worker and his wife were having coffee, the doorbell rang. It was a florist delivering a massive flower arrangement. The note attached to the flowers read, "With best wishes and profound appreciation from Donald and Ivana Trump. P.S.: We've paid off your mortgage."

Variations: In earlier versions of this legend, the good Samaritan stops to help the wife of a celebrity—Mrs. Nat King Cole, Mrs. Perry Como or Mrs. Leon Spinks. The reward is a pair of free tickets for a sold-out concert or prizefight.

The Unrecognized Celebrity

The vicar of a village church in England made a habit of visiting newcomers to the parish. He heard that a man had moved into the neighborhood, so he dropped by.

"Good morning. My name is Edmund Barset. I am the vicar here, and I wanted to welcome you to the village."

The man at the door smiled. "Call me Eric. Please come in, Vicar."

In the parlor, the vicar saw several guitars.

"Do you play?"

"A little," said Eric.

"I say, we're having an entertainment to benefit the building restoration fund. I don't suppose you'd consider playing for us?"

"Well…." the man said slowly.

Thinking that he needed a little reassurance, the vicar said, "Oh, you mustn't be nervous. I'm sure you're a fine musician. Maybe just a little more practice. The entertainment is not for two months. That should give you plenty of time to prepare, don't you think?"

"Yes it would," Eric said. "I'd be happy to play."

"Right. Very good. Well, I'll drop by with the details another time."

"That will be fine," Eric said, as he saw the vicar to the door.

Two months later, the villagers gathered for the benefit. They heard Eric Clapton, unplugged, in their parish hall.

Variations: Other versions of this legend feature a woman at an airport who mistakes a star from the NFL or the NBA for a porter, or American tourists at a historic villa in Europe who mistake a casually dressed film star for the gardener. The names of the athletes and the film stars change depending on who is popular at the time.

The Nervous Stargazer

A woman visiting Los Angeles walked into an ice cream store one afternoon. As she browsed along the case filled with different flavors, she noticed a man at the counter. Once she made her

selection and walked over to the counter to order, she realized that the man was Jack Nicholson.

"Be cool," she told herself. "This is L.A. The town is full of celebrities."

A clerk asked if he could take her order.

"Uh . . . Ice cream. I want ice cream. In a cone? Do you have ice cream cones here? Of course you do. What am I saying? This is an ice cream store. Every ice cream store has ice cream cones. Which is good. Because that's what I want.

"I'm babbling. But I'm going to stop now. There. See? Now I've stopped babbling. Now I can order. I'll have chocolate chip. Two scoops. I mean a double. On an ice cream cone. Or do you say in an ice cream cone? Whatever. I want a cone with two scoops of chocolate chip. Ice cream. Please. Thank you so very much."

The clerk went to make the woman's cone while another clerk filled pints of various kinds of ice cream for Jack Nicholson.

The poor woman wanted to remain calm, but it was hopeless. The proximity of Jack Nicholson was making her jumpy. She knew she had made a fool of herself. All she wanted was her cone so she could get out of the store.

After what seemed like an eternity, the clerk returned with her cone. She paid and walked out. But on the street, she realized that she did not have her ice cream cone. As she stared at her empty hands, Jack Nicholson came out of the store with two large bags. He leaned over the woman's shoulder and whispered in her ear, "The cone's in your purse."

John Carradine's Screen Test

This legend has been making the rounds in Hollywood for nearly 70 years.

John Barrymore was a Hollywood star in the 1930s. When he learned that his friend John Carradine wanted to move from the stage to the screen, Barrymore offered to help.

"This will be very simple," he told Carradine. "I've reserved a studio for your screen test. It will be me and the crew. No directors, no producers. No one who might make you nervous."

"This is more than decent of you," Carradine said.

"Not at all. Now here's what you have to do. I want you to step through that door there and pantomime a man who has just had a tremendously satisfying meal. No words, just gestures."

"I love it," said Carradine, as he vanished behind the door.

"Ready, John?"

"Ready!"

"Then . . . action!"

Carradine stepped out in front of the camera, a smile of perfect contentment on his face. He ran his tongue over his lips. He wiped his mouth with his handkerchief. He stroked his belly. He even gave a modest burp.

"Cut!" said Barrymore. "Print! Superb, John. Exactly what I was hoping for."

Carradine beamed.

"Tomorrow we'll show it to the studio heads together."

The next morning, Carradine, Barrymore and the studio's top

executives assembled in a private screening room.

Carradine's performance was perfect. Every gesture and facial expression confirmed that here was a man who had just eaten something delectable.

Carradine thought the clip was over, but then the camera cut back to the door. Now John Barrymore stepped in front of the camera—zipping up his fly.

Bill Gates Is the Antichrist

Many people in the computer industry believe that Bill Gates of Microsoft is evil incarnate. But one hardworking hacker has proven that Bill Gates is the devil himself—or least one of his really close subordinates.

Gates's full name is William Henry Gates III. If you convert the letters of Bill Gates (the name he goes by these days) to their ASCII numerical values and add the III, you get the following:

B	66	G	71	I	1
I	73	A	65	I	1
L	76	T	84	I	1
L	76	E	69		
		S	83		

The total is 666, the number of the Beast in the book of Revelation.

Short Takes 2

• Charlie Chaplin once anonymously entered a Charlie Chaplin look-alike contest. He lost.

• At the end of his career George Reeves, who played Superman in the television series, believed he could fly. He died when he leapt from a tall building in a single bound.

• The Gerber Baby is a portrait of the infant Humphrey Bogart, drawn by his mother.

• Marilyn Monroe was the model for Tinker Bell in the Disney animated cartoon version of *Peter Pan*.

• When he died, Walt Disney was frozen in liquid nitrogen in the hope that at some future date, medical technology would be able to bring him back to life.

• Barbra Streisand made her film debut in a porn flick.

• "Mama" Cass Elliot of the Mamas and the Papas choked to death on a ham sandwich. At the time of her death, she was pregnant with John Lennon's child.

• Fred Rogers of *Mister Rogers' Neighborhood* was a sniper in Vietnam.

• Jerry "the Beaver" Mathers of *Leave It to Beaver* was killed in Vietnam.

• Pia Zadora once appeared in the title role of *The Diary of Anne Frank*. Her performance was so terrible that when the Nazis arrived, someone in the audience cried out, "She's in the attic!"

• James Dean did not die in a car crash, but was horribly disfigured. He has lived as a recluse ever since.

• John F. Kennedy did not die of his bullet wounds, but survives in a coma in a secret room of a Dallas nursing home.

• Bruce Lee was killed by Chinese martial arts masters who were angry with him for teaching their ancient secrets to Westerners.

• Bruce Lee was killed by Hong Kong crime lords who were angry with him for refusing to work in their films.

• Brandon Lee, Bruce Lee's son, was murdered by Chinese martial arts masters or Hong Kong crime lords who were pursuing their vendetta into the next generation.

• The actual footage of the fatal shooting of Brandon Lee was left in the final cut of *The Crow*.

• After the show's final episode, the cast of *Green Acres* threw a farewell dinner in which the pig, Arnold Ziffel, was the main course.

• John Wayne turned down the role of Matt Dillon on *Gunsmoke*.

• Albert Einstein guest-starred on *Gunsmoke*.

• Charles Manson auditioned for the Monkees.

• Offended by the portrayal of Buckwheat, Bill Cosby bought the rights to *The Little Rascals* so the series would never appear on television again.

• At the 1992 Academy Awards, the Best Actress award was supposed to go to Vanessa Redgrave for her performance in *Howard's End*. But presenter Jack Palance was too confused or drunk (depending on which version you hear) to read the card. He could make out nominee Marisa Tomei's name on the teleprompter, however, so he announced that she had won the Oscar.

• Burt Reynolds is Tom Selleck's father.

• Clark Gable is Tom Selleck's father.

• During one of his concerts Ozzy Osborne, the *really* bad boy of rock 'n' roll, bit off the head of a live bat.

• Andrew Cunanan, who murdered fashion designer Gianni Versace and several other men, faked his own death and is now at large masquerading as a woman.

Alligators in the Sewers
and Other Classic Urban Legends

Alligators in the Sewers

The New York Times *first reported alligators in the city's sewer system in the 1920s.*

At one time, the hottest item in Florida's souvenir shops were baby alligators. But the trouble with baby alligators is that they grow up to be adult alligators—an inevitability that generally occurred to the tourists within a week or so of their arrival back home. Some owners gave their alligators to the zoo. But in New York City the preferred method of getting rid of an unwanted baby alligator was simply to flush it down the toilet.

The alligators thrived in the sewers of New York. There were plenty of rats and raw garbage to feed on. And for variety, an alligator would sometimes catch an unwary sanitation worker.

Over several generations, the New York alligators have evolved into a distinct species. Because they never see the sun, the alligators are all albinos.

Spanish Fly and the Stick Shift

Two high school sophomores in Tennessee had been going steady for three months. While the boy wanted to have sex, his girlfriend absolutely refused to go to bed with him.

"If I don't get something soon," he complained to his friends, "I'm going to explode."

Then one morning, a senior came up to the boy in the hallway

outside the chemistry lab. "Hey kid! The story is your girlfriend won't play nice."

"What business is that of yours?"

"Calm down, buddy," the senior said. "I've got a solution. It so happens that I have a little something that will get your girlfriend in the mood. Ever hear of Spanish fly?"

"You've got Spanish fly? That would solve my problem!"

"Easy does it, Romeo. For fifty bucks, I can give you enough so you can keep your girlfriend in the mood from now until you kids graduate. Bring me the money tomorrow and your troubles are over."

The next day, the boy met the senior under the bleachers on the football field. "Just remember, kid. A little of this stuff goes a long way. Put a tiny pinch in her soda and she'll be all over you."

"I'll remember," the boy said. "And thanks!"

On Friday night the boy took his girlfriend to a drive-in movie. When he went to the refreshment stand, he poured a tiny bit of the aphrodisiac in his girlfriend's soda. But when he considered how horny he felt and how determined his girlfriend was, he decided that more was better. He dumped a handful of the powder in her drink, stirred it with a straw and walked as casually as he could back to the car.

He handed his girlfriend her drink. "I'm so thirsty," she said. She took a long drink. Then she said, "You forgot the french fries!"

"I'll go back," the boy said. "It will only take a minute."

But there was a long line at the refreshment stand now, and 20 minutes passed before he returned with the french fries. As he approached the car, he saw that a crowd had gathered. And his car

was rocking violently. He pushed his way through the spectators and opened the door. There was his girlfriend on her knees, crying out in ecstasy as she made passionate love to the car's gearshift.

The Psycho Upstairs

A high school girl was babysitting two little kids for a neighbor when the phone rang. When she answered, a man's voice said, "You better get out of the house before I come down there and kill you."

The girl hung up without saying a word. "It's just some psycho," she told herself, and went back to watching television.

Fifteen minutes later, the phone rang again.

"Hello?"

"You better get out of the house now. I'm going to come down there and kill you."

"Stop calling me, you sick freak!" the babysitter shouted into the phone, and slammed it down.

But before she could get back to the couch, the phone rang a third time. It was the same voice on the other end.

"I warned you. I've killed the kids. And I'm gonna kill you."

Now the babysitter was frightened. She hung up, called the police and told them the story.

"We're sending a squad car over now, miss," said the officer. "But please hold so we can trace where the last three calls to your number came from."

A moment later the officer came back on the line, "Get out of the house now! Those calls came from the upstairs phone!"

Variation: In another version of this popular urban legend, two high school girls are babysitting together. Frightened by the phone calls, one goes upstairs to check on the kids and is stabbed by a killer lurking in the children's room. Before she dies, she manages to scream out to her friend, "The children are dead! The killer is coming for you! Get out of the house!"

The Poodle in the Microwave

A woman in Arkansas adored her miniature poodle. She took the poodle with her everywhere. She cooked all its meals herself and knitted it little outfits to wear in cold weather. She even bought it a pink leather collar studded with rhinestones.

So it broke her heart every week when she had to wash the poodle. No matter how thoroughly the woman dried the dog, it trembled violently for hours afterward until the last little bit of moisture had evaporated from its coat.

The woman had tried hairdryers, but the noise terrified the poodle and the hot air dried out its skin. It seemed hopeless.

Then one day the woman bought a microwave oven. And that's when she had an idea. If the microwave could heat up food in minutes, it could certainly dry Fluffy in the same amount of time.

On bath day she shampooed the dog and carried the trembling little creature into the kitchen. She popped open the door of the microwave and placed the dog inside. She shut the door securely and programmed the oven to eight minutes on high. Then she went back to the bathroom to clean out the tub.

Before she had finished, she heard an explosion. As she rushed downstairs, she recognized the aroma of cooked meat. To her horror, she found the microwave door blown off its hinges and bits of cooked poodle strewn all over her kitchen.

Curses! Broiled Again!

Over the Christmas and New Year's holiday, a South Dakota woman took a vacation in Miami. She returned home to the frozen north with a magnificent tan. But within a few days, the tan began to fade.

"I'm not going to be pale all winter long," she vowed, so she scheduled an appointment at the local tanning salon. But one 15-minute session on the tanning bed seemed to make no difference. She returned again the next day. And the next. And the day after that. It was no good. Daily 15-minute sessions were not restoring the deep golden tan she had acquired in Florida.

"I'd like to schedule a two-hour session for tomorrow," she told the young woman at the counter.

"But ma'am, we're not allowed to do that. Fifteen minutes is the limit. It's the law. The health department would shut us down."

"That's absurd. If I can lie out for two hours in the sun, I should be able to use your tanning beds just as long."

But arguing got her nowhere. The tanning salon would not let her tan for longer than 15 minutes.

The next morning, the woman had an idea. She got out the phone book and tore out the page that listed all the tanning salons in a 100-mile radius. She visited ten tanning salons that day and twelve

more the next day. She was very pleased with the results. Thanks to her tanning marathon, she was darker than she had ever been in her life.

On the third day, however, when she woke up, the woman felt very strange. She made an appointment with her doctor. He was surprised by the darkness of her tan. "Where have you been?" he asked.

She told him of her little scheme to sidestep the 15-minute limit. "So I expect I'm just a little dehydrated. That used to happen when I was in Miami," she said.

"We'll just run some tests to find out."

An hour or so later, the doctor called the woman into his office. "I really wish you had not gone to all those tanning salons," the doctor said.

"Why? Have I damaged my skin?"

"I wish that was all you'd done. I'm afraid you have about 24 hours to live. By spending all that time on the tanning beds, you cooked your internal organs."

Variations: Two common alternate versions of this story are slightly less grisly. In one version, only one arm was fried by prolonged tanning, but the arm had to be amputated. In the second version the young woman goes blind from her marathon tanning sessions.

The Runaway Grandmother

This story dates back at least to the 1970s and may have been the inspiration for a scene in the movie National Lampoon's Vacation. A family from Fort Worth, Texas, decided to take a vacation in Mexico. Mom and dad, the kids and grandma all piled into the station wagon for a trip south of the border. Then one morning, the family awoke to find that grandma had died in her sleep.

"We should call the authorities," the mother said.

"No way," said the father. "It will be weeks of red tape and filling out forms before the Mexican government releases my mother's body. And when they finally do let her go, it will cost me a fortune to ship her back to Fort Worth."

"So what's your solution?"

"I say we wrap her up in the picnic blanket, tie the body to the roof of the car and drive like hell for the border."

"I think you're nuts," the mother said. "But let's give it a try."

It was almost noon by the time the station wagon was packed, and grandma had been secured to the roof. The family had missed breakfast, and as they didn't want to delay any longer they also skipped lunch. "We'll eat when we're back in Texas," the father promised.

After six hours of nonstop driving, however, they were still about 100 miles from the border. Now everyone needed a break, so the father pulled over to a roadside restaurant.

"What about grandma?" the wife asked.

"She'll be fine where she is," the father answered.

An hour or so later, the family emerged from the restaurant.

The station wagon was gone, and grandma was gone with it.

The family notified the police in Mexico and Texas, but the car—and the body—were never recovered.

The Suspicious Birthday Boy

The owner of a construction firm suspected that his wife was cheating on him. On the morning of his birthday, as he was driving a truck full of fresh cement to a new construction site, he decided to take a detour. He turned down his street, and sure enough, the drapes in his bedroom were drawn, and parked in front of his house was a shiny new BMW convertible.

The humiliated husband was enraged. "The cheap little tramp has the nerve to cheat on me on my own birthday!"

He backed up the truck and when he was perfectly positioned, he began to pour cement into the BMW. As the car filled up, he leaned on the truck horn and shouted, "Come out and fight, you little weasel!"

The front door of his house swung open and his wife stepped outside. She stood on the front lawn watching. When the car was filled with wet cement, the husband climbed out of the truck and walked over to his wife.

"Where's your rich boyfriend?"

"I don't have a boyfriend."

"You don't have a boyfriend?"

"That's right. I don't have a boyfriend. And now you don't have the BMW convertible I bought you for your birthday."

"Beam Me Up, Scotty!"

A patient at a Des Moines hospital for the mentally disturbed was convinced that he was Captain James T. Kirk of the starship *Enterprise*. One night, he managed to slip past security and escape. When he was picked up the next day by the local police, he insisted that he was perfectly sane and was being held against his will in the hospital.

The officer who found the man said, "The hospital folks tell us you think you're Captain Kirk."

"That's a lie! I demand a hearing to prove that I'm sane."

A few days later, the patient, several doctors from the hospital and the police officer who picked the man up appeared before a judge. The judge asked the escaped patient his name, his address and his birth date. To all of these questions, the man gave the proper response.

Then the judge asked, "Sir, who is president of the United States?"

The escaped patient smiled and said, "Grover Cleveland."

The judge shuffled some papers on his desk, cleared his throat, and said, "For your own safety, I am sending you back to the hospital for a period of observation—"

But before the judge could finish, the man pulled his wallet out of his back pocket, flipped it open, and cried, "I'm in trouble down here! Beam me up, Scotty!"

Variation: In another version of this legend, the defendant is a young man convicted of drunk driving who shows his contempt for the court

by pulling out his wallet and saying, "Beam me up, Scotty. There's no intelligent life here."

Unusual Vacation Photos

Four college guys from Michigan State pooled their money and rented a condo on the beach in Jamaica for spring break. The condo was luxurious. Booze was cheap. The beaches were packed with beautiful women. The guys were living the good life in paradise. And they got just a little too obnoxious about it—especially with the two stewards assigned to their condo, whom they kept calling "Boy."

On the third day of their vacation, the guys returned to their condo to find it ransacked. Everything was gone—except their toothbrushes and a Leica camera.

American Express refunded their travelers' checks. The resort bought them new clothes and comped them on their meals and their bar tab. The boys were just grateful that at least they still had their camera.

Exhausted after their long day of running from office to office and filling out one form after another, the guys decided to crash early. They went back to their condo, brushed their teeth and went to bed.

When they returned to East Lansing, they sent the film out to be developed. A few hours later, they met in a bar off-campus to look at the photos. The first few pictures were shots of them on the beach and goofing around in Kingston.

But the next few pictures were different. They showed the two

stewards from the condo, naked, with the guys' toothbrushes stuck up their butts.

Variations: In the most common alternate version of this legend, the vacationers are newlyweds. The element of the story that varies most often is the setting—Florida, the Caribbean, even Europe—depending upon the preference of whoever is telling the legend.

The Mexican Pet

A woman from Colorado was on vacation in San Diego when she decided to take a day trip to Tijuana, Mexico. She didn't enjoy herself much. The town was noisy, the traffic was terrible, and the shops were filled with cheap trinkets. She was about to get in her car to go back to San Diego when she saw a tiny gray creature hiding behind a dumpster.

"What a darling little Chihuahua puppy," she said to herself. "The poor thing looks lost and hungry."

She dug around in her purse for a mint and offered it to the animal. It crept out from behind the dumpster and took the mint from the woman's hand. It was dirty and had no collar, so the woman assumed that no one owned it.

"I think I'll have to take you home with me," she said. "I'll call you Poncho." She picked him up, put him in the back seat of her car, and drove back to San Diego.

In the hotel, she gave Poncho a bath, and ordered him a hamburger from room service. Then she went to a pet store and

bought a cardboard carry-on box so she could take Poncho with her on the plane.

Back home in Fort Collins, the woman took Poncho to a veterinarian for his shots and a checkup.

"So what have we here?" the vet asked, pointing to the cardboard box.

As she opened the box, the woman said, "Doctor, I rescued the sweetest little Mexican Chihuahua when I was in Tijuana."

The vet glanced in the box and stepped back. "Lady, I'm afraid what you rescued is a little Mexican rat."

Short Takes 3

• The secret ingredient in the original formula of Coca-Cola was cocaine.

• If you drink Coke after you've eaten Pop Rocks candy, your stomach will explode. That's how little Mikey, the kid who would eat anything in the Life cereal commercial, died.

• For recreational sex, you can't beat a swimming pool. The chlorine is a foolproof contraceptive.

• Nine months after its 1965 blackout, New York City had the biggest baby boom in its history.

• Poinsettias are poisonous. Every Christmas, several small children die from eating the plants.

• At Halloween, sadists slip razor blades into apples and give them to trick-or-treaters.

• Blue Star lick-and-stick tattoos are laced with LSD.

• The fastest way to sell your house is to bury a small statue of St. Joseph in the front lawn. Make sure the head is pointing toward the house.

• The Beatles song "Lucy in the Sky with Diamonds" was really a secret code for the band's drug of choice at the time, LSD.

• A dying boy in England is trying to break the Guinness record for getting the most get-well cards.

• A dying boy in England is trying to break the Guinness record for collecting the most business cards.

• A dying boy in England is trying to break the Guinness record for receiving the most e-mails.

• An aluminum manufacturer will donate an hour of dialysis to a sick child for every 1,000 aluminum can flip tops it receives.

THE BABY ON THE CAR ROOF
AND OTHER AUTOMOTIVE MISHAPS

The Baby on the Car Roof

A young couple was driving across the Utah desert. Strapped into a car seat between them was their nine-month-old baby. After seven hours behind the wheel, the husband was beginning to get bleary-eyed.

"You look exhausted," the wife said. "Why don't you let me drive for a while."

"Thanks," the husband answered. "I could use a nap."

He slowed down and parked the car on the shoulder of the highway. The wife climbed out, and lifted the baby in its seat out of the car. "Here," she said, "just scoot over."

"I can't," the husband said. "You've got to move that duffel bag you call a purse out of the way first."

The wife reached up and put the baby on the roof, then reached back into the car and pulled out her large purse. She tossed it into the back seat, walked around the back of the car, and got behind the wheel.

"Sleep as long as you want. I've got everything under control," she said as she put the car in drive.

The wife hadn't driven more than two or three miles down the highway when she heard a siren and in the rear view mirror and saw a state trooper's car behind her with its lights flashing.

"Now what," the groggy husband said.

"I don't get it," the wife said as she pulled over. "What could I have done wrong?"

The state trooper walked slowly up to the car and leaned into

the driver's side window.

"Didn't you folks forget something?" he asked.

"Gosh officer," the wife said. "I'm sorry. I forgot to signal before I got back onto the road."

"No," the trooper said. "That's not what I meant."

He straightened up and lifted something off the car roof.

"Actually," he said, "I was referring to this."

He held before the stunned parents' eyes their baby, still strapped into the car seat.

The Elephant and the Volkswagen

Although this story seems to have originated in San Francisco about 1971, the most common version sets it in New York City at Madison Square Garden, the traditional venue for the circus in the Big Apple. The story even appeared in the New York Times *as a news item in 1975.*

A woman from New Jersey drove into Manhattan one morning to buy tickets for the circus that was appearing at Madison Square Garden. She couldn't believe her luck when she found a parking spot right in front of the Garden. Then, while she was in line at the ticket booth, she saw animal handlers lead one of the circus elephants onto the street for an airing.

"This is such a wonderful day," the woman said to the woman ahead of her in the line. "First a parking spot on the street, and now I get to see an elephant walking on Eighth Avenue!"

The other woman smiled.

"And look," the lady from New Jersey said. "The elephant is walking right over to my car. Oh, I wish I had my camera."

In fact, the elephant was hurrying over to the lady's car. Once it got to the curb, it turned itself around and very slowly sat down on the hood of the Volkswagen.

"You idiot! How could you let this happen," she shouted at the handler as she ran to her car.

"I'm really sorry, ma'am," the handler said. "Mambo must have mistaken your Beetle for the red stool she sits on during her act. Come inside with me and we'll straighten this whole thing out."

The woman was still extremely upset, but she followed the handler and Mambo into Madison Square Garden.

The circus manager couldn't have been more apologetic. He promised that the circus would pay for any repairs not covered by the woman's insurance, and he even gave her a notarized statement describing what happened to her car so she would have no trouble with her insurance company. Then he and the handler followed her back outside to make certain her car was still driveable.

The car may have looked ridiculous with its crushed hood, but because the VW Beetle's engine was in the rear, the car started up without any trouble. Slowly the woman pulled away and headed for the Lincoln Tunnel.

Once she was on the New Jersey Turnpike the woman leaned a little too heavily on the gas pedal. After a few miles, she heard a siren and saw a state trooper's car in her rear view mirror. Stressed and upset almost to the point of tears, she pulled onto the shoulder of the turnpike.

"Ma'am," the state trooper said, "do you know I clocked you doing 85 miles per hour? Let me see your license and registration."

"I know, officer," the woman said. "I'm sorry. I just want to get home."

The state trooper didn't say a word, but walked around to the front of the car to take down the woman's license plate number.

"Ma'am, what happened to your car? Don't you know driving it in this condition is hazardous?"

"Oh, that!" the woman said. "That's from the elephant that sat on my car this morning while I was waiting on line to buy tickets for the circus at Madison Square Garden."

"I see. Step out of the car, ma'am. Can you recite the alphabet backwards for me?"

"I am not drunk! I have a notarized statement signed by the elephant's handler and the manager of the circus!"

"Uh-huh. Good. Before we look at any paperwork, how about you take this breathalyzer test first."

Variations: A St. Louis version has an elephant sit on a family's car in the parking lot of the famous St. Louis Zoo. An English version has the elephant sit on the car when the driver stopped while cruising through a safari park.

The Rattle in the Cadillac

All his life, an insurance agent longed for a Cadillac. After 25 years of hard work during which he built a successful business, bought a nice home for his family, took his wife on an annual vacation to the Caribbean and put his children through college, he decided it was time to indulge himself. He went to a car dealer and bought the finest Cadillac on the market, loaded with every imaginable option.

The day he picked up his new car, the insurance agent was the happiest man in town. The first time he slid behind the wheel of the Cadillac, it was a sensuous experience for him. He ran his hands over the soft leather upholstery. He savored the new-car smell. He sat in the parking lot for a full 10 minutes listening to the low, sexy hum of the engine idling.

Finally, he pulled out of the dealer's lot and drove slowly back to his office about a half mile away.

The excitement of achieving his dream was too much for him, he couldn't get any work done, so the insurance agent took the rest of the day off. He decided he would pick up his wife, take her for a drive in the country, and then they would go have a romantic dinner to celebrate.

As he was heading home, however, he thought he heard a rattle. He tried to ignore it, but there was most definitely a rattling sound coming from his brand-new Cadillac. When he drove over the railroad tracks, the rattling became almost deafening. Now the man was furious. His life-long dream was be ruined by shoddy workmanship.

"Damn American cars!" he said to himself. "I should have bought a BMW."

He turned around and drove the Cadillac back to the dealer. For the next three days, the mechanics at the dealership carefully checked and tightened every single part on the Cadillac. But the car still rattled.

"Take it apart," the insurance agent said. "Disassemble it! Find out what's making that damn noise!"

Later that afternoon, the agent received a phone call from the Cadillac dealer.

"We've found the source of the trouble. Why don't you come over here and take a look."

The insurance agent hurried over to the dealership and into the garage. The entire staff was gathered around his car—the sales team, the mechanics, even the office staff.

"This is it," the owner of the dealership said as he handed the insurance agent a tin can suspended from a string. "We found it hanging inside the door panel on the passenger side of the car. We waited for you to open it up."

The insurance agent took a screwdriver from one of the mechanics and pried open the can. Inside were nuts and bolts, a few pennies, some small stones and a note .

"You rich SOB! So you finally found the rattle!" the note read. It was written on a letterhead from the Cadillac factory in Michigan.

Twenty-five Miles Per Hour

In the 1970s this was a very popular story, although its origins almost certainly go back to the 1950s when automatic transmission was a new option.

In 1970, a college kid had bought a used Volkswagen Beetle with automatic transmission. He was driving to work one morning when his car died in the middle of the street. A few moments later a friend from his fraternity pulled up in his big Chevy Impala.

"What's the trouble," the friend asked.

"The battery's died again," the owner of the Volkswagen said. "I can get it going if you give the car a push."

"I can do that," the friend said.

"There's one hitch," the owner of the Volkswagen said. "I've got automatic transmission. For the battery to kick over, you've got be going 25 miles per hour at least. Can you do that?"

"No problem," the friend said.

"All right," the guy in the Volkswagen yelled over his shoulder. "Start pushing."

Nothing happened.

He looked in his rear view mirror. Half a block away he saw his friend driving his Chevy straight for him at 25 miles per hour.

Cruise Control

In the late 1970s, a man decided to buy an RV for family vacations. One of the options he chose was a new device called cruise control. The salesman at the RV dealership explained that the man could set the speed of the RV, and it would remain constant until the driver touched the brake.

The day the man picked up the RV, he decided he'd take it out on the highway to see how it handled. He got the RV up to 60 miles per hour, set the cruise control, and then walked to the back of the RV to get a can of soda from the mini refrigerator.

Meanwhile, the highway curved to the left, but the RV continued cruising straight ahead—at 60 miles per hour—off the highway and into a dense stand of pine trees.

Not long afterward a state trooper pulled up beside the wreck. The man was badly bruised and had suffered a few scrapes, but he was okay. The new RV was totaled.

"I don't understand it," the man said to the cop. "I set the cruise control before I went into the back to get a soda."

"Mister," the cop said, "I think you mistook cruise control for automatic pilot."

Napping in the Nude

A husband and wife decided to drive their RV down to Baja California. After six hours behind the wheel, the husband asked his wife to drive for a while.

"If you don't mind," he said, "I think I'll go in the back and take a nap."

In the back of the RV, the man stripped off all his clothes, stretched out on the bed naked, and fell into a deep sleep.

An hour or so later, the wife heard a rattling sound. She pulled onto the shoulder of the road, got out of the RV, and found the source of the noise: The brace that held the spare gas can to the side of the RV had come loose. A couple turns of the screw and it was secure again.

Meanwhile, the husband woke up. He saw the RV was parked on a deserted stretch of highway. He went up to the driver's cabin, but his wife was not there. He went to the back of the RV and was about to step outside through the back door when he hesitated. Perhaps he should pull on his pants before he went outside. "The hell with it," he said to himself. "We're in the middle of nowhere." So, naked as he was, he stepped outside. But his wife was not in the back of the RV either.

The man was about to climb back inside when the RV pulled back onto the highway. He stood there stunned for just a moment. But even that was too long. By the time he started running after the RV, his wife was cruising along at 50 miles per hour.

The next vehicle that came along the highway was the Mexican highway patrol who arrested the man for indecent exposure.

Spunkball

A group of bored high school boys in rural Illinois came up with a way to generate a little excitement. They invented a game called Spunkball.

The boys split into two teams. Each team made a dozen "Spunkballs" by soaking rags in gasoline, wrapping the rags in aluminum foil, and duct-taping a firecracker to the exterior of each ball. Then each team got into separate cars and drove around town looking for likely targets.

The object of the game was to find empty parked cars with a window open. Then the boys would light the firecracker and throw the Spunkball into the car. The team that went through its arsenal of Spunkballs first, won.

One team had especially good luck finding parked cars with open windows. In 20 minutes they had tossed 11 Spunkballs. But then their luck ran out. They couldn't find any more targets. Worse, from neighboring streets they could hear explosions and shouts of triumph from their rivals. The opposing team was catching up.

While they sat at a traffic light, the boys argued about which part of town to head to next. Then a car pulled up beside them. Inside was a man and woman and all the car windows were open.

"This is our chance!" shouted the kid who was the keeper of the Spunkballs. He lit the firecracker on the last Spunkball and as the driver gunned the engine, threw it into the neighboring car. The light turned green and as their car raced down the street all the boys hung out the windows shouting "Spunkball!"

They heard the pop of the firecracker and saw a bright flame flare up in the back seat of the car that was still stopped at the intersection. A moment later a huge fireball exploded, destroying the car and killing the passengers.

What's In a Name? 1

In the late 1960s, General Motors began shipping the Chevy Nova to Mexico. The car had sold well in the United States, was priced right for the Mexican middle class and GM's marketing department was certain it would be a hit.

After several months in Mexico, not a single Nova had been sold. Back at headquarters, everyone was perplexed. What had gone wrong? The only way to find out was to organize a focus group.

A dozen GM executives flew down to Mexico with one of the best focus group facilitators in the United States. GM's Mexican office found a group of eight men and women who agreed to participate.

On the evening of the focus group, the facilitator showed the eight volunteers the Nova commercials and presented them with the sales brochures.

"Tell me, would you purchase a Chevy Nova?" she asked after she had given the panel a few minutes to review the material.

Everyone around the table laughed.

"Of course not," said a young woman.

"Tell why, specifically," the focus group facilitator said. "Is it the price? Performance? Appearance?"

"You don't understand," a well-dressed man said. "No one here will buy a car that doesn't go."

The facilitator looked confused.

"I'm not following you," she said. "What makes you think a Chevy Nova won't go?"

Everyone in the room laughed again.

"The name gives it away!" the man said. "In Spanish 'no va' means 'it doesn't go.'"

The Accident

A 15-year-old high school girl had just gotten her learner's permit, but her protective parents would not let her use any of the family's cars.

One Saturday night, when her parents had gone out for dinner and a play, the girl went to a party at a friend's house. At the party she met a nice looking soccer player and they decided to go somewhere quiet.

The boy drove to a famous make-out spot. He had brought a bottle of vodka along. After an hour or so he was pretty drunk and pretty obnoxious. The girl announced it was time to go back to the party, and that she was going to drive.

The boy didn't argue, but climbed into the back seat and passed out.

Once she was behind the wheel, the girl realized that her driving skills were not as good as she had thought. Worse, she had never driven at night. They had not gone far before the girl had a

serious head-on collision with another car.

When she came to in the hospital, a nurse was standing beside her bed.

"What happened?" the girl asked.

The nurse took her hand.

"It was a very bad accident. The boy in the back seat was killed. So was the couple in the other car. And you were very badly injured. We're doing everything we can for you."

The girl began to cry.

"Please. Please tell my parents that the boy was driving. I'm not allowed to drive. They'll be so angry with me."

"Don't worry," the nurse said. "They'll never find out."

Out in the hallway the nurse met the doctor who was handling the girl's case.

"Did you tell her that she's dying?" the doctor asked.

"No," the nurse said. "And I couldn't tell her that the couple in the car were her parents either."

The Body on the Grill

Since 1986, when it was first published in an Ann Landers' column, this story has grown in popularity.

After work, a construction worker went out with his friends for a few beers. What began as a couple of rounds of drinks turned into an all-night session. It was 2 a.m. when he staggered out of the bar, climbed into his pick-up truck and headed for home.

As he drove through his neighborhood, he felt a bump, but he

was too drunk to stop the truck. The man left the truck at the foot of his driveway, stumbled into his house, and passed out on the couch.

The next morning, while he was still in the shower trying to recover from his hangover, the man's wife was in the kitchen making coffee and listening to the radio. The lead news story was of an eight-year-old from the woman's own neighborhood who had disappeared during the night.

"How terrible," the woman thought. "I'll stop by the house this morning. Maybe the mother needs something." Then she went outside to get the newspaper.

Half-way down the driveway the woman let out a shriek her husband could hear in the shower. He grabbed a towel and ran outside. First, he saw his wife sprawled on the driveway where she had fainted. Then he saw embedded in the grill of his pickup truck, the body of an eight-year-old girl.

The Hook

Everyone in the towns and farms around Joliet, Illinois, were in a state of panic after a serial killer known as "The Hook" escaped from the penitentiary. The murderer had gotten his name after he lost his right hand while making a pipe bomb. Instead of getting a prosthesis, he had replaced his hand with a sharp steel hook—the same hook that he had used to kill 12 young women before he was captured and sentenced to life in prison.

A few days after the killer's escape, a young high school couple were out on a date. After the movie, the boy wanted to go to their

favorite spot for a little necking, but the girl refused.

"No," she said. "That lunatic is around here somewhere. Just take me home."

The boy pleaded, and whined, and made exaggerated promises until the girl relented.

"But we're keeping the windows rolled up, the doors locked, and the engine idling," she said.

"You're paranoid," the boy said.

"We do it my way or I go home," the girl answered.

So the boy agreed.

Their private place was the end of a driveway under a huge oak tree on an old abandoned farm. It was far off the road, surrounded by derelict corn fields. No car headlights or even roadside lights reached this dark corner.

The couple had been kissing for only a few minutes when the girl pulled away.

"I heard something," she whispered.

"That's your paranoia again," the boy said. He kissed her and the girl returned his kiss, but her heart was not in it. Again she pulled away.

"You had to hear that scratching sound," she said.

"No," the boy said. "I didn't hear anything." He tried to take his girlfriend in his arms again, but this time he stopped. He did hear a scratching sound against the passenger side door of the car.

"It's him!" the girl whispered.

"It's that huge raspberry bush," the boy said.

"Get me out of here," the girl said.

The boy started to protest, but the scratching sound was louder

and more distinct than ever now.

"Go! Go now!" the girl shrieked.

The boy threw the car into drive and hit the gas. The car lurched forward down the old driveway, spewing gravel and dust behind it.

All the way home the girl wept from fright. When he boy pulled up in front of her house, he got out and walked around to open her door and help her out of the car. He reached for the handle then yelled, jumped backward, tripped over his feet and fell flat on his back.

The girl threw open the door.

"What is it? What's wrong?"

"Look! Look!"

Hanging from the car handle was a bloody hook.

"No Radio"

A woman who lived in New York City had a car but couldn't afford the $250 a month to park it in a garage. That meant her car was out on the street, prey to car thieves and vandals. She could deal with getting up in the morning to find her car tagged by graffiti artists, but having a window smashed and her radio stolen time and again was maddening.

Finally, after the fifth radio had been ripped out of the dashboard, the woman went to her mechanic and told him to tape up the exposed wires and not bother putting in a new sound system.

That night, when she parked the car on the street, she placed in the windshield a large sign that read "NO RADIO!"

The next morning she went outside to find the driver side window smashed. Taped to the dashboard was a sign that read "JUST CHECKING."

A Tale from the Tollbooth

Two Goths took the New Jersey Turnpike to their college in Newark. Every day they stopped at the same tollbooth. Every day they asked the collector, "How much?" And every day they got the same answer. "Seventy-five cents, boys. Just like yesterday."

As pranks went, this was pretty dull. Even the tollbooth collector was bored with it. Then one of the boys had an idea that would make their next trip down the Turnpike memorable.

The next morning, the Goths pulled up to their usual tollbooth and asked their usual question.

"How much?"

"Same as yesterday," the collector said. "Seventy-five cents."

"That's a rip-off," the driver said. When he reached out his window, instead of dropping three quarters into the collector's outstretched hand, he clamped a handcuff around the man's wrist.

"What the hell are you doing?" the man said. And then the collector noticed that a rope was tied to the other cuff.

The driver gunned the engine and shot out of the tollbooth. As the rope uncoiled out the car window, the collector screamed and

tugged at the cuff, trying to free his hand. It wouldn't come off. His arm was going to be ripped out of its socket. The poor man began to weep.

Then he saw the frayed end of the rope flutter out of the car window.

300 Miles to the Gallon

In an effort to recapture the United States automobile market, an American car maker developed an engine that could run for 300 miles on one gallon of gasoline. The remarkable new engine was placed in a dozen cars, and these test models were sent out to dealers across the United States with instructions to road test the cars under the greatest variety of driving conditions.

A dealer in Minnesota received one of the experimental cars. Aside from its color—a metallic mint green—it looked like every other four-door sedan on the lot.

Not long after the experimental car arrived, an elderly woman came to the dealership to pick up her new sedan. She had special ordered her car in metallic mint green. The salesman went into the front office to get the new keys, grabbed the keys for the experimental car by mistake and escorted the lady out onto the lot. There, side by side, were two identical metallic mint green sedans.

The salesman tried the keys on one, but the door wouldn't unlock.

"Then this one must be yours, ma'am," he said as he unlocked the experimental car and held the door open for the customer.

She thanked him, took the keys, fired up the ignition and drove away.

For the next week, no one at the dealership had a spare moment to road test the experimental car. At the end of the week, the elderly lady came into the showroom looking very unhappy. Her salesman was out to lunch so the dealer himself asked if he could help her.

"The car handles beautifully," she said. "But the gas gauge is broken."

"How do you mean 'broken'?" the dealer asked her.

"I've driven more than 300 miles since I picked the car up last week, and the gas gauge hasn't moved a bit. Can your service people repair it?"

The dealer was stunned. He couldn't say a word.

"I don't want to make trouble," the woman said. "I saw another metallic mint green sedan on your lot last week. Would it be too much trouble to just trade my car for that one?"

The car dealer swallowed hard.

"No trouble at all. I'll make the trade right now. And I'll refund you half the purchase price of the car for your trouble. Just take a seat here. I'm going to pull your old car into the garage so it won't be sold by mistake to any other customer."

The Security System

A mid-life crisis hit a quiet, timid antique dealer in an odd way. He went out and bought a cherry red Alfa Romeo sports car.

The man loved his new car. When he raced it down the highway, he didn't feel middle-aged and prudent—he was young and hip. But after a few weeks the man began to worry. What if his car was stolen? It wasn't just a possession, it was now a vital part of his identity. He couldn't bear the thought of someone, undoubtedly younger and cooler than he, stealing his sports car.

So the antique dealer hired a contractor to tear down his old wooden garage and build a new one out of cinderblock with a reinforced concrete roof and no windows. It looked like a bunker, but that was only the beginning. Then he had a home-security service come in and install their finest alarm system. Finally, he bought the heaviest chain he could find and the most secure locks. Each night he chained the frame of the Alfa Romeo to bolts in the garage floor, set the alarm, locked the garage and went to bed.

At last, the antique dealer felt confident that his sports car was safe. Even a rash of car thefts in his neighborhood did not concern him.

One morning he opened his garage door and was stunned by what he saw. His beloved Alfa Romeo was still there, completely unharmed, but someone had turned the car around 180 degrees! And taped to the windshield was a note that read, "When we want it, we'll come and get it."

The Deadly Airbag

This story is the most recent of airbags-can-be-lethal folklore.

A man driving on Route 80 in Ohio stopped at a rest stop to use the men's room and get something to eat. When he returned to his car, he found that he locked the keys inside. Angry and embarrassed, he pulled out his cell phone and called the cops for help.

A few minutes later a highway patrol car pulled up. The officer took a metal rod he called "a slim jim" out of the trunk and slid it between the door window and the frame to unlock the car. After several attempts, the cop still hadn't hit the mechanism that controls the door lock release. Impatient and frustrated, the state trooper jammed the rod down hard, it slipped out of his hand, and struck the airbag panel in the steering wheel.

When the airbag inflated. The force propelled the rod out of the car and into the state trooper's skull. By the time the ambulance arrived he was dead.

The Exploding Cellphone

All versions of this urban legend can be traced back to Southeast Asia. Nonetheless, the story is so widespread in the United States that National Public Radio devoted a segment to it.

An executive was late for a meeting in downtown Los Angeles. As he sped along the freeway, he noticed that he was almost out of gas. Cursing furiously, he got off at the next exit and pulled into a gas station. He leapt out of his car, and jammed the nozzle into the gas tank.

"Damn! I'll never get there on time," he said to himself. So he reached into the car, opened his brief case, and took out his cellphone.

"Maybe I can get them to postpone the meeting for half an hour," he said.

The executive flipped open his phone and dialed the client's number. The spark from within the cellphone ignited the gas fumes, then the car's gas tank. A huge fireball engulfed the executive, followed by an explosion that leveled the gas station.

The Slasher Under the Car

A single woman bought a small house in a college town. After a couple of days, one of her neighbors dropped by to welcome her to the neighborhood.

"Forgive me for asking," the neighbor said, "but do you have hiking boots?"

The newcomer thought it was an odd question.

"No. Why do you ask? Are you a hiker?"

"Me? No way," the neighbor said, and laughed. "I hate walking anywhere. I'll drive around a parking lot for 15 minutes to find the closest spot to the mall door. And that is really my point. You see, we have some trouble here with the frat boys."

The newcomer poured her new friend another cup of coffee.

"One of the frat houses has a notorious shoe fetish. And the way the boys add to their collection is not nice. At night, they send pledges out to the mall parking lots. The boys lay underneath cars and wait for women wearing fine shoes to walk by. Then they reach out and slash the woman's ankle with a knife. While she's lying on the ground yelling, they steal her shoes and run back to the frat house."

"That's sick!" the newcomer said. "Has it happened to you?"

"Only once," the neighbor said. "I lost a $300 pair of Prada shoes. But now whenever I go shopping I wear heavy, ugly hiking boots that go halfway up my calf. And the frat boys keep their distance."

The Rest Stop

One summer a family from Maine decided to visit relatives in Arizona. The mother and father thought the visit would be a more memorable experience for their three children if they drove rather than flew. Initially, the trip was exciting, but day after day in the car made the children cranky.

There was one day when the children were just impossible. The family had been on the road for a week. It was hot. The drive through west Texas was boring. The kids were fighting constantly in the back seat.

"Just pull over somewhere," the mother said. "Maybe if we give them something to eat and let them run around for an hour they'll take a nap and we can get some peace."

Up ahead the father saw what appeared to be an exit.

"Maybe there will be something there."

He turned onto the ramp, but the exit led nowhere. The pavement ended abruptly and there was nothing but the endless plain.

"This is weird," the father said. "Whether they were planning an exit or a rest stop, the highway department must have abandoned the idea."

"I don't care about the reason," the mother said. "I'm just happy to get off the road for a while."

The father parked the car at the end of the pavement, and the mother laid out a blanket on the grass where the car provided a little shade.

While the family of travelers was eating lunch, back on the highway an 18-wheeler was in trouble. The truck's brakes were gone, and the trucker was desperate to find some grassy place where he could get off the road safely and just let the truck lose its momentum. Then he remembered the abandoned exit just up ahead.

The 18-wheeler was speeding along at 60 miles per hour when it began its descent down the ramp. The trucker saw the car parked dead ahead. He leaned on his horn. The low blaring sound was the last thing the family heard before the truck smashed through their car and crushed them all.

The Carjacker 1

After a full day of Christmas shopping at a mall, a woman returned to the parking lot just in time to see a man climb into her Mercedes.

"Stop!" she cried. "Get away from that car!"

The man looked at her with contempt.

"Get out of my way, lady," he said.

The angry woman dropped her shopping bags, opened her purse and took out a hand gun.

"Get out of that car or I'll shoot!" she said.

"You're out of your mind," the man said as he climbed out of the car and started to walk toward the woman. Before she knew what she was doing, the woman pulled the trigger and shot the man in the leg.

"You are insane!" the man screamed. Clutching his wounded

leg, he dragged himself away and hid under one of the neighboring cars.

Frightened and afraid that she would be arrested, the woman threw all her packages into the back seat of the car and climbed in behind the steering wheel and she realized this was not her car.

The Carjacker 2

A young woman was driving home in her 4x4 one evening when she saw the body of a man lying in the road up ahead of her. She slowed down, but realizing that this was a ploy carjackers often used, she decided to play it safe. She drove off the road, through the underbrush, and then returned to the highway again.

"Of course," she thought to herself, "it might actually be someone who needs help." To be on the safe side, she drove to the nearest police station and reported the incident.

When the cops got to the scene, there was no body lying in the road. There were, however, the bodies of four armed men lying in the underbrush. The woman had driven over them when she made her detour.

The Rhino and the Crazy Glue and Other Animal Stories

The Rhino and the Crazy Glue

A man just out of college was visiting a petting zoo with his girlfriend when another couple approached him. They spoke a language that sounded like Russian, and the woman had a tube of Crazy Glue in her hand. She asked the American a question which, of course, he didn't understand, and pantomimed applying the glue to her lips.

"Oh gosh, no!" the man said. "That stuff's not for chapped lips. It's Crazy Glue. It's super sticky stuff. Here, watch."

The American took the tube of Crazy Glue from the woman, applied a generous amount to his hands, and then put his hands on the posterior of Sally, a tame adult rhino that was part of the petting zoo.

"See! The rhino can't go anywhere now. This glue sticks like crazy!"

The Russian tourists clustered around the rhino's posterior to admire the adhesive qualities of Crazy Glue, but all this attention to her hindquarters made Sally nervous. She decided to trot over to the far side of the petting zoo enclosure. Naturally, she took the helpful American with her.

Now Sally was getting upset. No matter where she went or how fast she turned, she couldn't shake the human off her butt. Sally panicked and ran wildly around the enclosure. The other animals became terrified, too, and started a stampede.

In her frenzy, Sally chased all the visitors out of the enclosure, destroyed a concession stand, and trampled three miniature goats, a

Vietnamese pig, and a small flock of ducks. She only stopped when a zoo caretaker shot her with tranquilizer gun.

Sally collapsed on the ground, and the terrified, exhausted nimrod who had glued himself to the rhino's buttocks collapsed behind her. But the trouble didn't end there. A few moments after the rhino collapsed, the laxative the zoo's vet had given Sally earlier in the day went into action.

Thirty gallons of rhino dung erupted out of Sally and all over the hapless American. While two of the zoo's maintenance crews worked with shovels to clear away the dung so the poor man could breathe, one of the zoo's vets applied one solvent after another, trying to find something that would detach the man's hands from Sally's rear end. After an hour of effort, the man was free.

Gasping for air and gagging from the stench of the rhino dung that covered him from head to foot, the man staggered out of the petting zoo enclosure. At the gate stood the two Russian tourists and an elderly woman who was laughing and chatting with them in Russian.

"They want to thank you for the performance. They say you are better than the clowns in the Moscow Circus, and they want to know what time is your next show," she said in Russian-accented English.

The SUV on Ice

After a major score in the stock market, an investor from Detroit went out and bought himself a $50,000 Grand Cherokee. This SUV was loaded, and the guy was pretty proud of himself. So to show it off, he invited a friend to go duck hunting.

Early the next Saturday morning they loaded the guns, the beer, and the investor's labrador retriever into the Grand Cherokee and headed north to duck country.

It was late in the season, so their favorite lake was frozen solid, which gave the proud SUV owner an opportunity to drive his new baby out on the ice.

"Your Cherokee handles beautifully on ice, Eddie," the friend said, "but how are we gonna attract ducks? They only land on water, and we don't have any tools to cut a big enough hole in the ice."

"Sure we do," Eddie said. He climbed out and walked to the back of the SUV, followed by his friend and his retriever. Eddie opened his tool chest and took out a stick of dynamite with a 40-second fuse. "This should make a nice big hole in the ice," he said. "You light the fuse and I'll throw the dynamite."

As the fuse began to sizzle, Eddie put everything he had into the throw. The stick of dynamite soared high over the ice and landed far out on the lake. And as the stick of dynamite bounced on the ice, Eddie's lab took off like a shot to retrieve it.

Now both of the men are screaming at the dog.

"No! Stop! Come!"

But the lab was a dog with a purpose. He picked up the stick of dynamite, tossed his head back, and started prancing across the ice back toward the two hunters.

The two men are almost hysterical now.

"Down! Sit! Stay! Heel, dammit!"

But the dog and the dynamite kept coming.

Desperate, Eddie ran to the back of his SUV, took out his gun, and shot his dog.

Now the gun was loaded with bird shot, which will bring down a duck; it won't stop a 100-pound dog, but it will slow him down. The lab hesitated for a moment, but then kept walking toward his master.

Eddie fired again, and now the dog, hurt, confused, and frightened, looked for some place to hide. With the dynamite still in his mouth the lab took cover—underneath the Grand Cherokee.

As the two hunters scrambled to get away, the dynamite exploded, a huge hole opened up in the ice, and the Grand Cherokee sank to the bottom of the lake.

The two men were silent for several long minutes. Then the friend spoke up.

"So Eddie, you think your insurance will cover this?"

The Choking Doberman

This story dates at least from the 16th century. One peculiar modern version concludes with the vet telling the dog owner that the dog will have to be destroyed because once it has tasted human blood it will be a killer for the rest of its life.

A woman came home very late one evening to find her Doberman pinscher lying on the living room floor, blood coming from its mouth, and choking. She called her vet who told her to bring the dog to the animal hospital at once.

In the examination room the vet gave her an initial diagnosis.

"Whatever your dog tried to swallow is still lodged in its throat," the vet said. "And from the blood I'd say that whatever is down there has ruptured a blood vessel. I'll have to operate. Why don't you go home, and I'll call you in a couple of hours after surgery."

When the woman entered her house, she was surprised to hear her phone ringing. The vet couldn't have finished the operation already. She barely had time to say hello when she heard the vet shouting.

"Get out of your house now! Use your cell phone, call the police, and tell them you have an intruder. I'll meet you in front of your house in a few minutes," he said.

The poor woman was startled, even frightened, but she did as she was told. She ran out of the house and down the street where she called 911 on her cell phone. A few moments later two cops and the vet pulled up in front of the house.

"Did you call about a break-in, ma'am?" one of the cops asked.

"Yes," she said, "but I don't know anything about it. You'll have to talk to my veterinarian."

The two cops exchanged dubious looks, but the vet spoke up.

"It's like this officers. This lady found her dog choking to death tonight. When I examined the animal's throat I found these." From her coat pocket the vet drew out a clear plastic bag. Inside were three human fingers.

"It seems to me that the intruder could still be inside the house," the vet said.

"We get the picture," one of the cops said. "Both of you wait here while we search the house."

A few minutes later the police officers emerged from the house. They had a man with them, who was moaning and clutching his left hand which was covered with blood and missing three fingers.

The Hare Dryer

A man opened his back door one Monday morning to find his dog proudly holding a piece of dirty fur in its mouth. Upon closer inspection, the man was horrified to see that the dirty fur was actually his neighbor's prize rabbit.

He got the rabbit away from the dog and carried it into the house. The animal was dead, but there was no blood, no puncture wounds.

"The damned dog must have broken the bunny's neck," the man thought. And then he had an idea.

He carried the rabbit to the bathroom, placed it in the tub, and

grabbed the bottle of shampoo. He washed away all the dirt, used a little conditioner to make the rabbit's fur shine, and blew it dry.

Then, after reassuring himself that his neighbor was not home, he ran across the yard, placed the rabbit inside its hutch, and scurried back to his own house.

A few days later the man ran into his neighbor.

"The strangest thing happened," the neighbor said. "I found my rabbit dead in its hutch Monday morning."

"I'm sorry to hear that," the man said. "It must have been a shock."

"It was a shock," the neighbor said. "Because the rabbit died over the weekend and I buried it Sunday."

The Bump in the Rug

Three carpet installers pulled up in front of a house in suburban Illinois where they were scheduled to lay wall-to-wall carpeting on the first floor. The lady of the house met them on the porch with her seven-year-old daughter.

"I have some errands to run this morning," she told the men. "I should be back in two hours."

"That's fine," the foreman said. "We'll be finishing up by then."

The woman and her little girl went off on their errands, and the men went inside the house and got down to business.

It was a simple installation job. The crew finished in a little over an hour, so they sprawled out on the new carpet and relaxed until the woman returned. Then the foreman noticed something.

"Damn it! Look at the bump in the corner."

"It's not a big deal, boss," one of the men said. "I'll just tear up the corner and recut it."

The foreman glanced out the window and saw the woman's car pulling into the driveway. "She's home. Just take a hammer and pound that thing out."

After a couple of forceful blows of the hammer, the bump was flat. And a moment later the mother and daughter came through the front door.

"Mommy, I want to play with my hamster," the little girl said.

"You go ahead, sweetheart. I have to talk with these nice men."

The woman was delighted with her new carpet and that the men had finished the job so quickly. While she was writing them a check, the daughter came out of her bedroom crying.

"Mommy, the hamster's gone. The cage door is open and he's gone!"

The mother picked up her daughter and kissed her forehead. "These nice men are about to go, then you and I will look for the hamster. Okay?"

"I don't suppose you saw a hamster around while you were laying the carpet?" the woman said to the carpet installers.

The three men looked at each other, then glanced over to the corner. Where the bump in rug had been there was a now a fresh, wet, little puddle of blood.

Don't Leave Home Without Her

A Swiss couple from Zurich had no children, but they did have a poodle they were extremely fond of. They never went anywhere without their little dog, so when they planned a vacation to Hong Kong naturally they brought little Fritzie with them.

Their first night in Hong Kong they decided to dine out at a restaurant down by the harbor. As usual, they took the poodle with them. When their waiter came to their table, the woman handed her dog to him.

"While we have dinner, please take Fritzie to the kitchen and give him something to eat," she said.

The waiter did not speak much German. He looked at the couple strangely and was reluctant to take the dog from the woman's arms.

"It's alright," she said, "just take him to the kitchen."

The waiter shrugged, took the dog and walked away. Then he returned for the couple's order.

The travelers were ecstatic as course after course of delicious Chinese cuisine came to their table. Then the waiter emerged from the kitchen and rolled a cart bearing a large covered tray up to the Swiss couple's table.

He smiled warmly.

"I did as you asked," he said, then he lifted the cover. Lying on the tray surrounded by beautifully carved Chinese vegetables was little Fritzie, roasted to perfection.

Fetch!

Truman Capote is said to have told this story when he was a guest on Johnny Carson's *Tonight Show*.

A young man went to pick up his new girlfriend at her place on the twenty-third floor of an apartment tower on Manhattan's Upper East Side.

"I'm not ready to go yet," she said as she escorted him into the living room. "Have a seat. I only need a couple more minutes. You can get acquainted with my dog. He likes to play fetch."

Beside the couch was a pink rubber ball. The young man bounced it a few times off the floor, while the dog, a friendly little terrier, jumped up and down and yapped with excitement.

"Okay pooch, we'll start with something easy."

The young man tossed the ball against a bookcase. The dog caught it on the rebound in midair.

"Good boy! Try this one."

The young man threw ball against the far wall of the living room. Again the terrier snatched the ball out of the air and brought it back to the boyfriend.

"Okay, dog, show me what you've got." Now the young men threw the ball hard so that it bounced at the threshold of the French doors that opened on to the balcony.

The terrier dashed across the room after the ball, made a beautiful leap into the air, snatched the ball, and with it still in its teeth, sailed over the balcony railing.

"Bad Fifi!"

A wealthy couple in Miami hired an interior decorator to redecorate their apartment. It was a painless job—the clients were easy to please, had lots of money to spend, and stayed out of the decorator's way. The only trouble was the couple's obnoxious toy poodle, Fifi.

The dog followed the decorator wherever he went, yapping at him constantly, and running off with any tool or fabric swatch that he happened to put down. Not a day went by that the little mutt didn't sneak up from behind and bite the decorator in the ankle.

After weeks of this, the job was nearly complete. The husband and wife were sunning themselves on their deck while the decorator was going around the living room with a can of paint and a small brush doing touch-up work. Suddenly, he tripped and spilled the entire can of paint on the new $10,000 Persian silk carpet. The decorator was mortified to be so clumsy. But the thought of having to pay for another $10,000 carpet out of his pocket was what really upset him.

In the corner of the room was Fifi, yapping and snarling as usual. That's when the decorator had an idea. He reached into his pocket and took out a mint. Holding it in the palm of his hand, he got down on his knees. "Come here, Fifi. Come get the candy, sweetheart!"

The dog scampered across the room, and as it took the mint, the decorator grabbed him by the scruff of the neck and rolled the dog in the spilled paint.

"Oh, Fifi!" he shouted, loud enough so his clients would hear him. "Look what you've done!"

The Greenhorn

Stories of city slickers who can't tell the difference between wildlife and farm animals go back centuries. One modern version tells of farmers who paint "COW" and "HORSE" on the side of their animals for the benefit of clueless hunters from the big city.

A man from Manhattan who had never been outside New York City dreamed of the rugged life on the range. When he reached his forties, the man decided to act on his life-long dream. He bought an expensive hunting rifle and signed up for shooting lessons at a posh rifle club. After several months of practice, he felt he was ready to go hunting. At the beginning of the hunting season, he bought a first class ticket to Wyoming, rented a Jeep Cherokee at the airport, and drove up into the mountains.

He stopped at the first ranch house he saw and asked the owner if he could hunt on his land.

"That's fine with me," the rancher said. "Only watch out for my bull. It's grazing in the upper pasture, and if you shoot it, it will cost you $5,000."

The novice hunter promised to be careful.

A couple hours later the hunter stood at the rancher's door again.

"I'm terribly sorry," he said. "In spite of everything you told me, I mistook your bull for an elk and shot it. Will you accept a check?"

The rancher was angry, but at least he would be compensated for his loss. He took the New Yorker's check for $5,000 and watched him as he drove back to the main road. Then the rancher called one of his hands from the barn.

"That New York hunter shot the bull. Help collect the body and we'll have steaks tonight."

In the upper pasture, the two cowboys were surprised to see the bull grazing quietly amid the tall grass.

"What in hell did that city boy shoot?" the rancher said. As they wandered around the field, the ranch hand found the body of a magnificent eight-point buck.

"This is some day for you, boss," the hand said. "You've got a trophy buck, a freezer full of fresh venison and a $5,000 check."

"Yep," the rancher said. "I got to figure out a way to get more New York hunters up here."

The Deer Hunter

Every year for twenty-five years a Wisconsin man had gone deer hunting. Every year he bagged a deer. Still, he wasn't satisfied. Of all his friends, he alone had never shot a trophy buck.

Finally the hunter's day arrived. At the edge of an open field he spotted a magnificent buck with a huge rack. It was the most exciting moment of his life. None of his friends had ever gotten a deer as fine as this.

Slowly he drew his rifle up to his shoulder, aimed carefully, and squeezed the trigger. A moment later, the buck fell to the ground.

The hunter let out a pathetic imitation of a Tarzan yell and ran across the field. The deer was huge. And he had been right—it was an eight-point buck. If only his friends had gone hunting with him. Fortunately, he had brought a camera along. He propped up the deer's head, and rested his rifle in its antlers. Then he stepped back to mount the camera on a tree stump and set the timer.

As the timer buzzed, the hunter hurried over and crouched down beside the deer. A moment later, the camera went off, taking a series of beautiful shots of the buck coming to, standing up and bounding into the forest with the hunter's rifle still in its antlers.

The Hunter's Nightmare

A deer hunter had spent all day tramping the woods and fields of northern Michigan but did not see a single deer. In the late afternoon, he decided enough was enough.

As he was driving home, a deer leapt in front of the car. The hunter slammed on the brakes, but he struck the deer anyway. The impact threw the deer's body into a gully along the side of the road.

The hunter got out of his car to inspect the damage. Miraculously, his front end was intact. Then the hunter had an idea. He could still go home with a kill—he just wouldn't say how he had killed the deer. He dragged the deer out of the gully and stuffed it into the back seat of his car.

A few miles down the road, the deer came to. As the terrified animal thrashed around inside the car, the panicked hunter grabbed a tire iron and swung wildly at the deer. He missed, and hit his dog

in the head. The dog snarled and sank his teeth into his owner's arm. Somehow the man had managed to pull over to the side of the road. He ran from the car, pursued by his angry dog, and took refuge in a phone booth. He dialed 911.

"There's a deer in the back seat of my car kicking out all the windows!" he shouted into the phone.

"Sir," the 911 operator said, "I'm not sure how we can remedy this situation."

"Just send some cops! If they shoot the deer, I'll split the meat with them."

Don't Drink the Water

Two 10-year-old boys who lived in rural Montana went on a hike in the woods near their homes. Around noon they stopped by a stream to eat lunch. When they finished, both boys knelt beside the stream, cupped their hands, and drank some of the icy cold water.

"Snakes!" one of the boys yelled.

There, on the edge of the stream, was a nest teaming with baby snakes. The boys scrambled up the bank and ran for home.

A few months later, long after they had forgotten about the snake nest, one of the boys became very sick. He had severe stomach cramps. He was always hungry, yet he kept losing weight. His concerned parents took him to a pediatrician who sent him to the local hospital for a series of tests.

After studying an x-ray, a surgeon told the boy's parents that he was going to operate immediately.

"I'll explain everything after surgery," he said. "I can't waste any time."

In the operating room, the surgeon warned the rest of his surgical team.

"I don't want to frighten you, but be prepared for something out of the ordinary," he said.

Without any further explanation he cut open the boy's abdomen and removed a live, full-grown water snake.

The Watch Dog

This legend is at least 1,000 years old and is told in virtually every part of Europe. In Wales, the heroic dog's name is Gellert. In France, the dog's name is Guinefort. There is evidence that for many years French peasants prayed to Saint Guinefort to protect their children from harm.

After the death of his wife, a fur trapper took his infant and his large sled dog and moved to a cabin high in the Canadian Rockies, miles from any town or homestead. While the man set and checked his traps, the dog guarded the baby.

One winter's day while the hunter was out on his rounds, a blizzard struck. It took him hours to slog his way through the snow drifts back to his cabin. When he arrived, he found the door ajar. Cocking his rifle, he rushed into the house. To his horror, he saw the baby's crib overturned and no sign of the child. From behind the bed, crept the trapper's dog, its fur matted with blood.

With a cry of anger and despair, the trapper shot his dog dead.

Then the trapper heard the sound of his baby crying. He looked behind the bed and saw his son, safe and unharmed, lying on the floor. And sprawled beside the child was the body of a huge timber wolf, dead where the trapper's dog had killed it.

The Groaning Cactus

Southern California is basically desert, and it takes a lot of water—all of it imported from somewhere else—to keep the area's lawns and gardens green. Some residents would rather work with southern California's environment, so they build rock gardens around their homes and plant cactus and other native plants that require little water.

A woman new to the area decided that she would take the rock-garden-and-cactus approach to landscaping her new home. But when she visited local nurseries she found that a mature cactus cost thousands of dollars. She still wanted a cactus, but she didn't want to spend that kind of money for one. So she came up with an alternative.

She enlisted the help of a guy on her street, and together they drove her 4x4 out to the desert. In time, they found the perfect cactus, about five-feet tall. They dug it up, balled the roots, placed it carefully in the 4x4 and headed home where they planted it in the garden that night.

The next morning, as the woman was sipping coffee on her patio and admiring her garden, she heard a faint moaning sound that seemed to be coming from the cactus. As she got closer, she

noticed that the needles were quivering. It unnerved her, but she convinced herself it was just the breeze and went back into the house.

The next day the eerie sounds from the garden were considerably louder, and the cactus seemed to be heaving, as if it were trying to break loose from the ground. But once again, the woman convinced herself it was all in her imagination.

On the third day, high-pitched shrieks were emanating from the cactus and the sides of the plant were throbbing. Frightened, almost hysterical, the woman dialed 911.

"The cactus in my yard is alive!" she shrieked. "It's moving and making screaming sounds!"

"Stay indoors, ma'am," the 911 operator said. "I'll get a pest control emergency team over there in a couple of minutes."

The woman had scarcely hung up the phone when a large white van from the Department of Animal Services pulled into her driveway. Four men in heavy protective gear stepped out of the van and hurried into the back yard. Ignoring the advice of the 911 operator, the woman ran outside to meet them. One held a chain saw; the others carried canisters that resembled fire extinguishers.

"It's that one!" she said. "The one having convulsions!"

"Step back!" the crew shouted at her. "Get back in the house!"

Then, just as the man was about to fire up the chain saw, a loud, ugly ripping sound filled the yard and hundreds of poisonous tarantulas spilled out of the ruptured cactus.

The Mysterious Break-In

A family returned home one afternoon to find a huge hole in their roof and their dog dead in the living room, surrounded by a huge puddle of urine. Nothing was missing and no other damage had been done to the house.

The bewildered family called the police who were just as puzzled when they inspected the scene. At the family's request, the police department conducted an investigation.

Several weeks later the detective in charge of the investigation dropped by with the report.

"The key to solving this case was the urine," the detective said. "Our guys in forensics analyzed the samples and found that it represented the urine of a couple hundred individuals—men, women, and children."

"That makes no sense," the mother of the family said. "Why would 200 people come into our house to do nothing but urinate, kill the dog, and make a hole in the roof?"

"No one came into your house," the detective said. "And I'll explain why in a minute, but first, do you get a lot of plane traffic around here?"

"Oh yeah," the father said. "Planes are flying over the house everyday. This must be one of the main approaches to La Guardia."

"We thought so. You see, a plane was coming in for a landing at LaGuardia. It jettisoned the urine from its toilets. As the fluid dropped through the atmosphere, it froze. The block of frozen urine crashed through your roof and struck and killed your dog. By the

time you returned home, the ice had melted and formed the huge puddle of urine you found on your living room floor."

The Guest and the Dog

A woman who had just moved with her family to Bel Air was delighted when she received an invitation to tea at the home of one of the wealthiest and most socially prominent ladies in the community.

As the guest walked up to the front door, she encountered a large, shaggy, filthy dog. The pooch followed the woman up the front steps and sat down beside her. The hostess opened the door, but her smile of welcome faded when she saw that her guest had come to the house with a very dirty mutt. Nonetheless, she threw wide the front door. The newcomer stepped into the foyer, and the dog followed.

While the two women chatted and tried to ignore the dog, the animal ate finger sandwiches and cookies from the serving dishes, put its muddy paws on the furniture, and chased the cat through the house.

Finally, the guest was so uncomfortable that she made her excuses and got up to leave.

"Don't forget to take your dog," said the hostess, who had exercised heroic self-restraint throughout the visit.

The guest stared at the woman.

"My dog!" the guest said. "I thought it was yours!"

The Flying Cow

A man had stopped for lunch at a roadside diner in rural Nebraska. After his meal he went out to the parking lot and found the hood of his car crushed, with the body of a dead heifer sprawled across it. Soon the entire diner had emptied out as everyone speculated how such a thing could have happened.

Meanwhile the man went back inside to call his insurance company.

"I want to report an accident," said the man.

"Please describe the nature of the accident," said the insurance company's customer service representative.

"The front of my car was crushed by a cow."

"I see. You hit a car while you were driving."

"No," the man said. "The car was parked in a lot outside a diner. I was not even in the car at the time of the accident."

"Sir, how did the cow get onto the hood of your car?"

"I don't know," the man said. "It must have dropped onto the car."

"You're saying a flying cow landed in your car?"

"Not flying," the man said. "Cows can't fly. Something must have flung it in the air."

"So someone flung a cow onto the hood of your car."

"Yes," the man said. "That must be it."

The insurance company rep sighed.

"Sir, we'll have to investigate this accident and get back to you," he said.

Several days later the man received a phone call at his home from the same customer service rep.

"Sir, it appears that your car was indeed struck by a flying cow. The same day you called we received a claim from a trucking company. One of their drivers hit a cow near the diner where you were eating. The trucker saw the cow fly through the air, but he didn't know where it landed. We'll be sending out a check to you today."

The Flying Kitten

A young couple found a kitten in their backyard and decided to adopt it. One day the little thing escaped out the back door and raced up a tree. Coaxing, food, toys, catnip—nothing would lure the kitten down.

"I have a solution," the husband said. He went into the garage and came out with a long rope. He threw the rope over the branch the kitten clung to and began to pull. The branch bent and the kitten was nearly within the wife's reach when the rope snapped. The branch shot forward like a catapult and the kitten was hurled through the air. The heartbroken couple looked everyone for their pet, but they never found it.

A few weeks later the wife was shopping in the supermarket. At the check-out counter she met one of her neighbors from two blocks away. The neighbor was unloading cans of cat food from her shopping cart.

"I didn't know you had a cat," the woman said.

"We didn't until recently," the neighbor said. "About four weeks ago Ralph and I were sitting in the yard when out of no where this kitten flew over our backyard fence and landed safe and sound in Ralph's lap."

The Leashed Dog

It was a 12-year-old boy's job to take the family dog for a walk every day after he got home from school. He liked the dog, and he didn't mind taking it for a walk, but one day a friend stopped by and asked him to go swimming in his family's new pool.

"I've got to walk the dog first," he told his friend.

"No you don't," the other kid said. "Just tie the dog somewhere outside. It can do its business and you can go swimming."

This seemed like a good idea. So the boy walked his dog out to the garage and tied to the leash to the garage door handle.

An hour later the boy's mother was returning home from an errand. As she turned onto her street, she hit the remote for her garage door. When she pulled into the driveway, she saw the family dog hanging by the neck from the garage door. It was dead.

Variation: In another version of this story, the boy is traveling with his family in a camper. During a lunch break, the boy ties the dog to the rear bumper of the camper, and forgets about the animal. When the family drives away, the dog is dragged to death.

The Unusual Flower Arrangements

A woman had just bought a beautiful house in Los Angles and decided to throw a lavish house-warming party. She found a caterer and hired bartenders and several servers. All she needed was a distinctive decorative element that would make her party memorable.

She went to a fashionable florist and ordered a dozen flower arrangements in large clear glass bowls. Then she went to a pet store and bought several dozen goldfish.

On the morning of her party, the florist delivered the beautiful flower arrangements in large clear glass bowls. While the caterer and the servers and bartenders did the preparation work for the party, the hostess took her gold fish and placed six in each of the flower arrangements. The golden-colored fish looked lovely as they darted among the dark green stems of the flowers.

Soon the guests arrived and each one commented on the hostess' decorative flare. But as the party progressed, the guests become more and more silent, and the hostess found that they were congregating in small groups around each of the flower arrangements. The hostess sidled her way up to one of the little groups. Everyone was staring with glum expressions at the flower arrangement where the gold fish were all floating belly up in the bowl.

"That pet store sold me diseased gold fish," the hostess cried.

"Whether the fish were sick or not," one of her guests said, "they couldn't survive long in those bowls. The flowers sucked all the oxygen out of the water."

The Parakeet and the Splint

A man arrived at a veterinarian's office one morning with his parakeet. The bird had fallen off its swing and broken its leg. The vet placed a tiny wooden splint on the bird's leg, charged the man $35, and sent him home.

Before man and bird arrived home, the parakeet scratched and pecked at the splint until it broke. Back the man went to the vet who put on a new splint and charged the man another $35.

Five times this episode was repeated, and each time the vet charged the man the full $35 fee. So a day or two later, when the parakeet had broken yet another splint, the man felt that he could replace the splint himself.

The only piece of wood he had around the house that was comparable in size to the vet's splint was a wooden match. So the bird's owner bound the bird's leg to the match and returned the bird to its cage. Then he went outside to do some gardening.

The parakeet hopped around its cage scratching and pecking at the splint as usual, but it had the misfortune to drag the match stick against the rough surface of the cage liner. The match ignited, the bird's feathers caught fire, and an hour later when the man came back into the house he found the charred body of the parakeet lying on the floor of the cage.

"Don't Let the Cat Out"

A couple in Seattle was selling their house. They had a beautiful pure-bred Persian cat that they never allowed to go outside. Whenever the couple had to leave the house, they posted a note on the door for the real estate agents: "Please don't let the cat out."

One Saturday morning the husband and wife had a lot of errands to run. They knew at least one real estate agent would be showing their house to prospective buyers that day, so they posted the "Don't let the cat out" note on the front door.

When the couple returned in the afternoon, they found their beautiful Persian in the living room being mounted by a ragged tomcat.

They chased the stray out of the house and then found this note from the realtor.

"Another agent must have let your cat out by mistake. I found him sitting by the front door, so I let him in."

Three months later, the beautiful Persian cat gave birth to a litter of mongrel kittens.

The Cat Toys

Only a few weeks after a young couple got married, the wife came home with a kitten.

"I don't like cats," the husband said.

"But this one's so sweet," the wife answered. "And I promise never, ever to ask you to clean the litter box."

And so the husband gave in. After a couple of days, he found that he actually liked the kitten. It was a playful little thing. It especially liked to bat balls of yarn with its tiny paws.

The couple and the kitten had been living happily together for three weeks. One morning while the husband was in the shower the wife came into the bathroom.

"The garbage disposal has shut down again," she said. "Come out and reset it."

"I'm taking a shower," the husband told her. "You know where the reset button is."

"But that thing scares me. Please. You're good at these things."

The husband cursed under his breath, and to make a point walked dripping and naked to the kitchen. He squatted down beneath the kitchen sink and fumbled for the garbage disposal reset button. He never saw the kitten come bounding into the kitchen. But the kitten saw him. Or rather, it saw two balls swaying about a foot off the floor.

The kitten scampered over to the sink, leapt up and sank its needle-like claws into the man's scrotum sack.

With a blood-curdling scream, the husband jumped up,

slammed his skull against the underside of the stainless steel sink, and knocked himself out.

The wife rushed into the kitchen to find her husband, wet, naked and unconscious on the kitchen floor and her kitten mewing pitifully, its nasty little claws still caught in the man's scrotum.

When the husband came to, he was strapped to a gurney. All around him were paramedics and cops snorting and trying, unsuccessfully, to suppress their laughter.

"I want a divorce," he said to his wife who was standing at the foot of the gurney, holding the kitten and not saying a word.

John Wayne Was
a Draft Dodger
and Other Celebrity Legends

The Heckler

In 1970 Grand Funk Railroad was playing an arena in Los Angeles. In the middle of Mark Farner's featured guitar solo, someone in the front of the crowd shouted, "You suck!" and started to boo loudly. Farner kept his cool, and continued to play, but the heckler didn't stop. After a few minutes the booing and the insults were getting to Farner. He put down his guitar, motioned for the band to stop, and walked to the edge of the stage.

"You think you can do better, buddy?"

"Yeah," the heckler said. "I know I can."

"Fine. Get your ass up here and show us how good you are."

The heckler jumped up onto the stage, picked up the guitar, and played B.B. King's classic "Three O'Clock Blues."

The crowd went nuts, and even Farner was impressed. He took the stranger aside and asked him to wait for the band backstage.

After the show, Farner found the mystery guitarist. "You're great. You could make a career for yourself in this business. What's your name, man?"

"I'm Eric Clapton," the heckler said.

The Good Samaritan

Tales of mysterious strangers who come out of nowhere to help in a desperate situation date back at least as far as the Robin Hood legends of medieval England. They are an especially popular facet of the folklore of the American West.

A traveler got a flat tire on a desolate stretch of road west of Butte, Montana. He did not have a spare tire. He did not have a cell phone, and he had no idea how far it was to the next town or gas station.

Hour after hour slipped by, and not single car came along. The traveler was getting pretty nervous and wondered what he should do. Then he heard the rumble of a motorcycle far off in the distance. A few minutes later, a biker, wearing black leather and a shiny black and red helmet, was inspecting the flat tire.

"I can go to the next town and buy you a new tire. It will take me about an hour to get back," he said.

Before the traveler could give the stranger money for the new tire, the biker roared away.

An hour later the biker returned with a brand new tire and helped the traveler change the flat.

"I'm awfully grateful," the traveler said. "Now, what did that tire cost you?"

"Don't worry about it," the biker said. "I'm glad I could help."

"By the way," the traveler said. "You look familiar. What's your name?"

The biker picked up his shiny helmet.

"I'm Evel Knievel," he said.

Suicide on the Yellow Brick Road

A new employee at a video store was about to play *The Wizard of Oz* on the store TV when his fellow clerks stopped him.

"You don't want to play that movie," the store manager said. "It's got a really disturbing scene."

"You mean the flying monkeys?" the rookie said. "Everybody's use to them by now."

"No," the manager said. "I mean the suicide."

The new guy was stunned. "There's no suicide in *The Wizard of Oz*," he said.

"Come into my office," the manager said. "I'll prove it to you."

Inside his office, behind closed doors, the manager popped the video into his VCR and hit the fast forward button. He stopped at the scene of Dorothy, the Scarecrow, the Tin Man, and the Cowardly Lion about to set off together down the Yellow Brick Road.

"Look off to the edge of the screen," the store manager said. "There's a man by all those trees."

The rookie looked. A man, not in costume, stood beneath a tree. From the limb above his head hung a noose. The man climbed onto a wooden chair, but lost his footing. He tried again, got his balance on top of the chair, slipped the noose around his neck and tightened it. After a moment, the man kicked the chair out from under himself.

As Dorothy and her friends skip down the road to see the Wizard, the body of the hanged man swings slowly at the edge of the frame.

The Evil Twin

An Austrian couple were visiting relatives in a remote mountain village when the woman began to go into labor. The nearest doctor was in a town five miles away. While their relatives did what they could to assist the new mother, the husband hurried off to get the doctor.

A few hours later, the husband and the doctor arrived at the house to find that the woman had given birth to twin boys. They were very small, of extremely low birth weight, and they were blue. The doctor sat down beside the mother.

"Frau Hitler, the babies need oxygen, but I only have enough in my medical bag to save one of the children. I must ask you to choose," he said.

The new mother wept and kissed her two babies. Then she handed over one of the tiny infants.

"Here, doctor," she said. "Save my little Adolf."

The Lucky Landscaper

This story of the celebrity landscaper dates back to the 1940s.

A man had just moved to Beverly Hills and was looking for a good landscaper. One day, as he was driving home, he saw a black man tending a beautifully manicured lawn. The man pulled his car over to the curb and got out.

"Excuse me, " he said as he walked across the lawn, "do you

take care of this yard regularly?"

"Every week," said the man with the lawn mower.

"I just moved into the neighborhood and I need a landscaper. So I wanted to ask you Mr...."

"Murphy."

"Mr. Murphy."

"You can call me Eddie."

"Okay, Eddie it is then. So Eddie, how often do you work on this yard?

"Well, the lady of the house is happiest when I do a little work every day."

"And what does she pay you?"

"Nothing. She just lets me sleep with her every night."

Variations: The earliest version on record featured Bing Crosby. In later years the lucky landscaper was Bill Cosby or Flip Wilson.

The Bell Hop at the Plaza

Rev. Jesse Jackson was standing in front of the Plaza Hotel when a cab pulled up. Out stepped a white woman who looked at Jackson and smiled.

"The driver will open the trunk for you. Just leave my bags in the lobby, please," she said.

Without saying a word, Jackson lifted the woman's suitcases out of the trunk of the cab and carried them into the hotel. When he

returned to the curb, the woman was waiting for him.

"Thank you," she said. "You're very efficient." Then she handed him three dollars.

"I was happy to help ma'am," Jackson said.

Then, a limousine pulled up and the white driver stepped out to hold the door for the Jackson. As the limo pulled away, Jackson rolled down his window and gave the stunned woman a little wave.

Elvis's Farewell

East of Memphis was a farm owned by the McCoy family. The husband and wife knew Elvis Presley from the time he was a boy. When Elvis was just starting out in the music business in Memphis, the McCoys would have him out to the farm for Sunday dinner. The King never forgot the family's kindness. Even after he became a superstar, he stayed in touch with the McCoy's. When Elvis moved to Graceland, he often drove out to see his old friends. Several times when money was tight, Elvis helped the elderly couple.

One August day, Mr. McCoy was out in the field replacing some rotten fencing. He looked up and saw Elvis walking toward him. It seemed as if Elvis was wrapped in a blue mist, but at the time Mr. McCoy was so glad to see his old friend that he didn't think much of the phenomenon.

"Son, what are you doing out here in the fields in your city shoes? And where's your car?" he asked.

"I just stopped to say good-bye," Elvis said.

"You going back to Las Vegas?"

But before Elvis could answer, Mr. McCoy heard his wife calling him, and she sounded upset. He turned toward the sound of her voice, and when he turned back to ask Elvis to come with him into the house, the King was gone.

By that time, Mrs. McCoy was beside her husband. She was weeping.

"Oh Henry! It's the saddest thing. The man on the radio just said that nice boy, Elvis Presley, was found dead this morning."

Short Takes 4

• John Wayne dodged the draft during World War II.

• To expand her *Living* empire, Martha Stewart had herself cloned by a geneticist at Columbia University.

• During a program on how to cook duck, Julia Child dropped one of the birds on the floor. Without batting an eye, she picked it up, dusted it off, and placed it back in the roasting pan.

"Never let a little thing like that upset you," she said. "After all, you're alone in the kitchen."

• An episode of *Leave It to Beaver* made history when it showed the first toilet ever to appear on American television.

• The pilot for *Gilligan's Island* revealed Gilligan's first name was Willy.

• The producers of *Sesame Street* have decided to make Bert and Ernie a gay couple.

• The creators of *Star Trek* added the character Ensign Chekhov after an editorial in Pravda lambasted the show for failing to have a Russian aboard the U.S.S. Enterprise.

• Raquel Welch came on Johnny Carson's *Tonight Show* with a beautiful Persian cat.

"Would you like to pet my pussy?" she asked as she took her seat next to Johnny's desk.

"Sure, if you get that damn cat out of the way," he said.

• In the original 1940's radio program, *The Green Hornet*, Kato's character was Japanese. After the Japanese attack on Pearl Harbor, Kato's nationality was changed to Filipino.

• At the end of one of his broadcasts, Uncle Don, the host of a popular children's radio program in the 1930's, failed to notice that he was still on the air.

"There. That ought to hold the little bastards," he said.

• During the course of an interview, pop superstar Mariah Carey expressed her compassion for famine victims.

"I see those poor starving kids all over the world and I just cry. I'd love to be that thin, but not with all those flies and stuff."

• Ronald Reagan was originally cast to play Rick in *Casablanca*.

• Humphrey Bogart and Ed Sullivan were brothers.

• Humphrey Bogart developed his trademark lisp after his father hit him across the mouth when he was 10 years old.

• Humphrey Bogart developed his trademark lisp in the Navy after an inmate trying to escape from the brig hit him across the mouth with his handcuffs.

• Humphrey Bogart developed his trademark lisp in the Navy after a piece of shrapnel from an attacking Japanese submarine hit him across the mouth.

• During her *Larry King Live* interview, Monica Lewinsky said, "I've learned not to put things in my mouth that are bad for me."

• Star of *All My Children*, Susan Lucci, is the daughter of Phyllis Diller.

• Outrageous MTV comedian Tom Green had his show canceled after he attended a bar mitzvah dressed as Adolf Hitler.

• Phil Collins wrote "In the Air Tonight" about his brother's drowning. The first time Collins performed the song in concert, he sent free front row tickets to a man who had witnessed the drowning and done nothing to help.

• Phil Collins wrote "In the Air Tonight" about his wife's rape. The first time Collins performed the song in concert, he sent free front row tickets to the rapist.

• The will of movie critic Gene Siskel specified that he must be buried with his thumb pointing up.

THE HALL OF TORTURED SOULS
AND OTHER HIGH-TECH SCARES

The Hall of Tortured Souls

Users of Excel 95 found something uncanny in their software, something that has been removed from later versions of Excel. If you have Excel 95, you can experience it yourself. Here's how it works.

1. Open a new file.

2. Scroll down to row 95.

3. Click on the row 95 button, which will highlight the entire row.

4. Press tab to move to the second column.

5. With your mouse, click on Help, then click on About Microsoft Excel.

6. Press ctrl-alt-shift and click on the Tech Support button simultaneously.

7. A window will appear with the title, The Hall of Tortured Souls. The hall looks like a scene from Doom. Using your mouse, move around the chamber. On the wall you will see endless lists of names scrolling on the walls under the heading "Tortured Souls."

8. Go to the flight of stairs, walk up the stairs, then come back down and position your cursor in front of the blank wall. Type in EXCELKFA.

9. The blank wall will open to reveal a secret passage. Move carefully down the passage, be careful not to go over the edge. At that end of the passage a terrible secret will be revealed to you.

Intel's Revenge

One evening at a bar, two engineers from Intel were bitching about their favorite villain, Bill Gates, president of Microsoft.

"You guys are so predictable," the bartender said as he bought them a round. "Every night, it's the same song and dance about how awful Bill Gates is. But I got news for you boys, a hundred years from now, Bill Gates is going to be a corporate hero, like Carnegie and Rockefeller. Those guys were SOBs, too, but nobody remembers that now. Why don't you two techno-wizards figure out some way to express your feelings for Bill Gates that will last through the ages."

The two engineers looked at each, and they knew the bartender was right. They should be able to create some artifact that would be preserved in museums, something that would tell future generations that Bill Gates had not been everybody's hero.

The next day, they got their chance. Their boss assigned them to create a new version of the Pentium microprocessor.

For the next few months, the two engineers were positively giddy around the office. They came to work early and left late. They worked weekends. They were unfailingly cheerful, and the prototype of the new microprocessor they were designing was excellent. All the executives were pleased.

The day PCs with the new Pentium chip went on the market, the two engineers had cases of champagne brought in and threw the wildest office party in the history of Intel.

Months passed and the two engineers were still a happy couple

of guys. Then one day, a rumor began to spread through the computer industry that there was a secret message engraved on the new Pentium chip.

Executives at Intel tried to ignore the rumor, but the furor in the industry and the press, coupled with the unusual behavior of the two engineers responsible for the redesign of the chip, made them suspicious. At a special closed session of the company's executive board, the members voted unanimously to select Pentium chips at random and have them analyzed.

A few days later the executive board met again in a closed session.

"Ladies and gentlemen," the CEO said, "as you know analysts in our lab selected a random sampling of one dozen of the new Pentium chips. Examination of the chips under a powerful electron microscope detected the same message engraved on each chip. Here is what they found."

The executives turned toward the large monitor mounted on the board room wall. The CEO struck RETURN on the keyboard in front of him and there appeared a magnified image of the latest Pentium chip.

"BILL SUX" was engraved on it.

The Cupholder

A technical support rep at Apple sat down at her desk and picked up her first call of the day.

"This is Apple tech support. How can I help you today?" she said.

"Hi!," said a man on the other end of the line. "The cupholder on my new computer is jammed and I can't get it to close."

"Sir, you did say cupholder, correct?"

"That's right. It was working fine until this morning."

"Okay. First let me ask you a few questions. What model to you have?"

"I have a G4."

"Okay. I'm checking the specs on that model and I do not see a cupholder. Did you have your G4 customized by the dealer?"

"No. It was my understanding that this was standard equipment. It's built right in."

The customer service rep was silent for a moment.

"Sir, why don't you describe the location of the cupholder and how it operates."

"Well, there's an oblong button beneath it. When I press the button the cupholder comes out of the machine. It worked fine a few minutes ago, but when I put my coffee cup on it, the tray sagged and now it won't retract."

"Sir, that tray you've been using as cupholder, that's your CD-ROM drive."

Get a FREE Honda!

The get-something-for-nothing-just-by-sending-out-e-mail is a newcomer in the field of urban legends.

To become the number one car manufacturer in the world, Honda has launched an unusual campaign to promote its product.

Log on to the Honda webpage (www.Honda.com) and open an account in your name. Automatically the company will credit $1,000 to your account. For each person you e-mail about Honda, Honda will add $200 to your account. Every time a recipient of your e-mail forwards it to someone else, Honda will credit $100 to your account. Thanks to a powerful new BETA program, Honda will be able to track all of these e-mails accurately.

In a very short time, you could have enough in your account to get a Honda automobile FREE!

Variations: In other versions of this legend, the energetic e-mailers earn free cases of M&Ms, Pepsi, or Miller beer.

This Time Microsoft Has Gone Too Far

Sophisticated hackers have found proof that Bill Gates's evil empire, Microsoft, has become too cocky. It's not some wacky theory linking Gates with the Antichrist or demonstrating the links between Microsoft, the Rosecrucians, the Freemasons and the Illuminati. Instead, the secret is right where everyone can see it for themselves:

in MS Word's Thesaurus function.

Here's how it works.

Type in: "I hope Microsoft will rule the world."

"I should say so," the Thesaurus responds.

Another experiment uncovers Microsoft's fascist agenda.

Type in: "Kill all fags."

"Kill by beheading," the Thesaurus responds.

Type in: "All Jews must die."

"All over," the Thesaurus responds.

Type in: "I'd like all dikes dead."

"I'll drink to that," the Thesaurus responds.

If you have MS Word on your computer, try this yourself! It really works.

The Internet Psychic

In Ohio, a 15-year-old high school girl named Jennifer had a crush on the most popular guy in her school, a handsome football star named Danny. But Danny treated her like dirt. So Jennifer vowed that she would get revenge.

One night while she was answering her e-mail, she had an idea. She would mess with Danny's head.

The next day, she paid her school's best hacker $50 to get Danny's e-mail address. Then she gave him another $100 to keep his mouth shut about it.

That night Jennifer sent Danny an e-mail introducing herself as TawnyK. "I have psychic powers," she wrote. "I know all about

you." And to prove it, TawnyK/Jennifer supplied details about Danny's classes, friends, even the location of his locker.

Danny was definitely spooked. Night after night TawnyK sent him e-mail about where he lived, his activities during the day, even what he had said. It was freaking Danny out, so he showed the e-mails to his older brother.

"You moron," Danny's brother said. "It's probably somebody at school."

The next day Danny asked around school about TawnyK, but no one had ever heard of her. Nor would anyone admit to giving out Danny's e-mail address.

Meanwhile, TawnyK/Jennifer decided to make things more interesting. She downloaded porn from the web and sent it to Danny saying she wanted him to perform sexual favors for her. She was always afraid that she would go too far, that Danny would just stop signing on, or would change his e-mail address. But every night he waited to hear from TawnyK.

One Saturday night Danny did not log on. He was at a party— a party to which Jennifer had not been invited. She was sulking in her room when she heard "You've got mail!"

Jennifer opened her mailbox and there was e-mail from TawnyK.

"You bitch!" it read. "How dare you use my name and pretend to have my powers. I am the only TawnyK and I am a psychic. Stop playing your stupid schoolgirl games or I'll make you very sorry."

Jennifer flamed TawnyK, and went back to reading the other messages in her mailbox.

Later that night, when Jennifer's mother came into her room to say good-night, she found her daughter face down on the keyboard.

Jennifer was dead.

The autopsy revealed that Jennifer's brain had been fried by a powerful electrical shock. Mysteriously, an inspection of the wiring in her parents' house and of Jennifer's computer showed no trace of even a power surge let alone a deadly jolt of electricity.

Extend the Voters Rights Act!

Most Americans do not realize that the Voters Rights Act President Lyndon B. Johnson signed in 1965 was only an act, not a law. That's why in 1982, President Ronald Reagan extended the Voters Rights Act for another 25 years.

What does this mean? It means that in 2007, when the act expires, African Americans will lose their right to vote.

The only solution is an amendment to the United States Constitution that will guarantee the right to vote to all American adults irrespective of race. Because it takes the approval of 38 states to amend the Constitution, the Congressional Black Caucus has launched a massive e-mail campaign now to get the word out.

E-mail everyone in your address book and urge them to e-mail their representatives in Congress to begin the process of amending the Constitution. It is the only way to ensure that African Americans will not lose their right to vote.

A Call for Help

A Microsoft tech support representative received a call from a woman who was clearly very angry.

"Please tell me the problem, ma'am," the representative said. "I'll see if I can help you."

"It's about time!" the woman said. "I've been waiting for four hours."

"I'm sorry ma'am, I don't understand. Do you mean you've been on hold for four hours?"

"No! Of course not. I've been working in MS Word and I had a formatting problem so I pressed the Help key. That was four hours ago and I'm still waiting! What I want to know is how long it will take you people to get here?"

Just the Fax

A customer called Dell's tech support with a fax modem problem.

"I've been trying to fax a document for two hours now and nothing happens. I thought this model came with an internal fax modem," the customer said.

"Yes it does, sir," the Dell rep said. "Now let's walk through the process step by step and see if we can find the trouble."

Forty minutes later, the tech support rep was still unable to pinpoint the problem.

"Okay sir, tell me very simply how you have been trying to send

the fax," the representative said in desperation.

"I've got the document in my hand, I'm holding it in front of the monitor, and I press send but nothing happens!"

High-Tech Short Takes

• The Elf Bowling game (ELFBOWL.EXE) and the Frog-apult game (FROGAPULT.EXE) has a delayed virus attached to them that is activated every year on Christmas Day. It has already wiped out thousands of computer systems, including the databanks of the Royal Bank of Scotland!

• Do you know a child who is ill with cancer? Send an e-mail about him or her to the American Cancer Society. The organization will donate 3 cents toward the treatment of the child for each e-mail request it receives.

• Amy Jones, the mother of 5-year-old Kelsey Brooke Jones, wants you to help her find her missing child. E-mail everyone in your address book. Someone you know may have seen this little girl.

• Every December 25, unlucky computer users find an e-mail entitled Lump of Coal. Once they open it, the message unleashes a powerful virus that destroys their operating system.

• Atheists are targeting the computers of religious people, sending them an e-mail entitled "It takes guts to say the name JESUS." Once the user opens the e-mail, a virus devastates the computer's memory and the software.

• A congressman has introduced a bill that will charge a postage fee

for every e-mail computer users send. The congressman submitted the bill in response to complaints from the U.S. Postal Service that it was losing $230 million in revenue every year because of e-mail.

• Every year on the last day of February, the Internet shuts down for 24 hours for housekeeping that eliminates dead e-mail and inactive ftp, www and gopher sites.

• To express their outrage at AOL's ever rising prices, hackers will format an online riot next May 1 by sending viruses to thousands of AOL subscribers, shutting down chat rooms and terminating accounts.

• An e-mail entitled "How to Give a Cat a Colonic" may look amusing but it is anything but funny. Once you open the message, a powerful virus is released that erases all the documents and applications on the hard drive. It also destroys Netscape Navigator and Microsoft Internet Explorer.

• Anyone can log on to the list of Coke machines website and get the commands that will make any Coca-Cola vending machine deliver unlimited cans of Coke—FREE!

• A book was published in May 1994 with the e-mail addresses of movie stars and other celebrities.

• Compaq is considering changing the command "press any key" to

"press return key" because so many Compaq users call tech support asking where the "any" key is.

• In an effort to improve his image, Bill Gates will give $1,000 and a free copy of the latest version of Windows to anyone who sends a Bill-positive e-mail to 1,000 people.

THE $250 COOKIE RECIPE
AND OTHER CULINARY MISADVENTURES

The $250-Cookie Recipe

A mother and daughter were having lunch in the bistro of the Neiman-Marcus department store in Dallas, Texas. For dessert, they each ordered the Neiman-Marcus Cookie. From the first bite, the women knew they had found cookie nirvana. It was sweet, filled with rich chocolate and finely chopped nuts, and something else that they couldn't quite make out. So the mother called their waitress.

"This is a delicious cookie," the woman said. "We would love to have the recipe."

"I'm sorry," the waitress said. "We aren't permitted to give out the recipe."

"Well, if you can't give me the recipe, could you sell it to me?"

"Let me find out," the waitress said, and she walked away.

A few moments later she returned, beaming.

"Yes, ma'am. My manager says we can sell you the recipe. The price is two fifty."

"Wonderful! Just charge it to my Neiman-Marcus account."

Four weeks later, the woman's Neiman-Marcus bill arrived. When she opened it she was shocked to find an item from the bistro for $250. She called the store's billing department immediately.

"There's been a typographical error," the woman told the customer service representative. "I purchased the Neiman-Marcus Cookie recipe for two dollars and fifty cents and it was recorded on my bill as two hundred and fifty dollars."

"I'm sorry, ma'am," the customer service representative said.

"But the correct price for the cookie recipe is two hundred and fifty dollars. The recipe is unique to Neiman-Marcus and to keep it out of general circulation, the store charges a very high premium to anyone who wants a copy."

"Well, then I'll return it!" the woman said. "I'm not paying $250 for a cookie recipe!"

"Unfortunately, ma'am, the recipe is not a returnable item," the customer service representative said. "Consider it from the store's point of view. You've had the recipe for four weeks, by now you could have copied it and distributed it to everyone you know. I'm afraid I can't help you."

The woman was livid. She felt that she had been purposely misled by the store. But something the customer service representative said gave her an idea. She sat down at her computer and typed up the recipe. Then she e-mailed it to everyone she knew and encouraged them to do the same. Here is the recipe:

2 cups butter	2 tsp. vanilla
2 cups regular sugar	1 tsp. salt
2 cups brown sugar	2 tsp. baking powder
4 cups flour	1 8-oz. Hershey bar, grated
5 cups blended oatmeal*	24 oz. chocolate chips
3 cups chopped walnuts	
4 large eggs	

* measure oatmeal, then blend in blender until a fine powder

Cream butter and both sugars together.

Blend in eggs and vanilla.

Add flour, oatmeal, salt, and baking soda. Mix well.

Stir in grated chocolate, chocolate chips, and chopped nuts.

Roll batter into small balls and place two inches apart on a cookie sheet.

Bake at 375 for 10 minutes.

Makes approximately 112 cookies.

Straight from the Can

The mother of a high school girl was a meticulous lady who insisted that all beverages be drunk from a proper glass, not straight from a bottle or can.

"If you are away from home and there is no glass available, make sure you wash off the top of the can before you drink from it," the woman warned her daughter. "There's no telling what nastiness gets on those cans."

The teenage girl, of course, found her mother's rules boring and pointless. Everyday she bought a can of soda from a corner deli and drank it as she walked home from school without cleaning the top of the can.

One afternoon, the girl followed her usual routine. She stopped at the deli and bought a can of soda. The first sip tasted strange, but she did not give it a second thought.

A few blocks later, she began to feel sick, but she kept drinking the soda.

"The caffeine will help settle my stomach," she thought. Before she reached the next street she had severe stomach cramps. "I'll

gulp it down then I'll burp and the cramps will go away," the girl thought.

She took a long slug of the soda, emptying the can. A few moments later she staggered and fell face down on the sidewalk.

A cop who was driving down the street saw the girl fall. He called for an ambulance. The ambulance crew strapped the girl to the gurney. "Hand me her backpack so we can find out who she is," one of the paramedics said to the cop. "And give me that soda can, too, just in case."

The girl's mother was terribly upset when she received the call from the emergency room saying her daughter was there and unconscious. She drove to the hospital as quickly as she could. When she arrived, the medical team that had treated her daughter was waiting for her.

"I'm very sorry," the emergency room doctor said. "We did everything we could, but the toxin your daughter ingested works very fast."

"What do you mean toxin?" the poor woman cried. "Was she poisoned?"

"When the police and the paramedics found your daughter, she had an empty soft drink can in her hand," the doctor said. "Our lab tested it and found rat urine on the top of the can. It's a deadly, fast-acting toxin. Your daughter was dead by the time the ambulance got here."

The Package of Cookies

A New York woman was early for her train home, so she stepped into a coffee shop, ordered a cappuccino and bought a small package of cookies.

All the tables in the café were occupied, but there was a seat at a small table opposite a well-dressed man who was reading a newspaper.

"There are no other seats," the woman said. "Do you mind if I join you?"

"Not at all," the man said. Then he went back to reading his newspaper. He paid no attention to the woman until she opened her package of cookies. He folded his newspaper and set it on the table beside his coffee.

The woman took a cookie from the package. Without saying a word, the man took a cookie from the package.

The woman was utterly speechless. She had never seen such effrontery.

She glared at the man as she took a second cookie from the package. He returned her stare and took a cookie, too.

Finally, when there was only one cookie left, the man picked it up, broke it in two and offered half to the woman.

"Please. I insist," he said.

The woman lost her self-control.

"You insist! You help yourself to my food and then try to make a gallant gesture! You are the most insufferable oaf I've ever met!"

"I'm insufferable?" the man shouted back. "Who opened my

package of cookies and began to eat them?"

"No one!" the woman cried. "Look! Your package of cookies is still sitting there unopened on your briefcase!"

The Lab Report

Two biologists at UCLA went to dinner one night at a hole-in-the-wall restaurant in Los Angeles' Chinatown. One was a vegetarian, and the other a determined carnivore.

Halfway through their meal, the carnivore brought up his favorite topic.

"How you can you not eat meat? You have no idea what you're missing. This is the best stir-fried beef I've ever had. The meat is so tender and delectable."

"You want to eat meat," the vegetarian said. "Fine. But I think you're insane ordering meat in a place like this. Stick with the vegetables and rice. At least then you know what you're eating."

"I do know what I'm eating," the carnivore replied. "I've been eating meat all my life. And this is beef."

"Since you're so certain, you wouldn't mind placing a little bet?"

"No, of course not. What did you have in mind?"

"Pick a bone off your plate and let me analyze it back at the lab."

"Okay by me," the carnivore said. "But I get to watch the whole procedure. You might switch bones on me."

After dinner, the carnivore pulled a bone off his plate, wrapped it in a paper napkin, and handed it to his colleague.

Back at the lab, the vegetarian conducted a series of tests under the watchful eye of his meat-eating friend.

"Well, you've submitted it to half-a-dozen tests. Don't you trust your results?" the carnivore said.

"After half-a-dozen tests, yes, I do trust them," the vegetarian said. "I can say with complete confidence that tonight you dined on rat."

Discount Tuna

A woman in Toronto was shopping at her favorite warehouse supermarket when she saw a special sale: a case of brand-name tuna for only $20. She was delighted and congratulated herself for spending the money on a warehouse membership so she could take advantage of such great bargains.

Back at home, she took out one of the cans to make herself tuna salad for lunch. She chopped up fresh celery and onion, threw in a handful of fresh parsley and a judicious amount of mayonnaise. Then she poured herself a glass of mineral water, sat down at her kitchen table, and took the first forkful of tuna salad.

The tuna tasted a bit odd to her.

"I probably put in too much celery," she said to herself. She went on eating, but the peculiar taste became more and more pronounced. Suddenly the woman felt a sharp pain in her stomach. She jumped up and barely made it to the kitchen sink before becoming violently ill.

After the vomiting subsided, she rinsed out her mouth and went

into the living room to lay down on the couch.

She threw up all afternoon, and stomach pangs kept her awake most of the night. The next morning, however, she felt much better. She dumped the rest of the tuna salad down the garbage disposal and washed out the tuna fish can. As the woman rinsed the can, the label peeled off. But beneath the name-brand label, instead of a bare tin can, the woman saw another label that read "Generic Cat Food—Made from Decomposing Fish Parts."

Short Takes 5

• Bananas imported from Costa Rica are contaminated with necrotizing fasciitis, a bacteria that devours human flesh.

• The U.S. government forced Kentucky Fried Chicken to change its name to KFC because the meat the fast food giant was serving to its customers was so pumped up with additives it could not truthfully be called chicken.

• Kentucky Fried Chicken (in its pre-KFC days) paid millions of dollars to a customer who found a fried rat in his bucket of chicken.

• Never eat pizza in Scandinavian countries. The ground meat topping is actually dog food.

• The first McDonald's in Scandinavia was sued after garbage collectors found hundreds of empty dog food cans in the restaurant's dumpster.

• McDonald's places a small amount of a narcotic in its food to make it addictive.

• The secret ingredient in France's finest and most expensive wines is human blood.

• Because it is made from prunes, Dr. Pepper is a soft drink and a laxative.

- Mountain Dew shrinks testicles and makes men impotent.

- Mountain Dew is an effective spermicide.

- Coca-Cola is an effective spermicide.

- If you leave a human tooth in a glass of Coke overnight it will dissolve by morning.

- Coca-Cola paid millions of dollars to a woman who found a dead mouse in her bottle of Coke.

- Green M&M's are an aphrodisiac.

- Tropical Fantasy, an inexpensive fruit drink that is sold exclusively in minority neighborhoods, is owned by the Ku Klux Klan and contains a drug that causes sterility.

- Hostess Twinkies aren't baked; they congeal like Jello.

THE HOME-MADE
LIE DETECTOR
AND OTHER BIZARRE CRIMES

The Home-Made Lie Detector

This urban legend was dramatized in an episode of NYPD Blue.

Chicago police had arrested a suspected drug dealer. Although the suspect wasn't a very bright guy, he was stubborn. The arresting officers were getting nowhere with him. Finally, one of the cops had an idea.

He left the room and returned with a portable copy machine and a blood pressure monitor.

"Okay Willie," the cop said, "if you're telling the truth, you won't mind taking a lie detector test. Right?"

Willy looked worried, but he didn't see how he had much of a choice. He agreed to the test.

The cops wrapped the blood pressure band around Willy's upper arm, pretended to plug it into the copy machine, and began the test.

"We found a kilo of cocaine on you, Willy," the cop said. "Where did you get it?"

"It's not mine," Willy answered. "My brother asked me to hold it for him."

The cop hit the copy button and the machine printed out a sheet of paper bearing the word LIE.

"You were going to sell the coke, weren't you, Willy."

"No. I was just holding it for my brother."

Once again the machine printed out a sheet of paper bearing the word LIE.

Willy panicked.

"Your machine is messed up! I don't do coke! I don't sell coke! I don't know no dealers!"

Now the machine pumped out three sheets of paper, each one bearing the word LIE.

"Alright! I was gonna sell it. But I never was dealing before."

Once again, the machine printed out a sheet of paper bearing the word LIE.

The Shopping Mall Con Artist

Two weeks before Christmas 1999, a woman drove her new BMW to a shopping mall near her home in suburban Maryland. As she walked away from her car, a beautiful, well-dressed young woman wearing a button that read Chanel Sales Representative approached the shopper.

"Good morning!" the young woman said. "I represent Chanel and I want to tell you about an exciting holiday offer. Today only, you can purchase Chanel's new fragrance, Chanel 2000, which usually retails for $75 for only $8. Would you like to sample the perfume?"

The shopper was intrigued. She let the Chanel representative spray her wrist. But when the shopper smelled the perfume, she began to feel woozy and passed out.

When she came to, she was surrounded by paramedics, mall security and other shoppers.

"You'll be all right ma'am," one of the paramedics said. "You inhaled a powerful anesthesia. Thieves presenting themselves as

Chanel representatives have been victimizing shoppers for weeks now."

"Thieves!" the woman said. "What do they steal?"

"Ma'am," said one of the security guards, "your wallet is missing from your handbag. How much cash did you have on you?"

"I had $800 plus all my credit cards," the woman answered.

"And there's something else, ma'am," the security guard said. "Your car keys are missing."

"That can't be!" the woman said. "I left my new BMW right there." And she pointed to an empty parking space.

Variations: A man invites female shoppers to be in a pizza commercial, or an anti-drug public announcement or to help with a sick child. When the women follow the man outside the mall, they are robbed, abducted, or murdered, depending on who is telling the story.

The Cat in the Bag

A college girl was driving through the parking lot of a mall in Connecicut with a friend when her car accidentally hit and killed a cat.

"We can't just leave it here," one of the girls said.

"I have a shovel and a big Nordstrom shopping bag in the trunk," the girl driving the car said. "We can put the body in the bag and find some proper place to dispose of it."

She pulled the car into a nearby parking space. The girls scooped the dead cat into the Nordstrom shopping bag and began

walking around the outside of the mall looking for a dumpster.

"This wandering around is a waste of time," the driver said. "Let's just ask that security guard where we can find a dumpster."

"Fine," her friend said. "But leave the bag somewhere. We don't want him to see that we're trying to get rid of a dead cat."

They left the Nordstrom bag by a door to the mall and approached the guard. While they were talking to him, a woman hurried up to the Nordstrom bag, looked around quickly, then took the bag and started running across the parking lot.

The girls saw her and began to laugh.

"Let's follow her," the driver said. "I want to see the look on her face when she discovers what she's stolen."

They trailed the woman across the parking lot and saw her duck behind a large SUV. A moment later they heard screaming. The two girls hurried over to the scene, followed by other shoppers who were in the parking lot. The woman was lying on the ground, out cold.

One of the shoppers who had a cell phone called 911. As the paramedics rolled the woman into the ambulance, she regained consciousness and began to scream. "The bag! The bag!"

The kind shopper who called for help picked up the Nordstrom bag and slipped it inside the ambulance just before the door closed.

"The poor dear," the shopper said to the two college girls. "I wonder what was in that bag."

Six Inches of Steel

This urban legend is probably the basis for a famous scene from the movie, Crocodile Dundee.

A college student got a summer job playing a knight at a Renaissance festival in New Jersey. Every morning he got up, put on his costume of chain mail and strapped a 36-inch sword around his waist. Then, so he wouldn't look too weird on mass transit, he pulled on a long duster that reached to his ankles and covered his costume.

After a long day of jousting and rescuing damsels at the festival, the student caught a late train to New York. By the time he got on a subway for the final leg of his journey back to his apartment, it was nearly 1 a.m and he was the only passenger in his subway car.

Suddenly, between stations, a door at the end of the car crashed open. A hulking mugger with a knife in his hand ran up to the student, pulled him to his feet and held the knife in front of his face.

"I've got six inches of steel that says you're going to give me your wallet," the mugger said.

The student reached inside his coat and pulled out his sword.

"I'll see your six inches," he said, "and raise you thirty."

The Missing Gnomes

A lady in Arkansas decorated her garden with seven cement figurines of gnomes. One morning when she went outside to get the paper she found that all seven gnomes were gone.

The woman called the police who came out to the house and looked around, but they found no clues of who might have stolen the figurines. They advised the woman to go out and buy another set of gnomes.

A few days later the woman received a post card from Hawaii. "We decided we needed a change of scene. Hawaii is beautiful. Having a wonderful time. The Gnomes."

At first the woman was angry that the thief who stole her garden ornaments would play this type of prank on her. Then she noticed that the stamp on the card had been canceled at the post office on Maui. Now she was confused.

Two weeks later the woman answered her doorbell and found her seven gnomes on the front porch, all of them wearing Hawaiian shirts.

The Greedy Robber

A robber walked into a convenience store in Lawrence, Kansas, pulled a gun on the clerk behind the counter and demanded all the money in the cash register.

The clerk handed the thief $71 in bills.

"I've got about another $10 in change," the clerk said.

"This is it? Seventy-one bucks and change?" the robber said. "Where the hell is the rest of the money?"

"My boss took it to the bank half an hour ago," the frightened clerk said.

The robber thought for a minute.

"Okay. Into the store room," he said. He hog-tied the clerk and covered his mouth with duct tape. Then the robber took the clerk's place behind the counter.

The robber planned to stay only an hour or so, but he raked in over $300 in less than 60 minutes, and he got greedy.

"Maybe I should work the kid's whole shift," he thought. "Then I could walk out of here with some serious money."

After three hours, more than $1,000 was stuffed into the cash drawer. The robber was thrilled. But there was one thing he hadn't considered: Most of the patrons of the convenience store were regulars. When they saw a strange-looking man ringing up their purchases, they got suspicious.

The robber had just broken the $1,500 mark when four cops burst through the door and arrested him. The newspapers described the crime as the longest hold-up in the history of Kansas.

The Bikers and the All-American Boys

Forty big, loud, hairy biker dudes and their women barreled into a grocery store on a country road in Pennsylvania. The owner of the store was frightened as he watched these unruly customers scatter through the aisles and bring armloads of beer, soda, ice, potato chips, white bread, baloney and mustard up to the counter.

While the bikers were still shopping, four clean-cut college students in football jackets came into the grocery store and stood quietly to one side, waiting for the bikers to finish. The presence of these college jocks made the store owner feel a little more at ease. He even managed to smile at his biker customers and make a little small talk. By the time the bikers were finished, they had spent more than $400 in cash.

After the bikers had roared off down the road, the store owner turned to the four all-American boys.

"Boy, am I glad to see them gone," he said.

"So are we!" one of the college boys said. Then they all reached under their jackets and pulled out pistols. "Now hand over the cash!"

The Jogger's Wallet

A Wall Street executive was taking his early morning run on the narrow jogging path around New York's Central Park Reservoir. Suddenly another jogger coming from the opposite direction clipped him, almost knocking him off his feet. The man regained his balance, then checked his pocket for his wallet. It was gone.

He sprinted after the other runner, caught up to him, grabbed him by the shoulder.

"Hand over that wallet!" he demanded in the loudest, nastiest voice he could muster.

The runner looked frightened and gave the man the wallet immediately.

His adrenaline pumping and his ego swelling by the minute, the Wall Street executive ran two miles more than usual, then headed for his apartment on Central Park West. He took the stairs instead of the elevator and ran into his apartment, sweaty, out of breath, but still flushed from the excitement.

From the kitchen his wife called.

"I thought you'd come back sooner. Didn't you notice you forgot to take your wallet?"

The Double Theft

This story originated in England.

A woman spent the morning shopping at Harrod's department store. Before she left for home, she stopped in the ladies room. Inside the stall, she set her purse on the floor and made herself comfortable.

A moment later, a hand reached under the partition and snatched the purse. By the time the poor shopper made herself presentable and found a security guard the thief was long gone. At least the store called her a taxi and paid for the fare.

When she returned home, the building superintendent let the woman into her apartment. She had barely begun to make herself a cup of tea when the phone rang.

"Mrs. Waverly? This is Mr. Morison at Harrod's. We've found your purse. Would you like to come down to the store to collect?"

Naturally, the woman was relieved. She borrowed cab fare from a neighbor and returned to the store. But as it happened her purse had not been found at Harrod's. Furthermore, there was no Mr. Morison employed there.

Now the poor lady was upset. She hurried home where she found her front door wide open, her keys in the lock, her purse on the table and all of her valuables gone.

The Grateful Car Thief

One morning a couple discovered that their car had been stolen from their driveway. They called the police, but the cops offered them little hope that the car would ever be recovered.

"It's probably been stripped and sold for parts by now," said one of the police officers.

But two days later, the car reappeared in the driveway, perfectly intact, with an envelope taped to the dashboard.

"Forgive me for taking your car. It was an emergency. I can't go into the details, but you ought to know that a life was saved. As a token of my appreciation and to compensate you for your trouble, please accept these theater tickets," the note read.

"These are front row seats to the hottest show on Broadway!" the wife said.

That Saturday night, the couple drove into New York City and enjoyed a wonderful evening.

It was after midnight when they finally returned home. The husband unlocked the front door.

"That was great. I wonder how we can get these people to steal our car every week," he said.

But the couple's euphoria disappeared when they stepped inside their house. All their valuables were gone—the computers, televisions, stereo equipment, silver, jewelry, antiques. And scrawled on the mirror over the fireplace was this message.

"Hope you enjoyed the show!"

Wagger

The wife of a paramedic was accustomed to her husband being called to an emergency at all hours, but she never got used to him leaving her in the middle of the night. She was frightened to be in the house alone. So the husband went to the animal rescue shelter and brought home a big friendly mutt. They named the dog Wagger.

The next night, shortly after midnight, the paramedic's pager went off.

"It's another accident on the highway," he said to his wife. "At least now you have Wagger to protect you."

"Protect me!" the wife said. "This big, drooling furball? He's the lousiest guard dog in town. Why didn't you adopt a nice pit bull?"

The paramedic didn't answer. He just kissed his wife and left the house.

A few hours later the woman woke up to the sound of shattering glass. She could hear someone climbing in a window downstairs. Wagger heard the intruder, too. He stood at the bedroom door, growling. The woman didn't know what to do. She was afraid to go downstairs, and she felt helpless waiting in her bedroom.

Before she could make up her mind, she heard someone climbing the stairs. The intruder was coming directly to the woman's room. She watched in horror as the door knob turned and the door swung open. In the darkness she could make out a large dark figure.

"Get him, Wagger!" she screamed.

The dog leapt upon the intruder and knocked him to the floor. The woman ran to the phone and called the police.

"Call him off! Call him off!" she could hear the man shouting. Suddenly the intruder stopped shouting, and Wagger trotted over and sat down beside his mistress.

When the police arrived, they pronounced the intruder dead. Wagger had ripped open the man's throat.

"Take his mask off," one of the detectives said. As the cop removed the ski mask, the woman began to weep.

"Do you know this man?" the detective asked.

"He's my husband," the woman said.

"Why would your husband break into his own house?" the detective asked.

"I think he wanted to prove that Wagger is a good guard dog."

The Thief at the Wedding Reception

After dating for three years, a young couple from northern New Jersey got married. At the reception, guests approached the bride and handed her small white envelopes stuffed with cash, all of which she slipped into a large white silk bag.

At the end of the evening, when the bride and groom were in their hotel room, the bride could not find her silk bag. They called the reception hall, their parents, every member of their wedding party, but no one had the bag, nor had any one seen it. Clearly someone had stolen it.

The unhappy bride wept all night long.

The next day, the couple went off on their honeymoon to Aruba. After a few days, the sting of being robbed at their wedding began to diminish. They had a wonderful time together, and when they returned home they were resolved not to think of the theft any more.

A day or two after the newlyweds returned, they received their wedding video in the mail. That night, the husband and wife sat down on the couch together to watch it. About halfway through the footage of the wedding reception, they saw a man approach the head table, slip the white silk wedding purse under his tuxedo jacket, and walk away.

The thief was the bride's father.

The Well-Dressed Thief

A 19-year-old kid lived with his parents and went to college near their house. One night, while his mother and father were out of town, the kid worked until eleven o'clock at the college library. As he walked across the nearly deserted parking lot, someone grabbed him from behind and held a gun to his head.

"Get in your car, drive me to your house and you won't get hurt," the gunman said.

The boy was frightened so he did what he was told. At the house the thief ordered the boy into the cellar, tied him up, gagged him, and then went back upstairs. For the next hour the boy lay helpless in the cellar listening to the robber ransack the house.

The next morning the boy's parents returned. The thief had stolen televisions, stereo systems, computers, jewelry, silverware and

the boy's prize possession—his Versace sweater.

A week later, the police called the family to announce that they had arrested a suspect. They wanted the kid to come down to the station and identify the thief in a line-up.

When the boy looked through the glass, he recognized the thief immediately.

"That's him," he told the detective. "The second on the right."

"That was fast, son," the detective said. "How can you be so sure?"

"Because he's wearing my sweater."

In the Interest of Accuracy . . .

Police in Los Angeles arrested a man for armed robbery. A couple of hours later the victim came to the police station to see if she could identify the perpetrator.

The suspect was placed in a line-up with five other men.

"The man who robbed me was wearing a ski mask," the victim said. "I never saw his face. But I know I'd recognize his voice."

The detective who was running the line-up ordered each man to say, "Give me the money or I'll kill you."

One of the suspects refused.

"And what makes you better than everybody else," a detective asked him.

"Because that's not what I said!" the suspect answered.

The Burnt Hand

A wealthy widow lived in a fine old house in Philadelphia. One day, a young couple moved into the house next door. They were friendly young people, especially the husband who offered to do the widow's banking and help her with the heavy housework. The widow appreciated his help, and she also enjoyed his company. He was always willing to listen as she talked about her antiques, or her family silver, or the jewelry she had inherited from her great-grandmother.

One stormy winter evening, the widow built a large fire in her fireplace, but she neglected to remove the poker. An hour later, she finally noticed that the poker was still embedded in the burning logs. The widow was about to take the poker out of the fire when she heard a loud banging on her front door. She unbolted the door, but left the chain in place. On the porch stood a man in a ski mask.

"I've got a gun," the robber said. "Let me in."

The old woman was very frightened.

"No. Please don't come in. I'll give you something valuable."

"It better be good, Granny," the robber said.

"A diamond bracelet. I'll give you an antique diamond bracelet if you go away," she said.

"It's a deal," the robber said. "Hand it over."

He thrust his hand into the narrow opening. Meanwhile the widow hurried to the fireplace, took out the glowing red-hot poker. She thrust into the robber's hand.

The sound of the man's screams mingled with the hiss of his

burning flesh. The robber pulled back his hand and ran away. The widow slammed the door shut and bolted it.

The experience had her very upset, so she called her good neighbors next door.

"Mary, could you and Bill come over? The most terrible thing has just happened to me."

"I'm sorry, Mrs. Wentworth, we can't come over now," the widow's neighbor said. "Bill has just come in and his hand is terribly burned."

THE FINAL SPIN CYCLE
AND OTHER MYSTERIOUS MORTALITIES

The Final Spin Cycle

A man in Farmville, Virginia, was not having a good day. Once again he had postponed doing his laundry for weeks, and now he had no clean clothes. Worse, when he went down to the basement he found that his washing machine was broken. He would have to go to the laundromat, the one place he hated above all others.

Frustrated and angry, he filled the trunk and the back seat of his car with his dirty clothes and drove over to the strip mall where the laundromat was located. His only consolation was at least it was the middle of the week and the place would not be crowded. Sure enough, he had the place entirely to himself.

The laundromat had two dozen machines, and the man filled them all. But when he got to the final machine, a washer that held 40 pounds of laundry, he still had 65 pounds of dirty clothes, sheets and towels. No amount of cramming would make the final load fit into the last washing machine. Frustrated, the man climbed up on the machine and began to jump up and down on the 65 pounds of dirty clothes to force them into the 40-pound capacity wash basin. And that's when he did it. One foot kicked the ON button, and the washing machine began to turn.

The spinning laundry formed knots around the man's ankles and sucked him down knee-deep into the machine. He could not free himself. As the agitator went into high gear, the man was thrashed about. He struck his head sharply on a shelf over the washing machine and knocked over an open bottle of bleach. The bleach splashed onto the man's face, blinding him. He was

screaming for help now, but no one heard him.

When the washing machine went into its final high-speed spin cycle, the poor man was spun around at 70 miles per hour. He smashed his head on the steel beam behind the washer and was killed instantly.

The Flying Leap

A high school dropout who worked at a fast-food restaurant dreamed of a career as a professional bungee jumper. If there is such a thing as an Academy of Bungee Jumping, it wasn't located any place near this young man's home, so he decided he would teach himself.

One Saturday morning, he drove around to several hardware stores and bought a couple hundred short elasticized ropes with a hook at either end. Then he went home and in his parents' garage connected all the straps together into two bungee cords, each 85-feet long.

Very early the next morning he put the homemade bungee cords in his car and drove to a railroad trestle that passed above a highway. He secured one end of the cords to the steel beams of the trestle and the other end to his ankles. Then he stood on the end of the bridge, spread out his arms, and with dreams of fame and success as a dare-devil, leapt into open space. Moments later, his skull hit the pavement.

As the ambulance crew carted the body away, the two police officers who had been the first to arrive on the scene coiled up the

two home-made bungee cords.

"I don't care what you say," one cop said. "You've got to admire the kid's drive and determination. It took time to make two 85-foot bungee cords."

"Yep," the other cop agreed. "Too bad he didn't know the drop from the railroad trestle is only 70 feet."

Launched on the Fourth of July

Three high school seniors from a small town in Oklahoma were looking forward to the Fourth of July. They had pooled their money to buy some expensive fireworks, and they bragged to their friends that they were going to set off a display the whole town could see.

The trouble was finding a suitably prominent launching pad for the fireworks. There was nothing that could be considered a skyscraper in their town, and it being Oklahoma, there was no hill in the vicinity. The only elevated structure that could be seen from every part of town was the fuel storage tank beside the railroad tracks. It seemed awfully mundane for the extravaganza the boys were planning, but it would have to do.

On the evening of the Fourth, the boys climbed to the top of the fuel storage tank with the fireworks in their backpacks. On the ground a couple hundred feet from the tank stood a small crowd of high school kids.

From their perch, the boys could see the fireworks of neighboring towns off in the distance. Their own town did not squander tax dollars on anything so frivolous, which pleased the

boys—their show would have no local competition.

"Hey! Do you guys smell gas?" one of the boys said as they unpacked the fireworks.

"Of course we smell gas," one of friends said. "We're sitting on top of a gas tank. Now strike a match so we can light the first rocket."

A moment later a huge fireball erupted from the fuel tank.

The three boys got what they wanted. Everybody in town saw their fireworks display.

The Exploding Lighter

This story has circulated in train yards as well as on Navy installations where it has been a cautionary tale about on-the-job safety.

A worker at the railroad yard in Hoboken, New Jersey, always kept his Bic butane lighter in his pants pocket. One icy day in January, the railway worker walked a little too close to a fellow worker who was trying to thaw a switch with a blow torch.

A spark from the blow torch landed on the man's pants and burned through the fabric. When the spark touched the butane lighter it exploded with tremendous force and blew off both of the man's legs.

By the time an ambulance arrived, he had bled to death.

Lightning on the Lake

Three friends went fishing on Caddo Lake in Texas. Two of the three were having a great morning, pulling in one five-pound pike after another. But the third man in the boat, who happened to be a lawyer, wasn't getting so much as a nibble.

Each time one of his friends reeled in another fish, the lawyer would erupt with a string of foul curses in which God and Jesus Christ figured prominently. The other two in the boat were church-going men, and they didn't like what they were hearing.

"Settle down," one of them said. "And watch your mouth."

"Show some respect," the second one added.

"The two of you sound like a couple of old ladies," their angry attorney friend answered. "There is no God. And even if there were, why would God give a rat's ass about what one guy in a boat says?"

A few moments later, the sky began to darken, and the fishermen heard the deep, low rumble of thunder off in the distance. Suddenly a great bolt of lightning flashed over the water. The other fishermen on the lake headed for shore. The lawyer's friends reeled in their lines and started preparing to get off the lake, too.

"I suppose you think this is the wrath of God," the lawyer said.

"Whether it is or it isn't," one of his friend said, "only idiots stay out on the water in an aluminum boat during an electrical storm. Sit down! We're going in."

The lawyer let loose another barrage of obscenities.

"I'll prove there's nothing to worry about," he said. He stood up in the boat, stretched out his arms, turned his face to the dark, angry sky.

"Okay God! Let me have it!" he said.

The next bolt of lightning struck him full in the chest and hurled him out of the boat. His charred corpse hit the water with a large splash and sank beneath the waves.

Bride-and-Seek

It's thought that this story originated in West Palm Beach, Florida, in the mid-1970's.

A boy and girl who had been sweethearts all through high school decided to get married after graduation. The girl came from a wealthy family, and her parents planned an elaborate reception at their mansion in West Palm Beach, Florida.

It was a tremendous party, and toward the end of the evening, the groom, who had had a few drinks, suggested that they play hide and seek. The remaining family and friends were just drunk enough to get into the spirit of the game.

The groom was it and in half an hour he had found everyone except his bride. He and all the guests looked for hours, all through the house, but they couldn't find the girl. The groom was furious that his bride would play such a cruel trick on him on their wedding night. But when the bride still did not turn up the next day, the groom became frightened and called the police.

Weeks went by and still there was no sign of the girl. The groom was almost insane with grief and worry.

One day, months after the wedding, one of the maids at the bride's parents' mansion went up to the attic to dust the old

furniture the family kept there. In a corner she saw a large trunk, and out of curiosity she opened the lid.

Downstairs the other servants and the family heard horrible screams. The entire household raced upstairs.

"I found her!" the hysterical housemaid shrieked. "I found her!"

Inside the trunk was body of the bride, her mouth still open in a silent scream.

The Ball Pit

A young mother took her son to his favorite fast-food restaurant on his third birthday. After he had eaten his lunch, the mother let her little boy play in the ball pit. A few minutes later he crawled out of the ball pit.

"It hurts, Mommy," he whined and pulled at his pants. But the woman couldn't see anything. By this time, the little boy was crying so she took him home.

Back in the house, she undressed the child and found a red welt on his buttocks. It seemed to the mother that there was some kind of splinter lodged under the skin. She called her pediatrician, but while she made the appointment the little boy began to vomit violently. Then his eyes rolled back into his head. The woman slammed down the phone, picked up her son, and drove immediately to the nearest hospital emergency room.

As soon as they arrived, nurses rushed the little boy into an examining room, but he died a few minutes later. The attending physician examined the welt and found a one-inch piece of

hypodermic needle. The doctor sent the needle fragment to the lab for analysis.

An hour later, he found the heartbroken mother.

"The lab report has just came back," he said. "Can you tell me where your son was today."

"He was home with me all morning," the woman answered. "Then I took him out to lunch and let him play in the restaurant's ball pit. That's where he complained that something had hurt him."

The doctor took a deep breath.

"I'm sorry to tell you that your son died of a heroin overdose. Someone put a syringe full of heroin into the ball pit, and it just happened to be your little boy who ran into it."

Variation: In another popular version of this story, the little boy encounters a nest of poisonous snakes in the ball pit.

The Water Slide

Four Florida high school girls, all seniors, decided to cut school and spend the day together at a water park famous for its 300-foot-long water slide.

At 7:30 a.m on the appointed day, they all piled into a car as if they were going to school, but headed to the amusement park instead. Because they had left so early, they were the first ones there. The parking lot was empty. Since no was around, they changed inside the car into shorts and bikini tops—the perfect clothes for

water rides.

While they were waiting, they saw a strange looking man in dark, dirty clothes and greasy hair climb over the fence from inside the park and jump into the parking lot. Thinking he worked there, one of the girls shouted over to him.

"Excuse me! Is the park going to open soon?"

The man looked frightened at first. Then he smiled.

"Nine o'clock. They always open the gates at nine o'clock. I've just finished inspecting the rides and everything is ready."

As he walked away, he waved.

"If I were you, I'd go on the water slide first. Have a nice time!" he shouted.

Thirty minutes later, when the gates to the park opened, the four girls were the first in line. After they bought their tickets, they rushed to the water slide so they could be the first ones on it.

Four giant slides ran side by side down into a huge swimming pool. From the platform at the top the four girls looked down and shrieked with excitement and anticipation. They took their places at the top of the slides then, at the count of three, all four pushed off together.

A moment later the girls were screaming in pain and the water slide was red with blood. By the time the girls reached the pool at the bottom of the slide, park employees were running over to help them. They lifted them from the water and rushed them to the first aid station but the girls' major arteries had been slashed open. They were already dead.

The park's management closed the ride, shut off the water and

conducted a careful inspection. Attached to the bottom and sides of each slide they found a dozen razor blades embedded in chewing gum.

The Hair Fryer

This relatively new urban legend seems to be a spin off of the lady who tried to dry her wet poodle in the microwave.

All through her sophomore year, a high school girl in Miami had had a crush on a boy in her Spanish class. Just before the school year ended, he asked her out on a date.

When the big night arrived, the girl was running seriously late. She had been too long at the mall buying new clothes, and she spent over an hour in the bathtub. Now she had only five minutes to dry her hair and dress.

To save time, the girl ran down to the kitchen, set the microwave on "HIGH," and stuck her hair and just the top of her head inside.

Ten minutes later the boyfriend arrived. He rang the bell, but there was no answer. He knocked on the door, but there was still no answer. He called the girl's name, but the house remained silent. The boy walked around to the back of the house to try the kitchen door. It was open. And lying on the kitchen floor was his date—with the top of her head blown off.

The Lethal Ladies' Room

The staff at a Chicago hospital near O'Hare Airport was stumped by three inexplicable deaths. In less than a week, three airline hostesses had been brought to the hospital with the same symptoms: high fever, vomiting, and muscle cramps followed by paralysis and death. Their blood showed signs of toxins, but the lab couldn't determine the source of the poison.

The women all worked for different airlines; they had come from different parts of the world before landing at O'Hare. The only thing they had in common was all three had eaten at a restaurant in the airport.

The Department of Health descended on the restaurant and shut it down while they tested the food, the water, the air conditioning ducts, anything that might carry deadly microbes. But they found nothing.

A few days after the restaurant reopened, one of the waitresses showed up at the hospital with the same symptoms as the three women who had died. She said she had had nothing to eat or drink there, she had only stopped by to pick up her paycheck and use the ladies' room.

That gave a toxicologist at the hospital an idea. He drove out to the airport to inspect the restaurant's ladies' room. All he found was a small spider under one of the toilet seats. It seemed insignificant, but the toxicologist captured the spider and took it back to the hospital.

The spider turned out to be a South American Blush Spider. It

is a species that thrives in a cool, damp habitat. And it is extremely venomous.

The toxicologist filed his report with the Chicago Department of Health. They ordered a search of all rest rooms in the airport and of every plane flying in from South America. The other rest rooms in the airport were clean, but Blush Spider nests were found in the rest rooms of four planes.

The Jilted Wife

A wealthy executive lived with his wife on the twentieth floor of a high-rise overlooking Lake Michigan on Chicago's Gold Coast. One evening he returned home from work and announced that he wanted a divorce. He was in love with his 25-year-old secretary and he planned to marry her.

The wife was distracted with grief. She begged her husband not to divorce her. But nothing the poor woman said moved the man. He was determined to have his way. While his soon-to-be-ex-wife wept in the living room, the man packed two suitcases and walked out of the apartment.

"You can live here for the time being. But I'll want this place as part of the divorce settlement," he said on his way out the door.

After the husband slammed the door behind him, the wife burst into a new wave of hysterical weeping. She stumbled out to the terrace, looked at the magnificent view, then climbed over the railing and jumped.

As the woman's husband stepped out of the lobby of the

apartment building, he heard a strange sound above him. He looked up and saw his wife's plummeting body—just before it struck and killed him.

The View from the Tower

The first Saturday night after his girlfriend dumped him, a man from Hartford, Connecticut, was feeling pretty sorry for himself. He thought he needed a little time alone, a place where he would be far from the noise and demands of the world. From his apartment window, he saw the ideal spot: a 60-foot-high electrical transmission tower.

The man took a cold six pack of beer from his refrigerator, drove to the tower, and climbed up. Near the top he found a small platform where he could sit and think about his life.

After he had finished the fifth beer, the man felt pretty good about himself. But he also felt the urgent need to use the rest room. It didn't seem worth the effort to climb down the tower, so he stood up and unzipped. A beautiful stream arched out over the edge of the platform and struck one of the high voltage wires.

A charge of electricity, conducted by the urine, traveled up the stream to the source and instantly fried the man. It also knocked out the power for the entire city of Hartford.

A repair crew found the man dead at the base of the tower, his pants unzipped, his private parts charred and still smoking. On the platform they found a single unopened can of beer.

Variation: A related version of this story is set in a city subway station where a drunken man pees off the platform and is electrocuted when his stream of urine hits the third rail.

Fishing for Dummies

A man who lived beside a river in Alabama had invited 20 relatives and friends over for a fish dinner. When he went to the fish market that morning, he discovered it would cost him a fortune to buy enough for so many guests. There had to be a cheaper way to get fresh fish.

On his way back to his car, the man had an idea. At home he got a long pair of cables out of his garage and connected them to the main power source for his house. Then he stood on the riverbank and threw the other end of the cables out into the water. There was a tremendous explosion of sparks as the live cables hit the water, and soon dozens of fresh fish were floating belly up on the surface of the water.

Whooping with joy, the man waded into the river to collect his catch. Sadly, he forgot to reel in the cable. When his dinner guests arrived they found him floating belly up in the water, surrounded by dead fish.

Nothing's Biting Except the Worms

A man out for a walk encountered another man sitting on the bank of a stream, fishing.

"Catch anything?" the passerby asked.

"Nope," the fisherman said.

"What are you using for bait?" the passerby said.

"Just worms," the fisherman answered. "There's a nest of them right here. But instead of the fish biting them the worms keep biting me."

The passerby laughed.

"Nothing's biting except the worms. That's a good one." He continued on his way.

An hour later the man returned from his walk and passed the same stream. The fisherman was still there, but sprawled out face down on the ground, dead. When the passerby rolled over the body, he saw at once what had killed the fisherman. The nest of worms was in fact a nest of baby copperheads.

Pumping

From Thailand comes news of a bizarre new way to get a sexual high. Teenage boys have been inserting the nozzle of a standard bicycle pump up their rectum. The rush of air from the pump is said to cause an intense orgasm.

One boy became addicted to pumping, as it's called. He tried bicycle pumps of different kinds and power in search for the ultimate high. Then one day, on his way home school, he passed a gas station and he had an idea.

Very late that night he slipped out of his house and went to the gas station. Near the back of the lot, hidden in the shadows, he found the compressed air hose. The boy pulled down his jeans, slipped the nozzle up his rectum, set the machine on high and dropped a coin into the slot.

A moment later the entire neighborhood awoke to the sound of a terrible explosion. The first people to arrive at the scene found bits of bloody flesh and a pair of sneakers, but nothing else.

The Backward Jacket

When his mid-life crisis hit, a 45-year-old man went out and bought himself a Harley Davidson motorcycle and a black leather jacket. After his few times out with the bike, the man started wearing his leather jacket backward. It looked strange, but it was airtight that way and made his ride more comfortable.

One Sunday afternoon, the biker rode up to a lake in the mountains. As he came around a sharp bend in the road, he hit a patch of ice. The motorcycle tipped over and slammed into a tree. The man lay in the road unconscious.

A motorist witnessed the accident and stopped his car to help. He ran over to the biker.

"My God!" the good Samaritan said, "his head has twisted around!"

So he got a firm grip on the man's head, twisted it back to its "proper" position and broke the cyclist's neck.

The Last One

In the weeks and months immediately after the end of World War II, shelter, clothes, fuel, even food were in short supply in Berlin. People wandered the streets looking for a job or something they could salvage from the ruins and sell.

One day a young woman was scavenging in a bombed out apartment building when she bumped into a man. She was about to shout to tell him to watch where he was going, but she stopped herself. The man wore very dark glasses and held a long white cane in his hand. The poor man was blind.

"I am so sorry," the woman said. "I should be more careful."

"There's no harm done," the blind man assured her. And so they fell to talking.

"Could I ask you to do a small favor me? Would you mind delivering this letter? You will have an easier time finding the address than I will," the blind man asked after a few minutes.

The woman looked at the address on the envelope. It wasn't too far out of her way.

"Yes," she said. "I can deliver this for you."

"You are very kind," the blind man said. "Now if you will excuse me, I have an appointment."

The young woman watched as the blind man made his way slowly through the crowd. After he had inched his way to a street corner, he suddenly began to run, and as he ran he stuffed his dark glasses into his coat pocket and folded up his white cane.

Suspicious, the young woman looked for a policeman and

showed him the letter.

"A man I thought was blind asked me to deliver this for him," the woman said. "But then from the way he ran off it was obvious that he was not blind."

"Let's go to the address and see what happens," the policeman said. He called for help, and with half a dozen police officers the woman went to the mysterious address.

The woman stood at the curb while the policemen surrounded the house. A strange looking man opened the door. When he saw all the police he tried to run, but the officers arrested him. They searched the house, and in freezers in the cellar they found slabs of human flesh, wrapped in butcher's paper and priced for sale.

Out on the street, the policeman opened the envelope and took out the note.

"This is the last one I'm sending you today. Treat her like the rest," it read.

Oh, Susannah

Maggie and Sally were roommates at a college in Arkansas. Maggie was outgoing, while Sally was shy. When the drama department announced auditions for a school musical, Maggie tried out. She got a part singing the folk song, "Oh, Susannah."

Every night Maggie went off to rehearsal while Sally stayed in their dorm room studying. Maggie took her role so seriously that she practiced singing "Oh, Susannah" at every opportunity. The other girls on Maggie's floor were pretty tired of hearing the song

night after night, but Sally never said a word about it.

Finally the night of the play arrived. Maggie begged Sally to come and see her, but Sally wouldn't commit herself.

"I have a lot of reading to do this weekend," she said.

Maggie's performance wasn't quite the huge hit she had hoped it would be. In spite of all her practice, her voice cracked on stage.

The poor girl was humiliated.

After the play, Maggie skipped the cast party and went back to her room. The lights were out when she arrived, and she didn't want to turn them on in case Sally was sleeping.

As she started to undress in the dark, Maggie heard Sally's rocking chair creak.

"Sally? Why are you sitting here in the dark."

From the direction of the rocking chair a husky voice began to sing, "Oh, Susannah, don't you cry for me...."

"Don't be mean, Sally," Maggie said. "I've had a rough night."

But the voice sang again, "Oh, Susannah, don't you cry for me...."

"This isn't funny. Now knock it off."

Once again the voice sang, "Oh, Susannah, don't you cry for me...."

"All right, Sally, stop it!" And Maggie switched on the light.

There was Sally's body, rocking slowly in the chair. But her severed head was sitting on the little table under the window. And standing behind the chair, holding an enormous knife dripping with blood, was an insane looking man.

Maggie screamed.

"Help! Someone please help me!"

"There's no one here," the killer said. "Everyone went to see you in the play. I went too."

Maggie began to cry.

"Please don't hurt me. Please let me go. I won't tell anyone about you."

Maggie tried to edge toward the door, but the killer tackled her and pinned her to the floor. Maggie was screaming and weeping uncontrollably.

The killer sang, "Oh, Susannah, don't you cry for me...." as he sliced off Maggie's head.

The Phantom Car
and Other Supernatural Encounters

The Phantom Car

On a snowy night in 1930 in Lancaster, Pennsylvania, a farm family heard a car coming up the lane toward their house. As they gathered on the porch to see who could be visiting them, a sleek black Rolls Royce drove slowly past the house and headed for the barn. There the car stopped and a tall man dressed all in black climbed out of the Rolls, opened the double doors and then drove the car inside. For a moment, the interior of the barn was illuminated by the car's head lights, then all was dark again.

The father and the two oldest boys took lanterns and a shotgun to confront the trespasser. When they got to the barn, it was empty. There was no sign of the car, not even tire tracks in the snow.

Confused and frightened, the family got very little sleep that night. The next day, however, they forgot all about the strange event of the night before. The oldest son, who had gone out to the barn with his father and younger brother, had become deathly ill. He died before the doctor could get out to the farm.

The mother and father took the loss of their 17-year-old boy very hard. The mother confided to close relatives and friends that she believed the phantom car was a bad omen.

The months rolled by and soon it was winter again. The anniversary of the oldest boy's death came and went and the memory of the mysterious visitor had faded. One snowy night, the family heard the sound of a car driving up their lane. They collected on the porch and saw the same Rolls Royce heading slowly through the snow for the barn.

The father shouted at the driver to stop, but the car did not even slow down. At the barn, the driver, dressed all in black, climbed out, opened the barn doors and then drove the Rolls Royce inside. The father and his oldest surviving boy ran across the yard and reached the barn doors just as the car's headlights switched off. But there was no Rolls Royce in the barn and no trace of it in the snow.

The next morning, the boy who had gone to the barn with his father was stricken with the same mysterious illness that had carried off his older brother. And like his brother, the 16-year-old boy died before the doctor could get out to the farm.

Now the whole family was terribly frightened. The mother wanted to sell the farm and move into town, but the father refused. Instead, they invited their pastor to come pray over them and bless the farm.

When winter came again, the whole family was anxious, especially on snowy nights. But no phantom car appeared that winter or that spring, or summer. Perhaps the pastor's blessing had driven off the curse.

Then one autumn evening when it was still warm enough to keep the windows open, the family heard a car driving up their lane. They didn't go out on the porch. They didn't go out to the barn. They knew who it was.

All night the entire family sat up, the mother, the father, the four surviving children. When morning came, they were all very tired, but they were well. No one had fallen ill during the night.

After breakfast, the father went out to the fields. An hour or so later, one of the hired men ran into the kitchen. The father had

gotten caught in the combine. The machine chewed off both his arms. In a matter of minutes he had bled to death.

After the funeral, the mother sold the farm, auctioned off the machinery and the livestock, and moved her children to her sister's house in town. After they had settled in, the woman realized she had left her box of family photographs at the farmhouse. So she borrowed her brother-in-law's car and drove alone back to the farm.

The box of photographs was where she had left it on the floor of her now-empty bedroom. As she picked up the box and headed for the stairs, she heard the familiar sound of a Rolls Royce driving up the lane.

Hours went by and still the mother did not return to her sister's house. As it grew dark, the family began to worry. They borrowed a neighbor's car and drove out to the farm. There was no sign of the woman in the house, or in the garden, or in the yard. At last they found her in the barn, clutching her box of family photographs. Dead.

The Ghost Children

Many years ago in San Antonio, Texas, a school bus full of children stalled on railroad tracks. As the driver tried to get the engine to turnover, a freight train at top speed raced down the track, smashed into the bus and killed the driver and all the children.

A few weeks after the tragedy, a car full of kids from the local high school stalled on the same railroad tracks. The boys were

about to climb out of the car and push when everyone felt the car begin to rock gently forward. Then it glided over the tracks and rolled to safety on the other side.

The story spread throughout San Antonio. People began to drive to the railroad tracks and purposely cut the engine. Every time, the car rolled off the tracks to safety.

Finally a detective on the city's police force decided to conduct a little experiment. He dusted the entire surface of his car with the same powder he used at crime scenes to collect fingerprints. Then he drove to the railroad tracks and turned off his engine. Almost immediately he felt his car rocking gently, then it glided over the tracks.

When it stopped, the detective jumped out to examine the body of the car. In the powder on the rear and along the sides he saw the little handprints of dozens of children.

Variation: In Franklin Lakes, New Jersey, a similar story is told of the ghosts of teenagers who were killed when they ran a stop sign at the bottom of an exit off Route 208. Drivers that edge past the sign feel invisible hands pushing their car back up the exit.

The Baby's Bridge

One frigid Christmas night many years ago, after spending the holiday with their family, a young mother and father and their one-year-old baby set out for home.

The roads were slick with ice, but the husband drove slowly. When they reached the tollbooth of the Bear Mountain Bridge over the Hudson River, the toll collector warned them that the ice was especially thick on the bridge.

"Can't you folks take another route?" the toll collector said.

"Our house is only five miles on the other side," the husband said. "I'll be careful going across."

But the ice on the surface of the bridge was more treacherous than the family imagined. The tires couldn't get a grip on the road. The rear of the car shimmied dangerously. Anxious, even desperate to get off the bridge, the husband leaned heavily on the gas pedal. The car shot forward then spun out of control before it crashed through the railings and plunged into the Hudson River far below.

The next day, the bodies of the mother and father were found washed up on the shore a mile down river. The car was discovered and hauled out of the water a day or two later. The baby, however, was not inside. For a week, police divers worked in the terrible winter weather trying to find the infant's body. But it was never recovered.

Ever since that terrible Christmas, travelers who cross the Bear Mountain Bridge on a cold winter night say that they can hear the wailing of an infant.

The Sisters' Bridge

The Swarkestone Bridge in England stretches almost a mile across the River Trent. The first bridge on the site was erected in the 13th century by two sisters of a noble family.

The story goes that both young women were engaged to marry. Their future husbands were handsome young barons, and everyone expected that the double wedding would be a splendid affair. The day before the ceremony, the two young men waded across the Trent to attend a conference of local landowners. The meeting dragged on until after dark. By that time the tide was in, and the current in the Trent was stronger and swifter than it had been that morning. Yet the bridegrooms insisted that they would return to their brides that night. They urged their horses into the swift-flowing stream, but neither man ever made it to the other side. The horses and their riders all drowned in the powerful current of the River Trent.

The tragedy broke the sisters' hearts. They vowed that they would never marry, and they would use their dowries to build a bridge across the Trent.

It is said that on stormy nights when the river is high and the current is strong, you can see two ghostly young women weeping as they walk back and forth across the bridge, looking over the railing into the water for their lost lovers.

The Fisherman

The Nolichucky River in Tennessee is notorious for its treacherous undertow and the unseen underwater pits and caverns that have taken the lives of many swimmers and fishermen who waded too far out into the current. Some of the old folks tell of a fisherman from up North who went down to the Nolichucky to do a little fishing and never returned. The story goes that he appears on the river from time to time.

A few years back, a party of rafters in search of whitewater was drifting down the Nolichucky when they saw a fisherman standing waist-deep in the river. The rafters waved to the fisherman, and he waved back. Then, inexplicably, the fisherman disappeared.

Thinking the fisherman must have fallen victim to one of the underwater chasms, the leader of the expedition ordered the rafters to paddle over to the place where the man had been standing. As the raft drew near the spot, the guide pulled off his shirt and shoes and dove into the river. As he suspected, he found a large hole, the mouth of an underwater cave. After a moment's hesitation, the guide swam in, feeling his way in the semi-darkness. Up ahead of him he saw a flash of white and he swam for it, hoping it was the lost fisherman. What the guide found when he reached the spot was a human skull.

Frightened, the guide gave no more thought to the fisherman, but swam as fast he could out of the cave. He shot to the surface and dragged himself onto the riverbank where he lay gasping for air.

A few hours later, police divers brought up the skull and the rest

of a human skeleton. They also found an old pair of wadders and
the remnants of a wicker creel.

The congregation of a local church gave the bones a Christian
burial in their burial ground. Since that day, the ghostly fisherman
never appeared at the river again.

The Checker Cab

A cabbie with 10 years experience driving the night shift got a call
to go to Red Hook, a part of Brooklyn where he had never been
before. It was 4 a.m as he drove down the deserted streets of the
unfamiliar neighborhood, looking for his fare. Suddenly, as he
rounded a corner, a man came running out of an alley. The cab hit
the runner broadside. He flipped onto the hood of the cab and for
a few brief seconds clung to the windshield wipers and looked the
cabbie straight in the eye. Then the man rolled off the hood onto the
pavement.

The cabbie slammed on the brakes and jumped out of his
cab. He expected to find the man lying in the gutter, but there
was no one anywhere on the street. The cabbie inspected his car
for damage, but there wasn't a scratch on it. Nor were there any
handprints on the glass where the man had grabbed the windshield
wipers.

At the end of his shift, back at the garage, the cabbie told his
friends what had happened to him that night. No one believed him.

A week later, a different cabbie was driving down the same street
at the same unholy hour when a man ran out from an alley directly

into the path of the cab. When the driver got out to help, the man had vanished. The cabbie went back to the garage and told his story. Again, none of the other drivers believed him.

Yet week after week, drivers showed up at the end of the night shift telling the same story. Now, the laughing and hooting had stopped. The cabbies were definitely spooked.

Finally, the dispatcher decided to do a little research. He called up a friend at the *Daily News* and asked him to search for any accidents in Red Hook in which a man had been hit by a cab in the early hours of the morning.

A few days later, the reporter called back. A Red Hook man had indeed been struck by a cab and killed at the very intersection where the cabbies reported seeing him. The victim had been trying to get away from an angry drug dealer when he ran into the path of the cab, was struck and killed.

"Did this happen about eight weeks ago?" the dispatcher asked.

"No," said his friend at the *News*. "It happened five years ago."

The Ghosts of the S.S. Watertown

In the 1920s, a cargo ship was steaming across the Atlantic from England to Canada. A few days out from Southhampton, a gas pipe in the cargo hold developed a tiny leak. The two crewmen who were assigned to keep the hold in good order died from inhaling the toxic fumes. That same day they were buried at sea.

The morning after the funeral when the captain came on deck he found his entire crew gathered at the stern, pointing at the

ship's wake.

"What's going on here," the captain demanded of the first mate.

"Sir, it appears that the two men we buried yesterday are following the ship."

The captain looked at his first mate as if the man had lost his mind.

"Look for yourself, sir," the first mate said.

Although he felt foolish, the captain did look where the first mate pointed. To his horror, he could see the ghostly figures of both crewmen, floating above the wake of the ship.

"Who has a camera?" the captain said. "Bring it here immediately."

The ship's surgeon ran to his cabin, returning a few minutes later with a fine German camera.

"I want you to use all your film," the captain ordered. "We may all be suffering from mass hysteria. Or this may be a peculiar natural phenomenon. Whatever it is, I want a photographic record that can be investigated when we reach port."

The ship's surgeon did as he was ordered and took 24 shots of the ghostly figures.

Several days later, the *Watertown* docked in Halifax. The surgeon was the first man off the ship. Under orders from the captain, he hurried to a photographer's studio and asked him to develop the film at once. After he told the story of the apparitions, the surgeon also insisted that he be permitted to witness the entire developing process.

The ship surgeon's story of the ghosts intrigued the photographer. He put aside all his other work to develop this one

roll of film.

In the dark room, frame after frame emerged from the developing solution perfectly black. "You must have gotten a bad roll," the photographer said. "Too bad. I would like to see a ghost."

Then he lifted the final frame out of the basin. It was a perfectly clear photograph of the wake of the ship. And floating above the sea were the transparent figures of the two dead sailors.

The Haunted Bar

In the Greenwich Village neighborhood of New York City is a small bar in an old red brick rowhouse. Two hundred years ago, the property was owned by Aaron Burr. Whenever the bar's owner hired a new bartender or waitress, the rest of the staff always told the rookie that the place was haunted.

"Never go into the store room after midnight," they told the new employees. "That's where the ghost hangs out."

One young woman who took a job as a waitress at the bar was not impressed by ghost stories. No matter what horrors the rest of the staff told her, she wasn't buying it.

Late one Saturday night in summer, after she had been working at the bar for only a few weeks, the waitress went into the storeroom to get some pretzels. When she flipped on the light, she saw a man in an antique costume standing among the boxes.

"Who are you?" she said. "What are you doing back here?"

The man looked the waitress straight in the eye.

"Where is Theodora?"

The waitress frowned. "Nobody named Theodora works here. Now get out."

But the man didn't move. He repeated his question.

"Where is Theodora?"

"Are you high?" the waitress said. "I told you, there's no Theodora here. Now get out before I call the bouncer."

Now the man wailed, "Where is Theodora?"

Thinking this nut case might be dangerous, the waitress backed out of the store room and ran for the bouncer.

"There's a guy dressed up in weird old clothes in the store room. He wants some chick named Theodora," she told the bouncer.

"Do you want to handle this, or should I call the cops?"

"Cops don't arrest ghosts," the bouncer said.

"What are you talking about," the waitress said.

"You just saw Aaron Burr's ghost," the bouncer said. "He's looking for his daughter, Theodora. She was lost at sea."

The Ghostly Handprint

This legend is one of the most famous ghost stories in the city of Chicago.

On an April day in the 1920s, a fireman named Frank Leavy was washing the windows at his firehouse. While he washed the glass, he chatted with a fellow firefighter. Suddenly, Frank put down his wash rag, leaned his hand against the glass window pane.

"You know, I just had a strange premonition that I would die

today," he said to his friend.

At that moment, the station's alarm went off. Frank left his bucket and wash rags and ran for the fire truck. Soon Frank and dozens of other Chicago firefighters were battling a blaze at a huge downtown office building. In the middle of the battle, a wall collapsed, killing eight firemen. Frank Leavy was among the dead.

The next day, Frank's friend saw something odd on one of the station house's window panes. It was the imprint of a hand, and it was on the exact spot where Frank had been leaning the day before, the place where he predicted that he would die.

The firemen tried every cleaning solution on the market to remove the imprint, but nothing worked. When the story of the indelible hand print spread around the city, an expert from a Chicago glass manufacturer guaranteed the fire department that he could remove the stain. But he failed.

Some of the firefighters argued that the glass pane was bad luck and it should be removed, but Frank's friends at the firehouse—and he had lots of them—said it would be disrespectful to the dead to take the window away.

For more than 20 years, the ghostly handprint remained intact at the firehouse, until one morning a paperboy made a bad throw with the newspaper and shattered the mysterious window.

The Naked Ghost of the Rue Royale

Several decades before the start of the Civil War a woman of mixed race who was a slave in a fine house on New Orleans' Rue Royale fell desperately in love with her master. One day she dared to confess her love and begged her master to make her his wife.

A cruel master might have killed the slave for such boldness, or at least sold her off, but this man did not have a harsh disposition. He did not even want to hurt the poor woman's feelings. So he thought he would set an impossible condition that the woman would not even consider performing.

"If you spend an entire winter's night naked on the roof of the house," the master said, "I will marry you."

The woman went away heartbroken and never spoke of marriage to her master again.

During the week before Christmas, the master invited a friend over for a game of chess. It was a damp, cold night for New Orleans. While the men played before a warm fire, the lovelorn slave woman stripped off all her clothes and climbed onto the roof of the house. There she stayed all night long. And that's where the other house slaves found her the next morning—naked, cold as ice, and dead.

For his part, when the master learned that his little jest had cost the woman her life, he went mad.

Today, residents of the Rue Royale say that on cold December nights, they still see the slave woman standing naked on the roof, while the master fills the house with cries of despair.

The Dead Lover's Advice

A young New Orleans couple fell in love in the weeks before the United States entered World War I. They planned to marry. But when the war broke out, the young man enlisted. He promised his fiancee that they would be married when he came home.

Faithfully, every week, the young woman received a letter from her husband-to-be. Then there was a week when no letter came. One week stretched to three and then to six weeks without any news from the boy. Finally, the young woman learned from her fiancee's mother that he had been badly wounded in France. The Army was shipping him home.

The long journey back to New Orleans proved to be too much for the poor soldier. He died less than a week after his return.

The young woman could not be consoled. She went to the dead man's grave everyday and sat there for hours. She said her dead lover communicated with her.

A year after the soldier's death, the young woman met a stranger to New Orleans. He was rich, handsome, and he pursued her with a passion she had never known before. Then the wealthy stranger asked the young woman to marry him. She didn't know what to say. She was still mourning her first love. So she asked for time to consider the proposal.

That night the woman went to the soldier's grave. She sat on the bench opposite the headstone.

"There's a newcomer in town who wants to marry me," she said. "He's very successful, good-looking, he appears to love me

very much. But I don't know if I should accept his proposal. We know so little about him, and I am still so sad that I lost you. Tell me what I should tell him."

Now, planted on either side of the dead soldier's headstone were rose bushes, one red, the other white. It was winter, the flowers had all faded away months before, yet now the two bushes burst into bloom. Fourteen buds appeared on the red bush, fifteen on the white. The woman collected the flowers, held them in her lap, counting them over and over again as she wondered what the message signified.

Then it came to her: The fourteenth letter of the alphabet is N, the fifteenth is O. Her dead fiancee had sent her an answer.

Soon after the young woman refused the stranger's offer of marriage, he left town. Months later the story came back that he was already married—to three different women, in three different parts of the South.

Laura

A visitor to Alexandria, Virginia, took a walk through the historic Old Town. At one point, she wandered into a lovely old house that had been converted to a Christmas shop. She selected a few ornaments and some other Christmas decorations and took them to the counter.

While the cashier rang up the woman's purchase, the shopper felt a cold draft rush past her. Then she thought she heard a woman

screaming. She looked around, but there was no one else in the store other than herself and the clerk.

"Don't be concerned," the cashier said.

"What do you mean?" the shopper said.

"You felt a cold wind and you heard a woman screaming, didn't you?"

"Yes! Did you feel it and hear it, too?"

"I experience it at least three times a day. It's Laura," the clerk said. "Do you have time to hear an old story?"

"Absolutely," the woman said.

"Well, about a 150 years ago, this house belonged to a prominent family. Their daughter, Laura, was engaged to be married. On her wedding day she was dressed and ready to go to church when she brushed too close to a candle flame. Before she knew what had happened, her dress caught fire. In panic, she ran out of her bedroom. By the time she reached this staircase she was a ball of fire. She was dead before she reached the bottom.

"As I said, Laura's ghost races through the shop several times a day. Some folks say she is trying to get to the river to extinguish the fire. But her ghost never leaves this old house," the sales clerk said. "Perhaps if she could get to the water her soul would know some peace."

The Blue Light

This story originates in Ohio.

In the first years of the 20th century, a young woman named Nora fell in love with a young man who was good-looking and ambitious but nonetheless selfish and cruel. Her family and friends warned Nora to give him up, but the young woman insisted that she could change him.

They had been dating for a few months when Nora discovered that her beau was cheating on her with a woman in a neighboring town. They had a tremendous fight. Everyone was certain that the love match was over. But the next day, Nora and her bad boy were still a couple.

The Saturday night after their quarrel, Nora and her man walked out to an old covered bridge. They kissed in the shadows beneath the bridge. Then the boyfriend stretched out and fell asleep with his head in Nora's lap. As he dozed, Nora took a long sharp knife from her purse and slit her lover's throat.

Then she lifted the knife again and cut her own throat.

When a fisherman found the two bloody corpses the next day, Nora still had her fingers wrapped in her cheating lover's hair.

The old wooden bridge is long gone and a new, concrete one stands in its place. But if you stand on the bridge after midnight and call Nora's name, a blue light will appear down by the stream and slowly make its way up to the bridge.

The Boy in the Bleachers

After a long day, a guidance counselor at a high school in rural Indiana decided to hit the gym before he went home. It was after 8 p.m. All the teachers, students and staff had gone home long before.

In the boys' locker room the counselor changed into a T-shirt, shorts and running shoes, then he sprinted up the stairs to the gym. He had done a few laps around the gym when he noticed a boy standing at the top of the bleachers watching him. The counselor waved as he ran by and shouted hello, but the boy didn't respond.

For the next half hour while the counselor worked out the boy never left his spot on the bleachers. He did not even change his facial expression. The counselor was beginning to feel uneasy. Maybe the kid was on something and needed a doctor. He stopped running and walked toward the bleachers to confront the kid, but the boy was gone.

The counselor was searching for the boy when he met one of the school's custodians.

"Have you seen a boy around here tonight?" the counselor asked.

"No," the custodian said. "Have you?"

"Yeah. I was doing laps in the gym when I spotted this kid standing on the top of bleachers watching me," the counselor said. "He was as still as a statue. I thought I'd ask him if he needed some help, or a ride home, but the moment I started walking toward the bleachers, the kid disappeared. I've been looking for him everywhere. I don't suppose you saw him?"

"You won't find that boy," the custodian said. "He's long gone."

"Then you saw him leave the building?"

"Nope. But I saw him die."

The counselor was speechless.

"At a basketball game in the gym, Mike Horgan fell off the topmost bleacher and split his head open. He was dead before anyone got to him. That was 25 years ago this very night. Mike always comes back to the gym for an hour or so on the anniversary."

The Bloody Angel

In an old graveyard in Baltimore stands the statue of an angel. The sculpture marks a double grave. The first body buried there was a 9-year-old girl who was murdered by her own mother. It was the child's grief-stricken relatives who erected a large sculpture of an angel over the little girl.

Meanwhile, the mother was tried, convicted and sentenced to life in prison. For the next 10 years, she was a model of the repentant sinner. She wrote letter after letter to her family begging them to forgive her. She became a devout Christian. She volunteered to work in the prison hospital where she performed the most unpleasant tasks cheerfully.

Then one morning the matron found the woman dead in her cell.

Now the family faced a dilemma? Where should they bury

this woman? Some argued that she should be buried in the prison cemetery. Others insisted because the woman had shown every sign of sorrow for her crime, she ought to be buried beside the child she killed. In the end, the family agreed to bury the woman in the same plot with her dead daughter.

Aside from the large crowd that gathered around the statue of the angel, the woman's burial service was no different than any other. When the final prayer had been said, the pallbearers lowered the coffin into the grave. As it came to rest at the bottom, the entire crowd could hear the distinct sound of droplets striking the coffin's wooden lid. The mourners looked up to see if it was beginning to rain, but the sky was clear and the sun was bright. Then the dead woman's sister pointed at the angel.

"She has blood on her hands!" she shrieked.

The angel's hands were indeed red with blood, which trickled off the sculpture's fingertips and struck the coffin of the little girl's killer.

How the Modern World Went to Hell

It's said that beneath the Vatican are vast catacombs that serve as storage areas for strange artifacts, forgotten sacred objects and bogus relics.

One day in 1914, a novice monk was pestering an elderly monsignor with questions about the "secrets of the Vatican."

"There are no secrets anymore," the old priest said. "Every document in the Archive, every book and manuscript in the library,

every work of art in the museums has been catalogued."

But the novice persisted.

"That can't be true. There must be some things that were overlooked."

The old man sighed. It was past noon and he wanted his lunch. More to the point, he wanted this chatty, irritating, would-be monk to leave him in peace.

"Yes. There is one place that is still secret. The ancient cellars of the Vatican are filled with peculiar objects that have not seen the sunlight in centuries. Adam's rib is said to be down there, and a feather from the wings of the Angel Gabriel and no less than 27 skulls, all purporting to be the true head of St. John the Baptist."

"It sounds wonderful!" the novice said.

"You would think so. But other objects are down there, too, things that should remain hidden and forgotten. You're too curious, boy. It will only get you into trouble."

But the novice begged and pleaded to be allowed to explore the storage rooms. Finally, the monsignor relented.

"Go to the Security Office. Tell Fabrizio I said he should open the door for you."

"Oh! Thank you monsignor!"

"Good. Fine. Enjoy yourself," the old man said as he walked away.

An hour later, the novice was wandering happily through the storage area. The old monsignor had been right, most of what the novice saw was junk. But then he spotted something out of the ordinary.

In a cabinet all by itself was a clay jar of great age. The novice

held his lamp closer to the ancient jar and saw a label that read "Tenebrae Aegypti"—the Darkness of Egypt. Below the heading was this verse from the Book of Exodus, "And the Lord said to Moses: Stretch out thy hand towards heaven: and may there be darkness upon the Land of Egypt, so thick it may be felt. And Moses stretched forth his hand towards heaven: and there came horrible darkness."

A shiver of terror ran up the novice's spine. The jar slipped from his grasp, shattering on the filthy stone pavement. From the fragments rose a dense black cloud that began to spread through the catacomb.

With a cry of horror the novice ran for the door, slammed it and locked it behind him. But the dark cloud seeped out from under the door and through every crack in the wood.

Once again the novice took to his heels, running back the way he came, up through the catacombs, through the sub-basements and cellars of the Vatican, back to the light of day and the crowded, noisy streets of Rome. Yet he felt no relief when he stood in the sunlight. He knew the darkness would spread over the city, perhaps over the whole world, and there was nothing the novice could do to stop it.

Within a few weeks, the novice saw the first sign that the supernatural darkness was at work. First came the horrors of World War I and then the bloody chaos of the Russian Revolution. This was followed by the rise of Stalin and then Hitler, World War II, the dropping of the atomic bomb, the Communist takeover in China. Year after year the monk saw bloodshed, hatred, and the collapse of the old social order.

And he knew it was all his fault.

THE NAVY PILOT'S
COLLISION COURSE
AND OTHER ON-THE-JOB FOIBLES

The Navy Pilot's Collision Course

A Navy fighter pilot was out on a routine test flight along the coast of New England when a heavy fog set in. Suddenly, straight ahead of him, the pilot saw a light.

"Change your course. You are endangering us both," he radioed to the approaching plane.

He heard a man's voice over the radio.

"No. It's up to you to change your course."

The Navy pilot was furious. Who was this idiot?

"Look, buddy," he said, "do realize that you're talking to the U.S. Navy?"

"And do you realize that you're flying straight into the Cape Neddick Lighthouse?"

The Backyard Archaeologist

Scott Williams of Vermont is an amateur archaeologist whose backyard has proven to be a treasure trove of rare artifacts, all of which he donates to the Smithsonian. After his latest bequest, Williams received this reply from one of the museum's curators.

Smithsonian Institute
207 Pennsylvania Avenue
Washington, DC 20078

Dear Mr. Williams:

Thank you for your latest submission to the Institute, labeled "93211-D, layer seven, next to the clothesline post...Hominid skull." Naturally, we have given this specimen a careful and detailed examination. After reviewing the lab report, it is my sad duty to inform you that we cannot concur with your theory that the skull is conclusive proof that Early Man was living in Vermont 12 million years ago.

Rather, it appears that what you have found is the head of a Barbie doll. We consulted a specialist in this field, Tiffany DiStefano, the seven-year-old daughter of one of our curators. Miss DiStefano informs me that the head belongs to "Malibu Barbie," and can be dated no earlier than 1995.

All of us at the museum respect the effort you expended analyzing this specimen. Those of us who are familiar with your prior work in the field were loath to contradict your findings. Nonetheless, we feel compelled to highlight several physical attributes of the specimen which might have tipped you off to its modern origin:

1. The material is molded plastic. Ancient hominid remains are fossilized bone.

2. The cranial capacity of the specimen is approximately 9 cubic centimeters, well below the threshold of even the earliest identified proto-hominids.

3. The bite pattern found on the skull is more consistent with the common domesticated dog than it is with the ravenous man-eating Pliocene clams you speculate roamed the wetlands of southern Vermont 12 million years ago.

All of us at the Smithsonian were especially intrigued by your man-eating clams hypotheses. Alas, in your zeal for science you overlooked a minor but telling point: clams don't have teeth.

It is with feelings tinged with melancholy that we must deny your request to have the specimen carbon-dated. Our reasons are twofold. Surely you can appreciate the heavy burden our lab must bear in its normal operation, and to the best of our knowledge, no Barbie dolls were produced prior to 1956.

We must also deny your request to assign your specimen the scientific name "Australopithecus spiff-arino."

While I, and several others, fought tenaciously on your behalf, in the end the committee voted down your proposal. They explained that common usage within the scientific community bars species names that are hyphenated. Furthermore, the committee members felt that Australopithecus spiff-arino didn't really sound much like Latin.

I do have some good news for you. We are pleased to accept your generous donation of this fascinating specimen to the museum. It is yet another riveting example of the great body of work you have accumulated here. You should know that our Director has reserved a special shelf in his own office for the display of the specimens you have previously submitted to the Institution, and the entire staff speculates daily on what you will happen upon next in your digs in your back yard.

We eagerly anticipate your trip to our nation's capital, and several of us are pressing the Director to pay for your travel expenses. We are particularly interested in hearing you expand upon your theories regarding the trans-positating fillifitation of

ferrous ions in a structural matrix that makes the excellent juvenile Tyrannosaurus rex femur you recently discovered take on the deceptive appearance of a rusty 9-mm Sears Craftsman automotive crescent wrench.

Yours in Science,
Harvey Rowe, Chief Curator–Antiquities

Airborne Chickens

Early in its career, the Royal Canadian Air Force had suffered several casualties when birds collided with an aircraft's windshield. To test the strength of newly designed windshields, the RCAF developed a device that shot a chicken carcass at the glass at the usual speed of the aircraft. If the windshield didn't break, then it was likely that the plane would survive any midair collision with birds.

When officials of the FAA in the United States heard about this device, they were impressed and asked their Canadian colleagues to come down and show them how to conduct the test.

The first test took place at Andrews Air Force Base. The Canadian engineers positioned their device in front of a fighter plane. The Americans loaded the chicken carcass into the barrel of the device and set the discharge to an American fighter plane's maximum speed. Then they fired.

The chicken carcass was hurled out of the device, shattered the windshield, smashed through the headrest of the pilot's seat, and embedded itself into the rear wall of the cockpit.

"I don't understand," the chief FAA engineer said to the Canadians. "What did we do wrong?"

"Well," the Canadian engineer said, "Next time you might want to let the chicken thaw."

Built in a Day

Stories about difficult American tourists are more than a century old. One of the classic examples comes from Mark Twain's comic novel, Innocents Abroad *(1869), in which American travelers to Italy torment their guide by pretending that they are not impressed by anything they see.*

A cab driver in Rome picked up an American tourist in front of the Hassler Hotel. "I've never been to Rome before," the American said, "so how about driving me around and pointing out the most important sights."

"Sure. Okay. No problem," the cabbie said.

First he drove to the Colosseum. "Wow! That's impressive," the American said. "How long did it to take to built the Colosseum?"

"Oh, maybe three, four years," the cabbie said.

"Really? That long? In the States we could have that up in a little over a year. And we'd have Sky Boxes."

The cab driver was silent.

Next he pulled up in front of the Pantheon. "This is an intact Roman temple. The dome is the largest ever built in the ancient world."

"Beautiful," the American said. "How long did it take the

emperors to build this temple?"

"No more than two years. They worked very fast," the driver said.

"That's not so fast. For a little thing like this our contractors back home would be done in under a year."

Now the cabbie was beginning to get angry. So he drove the American to St. Peter's Basilica.

"Spectacular!" the American said. "What is this church called?"

"I don't know," the cabbie said. "It was not here this morning."

The Roughneck's Revenge

On an oil rig off the coast of Alaska, a roughneck, as members of the drilling crew are called, lost his grip on a twelve-pound sledgehammer and dropped it down a newly drilled oil well. Naturally the hammer wedged itself in the worst possible position so the pump would not operate. The rig's foreman had no choice but to call the mainland and have a repair crew bring equipment out to the rig to extract the hammer.

The whole procedure cost a small fortune, and it was two days before the hammer was finally dislodged. Once it was brought back up to the surface, the foreman handed the sledgehammer to the roughneck who'd dropped it in the first place and said, "Here. You're fired."

"Then I guess I won't need this anymore," said the roughneck as he tossed the hammer down the well again.

The Seventh Boy

Every afternoon, immediately before supper, the headmaster of a boy's school in northern England dealt with students who had broken the school regulations that day. He had an established routine. The miscreants lined up in the hallway outside the headmaster's office. The boys were ordered to hold out their hands, palms upward. Then the headmaster went down the line with a bamboo cane and gave each offender half a dozen sharp blows.

One day the headmaster stepped out of his office to find seven boys lined up and waiting.

"Assume the position," he ordered. All the boys extended their hands except for the tall boy at the end of the line.

When the headmaster got to him, he shouted, "I said assume the position."

The frightened boy could only stammer, "B-b-b-but…."

"Hold out your hands, damn you!"

Slowly the tall boy extended his hands. After the first blow of the cane, he snatched them back and began to cry.

"What's the matter with you, boy," the headmaster said. "And who are you? Why haven't I seen you before."

"I'm Willis, sir," the boy said.

"Don't be foolish. There is no Willis at this school."

"I don't go to the school, sir," the tall boy said. "I work at the telegraph office. I just came to deliver a telegram to you."

The Missing Co-Pilot

Halfway between a DC-9's flight from Miami to Washington, D.C., the co-pilot left the cockpit to use the bathroom. Fifteen minutes later he had not returned so the pilot called one of the flight attendants on the intercom and asked her to tap on the lavatory door to see if the co-pilot needed anything.

"Sorry, Captain," the flight attendant said. "We're in the middle of beverage service. The carts are blocking the aisles."

So the captain activated autopilot, stepped outside the cockpit and shut the door behind him.

At that moment, the co-pilot emerged from the bathroom.

"What are you doing out here?" he asked the pilot.

"You were gone an awfully long time. I wanted to make sure you weren't sick."

"I'm fine," the co-pilot said. "But the next time we're in Miami, remind me to stay away from refried beans. You got the key?"

The pilot was quiet for a moment. "No. I thought you had the key."

"Great. How do we get back in?"

"The important thing is not to panic the passengers," the co-pilot said. "Here. I've got an idea."

The co-pilot opened the compartment that held fire equipment and removed the ax. With one blow he smashed open the cockpit door.

The plane erupted in pandemonium as passengers screamed. "There are terrorists on the plane! They're going to kill the pilot!"

"Nice work," the captain said. "I can't wait to see the letters we

get from the passengers about this flight."

Variation: The pilot is locked out when he leaves the cockpit to greet the passengers, or to get sugar for his coffee.

Dead Again

A funeral director received a call one rainy night from a man whose elderly mother had just died.

Within an hour, the director and one of his employees had driven to the man's home, removed the body and were returning it to the funeral home.

Suddenly they heard a gurgling sound from the back of the hearse. The employee gave the funeral director a quizzical look. "It's nothing. Just an air bubble escaping from the lungs. Happens all the time."

When the hearse went over several potholes and some railroad tracks, the two men heard a distinct groan. They pulled over, checked the woman, and found that she was alive. "Let's get to a hospital!" the funeral director said.

The driver of the hearse raced for the nearest emergency room, but bad roads and bad weather were working against him. He lost control of the hearse on a slick stretch of road. The car spun around and the rear half of the hearse smashed into a huge tree.

When an ambulance arrived a few minutes later, the paramedics found the driver and the funeral director alive but unconscious. But the woman in the back was dead.

The Jaws of Death

A dentist was working on an elderly patient's teeth when the man convulsed in the chair and died.

The panic-stricken dentist did something desperate. He locked the examination room door. Then he hoisted the dead man onto his shoulder, bounced the corpse up and down a few times to make sure he had a good grip on the body, and carried it out of the office the back way.

After staggering down several flights of stairs to the building maintenance crew's men's room, the dentist kicked open a stall door, dumped the dead man on the toilet, and then ran back up the stairs to the his private office.

While he was still trying to recover from his ordeal, his nurse came in. "Doctor, I thought you were treating Mr. Quincy, but he's in the reception area. He says to tell you that was some weird CPR maneuver you used on him, but he's grateful that it worked."

The Butcher's Prank

A butcher saw a friend heading toward his shop, so he took a sausage and slipped it into his pants, letting the top two inches protrude over the top of his belt.

The friend entered the shop, ordered some steaks, some chicken breasts, and a roast. When the butcher came back from the freezer with the meat, his friend said, "Uh, Frank? Your equipment

is showing."

Feigning surprise, the butcher glanced down at his crotch.

"Damn it! It always does that. I just can't take the embarrassment any more."

Then the butcher walked over the cutting board, opened his pants, laid the sausage on the board, grabbed a cleaver, and chopped off three inches of meat.

The shock was too much for the butcher's friend. He suffered a massive heart attack and dropped dead on the shop floor.

The friend's wife sued the butcher for $500,000—and won.

The Deadbeat Client

A stonemason spent three weeks building a beautiful fieldstone fireplace for a wealthy man in Greenwich, Connecticut. When the job was done, the mason presented the client with his bill.

"I'm a little embarrassed," the client said. "I forgot to go to the bank this morning. I don't have $5,000 in cash on me."

"That's not a problem," the stonemason said. "I'll take a personal check."

"You know, I can't even do that," the wealthy man said. "I ran out of checks yesterday. It will be two weeks before the new set of checks arrive."

"Then I'll make a deal with you," the mason said. "If I have to wait for my money, you have to wait to use your new fireplace." "Agreed," the client said. "I won't build a fire until I get you the money."

That night the stonemason received a phone call from his wealthy client. "Dammit! What the hell did you do? My house is full of smoke!"

"I told you not to use the fireplace until you paid me," the mason said.

"I have the money. I'll give you the full $5,000 in cash," the client said. "Just get over here now and fix this!"

The stonemason found the rich man waiting on his front lawn. The doors and all the windows were wide open to air out the house.

"Have you got the money?" the stonemason asked.

"Yes. Here it is," the rich man said, as he handed the mason a large envelope. "Take it! Just fix the chimney."

The mason opened the envelope and counted the cash. The full $5,000 was there. Then he took a long aluminum ladder and a single red brick from the back of his truck. He leaned the ladder against the house, climbed to the top, and dropped the brick down the chimney. A moment later the two men heard the sound of shattering glass.

"What the hell was that?" the rich client said.

"That was my personal insurance policy," the stonemason said. "Whenever I build a chimney I mortar a pane of glass across the flue. If the client pays me right away, I break the glass before I leave the job. If the client tries to put me off... well, you know what happens then."

The Lipstick Mafia

Some of the cheerleaders at a middle school in Tennessee thought it was cute to crowd into the girls room, apply a fresh coat of lipstick, and then kiss the mirror to see who could leave the best lip prints.

The principal had scolded the girls for making a mess. "Do you have any idea how hard it is to get all that lipstick off half a dozen mirrors?" he said. But neither lectures nor detention made any impression on the cheerleaders. They started calling themselves "The Lipstick Mafia."

Late one Friday afternoon, after practice, the cheerleaders were back in the girls room indulging in their favorite little act of rebellion when a school custodian emerged from one of the stalls with a can of scouring cleanser in one hand and a toilet brush in the other. The girls were a little embarrassed to be caught in the act by the guy who had to clean-up after them.

The captain of the squad said, "You know, we're sorry we've made extra work for you. But why is it so hard to get lipstick off a mirror?"

"It was only tough in the beginning," the custodian said. "But for the past few months I've used this and it comes right off."

To demonstrate, he dipped the brush in the nearest toilet and scrubbed off the lip prints.

That was the last time the cheerleaders kissed the girls room mirrors.

The Soap Saga

A businessman checked into a fine hotel in Atlanta for a week-long stay. He traveled frequently and had gotten into the habit of bringing his own toiletries. He even carried along bath-size bars of his favorite soap; he didn't like the soap hotels provided—the bars were too small, and they made his skin break out. After his first night in the hotel, he left this note for the maid.

Dear Maid,
Please do not leave any more of those little bars of soap in my bathroom. I always bring my own soap. You will find three unopened little bars on the shelf under the medicine chest and another three in the shower soap dish. Please remove them. They are in my way.
Thank you,
Sam Berman

Dear Mr. Berman,
I am not the regular maid for your room. She had today off, but she will be back tomorrow. In the meantime, I removed the 3 hotel soaps from the shower soap dish as you requested. I moved the 3 bars from under your medicine chest and left them on top of your Kleenex dispenser in case you should change your mind. The hotel management requires us to leave 3 fresh bars of soap in each room every day. I hope this is satisfactory.
Kathy, Relief Maid

Dear Maid,
I hope you are my regular maid. Apparently Kathy, the relief maid,
did not tell you about my note concerning the little bars of soap.
When I got back to my room this evening I found you had added
three little bars of soap to the shelf under my medicine cabinet. Now
I have six, but I don't want any of them. I always travel with my own
soap. Furthermore, those six little bars of soap on the medicine
chest shelf get in the way when I'm brushing my teeth and shaving.
Please remove them. Thank you.
S. Berman

Dear Mr. Berman,
We are instructed by the management to bring 3 fresh bars of soap
to each room every day. But since these soaps are in your way, I have
moved them from the medicine cabinet shelf to the soap dish in the
shower. Of course, I had to leave another 3 bars of soap, but I hid
these inside your medicine cabinet. Please let me know if I can be of
further assistance.
Your regular maid,
Dotty

Dear Mr. Berman,
Mr. Davis, the hotel's assistant manager, informed me this morning
that you called him last evening and said you were unhappy with
your maid service. I have assigned a new girl to your room. I hope
you will accept my apologies for any past inconvenience. If there is
anything I can do to make your stay more pleasant, please call me

directly at extension 1108 between 8 a.m and 5 p.m.
Thank you,
Elaine Carmen, Housekeeper

Dear Miss Carmen,
It is impossible to contact you by phone since I leave the hotel for
business at 7:45 a.m and don't get back before 6 p.m. That's the
reason I called the assistant manager last night. You were already
off duty. I only asked the assistant manager if he could waive
housekeeping's policy of leaving little bars of soap in my room
everyday. The new maid you assigned to my room apparently does
not know about my notes to the two previous maids, Kathy and
Dotty. She has left me three bars of soap in my shower and three
more on the shelf under my medicine chest. I have accumulated 24
little bars of soap and I don't want any of them!
S. Berman

Dear Mr. Berman,
Your new maid, Michele, has been instructed to stop delivering
soap to your room and remove the extra soaps. If I can be of further
assistance, please call extension 1108 between 8 a.m and 5 p.m.
Thank you,
Elaine Carmen, Housekeeper

Dear Mr. Davis,
My personal bath-size bar of soap which I brought with me is
missing. In fact, there was no soap in my room at all. I came in

late last night and had to call the bellhop. He brought me 4 little Cashmere Bouquets.
S. Berman

Dear Mr. Berman,
I have informed our housekeeper, Elaine Carmen, of your soap problem. I cannot understand why there was no soap in your room since our maids are instructed to leave 3 bars of soap each time they service a room. The situation will be rectified immediately. Please accept my apologies for the inconvenience.
Martin L. Davis, Assistant Manager

Dear Mrs. Carmen,
Who the hell left 54 little bars of soap in my room? I came in last night and found 54 little bars of soap. I don't want them. All I want is the bath-size bar of soap I brought with me. Give me back my soap!
S. Berman

Dear Mr. Berman,
You complained of too much soap in your room so I had them removed. Then you complained to Mr. Davis that all your soap was missing so I personally returned the 24 bars which had been taken away by Michele plus the 3 bars you are supposed to receive daily. Obviously your maid did not know I had returned your soaps so she also brought 24 bars plus the 3 daily soaps. I don't know where you got the idea that this hotel issues bath-size bars of soap.
Elaine Carmen, Housekeeper

Dear Mrs. Camen,

Just a short note to bring you up-to-date on my latest soap inventory. As of today I possess:

• On the shelf under medicine cabinet, 18 bars in four stacks of four and one stack of two.

• On the Kleenex dispenser, 11 bars in two stacks of four and one stack of three.

• On the bedroom dresser, 1 stack of 3 Cashmere Bouquet, and eight additional bars of Cashmere Bouquet in two stacks of four.

• Inside the medicine cabinet, 14 bars in three stacks of four and one stack of two.

• In the shower soap dish, six bars, very moist.

• On the northeast corner of the bath tub, one Cashmere Bouquet, slightly used.

• On the northwest corner of the bath tub, six bars in two stacks of three.

Please ask Michele when she services my room to make sure the stacks are neatly piled and dusted. Also, please advise her that stacks of more than 4 have a tendency to tip. I would l like to point out that the window sill is empty and would make an excellent spot for future soap deliveries. One more item, I have purchased another bar of bath-sized of soap, which I am keeping in the hotel vault in order to avoid further misunderstandings.

S. Berman

The Penguin Fly-By

The Falkland Islands is one of the most boring assignments for pilots of the British Royal Air Force. After one of the pilots noticed that the thousands of penguins that inhabit the islands were fascinated by fighter jets, some of the Royal Air Force's top guns invented a unique game they called the Penguin Fly-By.

The pilots find the beach with the highest density of penguins and fly slowly just above the water's edge. The guys get a real kick watching thousand penguins slowly turn their heads in unison as they watch the planes go by.

When the pilots fly back, the birds turn their heads slowly in the opposite direction. One of the pilots has said its like seeing a stadium full of spectators at Wimbledon watching a slow-motion tennis match.

But the hot shots save the best part for last. They take the jets out to sea, turn around, and fly straight for the penguin colony. As they pass over the birds strain their necks to look up until ten thousand penguins topple over onto their backs.

A Bad Day at the Office

Dear Sue,

Yep, it's another note from your bottom-dwelling brother. Last week I had a really bad day at the office. I was testing a new device that would enable oceanographers like me to work at the bottom of the sea even in the coldest temperatures.

Here's how it works. On the dock of the ship we have a diesel-powered water heater. It sucks water out of the sea and heats it to the temperature of bath water. The warm water is pumped into the diver's wet suit through a very long hose.

It sounded like a good plan to me, so I put on my wet suit, attached the hose to the opening at the back of my neck, and went down. My whole suit was flooded with warm water. It was like working in a Jacuzzi. Everything was going great until my ass started to itch. Naturally, I scratched it. But within a few seconds my itchy ass started to burn. I'm not talking mild discomfort here; I mean someone's holding a flame-thrower set on high to my rectum.

In agony, I realized what had happened. The pump back on deck had sucked up a jellyfish and pumped it down the hose and into my suit. The little jellyfish had slid effortlessly down my smooth, hairless back and finally found a place to grab onto when it reached the definitely-not-hairless crack of my ass. By scratching I had actually driven the jellyfish further up my butt.

I radioed the dive supervisor of my situation and that I wanted to come up to the surface NOW. All I heard in response over the communications system was hysterical laughter.

Since I was instructed to make 3 hellish in-water decompression stops, it took over 35 minutes for me to reach the surface. When I climbed on board, the medic, with tears of laughter streaming down his face, handed me a tube of cream and told me to coat my ass when I got in the decompression chamber. The cream put the fire out, but I couldn't shit for two days because my asshole was swollen shut.

Since then we've modified the equipment to filter out sea creatures. And we've sent our recommendation to the manufacturer.

Anyway, the next time you have a bad day at the office, remember that it can't be as bad as squashing a jellyfish up your ass. Your loving brother,
Ned

I Know That Corpse!

Since this story was first published in London in 1896, it has been a perennial favorite in newspapers around the world. Variants have been collected from as far away as New Delhi.

A medical student at Johns Hopkins had a reputation for being completely cool in anatomy lab. The most gruesome dissection assignments, the most horribly mangled corpses of accident victims—nothing fazed this guy.

One morning, the medical student reported to the anatomy lab as usual. He pulled back the sheet, took one look at the body, and ran out of the room.

No one in the class could understand what had upset him. The body wasn't disfigured in any way.

After class, the medical student's lab partner tracked him down in a bar near campus. "What freaked you out in the lab today?" he asked. "There wasn't a thing wrong with the body."

"There was a lot wrong with that body," the medical student said. "I knew that guy. I hadn't seen him in over five years, but I recognized him right away."

"That is freaky," his friend said. "What are the chances of getting an acquaintance's corpse as your lab assignment."

"He wasn't an acquaintance," the medical student said. "He was my father."

Variation: The medical student finds his mother on the dissecting table; she had disappeared a few weeks earlier.

Skylight Tanner

Playboy *magazine featured this legend as a cartoon in the 1960s. In the 1990s, it was part of an episode of the Emmy-winning comedy,* Frasier.

A woman from North Dakota decided to escape the frigid winter weather and take a vacation in Florida. The day she arrived, she explored her hotel and found that the roof had a wonderful view of the ocean.

That afternoon she put on her bikini, grabbed a towel, and

headed for the roof to begin working on her tan. She had the place all to herself—no other guest of the hotel ventured up on the roof.

The next morning the woman went back to the roof again. By noon, after a morning of complete solitude, she was convinced that she had found the perfect place to get an all-over tan. She removed her bikini and stretched out in the warm Florida sun. But a few minutes later she heard the sound of footsteps hurrying up the stairs. She rolled over onto her stomach and threw the towel over her bottom.

A moment later the hotel's assistant manager stood before her, flustered and out of breath.

"I'm sorry, ma'am. You're welcome to sun yourself on the hotel roof, but we must insist that you wear your bathing suit."

"I can't see why," the woman said. "No one can see me up here."

"I'm afraid that's not true," the assistant manager said. "You're lying on the skylight over the restaurant."

The Concrete Tomb

At the turn of the 20th century, a new bridge was being constructed over the Ohio River. It was dangerous work and there were no safety regulations on the work site.

One blistering day in August, a man working on the framework where concrete was being poured for a massive pylon suffered a case of sunstroke, lost his footing, and plunged into the wet concrete. Before anyone could reach him, the workman sank without a trace.

The trustees who supervised the construction of the bridge rejected the idea of destroying the new pylon to recover the worker's body. It would cost tens of thousands of dollars and delay the work by several weeks. Instead, the board authorized a large payment to the dead man's wife and children and, under pressure from public opinion, agreed to place a small bronze plaque bearing the workman's name and the dates of his birth and death on the pylon in which he lies buried.

The plaque is still there to this day.

Home at Last

A British diplomat returned to England after 20 years of service in distant corners of the world. During his first week back in London, a member of the House of Lords invited the diplomat to a party.

The diplomat was mingling rather successfully when he came face to face with a woman who looked very familiar, but he could not recall her name. In an effort to get his bearings he said, "What a pleasure to see you again! How is your father."

"My father is dead," the woman replied.

"Oh, terribly sorry," the man said. "I've been away so long, I hadn't heard."

Still trying to get a clue who he was talking to, the diplomat said, "Then how's your brother?"

"I don't have a brother," the woman said. "Just one sister."

"Of course, how stupid of me," the diplomat replied. "Now

I remember. And what is your sister doing these days?"

"The same thing," the woman said. "She's still Queen."

THE HOTEL RESERVATIONIST
AND OTHER TALES OF REVENGE

The Hotel Reservationist

An international hotel chain built a $10 million hotel outside Memphis. From the day the hotel opened for business, a woman who lived in the town began getting phone calls for the hotel— dozens of them, everyday. She appealed to the hotel management, but they refused to change their phone number, saying that they would have to alter all their advertisements, their stationery, and their listing in every hotel directory. The phone company would not help either. So the woman decided to take matters into her own hands.

The next time someone called and asked to book a room, she took the reservation. When a business executive called and requested a two-bedroom suite for seven nights, she offered him the Penthouse and quoted him a price of only $75 per night.

For weeks, she booked conventions, proms, reunions, wedding receptions, bar mitzvahs, and sweet sixteen parties. She accepted reservations for the hotel's restaurant. Then she sat back and watched as the hotel was inundated by furious clients who insisted that they had booked rooms, or a table for dinner, or a ballroom for a special event. Of course, the hotel computer system had no record of any of these reservations. Soon the hotel filed for bankruptcy.

Then the woman's phone rang again. A representative from Marriott made an offer for the defunct hotel. "I'll take it," she said. "But only if you get a new telephone number for the hotel."

Age Has Its Advantages

An elderly woman drove her Mercedes into a shopping mall's crowded parking lot on a Saturday morning before Christmas. There were no spaces available, so she pulled to one side and waited. A shopper came out of the mall, and saw the woman waiting.

"I'm leaving now," she said. "You can have my space."

The shopper loaded her purchases into her car's trunk and backed out. But before the woman in the Mercedes could park, a young man in a shiny red MG cut ahead of her and took the parking space.

"Face it! I'm younger and faster!" he shouted as he ran toward the mall.

The woman was quiet for a moment. Then she backed up, hit the gas, and slammed into the MG. She backed up and did it again. And again. And again.

The young man ran back to his crumpled MG.

"What are you doing? Are you crazy?"

"Face it! I'm older and I have more insurance," the elderly woman said. Then she drove away.

The Bothered Bride

After dating for three years, Tony and Tina decided to get married. Tina's friends were not sure this was such a great idea—Tony had a well-earned reputation for being a babe-hound. He had strayed several times while dating Tina, yet she always forgave him. Once the engagement was announced, however, Tony was a changed man. He was attentive, considerate, and showed no signs of chasing other women. Everyone was relieved.

The wedding day came, and it was perfect. It was the loveliest day in June. The bride was radiant. The groom was handsome.

At the reception, family members and friends competed with one another to give the funniest, sweetest toast to the happy couple. And after all the toasts were done, the bride stood up. This was unexpected, and everyone fell silent to hear what Tina had to say.

"First," she began, "I want to say how touched I am that all of my relatives and all of my friends are here with me today. You are very dear to me. Next, I want to thank my mom and dad who gave me this beautiful wedding. You are the most important people in the world to me."

Everyone in the reception hall beamed as Tina's parents wiped tears from their eyes.

"Finally," Tina said, "I have a special wedding favor for all of my guests. Please reach underneath your chairs and open the envelope you'll find there."

The bride waited as all her guests opened the envelopes. Inside were photographs of Tony having sex with the maid of honor.

Then Tina turned to Tony.

"You sonofabitch! Did you really think I'd fall for all those lame excuses why you had to leave the apartment 'just for a couple of hours' every night for the past month? I knew you were cheating on me and I hired a private detective to find out who it was."

Tina picked up her bouquet and slapped the maid of honor across the face.

"You're a slut!" she cried. Then she slapped Tony. "And you're going to get the bill for this wedding," she said.

With that, Tina stomped out of the reception hall.

The Frat Boys' Peace-Offering

At the University of Wisconsin in Madison, a sorority house stood next door to a fraternity house. The sisters and brothers hung out and studied together on school nights and partied together on weekends. There was only one weekend of the year when relations between the sorority and the fraternity broke down—at the annual Men's Aggression Night it was guys only at the frat house.

Typically, the evening was a testosterone fest of ear-shattering music, brawling in the street, and vomiting in the bushes, followed by deathly silence the next day as the boys tried to recover from their killer hangovers. But one year the party turned ugly. The frat boys directed all their aggression on the sorority house—brawling on their lawn, puking in their bushes, and even trying to break down the front door.

The sisters called the cops and about a dozen frat boys were hauled away for disorderly conduct.

About 9 a.m the next morning, there was knock at the battered front door of the sorority house. There stood the officers and executive committee of the frat.

"We've come to apologize," the president said. "We were animals last night. We deserved to have the police shut us down. And even though twelve brothers spent the night in jail, we wanted to prove to you that there are no hard feelings."

At this, the president and the other officers handed over four boxes of donuts from the best bakery in town.

"Please accept this with our compliments," the frat president said. "You deserve it."

The sorority girls were very pleased with the boys' abject apology and the peace offering. They put on more coffee and sat down to a breakfast of donuts.

The donuts were almost gone when one of the sorority sisters noticed a Polaroid at the bottom of one of the boxes.

"Omigod!" she shrieked. "Look at this."

The photo showed all the frat brothers, naked, and wearing donuts on the erect portion of their anatomies.

Extra Cheese

A high school boy in Milwaukee got a night job delivering pizza. It was decent work and most of his customer's were good tippers, but there was one address he hated going to. Half a mile from Marquette University was a house where 10 college guys all lived together. At least four times a week they ordered pizzas, and they always did something to make the delivery boy's life miserable.

Once, while he was at the door with the order, a couple of the guys let the air out of the tires of his delivery truck. Another time, when the delivery boy brought 30 pizzas to the house for a party, the college guys took the pizzas and refused to pay.

After months of enduring their pranks and abuse, the delivery boy had had enough. One stormy night, he got a call to deliver a pizza with extra cheese to the college guys' house. The rain was coming down in sheets and driving was hazardous, but the kid's boss insisted that he make the delivery. When he arrived at the door, the guys complained that this wasn't their order.

"We said 'extra cheese.' Take it back and bring us another pizza."

The delivery boy returned to the pizzeria, sprinkled another handful of mozzarella over the pizza, placed it back in the oven, and then went out in the storm again to make the delivery.

Again, the college guys complained that there wasn't enough cheese on the pizza. And once again the delivery boy went back to the pizzeria to add more cheese.

The next time he returned to the house, one of the guys said, "Well, it looks like it has extra cheese, but it doesn't have any string

cheese. Take it back and put some string cheese on it."

The kid wanted to slug the idiot, but with 10 against one, he would have gotten the crap beaten out of him. So he climbed back into his truck and headed for the pizzeria. He didn't know what he was going to tell his boss. They didn't have string cheese at the pizzeria—it wasn't an ingredient people asked for. That's when the kid had an idea.

At the pizzeria he added even more mozzarella, popped the pizza back in the oven, then hurried out to the truck. When he was a couple of blocks from the house, he parked the truck and climbed into the back. It was dark and warm and there were no windows. Nobody could see him as he unzipped his jeans and began to rub his penis. When he felt that he was ready to shoot, he opened the pizza box and came all over the pizza. Then he closed the box and made the delivery.

The college kid who opened the door checked the pizza.

"Good. You added the string cheese. You even managed to get it on every part of the pizza. Nice job, kid."

The Heiress' Revenge

There is an abandoned family graveyard near a burned out plantation in Georgia. All the graves are marked with conventional headstones and obelisks, except for one. Over that singular grave the family erected a life-size sculpture of a young woman seated on a bench, her arms stretched out as if she were inviting someone to embrace her.

Local legend says this is the grave of the heiress to the plantation. She had fallen in love with a dashing young man from Charleston named Morgan. He asked her to marry him. But the night before their wedding, Morgan came to see his fiancée, and told her he could not marry her. His family would not give their consent, he said, and they had already arranged for him to marry someone else. The poor jilted bride died of a broken heart.

It became a tradition among the sororities at a college near the graveyard that new pledges should spend the night sitting in the statue's lap—keeping company to the sad, lonely woman.

One year, a freshman from Charleston pledged the sorority. The sisters told her the story of the jilted plantation heiress and her hard-hearted lover, Morgan.

"What a coincidence," the new pledge said. "I'm from Charleston and my name is Morgan. I wonder if we're related."

On the final night of pledge week, the sisters took the new girl to the graveyard. They watched as she climbed onto the statue's lap.

"We'll see you in the morning," the president of the sorority said. Then the girls left the pledge alone.

Early the next morning all the sorority sisters returned to the graveyard with hot coffee and donuts to welcome their new sister. They could see that she was still sitting in the statue's lap, but she didn't respond to any of their calls. "She must have fallen asleep," one of the girls said. She strolled over to wake her new sister, but when she got to the statue she began to scream.

The new pledge was indeed still in the statue's lap. But the arms of the statue no longer reached out. Now they were wrapped tightly around the girl. On the dead girl's face was a look of terror. But the statue's old expression of sorrow had been replaced by a look of joy and triumph.

The heiress had avenged herself on the family of Morgan.

The Boyfriend's Revenge

Jenny and Marty met at orientation on the first day of high school and were inseparable for the next four years. Neither one ever dated anyone else, and they lost their virginity to each other on the night of their senior prom. They had planned to go to the same college and then get married, but there was one glitch. Jenny got into Boston College; Marty did not. Marty got into UCLA; Jenny did not. The disappointment almost broke the two lovers' hearts, but they promised each other to remain faithful.

At first Jenny and Marty spoke to each other on the phone every night and sent each other e-mail throughout the day. But as time went by Jenny started to get into Boston College's party scene. She especially liked the out-of-control frat house parties. Lots of the

guys at these parties asked her out, and she was getting tired of saying no and spending her nights alone while her roommate and other new friends went out on dates.

Marty was so far away, and four years was such a long time— Jenny began to think that she had been an idiot to promise to remain monogamous all though college.

Meanwhile, Marty was running into lots of temptations himself. Southern California was full of beautiful girls. His roommate and his new friends thought he was out of his mind to pass up so many opportunities for a good time. But Marty was determined to stay faithful to Jenny. Since he had to do something with his sexual energy, he put it all into his schoolwork and became a straight-A student for the first time in his life.

Jenny, on the other hand, had decided to take advantage of her opportunities. At the next frat party a handsome junior, a member of the college's hockey team, asked her out and she accepted. At the end of the evening, Jenny went back to the hockey player's room and spent the night with him.

The next morning she felt guilty. She decided the best thing to do was break it off with Marty. So she sent him an e-mail saying their relationship was over, that she was dating someone else and he should, too.

Marty was stunned. He couldn't believe it. He called Jenny, but she wouldn't speak to him. He sent e-mails that he would wait for her. She sent e-mails back saying he shouldn't. It would be pointless. It was over.

Marty was certain once they saw each other at Christmas they would be together again. He kept pestering Jenny with phone calls,

letters, e-mails, faxes, flowers, candy, teddy bears and mylar balloons. Jenny could see that Marty was not going to go away quietly.

She had an idea. Jenny asked her roommate to photograph her making love to the hockey player. Jenny's boyfriend said it was fine with him! In fact, he really liked the idea.

The next day, Jenny sent the photographs to Marty with a note that read: "Marty—I have a new boyfriend. Get lost."

At first Marty was crushed. Then he was angry. Finally, he decided to get even. He took out a piece of stationery.

"Dear Mom and Dad, College is so wonderful! I'm having a great time! But my sheets are wearing out. Please send money so I can buy more. Love, Jenny," he wrote.

Marty put the note and photographs into an envelope and sent it that day to Jenny's parents.

"He's Not Much of a Man"

A trucker stopped at an all-night diner in the Ozarks. He ordered a couple of hamburgers, a large plate of french fries, and a cup of coffee. Soon after his food arrived, two redneck kids roared up to the diner on motorcycles. They walked inside and sat down at the counter next to the trucker, one on either side.

They ate one of the man's burgers, grabbed handfuls of fries off his plate and drank his coffee. Through all this, the trucker did not say a word. He ate what the boys had not touched, left a tip, paid his bill, and walked out of the diner.

"He's not much of a man, is he?" one of the rednecks said to the guy behind the counter.

"And he's not much of a driver either," the counterman said. "He just ran his truck over your bikes."

Rough Justice

A lawyer found that she had left at home a file she would need at her afternoon meeting. During lunch she drove back to her house and she was surprised to see her husband's car in the driveway. As she stepped into the kitchen, she could hear the sounds of a man and a woman making love in the family room. The lawyer took off her shoes and tiptoed to the doorway. There on the floor in front of the fireplace was her husband making love to his secretary.

Without making a sound, the woman returned to kitchen, picked up the file she needed from the counter, and drove back to the office. She called her mother and asked her to pick up the kids after school and let them stay at her place that night.

That evening the woman stopped at the fish market and bought two lobsters and two dozen raw oysters. At the wine shop she picked up a bottle of Dom Perignon. Once she was home, she set the table, lit the candles, chilled the champagne, put the oysters on ice, and boiled the lobster. Her husband was delighted to find his wife had prepared a romantic evening just for the two of them.

After the meal, the woman put on her sexiest underwear and slipped into bed beside her husband. Soon he was fully aroused, but his wife insisted that he wait a little longer.

"I have one last surprise for you," she whispered.

As she took a small tube from her nightstand, the husband asked, "Have you found some sexy new lubricant?"

"Yeah," his wife said. "Something like that. Just wait."

The woman squeezed the liquid from the tube onto her husband's belly and then pressed his erect penis against it.

"It's cold and sticky," he said. "What's this stuff called?"

"It's called Super Glue," she said. "Now while you call the ambulance, I'm going to get my cell phone and call a divorce lawyer."

Call Waiting

A man and a woman had been living together for two years. The woman expected they would get married, but the guy was bored with his girlfriend. He wanted to be single again.

"I'm sorry to say this, but I don't want to live with you anymore. I want to see other women. And since this is my apartment, I'm afraid I'll have to ask you to move out. I know it sounds cruel, but I want all of your things out of here by the time I get back two weeks from now," the guy told his girlfriend the morning he was leaving on a two-week business trip.

The poor woman was stunned. She just stared and couldn't say a word. The man picked up his briefcase and his luggage.

"This is good-bye," he said.

During the two weeks he was traveling, the guy had to admit that he had been harsh.

"It's better this way," he told himself. "At least I was honest."

He was worried, however, that when he returned home his apartment would be trashed, or his girlfriend would still be there and refuse to leave. Given a choice, he would prefer a trashed apartment.

The two weeks passed and the man returned home. He took a deep breath and then opened his apartment door. Everything looked fine. It fact, the place was immaculate. His girlfriend had cleaned before she left. As he wandered from room to room, he found no trace of her. She had taken everything that was hers and nothing that was his.

Then the man heard a strange sound. He raced in to the bedroom where he found the telephone off the hook and gibberish coming from the speaker. The man put the phone back on its base and then, just to be certain it was in working order, he called his best friend. The call went through with no trouble. He never gave the phone being off the hook another thought.

A week later his telephone bill arrived. On it were charges for a call to the time and weather information number in Beijing, China. According to the bill, the call had been made the day he left on his business trip and had continued uninterrupted for the next two weeks until the day he returned and put the phone back on the hook. The charge for the 14-day long distance phone call was $75,000.

The Vigilante Grandmother

An 81-year-old grandmother in Sydney, Australia, was very upset when her granddaughter's latest boyfriend hit the girl and gave her a black eye.

"Stop seeing him," the grandmother said. "Anyone who does this to you is an animal. Get rid of him now."

The girl wouldn't listen, so the grandmother decided to speak to the boyfriend.

"If you ever touch my granddaughter again, I am going to make you very sorry," she said.

The boy smirked. "Yeah. Sure. No problem, Granny. By the way, you really scare me," he said.

"Just remember what I said," the grandmother replied.

Although the boyfriend no longer hit the girl, he took every opportunity to humiliate her in public. He shouted obscenities at her in restaurants and movie theaters, insulted her and belittled her in front of his friends. After several months of this, the girlfriend had had enough and broke up with the slob. Her grandmother was greatly relieved.

Late one night a week after the break-up, the girl was walking home from a friend's house when she saw her ex-boyfriend and one of his friends leaning against a lamp post at the corner. She turned around and began walking back to her friend's house, but the two young men ran after her, caught her and dragged her into an alley where they raped the poor girl.

The grandmother was heartbroken when she heard what had

happened to her granddaughter. She hurried to the hospital to see the poor girl.

"Have the police arrested them yet?" she asked.

"No," the girl answered. "I told the police I didn't know who the men were and I couldn't give a description because it was too dark to see their faces."

The grandmother was stunned.

"Dear child, why did you say such a thing?"

"They said they would kill me if I turned them in," the girl answered. Then she began to cry.

The grandmother kissed her granddaughter and left the hospital. She stopped at her house to get something from her late husband's room, then she climbed back into her car and began driving around town. She drove to every place her granddaughter had ever mentioned going with her ex-boyfriend. At last she found him and his friend on a rotting wharf down by the harbor.

The guys laughed when they saw an 81-year-old woman walking toward them carrying a shotgun.

"I said you would be sorry if you ever hurt my granddaughter," the old woman said.

"What are you gonna do, Granny," the boyfriend said. "You gonna kill us?"

"No. I'm going to make sure you never hurt another girl again." Then the grandmother raised the shotgun and shot both boys in the groin.

The Innkeeper's Revenge

A little boy had been cast as St. Joseph in his parish's Christmas pageant. He was a cute little guy, but he couldn't remember his lines. After four weeks of rehearsal and with the date of the pageant only three days away, the boy still couldn't get his lines right.

Reluctantly, the nun who was directing the pageant gave the boy the part of the innkeeper, a role with only one line, and promoted the innkeeper to the part of St. Joseph.

The original St. Joseph was not happy about being demoted. "It's your own fault," his rival said. "You should have studied your lines like Sister said. Now I'm the star of the show, and you're a nobody."

This observation did not sit well.

Nonetheless, at dress rehearsal the new innkeeper recited his one line perfectly and gave no sign of resentment. The nun still felt bad about making the switch, but at least the boy had taken it well.

The next night the church hall was packed with parents and relatives. The nun was pleased that all the children were remembering their lines. Then came the scene in which Mary and Joseph meet the innkeeper.

The boy playing Joseph recited his line.

"Master Innkeeper, do you have a room for me and my wife Mary. She's about to have a baby."

The innkeeper glared at Joseph. "I have a deluxe room for Mary," he said, "but you can go to hell!"

Cheating Stinks

A woman and her boyfriend had bought a beautiful house together overlooking Long Island Sound. One day she came home from work early to find her boyfriend in bed with another woman. Much as she would have liked to start a brawl, the jilted girlfriend kept her self-control.

"I'll be back tomorrow to clean out my stuff. I don't want to find either one of you here," she said.

The next day the woman returned to the house with a couple of friends and began packing up her things. While her helpers carried the last boxes out to the moving truck, the woman went into the master bedroom with a shopping bag. She took down the shiny brass curtain rod over the bedroom window and unscrewed one of the finials. From the shopping bag she took a half dozen jumbo shrimp, stuffed them into the hollow rod, screwed the finial on again, hung the rod over the window, and left the house.

The next morning, the new girlfriend complained that something smelled odd in the bedroom. So the man took all his dirty clothes down to the basement and threw them in the washer.

But the smell persisted.

The couple sent all the bedding and the Oriental carpets to the dry cleaner. They bought new pillows. They scrubbed down the walls, ceiling and floor. They hung air fresheners throughout the room. They burned incense.

Still, the smell persisted. In fact, it got worse.

"Maybe a mouse died inside the walls or under the floor," the

man suggested. So he tore down the bedroom walls and ripped up the floor. But he found nothing. And the stench was getting worse.

Now it was July and the couple couldn't bear to go into the master bedroom. They slept in the guest room on the first floor, but the stink had invaded every room of the house. In desperation, they put the house up for sale.

The old girlfriend heard that her ex and his new girlfriend had bought a new house together. On moving day the old girlfriend sat in her car at the end of the block and watched the movers carry furniture and boxes into the moving truck. She sat and watched for three hours, and she only drove away when she saw the movers place the brass curtain rod in the truck.

WAITING FOR THE ICEMAN
AND OTHER SEXUAL ESCAPADES

Waiting for the Iceman

Back at the turn of the 20th century, a woman was about to step into the bath tub when she realized that she had forgotten to leave the back door open for the ice man.

Without even putting on her bathrobe, she raced downstairs to the kitchen and threw open the back door. Standing on the back porch was her next door neighbor.

The naked woman froze. The man stared.

"My wife sent me over to borrow a couple of eggs," he finally managed to stammer.

"Oh," said the naked woman. "Well, I was just waiting for the iceman."

She Found Her Thrill on Hyde Street Hill

A 23-year-old woman from Holland, Michigan, traveled to San Francisco to visit her cousin. It was her first trip to the City by the Bay, and she enjoyed doing all the typical tourist things. But she could not get enough of riding the cable cars. She tried to plan her sightseeing around the cable car routes, and even then she often concluded her day with a few extra trips up and down the hills of San Francisco.

On her fifth day in the city, she was taking a cable car up Hyde Street when the car lost its grip and began to plunge backward down the hill. The young woman was thrown to the back of the car.

When the police and paramedics arrived, they found the Michigan tourist unconscious, with two black eyes, some serious bruises, and her legs wrapped around an upright pole at the rear of the car.

Her cousin was at her bedside when the Michigan tourist regained consciousness.

"I feel so strange," the woman said.

"Of course you do, honey," her cousin said. "You were in a nasty accident. All those bruises. And two black eyes. It must be painful. Do you want me to call a nurse to give you a pain killer?"

"No, I really don't feel that much pain. What I do feel is incredibly horny," she said.

Poor girl, her cousin thought. She's delirious from the accident.

But delirium, like the bruises, was not the Michigan tourist's problem. Her trouble was her libido. Something happened during the accident that set her G-spot on overdrive, and now she could barely control herself. Throughout her hospital stay, she tried to seduce every man who walked into her room: doctors, orderlies, male nurses, hospital administrators. She even lured into her room men who had come to the hospital to visit other patients. She was very insistent, and some of the men were only too happy to respond.

The woman's attending physician was perplexed. The cousin told him that the woman had had several relationships in the past few years, but she had always been discrete. So the doctor called for a psychiatric consultation.

The psychiatrist's diagnosis was nymphomania.

"I don't know why a cable car accident would set off nymphomania," the psychiatrist said. "But this is a textbook case nonetheless."

Once she was released from the hospital, the woman gave her new insatiable appetite full rein. She moved out of her cousin's apartment and into a hotel, but the hotel management suspected that any woman who saw men in that volume had to be a prostitute. They asked her to leave.

The poor woman's appetite was still insatiable, but now she was ashamed. She knew that something strange had happened, that she needed professional help, and she suspected that it would be expensive. So she sued the cable car company.

In court, several San Francisco psychiatrists testified the woman did indeed suffer from nymphomania, that it dated from the cable car accident and the condition was destroying her life. The jury—eight women and four men—was sympathetic. They awarded the woman $1 million. And all four male jurors offered to take her out for a celebration dinner.

A Boy's Best Friend

A 15-year-old boy was playing with himself in his bedroom when he heard his mother calling him.

"Your grandparents are coming over for dinner tonight," she said. "I have to go to the supermarket. While I'm gone, you can vacuum the house."

The kid started to whine, but his mother pretended not to notice.

"I'll be back in an hour and a half. That will give you more than enough time. And use the new vacuum." Then she walked out the door.

The boy moped around for ten minutes or so, then he went to the utility closet and took out the new vacuum cleaner. His mother had just spent $500 on this deluxe model. The suction was supposed to be strong enough to lift a bowling ball, but since no one in the family bowled they weren't able to test it.

The kid vacuumed the kitchen, the dining room and the living room. Then he went back to the closet to get the attachments to vacuum the furniture. There was a long flexible vinyl hose with a soft brush at the end. He ran the bristles over his arm, they gave him goosebumps. He placed his hand over the hose and felt the force of suction. That's when he had an idea.

He locked the front and back doors, dragged the machine to a windowless corner of the living room, and unzipped his pants. He slipped his penis into the hose and turned the vacuum on low. The sensation was electric. He had never known anything that felt so wonderful. It didn't take long before he came.

He went back to vacuuming the furniture, but his mind was on his last orgasm. The thought of it got him excited, and soon he was ready again. Once more he unzipped his pants, slid his penis inside the hose, and this time put the setting on medium. It was as if every nerve in his body had caught fire. A few moments later he dropped to his knees from the intensity of the most explosive orgasm of his life.

Afterward, the kid lay on the living room floor. All thought of going back to housekeeping had vanished. He was just giving himself enough time to recover so he could experience the ultimate—the vacuum cleaner set on high.

He remained flat on his back as he slipped the hose over his

penis, then reached over, turned the vacuum's setting up, and hit the ON button. The boy almost blacked out from the force of the suction, but within moments the pleasure had changed to excruciating pain. He curled into the fetal position and cried out in agony—he felt as if the vacuum cleaner would rip his penis off. He reached for the OFF button and knocked the vacuum over instead. He was screaming from the pain as he dragged himself across the floor and hit the OFF button.

He wept tears of relief as the vacuum fell silent and the suction stopped. Afraid of what he would see, he closed his eyes and slowly, gently, slid the hose off his penis. Wave after wave of agony came over him. When at last he did open his eyes, he began to wail. His penis was raw and bruised—and stretched 20-inches long.

The Girl Who Loved Her Cat

The game show version of this classic urban legend first started circulating in 1999.

A game show in Puerto Rico ran a contest in which first prize was a chance to meet the Latin pop superstar Ricky Martin. The parents of a 15-year-old girl, who was a huge Ricky Martin fan, entered her name in the contest and won!

While the girl was at school, a camera crew from the game show came to the family's home, placed tiny cameras discreetly throughout the house, hid Ricky Martin in the girl's bedroom closet, and took the parents back to the studio so they could witness their daughter's surprise with millions of other viewers.

A few moments after the game show went on the air, the girl came home from school. The cameras caught her every movement. She dropped her school books on the kitchen table, opened the refrigerator, and took out a can of paté. With the paté, she walked through the house and upstairs to her bedroom. The cameras in her room recorded her as she stood before a full-length mirror and stripped off all her clothes. Then she spread the paté on her erogenous zones, lay down on her bed, and called the family cat. The animal raced into the bedroom, leapt onto the bed, and began nibbling at the paté while the girl moaned with pleasure.

Meanwhile, the girl's parents had left the studio in shame. They never saw Ricky Martin step out of the closet. He took one look at the naked girl, the paté, and the cat.

"Well, I guess you don't need me," he said.

Variation: The classic version of this urban legend tells of a young woman who smeared peanut butter on her private parts and let her dog lick it off. She was discovered in the act by her fiancée, family, and friends who had hidden in her apartment to throw her a surprise party.

The Blind Man

This story originated in New Zealand in the 1950s.

A woman had just undressed and was about to step into the shower when she heard the doorbell ring.

"Who is it?" she shouted from the bathroom window.

"Blind man," a man answered.

The woman sighed. It was too much trouble to get dressed again, so she thought she would just run downstairs and give the poor man some money as she was.

"There's nothing to be ashamed of," she told herself. "He can't see a thing."

The naked woman grabbed a few dollars from her purse and threw open the door.

The man on the back porch gasped. Then he smiled. "Good morning, ma'am," he said. "Where would you like me to hang the blinds?"

The Amazing Breath Freshener

Two marketing executives, Sally and Victoria, were having lunch. "I saw that huge flower arrangement in your office," Sally said. "Why is your boyfriend apologizing? How did he screw up?"

"Actually," Victoria said, "those aren't 'Forgive me' flowers; those are 'Thank you, you were fantastic flowers.'"

Sally leaned across the table, "What did you do, girl?"

Victoria glanced around at the neighboring tables to make sure no one was close enough to hear.

"Okay. Last night Michael and I went out to dinner and then I wound up back at his place. I didn't have my toothbrush with me, so before we went to bed, I chewed four Altoids."

"You mean those really obnoxious mints?"

"Exactly. Well, I had had a few glasses of wine at dinner and I found myself doing what Michael has always asked me to do."

"Oral sex?!"

"Uh huh. And he says it was amazing. He was literally screaming. And this morning he left this steamy message on my voice mail calling me the oral goddess. Thank God I didn't have it set on speaker phone."

"And you think the Altoids made the difference?" Sally said.

"Honey," Victoria said, "buy a box and try it tonight yourself. The mints have this lasting tingling sensation, it drove Michael wild."

And Sally did that just that. The next morning she had a huge, gorgeous bouquet of flowers on her desk from her husband. She told two or three select friends why, and they told a few of their friends in the office. At lunch time, the women and gay men in the office were stampeding to drug stores and newspaper stands to buy Altoids. And the straight guys in the office were trying to figure out how they could get their wives and girlfriends to chew a few Altoids before sex.

Meanwhile, Victoria was on the phone to her broker. "Get me 1,000 shares of Altoid's stock," she told him. "It's going to be bigger than Viagra."

Bad Kitty!

A man went to visit his brother and sister-in-law at their new home in Murfreesboro, Tennessee. The couple had just moved in a few days earlier, and their guestroom was full of boxes.

"You can use the den as your room," the woman told her brother-in-law. "The couch folds out, and you'll have plenty of privacy."

That night the houseguest climbed into the hide-a-bed naked. The bed was comfortable and he slept so well that he decided to sleep in the next morning when his brother and sister-in-law went off to work.

While the man dozed, the family cat found its way into the den. She sniffed the guest's clothes and decided she didn't like his scent. She jumped up on to the bed, settled herself on the houseguest's pillow and peed.

The guest jumped out of bed, grabbed the cat by the scruff of the neck, and threw her across the room. She landed, claws fully extended, on the heavy drapes that covered a large picture window. Her frantic clawing tore the drapes from the window, and the cat fled the room.

The man hurried to the window and then stood with his hands on his hips surveying the damage. A loud ruckus from outside broke his concentration. When he looked up, he saw a dozen grammar school kids laughing and pointing, and getting their first lesson in the anatomy of an adult male.

What Grows to Six Times Its Normal Size?

The biology instructor at a small college in Virginia was reviewing material for his class's upcoming midterm. "Miss Spencer," he said, "under proper conditions a certain organ of the human body expands to six times its normal size. Name the organ and the necessary conditions for its expansion."

The young woman was silent for a moment. Then she said, "Professor, that is an indecent question. We have not covered any material on human reproduction. And I am going to file a complaint of sexual harassment with the dean." Miss Spencer collected her books and was beginning to walk out of the room when the professor stopped her.

"Before you leave, Miss Spencer, you should know that the correct answer is the pupil of the eye, which expands to six times its normal size in dim light."

"I think if any one has a dirty mind, Miss Spencer," the professor said, "it's you. And by the way, when you do get around to experiencing human reproduction, I'm afraid that you're in for a big disappointment."

The Stamp Dispenser

A woman had an appointment with her gynecologist. When she arrived at his office the receptionist said the doctor was running late. After half an hour, the woman left the waiting room and went down the hall to the ladies room.

When she finished, she found that there was no toilet paper in her stall. So she used some tissues she had in her purse. What she didn't know was a strip of postage stamps was stuck to the tissue, and when she wiped herself they transferred to her private parts.

A few minutes after she returned to the waiting room, the doctor was finally ready to see her.

The woman climbed up on the table and the gynecologist began the examination. Very gently he removed the stamps, held them up for his patient to see.

"That's a very interesting stamp dispenser you have, Mrs. Wilson!" he said.

The License

A newlywed couple spent their honeymoon in Mexico. One afternoon they went to the hotel's exchange desk to buy pesos, but the hotel had run out.

"There is a cash machine at a bank two blocks from here that accepts American ATM cards," the desk clerk said.

While the husband ran off to the bank, the wife waited in front

of the hotel. But there was a long line at the ATM. A five-minute errand took more than half an hour. Meanwhile, the young woman was pacing impatiently back and forth in front of the hotel.

Then a police officer approached the woman. "Business is slow today."

"Excuse me?" she said.

"No customers," the policeman said. "I have been watching you for the last 30 minutes."

"I don't know what you're talking about," the woman said.

"You American streetwalkers are so obvious. Don't you know better than to be try to solicit customers right in front of a fine resort hotel? I must write you a summons."

"Streetwalker! I'm waiting for my husband. He went to the bank."

At that moment the husband arrived and assured the police officer he had made a terrible mistake.

"It is too late, señor," the policeman said. "I have already written the summons. Your wife must appear in court to answer a charge of soliciting."

"But isn't there another solution?" the husband said. "Can't we just pay a fine instead of going to court?"

"A fine, no," the policeman said. "But I can issue you a license."

"I don't understand," the woman said.

"Streetwalking is not illegal here," the policeman said. "Just unlicensed streetwalking. For 25 pesos the lady will be licensed by the city of Cancun to conduct her business anywhere she chooses."

"And we can get this license now?" the husband said. "We don't have to go to court?"

"Absolutely," the policeman said.

"Then here's the 25 pesos," the husband said.

When the newlyweds returned home, they had the wife's streetwalking license framed and hung it in their bedroom.

The Amorous Dentist

A dentist in Detroit had a strange fetish. Whenever an attractive woman came to him for an examination, he told her she had a bad tooth that would require very painful drilling. He urged the patient, for her own sake, to let him put her under with anesthesia so she wouldn't feel the pain of the procedure. Then, while the woman was asleep, the dentist had sex with her inert body.

The dentist had been doing this for a couple of years when one day an underwear model came to his office. One of her fillings had fallen out, and she was in a lot of pain.

Having sex with a model was a fantasy come true for the dentist. But in his excitement, he didn't use as much anesthesia as usual. The woman woke up while he was on top of her. She pressed charges, and the story was picked up by newspapers and entertainment magazines.

After a brief trial, the dentist was found guilty. The headline for the story that ran in *Entertainment Weekly* read, "Dentist convicted of filling wrong cavity."

The Misunderstood Note

At a sexual assault trial, the victim, a young woman barely 18 years old, could not bring herself to repeat on the stand what the rapist had said to her.

"I won't force you, Miss," the judge told her. "Just write down what he said on this slip of paper and I'll pass it along to the jury."

The woman took the paper and pen from the judge and wrote, "I want to f**k you until you die."

The judge read the note, then directed the bailiff to give it to the foreman of the jury. The jurors passed the note silently among themselves. Finally a woman handed the note to the last juror, a man who had dosed off during the proceedings. She shook him awake and gave him the paper.

He read it, smiled at the woman juror, and stuck the note in his pocket.

"Sir, you must give that paper to me," the judge told the man.

"I don't think so, judge," the man answered. "This is a private note from this lady here to me."

The Policeman's Ball

A very beautiful young woman was driving her sports car more than 90 miles per hour down a highway in Tennessee when a state trooper pulled her over.

She gave the police officer her most dazzling smile, apologized in the most earnest manner and even shed a few tears. But to all of these ploys, the state trooper was unmoved. He just kept writing out the ticket.

Finally, the young lady tried a different approach.

"Please, officer, my husband will have a fit if I come home with a speeding ticket. Could you forget about this incident if bought a few tickets for the policemen's ball?"

The state trooper stopped writing, looked the young woman in the eye.

"Ma'am, I'm a state trooper. State policeman don't have balls," he said.

The young woman was silent for a moment.

"From the way you look, I never would have guessed," she said.

The cop blushed deep red, tore up the ticket and walked back to his car.

The Cheating Wife

A man knew his wife was having an affair. When she announced that she was pregnant, the husband disowned the baby.

The wife's boyfriend also refused any responsibility for the child. So the woman did the only thing she could do: wait.

Six months later the woman gave birth to twin boys. To determine paternity, she demanded a blood test.

A few hours later, her obstetrician returned to the new mother's room with the results of the blood test.

"In twenty years of medical practice, I've never even heard of such a thing," he said. "One of your babies was fathered by your husband. The other twin was fathered by your boyfriend. Lady, you've just hit the child support jackpot."

The Tell-tale Condom

A gynecologist was out playing golf with a long-time friend. After 18 holes, they went to the club house for a couple of drinks. Halfway through the third martini the gynecologist got talkative.

"You know," he said to his friend, "your wife came to see me the other day."

"She comes to see you all the time," the other golfer said. "You're her doctor."

"Yes, but this time the examination has something to do with you," the doctor said. Then he took a deep breath. "I'm probably in

breech of medical ethics, but we've been friends for years and your wife's health is involved."

"Now you've got me nervous," the doctor's friend said. "What did you find?"

"Well, during the examination, I removed a used condom that was stuck inside your wife. I'm sorry if I'm intruding on your privacy, but you just can't do that type of thing. The impact it could have on your wife's health is staggering."

The gynecologist could tell that his friend was furious.

"Look, I'm not being critical, I'm just urging you to be more careful next time," he said.

"You don't get it," his friend said. "I'm not angry with you. I'm furious with my wife."

"You can't blame her for this," the gynecologist said.

"Oh yes I can. In fifteen years of making love to that woman, I've never used a condom!"

Caught in the Act

Two 16-year-old sweethearts were delighted when their parents agreed that the two families would go camping together in Wyoming. The camp site the families chose was perfect, with spectacular views of the mountains, a beautiful forest and, just a couple hundred yards from the camp site, a lovely waterfall.

After three days in paradise, the young couple decided this was the perfect place to consummate their love. One afternoon, after telling their parents they were going for a hike, the boy and girl

slipped away to the waterfall and made love. But their passion made them lose all sense of time.

When five hours had passed and the young couple still had not returned to the camp site, their parents went looking for them. Eventually they found their children at the waterfall, lying together on a large flat rock, naked, the boy on top of the girl.

Panicked at the sight of her parents, the girl experienced a bizarre physiological reaction: her pelvis muscles locked. The boy couldn't withdraw, the girl couldn't release him. Everything the parents said or did to help only increased the girl's humiliation. Her pelvic muscles clamped tighter and tighter.

By the time the ambulance crew finally reached the waterfall, the girl was weeping with shame and the boy was screaming in agony.

The Substitute

A 20-year-old American sailor had shore leave in Singapore. While he was having a few drinks in a bar, an elderly, well-dressed man approached him.

"You are from the United States?" the old man asked. "How long will your ship be in port?"

"The captain says we'll be here a week," the sailor said.

"Perhaps," the old man said, "you would like some female company while you are in Singapore?"

"Absolutely!" the sailor said. "How much?"

"There is no charge. Consider it a gesture of friendship. Come with me."

The sailor was suspicious, but he decided to go along. Outside the bar, a black stretch limousine was waiting for the elderly gentleman. The driver took them to a magnificent villa on a hill high above the harbor.

"This is my home," the old man explained.

Inside, the sailor could scarcely believe his eyes. No cat house he had ever seen was so richly furnished. Fine paintings hung on the walls, every room was furnished with antiques. The old man led the sailor upstairs to a large bedroom where a beautiful young woman was waiting.

"I will call for you in the morning in time for you to return to your ship," the old man said. Then he closed the bedroom door.

The sailor and the beautiful woman made love all night long. Before sunrise, the limo took him back to his ship.

That evening, when the sailor went ashore again, the limo was waiting for him on the dock, along with a written invitation from the old man to visit the young woman again.

Every night for the next six nights, the pattern was repeated. As he climbed into the limo to be taken back to his ship for the last time, the driver handed the sailor an envelope. Inside was a letter from the old man.

"As you must have guessed by now, I am a wealthy man. None of my relatives are worthy to be my heirs, but I am too old to father a child. You have been my substitute. Already my beautiful young wife feels certain she has conceived by you. Please accept this small gift as a token of our gratitude."

Attached to the bottom of the letter was a check for $1 million.

The Cyberlover

Emily, a freshman at an all-women's college in western Massachusetts, missed her boyfriend. One dull Saturday night she logged onto a cybersex chat room. There she met the usual number of giggly 13-year-old boys and 60-year-old perverts. But there was one guy, RealMan4U, who seemed mature, experienced, and romantic.

After their first meeting in the chat room, Emily and RealMan4U met each other online every night for long conversations. By the second week, Emily wanted to see RealMan4U in the flesh.

"Let's hook up tomorrow night," she said.

"Can you get to Boston?" RealMan4U answered.

"Sure. It's a little over an hour's drive."

RealMan4U sent a message back.

"Excellent. Meet me at the Boylston Street Coffee Shop. I'll sit at the end of the bar. And I'll be wearing a yellow cotton sweater."

The next night Emily borrowed a friend's car and drove to Boston. Her heart was racing as she walked to the coffee shop. At the door, she took a deep breath, then stepped inside.

At the end of the bar sat a good looking older man in a yellow cotton sweater. The man turned toward the door as she walked in.

"Emily!"

"Daddy!"

The Gravy Ladle

Not long after a guy named Jack graduated from college he rented an apartment with a young woman named Ann Marie. Once the place was cleaned and painted, Jack invited his mother over for dinner.

Jack's mom had been suspicious about her son's living arrangements, but now that she saw Jack and Ann Marie together she was pretty sure that they were lovers.

At one point, when Ann Marie was in the kitchen, Jack said to his mother, "Look, Mom, I know what you're thinking. But you've got it all wrong. Ann Marie and I are just roommates. This is the only way either one of us can afford to pay the rent."

"Did I say a word?" his mother asked.

So Jack dropped the subject. The three of them had a nice meal, Jack's mom helped with the dishes, and then she went home.

A week later, Ann Marie asked Jack, "What did you do with the silver gravy ladle?"

"What are you talking about?"

"I used my grandmother's silver gravy ladle when your mother came for dinner last week," Ann Marie said. "Now I can't find it."

"You're not suggesting my mother swiped a gravy ladle?"

"No. Of course not. But maybe she put it away somewhere."

"To set your mind at ease," Jack said, "I'll e-mail my mom."

Jack went to the computer and sent his mother an e-mail.

"Mom, do you remember what happened to the silver gravy ladle Ann Marie brought to the table last week? I'm not saying you have it and I'm not saying you don't, but Ann Marie can't find it."

A few hours later, Jack's mother e-mailed back.

"Jack, I'm not saying you do sleep with Ann Marie and I'm not saying you don't. But if Ann Marie really sleeps in her own bed, by now she would have found the gravy ladle."

The Specimen

A college boy had biology lab at 8 a.m. One day the professor announced that he would be conducting an experiment personally and he needed some volunteers.

"I'm going to scrape the inside of each volunteer's cheek, analyze the scrapings and then tell each of them what they ate during the past 12 hours," he said.

Three students volunteered, two girls and boy.

After studying the scrapings from the first girl the professor reported that he had found evidence of pizza, potato chips, toasted bagel, coffee, and mouthwash.

"That's right!" the first volunteer said. "You didn't miss a thing!"

The scrapings from the second girl's mouth showed traces of spinach salad, grapefruit, dry toast, and coffee.

"Yes!" the second girl said. "I'm dieting for Spring Break."

Finally the professor studied the scrapings from the boy's mouth.

After a few minutes he glanced up from the microscope and gave the boy a strange look.

"What's the matter, professor?"

The professor didn't answer but went back to studying the specimen.

"I can't make a definite reading," the professor said.

"Come on, professor," the boy said. "You can at least make an educated guess."

"Yeah," another guy in the class said. "Tell us what he's put his mouth over the last 12 hours!"

"You insist?" the professor asked his volunteer.

"Absolutely. I've got nothing to hide," the student said.

"Very well. My analysis shows traces of pizza. I've also found evidence of beer. And there's one more thing I've found in the scraping taken from your mouth," the professor said. "Sperm."

The Blind Date

A 19-year-old kid home from college for the summer was feeling lonely, so his best friend decided to fix him up with a blind date.

"This girl's a sure thing," the friend said. "I've spent a few wild nights with her myself, so when you pick her up tonight, make sure you're prepared."

That afternoon, the college boy went to the drug store to buy some condoms. To his dismay, he saw the condoms were kept on a shelf behind the pharmacist's counter. He would have to go up and ask for them. But every time he approached the counter, there was some sweet old lady there, or a young mother with small children.

After loitering around the store for half an hour, the pharmacist called to the boy.

"Young man, would step back here please?" In the storage room, out of sight of the other customers, the pharmacist held out a box of condoms. "Is this what you're looking for?" he said.

"How did you know?" the college kid said.

"Hey, I was young once," the pharmacist said. "I remember how embarrassing it was to have to walk into a drug store and ask for rubbers. So you've got a hot date tonight?"

"Yeah," said the relieved college kid. "She's supposed to be pretty hot. All the guys in town say she's a sure thing."

"Enjoy yourself, son," the pharmacist said. "And I'm glad you're being careful. Now get out of here and go rest up for your date."

At 8 p.m. the boy stood on the front porch of his date's house and rang the doorbell. But when the door opened and the kid saw his date's father, he vaulted over the porch railing and ran for his car.

It was the pharmacist.

Fun with Gerbils

David and Zander, a gay couple, heard of a famous movie star who had had the orgasm of a lifetime when his partner slipped a live gerbil up his anus. They decided to try it themselves.

On the appointed night, David pushed a cardboard toilet paper tube up Zander's rectum and then slipped in a gerbil they had bought at a pet shop that morning. In a few moments, Zander was shouting, "Enough! Enough! I can't take any more!"

David tried to grab the gerbil, but the critter was out of reach. Thinking the gerbil might be attracted by light, David struck a

match and held it to the opening of the toilet paper tube. The flame ignited a pocket of gas inside Zander's colon and a small fireball shot out of the tube, severely burning David's face and setting his hair on fire.

The fireball also set fire to the gerbil's fur. It burrowed deeper into Zander's colon. Unfortunately, the gerbil ignited another, larger pocket of gas which shot the little creature out of the tube, straight into David's face. The gerbil's velocity broke David's nose.

At the hospital, David and Zander were treated for first and second degree burns. But the gerbil didn't make it.

THE JINX OF THE SPORTS ILLUSTRATED COVER
AND OTHER HIGH-PROFILE PROBLEMS

The Jinx of the Sports Illustrated Cover

Since 1954, the first year *Sports Illustrated* was published, athletes, teams and coaches have dreaded appearing on the magazine's cover. This dubious honor has proved to be bad juju for more careers and sabotaged more winning seasons than anything short of a pact with the Devil.

Let's look at the mayhem that appearing on the *Sports Illustrated* cover has wrought.

• October 29, 1956: The Saturday after Paul Hornung of Notre Dame appeared on the cover, the Fighting Irish went down to ignominious defeat—40-0—to Oklahoma. Notre Dame went on to lose games to Navy and Pitt, finishing the season 2-8.

• April 18, 1960: If anyone seemed a shoo-in for the U.S. Olympic swimming team, it was Carin Cone. For four years she had been undefeated in the 100-meter backstroke. At the nationals, a few weeks after she appeared on the cover of *SI*, Cone finished second. As if that weren't bad enough, at her next meet she failed to qualify for the Olympics.

• October 30, 1978: Runner Bill Rodgers had just won his seventh marathon in a row when he was invited to be *SI*'s cover boy. He agreed—and in his next marathon he came in sixth.

• December 6, 1982: The undefeated Redskins made *SI*'s cover.

The week the magazine came out, the Redskins played the Cowboys and lost 24-10.

• March 27, 1989: Steffi Graf looked great on *SI*'s cover. She didn't look so good two weeks later when she suffered her first loss of the 1989 season.

• May 24, 1993: Barry Bonds of the Giants seemed unstoppable. Within two weeks of appearing on the *SI* cover, his batting average plummeted 40 points.

• January 14, 2002: The *SI* issue with Michael Jordan on the cover was at the printer when word came out that Jordan's wife had filed for divorce.

Martha Stewart Can't Phone Home

Martha Stewart was vacationing near Kennebunkport, Maine, when her car broke down on a country road in the middle of a torrential rainstorm. The only building in sight was a general store about 100 yards away. She wrapped herself in a yellow rain slicker and made a dash for the shop.

Inside, a single clerk assisted a long line of customers. Martha joined the line to wait her turn. She became more and more impatient as each minute passed, but she managed to control her temper. After forty-five minutes, she finally reached the counter.

In her most pleasant voice, Martha said to the clerk, "Good

morning. My car broke down. I'd like to use your pay phone to call AAA."

"We don't have a pay phone," the clerk said.

"Then perhaps you would let me use the store's phone," Martha said.

"You can't. Nobody gets to use the store phone," the clerk answered.

"It's a toll-free call," Martha said. "It won't cost anyone a thing."

"Store policy," the clerk said. "Nobody can use the phone."

Martha snapped, "This may be the policy for the local hayseeds, but it doesn't apply to me. Do you have any idea who I am? I'm Martha Stewart!"

Before the clerk could reply, the man standing behind Martha tapped her on the shoulder and said, "I'm George Bush, and they won't let me use the phone either."

Lee Greenwood: Draft Dodger

Since the mid-1980s singer/songwriter Lee Greenwood's "God Bless the USA" has been one of America's most popular patriotic songs. In 1985 the Country Music Association named the anthem "Song of the Year." During the Persian Gulf War, it was played daily on radio stations across the country, and it was the favorite song of America's fighting men and women stationed in the Gulf. It is a regular feature at Fourth of July and Memorial Day celebrations, and since the September 11 attacks, it has been the only song to rival the Irving Berlin classic, "God Bless America," in popularity.

Yet in spite of his reputation as a red-blooded American patriot, Greenwood harbors a nasty little secret: In the late 1960s he dodged the draft and fled to Canada.

Silent Bruce Crampton

Senior PGA golfer Bruce Crampton was a sports reporter's worst nightmare. No matter what the question was, Crampton never gave more than one- or two-word answers.

One afternoon at Pebble Beach, a woman approached Crampton in the clubhouse and said, "Mr. Crampton, I made a $50 bet with my friend that I could get you to say five words to me."

Crampton looked at her for a moment with a blank expression on his face, then said, "Sorry, lady. You lose."

Variation: The classic rendition of the story features Calvin "Silent Cal" Coolidge, the least talkative president the United States has ever had. In this older version, a congressman's garrulous wife is seated next to Coolidge at a state dinner. She tells the president that she had made a bet that she could get him to say more than three words to her. Coolidge responds, "You lose."

What's In a Name? 2

In the mid-1960s, Jerry Rivers, a young Jewish man from the Bronx, was trying to break into television as a newsman. Although he was a perfectly competent reporter, he didn't have anything that set him apart from every other Walter Cronkite wannabe.

Plenty of television stations offered him a job working on the copy desk, but none of the networks was willing to put Jerry in front of the camera.

In desperation, Jerry decided to reinvent himself. It was the 60s and ethnic chic was cool, so he changed his name, grew a moustache and went back to the networks that had refused to hire him.

Soon after, a New York television station issued a press release stating that it was proud to be the first network in New York City to hire a Hispanic newscaster. His name was Geraldo Rivera.

Playing Hardball in Chicago

It seems anything goes in Chicago's rough-and-tumble political campaigns, and the 1980 presidential race was no exception.

Senator Ted Kennedy was challenging incumbent Jimmy Carter for the Democratic nomination. Although the majority of the Illinois Democratic Party was firmly behind Carter, the mayor of Chicago, Jane Byrne, supported Kennedy. At the mayor's invitation, Kennedy came to town a couple of days ahead of the primary to walk at

Byrne's side during Chicago's St. Patrick's Day Parade.

In response, the Illinois State Democratic Party pulled a stunt that cleverly revealed its political candidate of choice: An empty car was rolled off the Michigan Avenue Bridge as a subtle reminder of the Chappaquiddick fiasco, the most notorious scandal in Kennedy's career.

Tiger Woods Gets Carded

Golf superstar Tiger Woods was playing a tournament in Las Vegas. Late one night he and a group of friends headed for a strip club.

The bouncer took one look at the boyish young man and demanded to see his driver's license.

"It says here you're 20 years old," the bouncer said. "Nobody under 21 gets to see this show. Sorry, kid."

Woods was stunned. He was certain his celebrity status would make him welcome anywhere.

"But I'm the Tiger!" he said.

"Kid," the bouncer said, "I don't care if you're the Lion King. You ain't comin' in here until you're 21."

The Books Satan Loves

The Harry Potter novels are luring children into the practice of the dark arts!

Shortly after the first Harry Potter movie was released in 2001, an unnamed ex-witch revealed that author J.K. Rowling is a practicing witch; that a coven of witches were on the set of the movie to ensure complete authenticity; and that the spells, charms and incantations used in the books and the movie are actual demonic formulas.

It's not surprising that Rowling would use her powers to boost the sales of her novels. What author wouldn't? The popularity of the Potter books has surpassed that of any other children's book ever published, a feat attributable to the malevolent spirits Rowling assigned to each of the works. These spirits first entice, then enchant, readers so they will turn their backs on God and give themselves entirely to the practice of evil.

Since the first Harry Potter novel was published, thousands of young candidates have applied to join covens. Before the Potter phenomenon, the minimum age to join a coven was 18. Today witches are accepting children as young as 12 or 13.

Rent-a-Staff

Today, from their home office in London, the Saatchi brothers, Charles and Maurice, rule an advertising empire. But in 1970 they were two novices with no reputation and no clients.

In an act of real bravado they pitched themselves to Jacob's Biscuits, a huge snack-food manufacturer, the British equivalent of Hostess. Several Jacob's vice presidents were intrigued by the Saatchi brothers' presentation; they announced they'd stop by the Saatchi offices the next day.

Charles and Maurice had rented a suite of offices in the center of London, but they had no employees. To win the account, the brothers thought they had to make the Jacob's executives believe that Saatchi & Saatchi was a thriving agency. But how?

Charles had an idea. Early the next morning he went out into the streets of London with a fistful of cash. He approached stylishly dressed young men and women and offered each one 100 pounds if they would spend the morning in the Saatchi offices and pretend to be busy advertising copywriters, designers and executives.

By the time the Jacob's group arrived, the Saatchi offices were humming with attractive young people working the phones, hammering away at typewriters and brainstorming in conference rooms. It set the perfect backdrop for Charles and Maurice's final sales pitch. The brothers got Jacob's as a client and were on their way to becoming giants in the advertising industry.

Let the Man Talk!

Actor Jack Benny starred in the now-classic comedy, *To Be or Not to Be*, directed by Ernst Lubitsch. After the filming was completed, Lubitsch held a wrap party at his house in Bel Air. At one point in the evening, Benny, Lubitsch, producer Billy Wilder and a new up-and-coming director in Hollywood were talking among themselves outside, by the pool.

The director was a tireless yakker and began a lengthy discussion of Lubitsch's gifts and failings. Every time Lubitsch tried to respond, the director cut him off and kept up the endless monologue.

After ten minutes of this, Jack Benny excused himself and went into the house. When he emerged, the director was still holding court. A few minutes later, one of Lubitsch's servants delivered a telegram to the director. The director was very pleased—to receive a telegram while at a party made him look very important. He opened the telegram and read the message: "Why don't you shut up and let Lubitsch talk? Signed,
Jack Benny."

Back to the Future II Predicted the Florida Marlins Would Win the 1997 World Series

One of the essential points in the plot of *Back to the Future II* is that the oafish villain, Biff, goes into the future, to the year 2015, steals a copy of *The Sports Almanac*, then returns with it to the past.

Thanks to this handy volume, Biff becomes incredibly wealthy by accurately predicting the outcome of every sporting event and winning each bet he makes.

At one point in the movie, Biff is flipping through *The Sports Almanac* and says, "Florida is going to win the World Series in 1997. Yeah, right."

Incredibly, *Back to the Future II* came out in 1987, ten years before the Florida Marlins did in fact win the World Series. Even weirder is that Florida didn't have a baseball team in 1987.

Origins: After the Florida Marlins won the 1997 World Series against the Cleveland Indians, this story started making the rounds via e-mail and websites. But Back to the Future II *does not predict that Florida wins a World Series, it predicts that in 2015 the Chicago Cubs will be the champs. This is a cruel dig at Cubs fans whose team has not played in a World Series since 1945 or won a World Series since 1908.*

It is routine for urban legends to suggest (wrongly, of course) that some of our warmest, most cuddly celebrities actually have a sinister past. Fred Rogers (of Mister Rogers' Neighborhood*) is said to have*

been a sniper in Vietnam. Barbra Streisand is supposed to have started out as a porn actress. The Monkees are rumored to have auditioned Charles Manson. In the realm of urban legends, an innocent demeanor must conceal some dire secret.

Dave Thomas's Secret

Until his death, Dave Thomas appeared in commercials as the friendly, benign owner of Wendy's fast-food restaurants. Thomas, however, was harboring a painful secret.

In 1970 Dave Thomas was a member of the National Guard. He was among the troops sent to Kent State University on May 4, 1970, to quell student demonstrations that threatened to spin out of control.

In the confrontation between student demonstrators and National Guardsmen, four students were killed. Dave Thomas was the trooper who fired the first fatal shot.

John Denver's Secret

John Denver was not always a singer of folksy, sentimental (some might say sappy) hit singles. In the mid-1960s, when he was still going by his given name, John Henry Deutchendorff, he was a sniper for the U.S. Army in Vietnam.

Deutchendorff had a favorite way of picking off Viet Cong. He would climb into a tree and position himself so the sun was behind him. When an enemy came into view, Deutchendorff whistled. The Viet Cong foot soldier would look toward the sound and be blinded by the sunlight. In that split second, Deutchendorff would pick off his prey.

By the time he finished his tour of duty, the future John Denver had compiled an impressive number of kills and earned a chestful of medals. But the memory of all those dead men tortured Denver's conscience, and he became an outspoken pacifist. His hit single, "Sunshine on My Shoulders," was Denver's way of wrestling with the memories of the years he spent as a trained killer.

Short Takes 6

• Michael Jackson wears a glove on one hand because it is the only part of his body that did not respond to the radical skin-lightening treatment. The hand retains its original skin color.

• The promoters of the Britney Spears Look-a-Like Contest persuaded the sexy pop star and her N'Sync boyfriend, Justin Timberlake, to act as one of the contest judges. After watching three dozen contestants bump, grind and lip-synch their way through "I Did It Again," Britney and Justin picked the winner. The next day the press reported that the Britney Spears Look-a-Like was a transvestite.

• At the end of the recording of Johnny Rivers's classic, "Memphis," you can hear a crowd whooping it up and carrying on. The cause of the excitement was not Rivers's performance, but a dog that sneaked into the recording studio, took a fancy to the performer's left leg, and humped it as soon as the song was over.

• Mariah Carey was in the middle of a live interview on MTV when breaking news announced that King Hussein I of Jordan had died. Carey exclaimed, "What a terrible loss for professional basketball!"

• The first couple shown in bed together on television was Fred and Wilma Flintstone.

• Mel Blanc, who did the voice for Bugs Bunny, was allergic to carrots.

• In August 1997, Orioles infielder Cal Ripken Jr. walked into his bedroom and found his wife having sex with actor Kevin Costner. Ripken had not missed a ballgame in a record number of games, but his wife's infidelity had him so upset he refused to play that night. Rather than break Ripken's consecutive-game streak, the Orioles management canceled the game.

• In the early 1970s, actor Rock Hudson and singer/actor Jim Nabors were married in a public ceremony in Huntington Beach, California.

• Lars Ulrich, the drummer for Metallica, was shot and killed as he left a hotel in Austin, Texas. The culprit was a well-dressed man who, before firing the fatal shot, shouted, "You killed Napster!"

• Everybody stayed home from 8-9 P.M. on February 9, 1964, to see the Beatles in their first appearance on *The Ed Sullivan Show*. In New York, the program's high rating translated into a phenomenon never recorded before or since: Not a single serious crime was committed in the city throughout the entire live broadcast.

• Marilyn Monroe never wore open-toed sandals because she had six toes on each foot.

• Cher had several of her ribs surgically removed so she would look thinner.

• Fashion designer Tommy Hilfiger appeared on *Oprah* saying he wished African-Americans would stop wearing his clothes. "My designs," he said, "are intended for white people."

• Through subtle references in their lyrics, Led Zeppelin tried to send a message to fans that Jimmy Page had sold his soul to Satan.

THE SPAGHETTI ORCHARDS
OF SWITZERLAND
AND OTHER SCAMS, PRANKS, AND HOAXES

The Spaghetti Orchards of Switzerland

Spaghetti does grow on trees! On April 1, 1957, *Panorama*, a British news program, ran a segment on the spaghetti harvest in one of Switzerland's southern cantons. While the program's host praised the harvest's record crop yield, film footage showed dozens of happy Swiss peasants plucking ripe strands of spaghetti from trees and placing them in baskets.

That year's bumper crop was due to a new insecticide that had greatly reduced the numbers of the voracious spaghetti weevil, a pest that had ruined many harvests in previous years. But the spaghetti farmers were not entirely home free. Since the harvest comes at the beginning of April, there is always the risk of late frost. While a cold snap doesn't destroy a spaghetti crop, it does sap some of the flavor, which in turn affects market price. And of course, the farmers must also deal with the pasta mega-farmers of northern Italy.

Recognizing that many of their British viewers were avid gardeners, the program concluded with directions on how to plant one's own spaghetti tree.

"Take a single strand of dried spaghetti," the host instructed, "insert it upright in a can of tomato paste, and wait for nature to take its course."

Royal African Millionaires Need Your Help!

From: PRINCE WILLIAMS & PRINCESS MARY EDWARD
 princes@invest4us.com

RE: BUSINESS PROPOSAL AND INVESTMENT
 IN YOUR COMPANY

Dear Sir,

It is a pleasure to send you this proposal for the purpose of making a joint business investment with you and your company.

My sister and I are orphans. We are the children of the late chief Martins Edward who was a personal confidant of the arrested warlord, Mr. FODAY SANKOH, of the Republic of Sierra Leone. Before the arrest of Mr. FODAY SANKOH, our late father left Sierra Leone with a box containing US $20,000,000 for Abidjan, Côte d'Ivoire, West Africa, where he deposited the box in a private security-and-trust company. He registered the contents as family treasures and important family documents for his children.

Unfortunately, our father died in the heat of the crisis when Mr. FODAY SANKOH was about to be arrested. Before his death, our father gave us his documents and revealed to us that the real contents of the box was money. He instructed us to leave Sierra Leone immediately, go to Abidjan, claim the box and make use of the money with the help of an honest and trustworthy foreigner who would assist us in managing it.

We are currently undercover in Abidjan and seeking a reliable and trustworthy individual or company to assist us in obtaining the

money. We would then like to transfer the money to his company and then invest it in a reliable business. We also hope you will arrange for our permanent settlement in your country as we have no interest in staying in Africa.

We are ignorant of the business world and need your assistance. We hope you are honest and trustworthy enough to render your assistance to us. For your efforts, we would offer you 20% of the total sum of US $20 million. We have mapped out 5% for any expenses that might be incurred in the course of transferring the money to a secure place.

Please, as soon as you receive this message, send us an e-mail to the above address for more details. We expect your positive response.

Thanks, and God bless.
Best regards,
PRINCE WILLIAMS
& PRINCESS MARY EDWARD

NOTE: To move the funds out of the country, we need the
 following:
 1) Your bank account number and the telephone and fax numbers of the same bank.
 2) Your private telephone and fax numbers for easy and confidential communication.

As soon as I receive your banking information, we will arrange to handle the transfer of the funds with a bank here after the money

is withdrawn from its current location.

When the transaction is complete, I will send you 20% of $20 million United States dollars to thank you for your help!

Variation: Another version of this letter comes from a Nigerian government official who is being persecuted by a corrupt regime. He begs the recipient to send him his or her bank account number so he can deposit millions of dollars for safekeeping. In return, he promises to pay the American a generous commission.

You're Sitting on Anthrax

After anthrax was detected in a Washington, D.C., congressional office, Americans across the country feared exposure to the disease. Residents of the capital and the surrounding suburbs were especially tense.

A few weeks after the discovery, a woman in Arlington, Virginia, just across the Potomac from the capital, left her desk to use the ladies' room. As she finished, she unwound a length of toilet paper from the dispenser. Taped to one of the sheets was a note that read, "You're sitting on anthrax, and you're going to die."

The woman was so terrified that she had a heart attack that killed her on the spot.

Investigators later found that the toilet seat, the ladies' room and the entire building were anthrax free and determined that the unfortunate woman had been the victim of a cruel prank.

Weather or Not

A supermarket tabloid reported that China's Communist government had come up with a foolproof plan to destroy the power of the capitalist West. It designated May 1 as "Strike a Blow for the People Against the Bloodsucking Capitalist Leeches Day."

At noon on the appointed day, every man, woman and child in China would be required to jump up and down. The impact of one billion people jumping simultaneously would be powerful enough to jolt the earth off its axis. The West would then be scorched by searing heat, or frozen back into the Ice Age—depending on whether the planet veered closer to or farther away from the sun (China's scientists were a bit vague on this point).

An alert citizen in Hoboken, New Jersey, read the report while standing in line at the local supermarket. Immediately he began organizing a counter jump. He reasoned that if he could get one billion people to jump on May 1 at the same time the Chinese were jumping, the capitalist jump would cancel out the Communist jump, and the earth would remain in balance.

Microsoft and AOL Want to Pay You for Sending E-mail!

The merger between AOL and Time Warner was huge, but the AOL-Microsoft merger is even bigger. To win over the Internet-surfing public (and to ensure that Microsoft's Explorer remains top dog among the Web browsers), AOL-Microsoft is making a very generous offer.

If you use Microsoft Explorer, or if you subscribe to AOL, you will receive a reply e-mail from AOL-Microsoft. Forward it to all your friends; AOL-Microsoft will pay you $245 for every person you send it to.

Microsoft will pay you $243 for each friend who then forwards it to his or her friends. For every person (three removed from you) who receives the e-mail, you will be paid $241.

AOL-Microsoft will track the e-mails for only two weeks, so your window of opportunity is limited. At the end of the two weeks, the company will contact you for your snail mail address. Soon after, you'll receive a check. Your earnings, just for forwarding an e-mail, could easily exceed $25,000!

Variation: In another version, AOL merges with Intel, but rewards for forwarding the new company's e-mail are not nearly as generous as in the AOL-Microsoft merger: AOL-Intel only pays $203.15 for each person you send it to, $156.29 for every person your friends send it to, and a measly $17.65 for each e-mail at the third remove from your original e-mail.

Let's Saw Manhattan in Half

In the spring of 1823, two men by the names of DeVoe and Lozier announced to a crowd at New York City Center Market that Manhattan was sinking due to the number of people living on the island. According to the men, the weight of the existing population compounded by the daily influx of immigrants was sinking Manhattan deeper and deeper into New York Bay.

Distressing as that news may have been, all was not lost. DeVoe and Lozier claimed that Stephen Allen, the mayor of New York, had commissioned them to save Manhattan by sawing the island in half, towing the lower portion into the harbor, turning it 180 degrees and reattaching it to the upper half. Thus, Lower Manhattan, the most densely populated area of the city, would be centrally located, and the island would not tip and dump its inhabitants into the bay.

Hundreds of workingmen signed up to help cut the island in half. The volunteers waited and waited the day the project was to begin, but DeVoe and Lozier never showed. Instead, they sent a message stating that their health compelled them, unexpectedly, to leave the city.

It only took a few minutes before the volunteers realized the con men had made fools of them.

Short Takes 7

• Young people in England began eating bag after bag of Walker potato chips after a report circulated that the company would buy a dialysis machine for a little girl suffering from kidney disease as soon as it received a million empty potato chip bags.

• Nina Totenberg has written an e-mail warning the American public that there is a bill in Congress to pull PBS off the air because certain reactionary elements believe *Sesame Street's* Big Bird is part of a plot to train children to accept the Orwellian world of Big Brother.

• McWhortle Enterprises, Inc., received high marks from stockmarket analysts thanks to its Biohazard-Alert Detector. This battery-operated device is small enough to fit in a pocket and beeps when the carrier comes in contact with anthrax or any other deadly microorganism.

• African-American taxpayers are entitled to a credit on their federal income taxes in reparation for slavery.

• A company called IQ Inkjet Products has announced that for every empty inkjet cartridge it receives, it will donate a dollar to the Families of Freedom Scholarship Fund, an organization founded by former President Bill Clinton and retired Senator Bob Dole to provide college education for children of the victims of the September 11 attacks.

• The government is now able to track every purchase you make thanks to a strip implanted in the newly designed U.S. paper currency. But don't panic! At this point, the feds are only interested in radical political, religious and social activists.

• The CIA conspired with the Contras in Nicaragua to introduce crack cocaine into African-American neighborhoods as a way to further oppress black Americans.

• Scientists working for a secret U.S. intelligence agency invented the AIDS virus as a way to eliminate homosexuals, drug addicts and minority groups.

• The alligators in the sewers of New York City are dying! The international organization "Save the Sewer Gators Coalition" is urging the alligator-loving public to join in petitioning New York City officials to clean up the toxic chemicals destroying the gators' unique sewer habitat.

THE DAY THE SUPERMARKETS
RUN OUT OF AVOCADOS
AND OTHER LORE FOR SPECIAL OCCASIONS

The Day the Supermarkets Run Out of Avocados

Super Bowl Sunday is an exciting day for football fans and the best program for corporations to broadcast new television commercials. But this legendary day also impacts Americans in a host of unexpected ways.

During the days leading up to Super Bowl Sunday, there is a run on avocados at supermarkets (for the guacamole, of course).

Pizzerias start preparing days before Super Bowl Sunday for their busiest day of the year. And the busiest time of the busiest day of the year for pizza parlors is halftime when everyone tries to pick up their order before the game resumes.

In the hours after the game, the number of cases of wife-beating soars—especially if the team the husband was backing loses.

While some viewers actually look forward to the commercials during the Super Bowl, other viewers wait for these breaks to make a mad dash to the bathroom. The flushing of millions of toilets at the same time has caused the water pressure in some urban areas to drop to dangerously low levels.

The Hidden Meaning of
"The Twelve Days of Christmas"

Who would give their true love a partridge in a pear tree? And how could you wrap it? It turns out this whimsical Christmas carol actually contains a coded message for persecuted English Catholics.

From 1558 to 1829, Roman Catholics in England were not permitted to practice their faith openly. Jesuit priests wrote "The Twelve Days of Christmas" as a simple but secret way to teach English Catholic children their catechism.

The partridge in a pear tree is Jesus Christ.

The two turtledoves are the Old and New Testaments.

The three French hens represent faith, hope and charity.

The four calling birds are the four gospels of Matthew, Mark, Luke and John.

The five golden rings symbolize the Books of Moses, the first five books of the Old Testament.

The six geese a-laying represent the six days of creation.

The seven swans a-swimming represent the seven gifts of the Holy Spirit: wisdom, understanding, counsel, fortitude, knowledge, piety and fear of the Lord.

The eight maids a-milking are the eight Beatitudes.

The nine ladies dancing are the nine ways one can be an accessory to another's sin: by counsel, by command, by consent, by provocation, by praise or flattery, by concealment, by sharing, by silence and by defending wrong that has been committed.

The ten lords a-leaping are the Ten Commandments.

The eleven pipers piping stand for the eleven apostles who remained faithful to Christ (the twelfth, Judas, hanged himself).

The twelve drummers drumming symbolize the twelve points of belief in the Apostles' Creed.

The Free Air Guitar

A grandmother stopped in at the Times Square Virgin Megastore to buy a CD for her teenaged grandson. She told the sales clerk that her grandson enjoyed playing the guitar, and the clerk recommended a new Virgin release, "The World's Greatest Air Guitar Album Ever," with tracks by Jimi Hendrix, Queen and Van Halen. A sticker on the outside of the CD case read: "Get your own air guitar FREE!"

"I'll take it," said the grandmother. "Now where do I pick up the free air guitar?"

The clerk smiled. "It's a joke, ma'am. There is no free air guitar."

"It says right here that I'm entitled to a free air guitar with purchase. Are you trying to cheat me?"

"No, lady, really. An air guitar is an imaginary instrument. It's something you pretend to play while listening to the CD. Watch!" In the middle of the store, the clerk did a creditable job imitating Jimi Hendrix.

"See," the clerk said. "That's an air guitar."

"Do you take me for an idiot?" the woman asked. "You weren't playing any instrument at all!"

The angry shopper threw the CD at the clerk and stormed out of the store.

The clerk explained to his manager what had happened and asked, "Do you want me to pull the CDs from the shelves?"

"No," the manager said. "Just try not sell them to grandmothers."

The Canadian Flag at the Olympics Jinx

Since 1976, Canada's Olympic hopefuls have tried to avoid being selected to carry the Maple Leaf Flag at the Opening Ceremonies of the Olympics. Experience has proven that being the flag bearer is a jinx: Of 16 Canadian flag bearers, 11 met with disaster at the Olympic Games.

In 1976, three weeks before the Winter Games at Innsbruck, Austria, skier Dave Irwin, who had already been chosen to carry the flag on opening day, took a nasty tumble on the slopes in Switzerland. He insisted on competing and finished eighth in the men's downhill event.

In 1980, at Lake Placid, New York, flag bearer Ken Read lost a ski at the starting gate.

At the 1988 Olympics in Calgary, Canada, Brian Orser carried the flag and lost the gold medal to Brian Boitano, proof that the jinx even works on home turf.

Great things were expected of the sprint speed-skating world champion Sylvie Daigle in the 1992 Games in Albertville, France. Instead of bringing home the gold medal, Daigle, the flag bearer,

took an ignominious spill on the ice in mid race.

At the 1992 Summer Games in Barcelona, Spain, Canada's designated flag carrier and golden boy, decathlete Michael Smith, pulled a hamstring.

Kurt Browning arrived at the 1994 Olympics in Lillehammer, Norway, as the four-time world figure-skating champion. But after carrying the flag he came in fifth in the Games.

Freestyle skier Jean-Luc Brassard took a gold medal at the 1994 Winter Olympics in Lillehammer, Norway (where he did not touch the flag). At the 1998 Winter Olympics in Nagano, Japan, Brassard carried his country's flag—and finished in fourth place.

The Stung Bride

Some brides may worry about the number of bridesmaids, or the quality of the band, or the number of courses at the dinner, but the primary concern of a young bride in Helsinki, Finland, was filling the church and reception hall with magnificent floral arrangements. Equal care went into the selection of her bouquet, a large spray of white roses. The bride thought the bouquet to be so beautiful that she could not bring herself to follow the custom of tossing it to the crowd of unmarried women in the reception hall. Instead, she threw the bouquet of one of her bridesmaids and carried her own up to the bridal suite and placed it carefully on her pillow.

The bride had been determined to save her virginity until her wedding night, and the groom had long been looking forward to the moment. He made love to his new wife with real vigor, and she

responded passionately. At one point, the bride's head crushed her bouquet of roses, and seconds later she began to thrash about wildly and scream.

The groom thought he was the cause of his new wife's frenzy—until he saw angry bees swarming from the crushed flowers and stinging his new wife. He leaped from the bed, wrapped a sheet around his waist and ran for help. By the time he returned with a doctor, the poor bride had been stung to death.

Variation: In another version set in Singapore, the bride wants her wedding pictures taken in a botanical garden. While the newlyweds are posing amid exotic flowers, a poisonous serpent bites and kills the bride.

The Sailor's Christmas

An American tourist who had taken his family to France for the Christmas holidays sent this letter to Admiral David L. McDonald of the United States Navy.

Admiral David L. McDonald, USN
Department of the Navy
Washington, DC

Dear Admiral McDonald,
The story I want to tell you is a long one, but I hope you will bear with me.

Last Christmas my wife and I took our three sons to France for Christmas. We were hoping for a memorable family holiday in a beautiful part of the world, but nothing went as planned. We were bumped from our flight to Paris and could not catch another flight until late the next day. When we arrived at our hotel, the manager explained that he had given our rooms to other travelers, but he would book rooms for us in another hotel. The hotel he found for us was a flea bag in a deteriorating neighborhood far from the heart of the city.

Rather than spend a gloomy Christmas there, we rented a car and set out for Nice where we expected we would have better luck. On the highway the car broke down. We arrived in Nice after dark on a cold and rainy Christmas Eve. The only hotel that had any vacancies was just as dismal as the hotel we had left in Paris.

All of us were tired and irritable from the trip and very hungry. After leaving our luggage in our rooms, we went out to find a restaurant. Every place was booked, except a drab little bistro. A few pathetic Christmas decorations hung in the window. At an out-of-tune piano in the corner a man tried to play Christmas music. There were three other families in the place, and all of them looked as depressed as we felt. The only sign of Christmas spirit in the entire restaurant was a handsome young American sailor who sat at a table alone, beaming as he wrote a letter.

Although my wife ordered our meal in French, the waiter brought us nothing that we had asked for. In frustration my children began to squabble. At the table on our left a father slapped his son for knocking over a glass of water. At the table on our right a husband and wife were quarreling at the top of their voices.

Then the door to the restaurant opened and an elderly flower lady shuffled in. She offered her flowers at every table, but no one bought any. With a weary sigh she sat down at a table in the far corner near the piano. She called the waiter over and ordered a bowl of soup. As the waiter moved off to the kitchen, the flower woman leaned over to the piano player and said, "What a miserable Christmas. I haven't sold a single flower all day, and now my dinner is a measly bowl of soup." The piano player commiserated with her and pointed to his own empty tip plate.

Then the young sailor stood up, pulled on his coat, and walked over to the flower woman. He chose two white roses from her basket and asked, "How much?" "Two francs, m'sieur," she answered. The sailor pulled out a 50 franc note and handed it to her. "I do not have change, m'sieur," the flower woman said. "Wait, I will get some from the bar."

"Don't bother," the sailor said. "It's my gift to you. Merry Christmas!"

While the stunned flower woman stared at him in disbelief, the sailor pressed one white rose with his hand and slipped it into his letter. Then he took the second rose and walked over to our table. "Sir," he said to me, "with your permission I'd like to offer this rose to your beautiful wife. Merry Christmas!" A moment later he was out the door and vanished into the night.

Everyone in the restaurant was silent for several long moments. Then suddenly the Christmas spirit erupted in the restaurant. The flower seller called the waiter and ordered a feast for herself and the piano player. The piano player began to bang out a lively French

carol. The French families began to sing along. And my wife and I got up to dance.

The squabbling couple kissed, made up, and ordered wine for everyone in the restaurant. The music and laughter and dancing attracted passersby, and soon every table in the restaurant was packed with merry diners. Our celebration lasted long past midnight, and it was all thanks to the warm, generous spirit of one of your sailors. Thank you, Admiral McDonald, for instilling in our servicemen and women such a joyful, selfless spirit.

Merry Christmas
William J. Lederer

THE KID WHO FELL ASLEEP IN THE CASKET
IN THE CASKET
AND OTHER CREEPY TALES

The Kid Who Fell Asleep in the Casket

As a practical joke, the 12-year-old son of a funeral director invited all of his friends to meet him in the showroom of his father's funeral home, where he hid in a casket and waited to surprise them. When the kids had assembled, the boy slowly raised the coffin's lid and sat upright, scaring the hell out of all of his friends.

The boy enjoyed seeing the looks of terror on the faces of his friends, but he also found pleasure just lying in the coffin. He thought it might be the perfect place to nap undisturbed. More than once his parents found him asleep in one of the floor models.

When the boy's father set up a $20,000 mahogany casket in his showroom, he proudly pointed out its special features to his son. "It's made of mahogany from the West Indies," said the funeral director, "The handles are solid bronze. And inside, there's a quilted silk lining and a goosedown cushion. This baby is the top of the line."

"It's great!" the kid said. "It looks really comfortable."

"Don't get any ideas," the father said. "This isn't some floor model you can goof around in. A customer has already bought this casket." He then walked his son out of the showroom and bolted the door.

About an hour later the kid stole his father's keys, sneaked back into the showroom and climbed inside the mahogany box. It was as comfortable as a feather bed, but the fluorescent lights overhead annoyed the boy, so he closed the casket lid. A few minutes later he was fast asleep.

While the boy snoozed, two men who worked for the funeral home came into the showroom.

"Which one is mahogany?" asked the first man.

"The one with the closed lid," his friend said.

The men positioned themselves at either end of the mahogany box, picked it up and carried it to the door.

"Does this one go to Gate of Heaven or Oak Park?" the first man asked.

"Nah. This isn't a burial," his friend said. "This one's a cremation."

The Haunted Orphanage

After housing children for more than a century, Holy Family Orphanage in Belfast, Northern Ireland, shut its doors in 1970. For thirty years the massive stone building stood abandoned, until the city council decided to demolish it and build an apartment complex on the site.

From the day the demolition crew arrived, it had one peculiar experience after another. Wrecking cranes would not operate. Tools vanished and could not be found again. Piping hot cups of tea from the workmen's Thermoses turned icy cold in an instant. In the large room that had once been the nursery, the workmen heard babies crying. In the cellar where the morgue had been, the sound of children wailing echoed down the long, dark corridors.

As the story of the haunted orphanage spread through Belfast,

a local news station sent a camera crew to the site to do a story on the eerie events. A cameraman was filming in the dormitory when a small boy approached him.

"Excuse me, sir," the boy said. "Would you tell my sister, Mary Maguire, that I'm alright, and that I'll wait for her here."

The cameraman was surprised. Mary Maguire was the manager of the station's evening news program. How could a woman over 60 years old have a brother who could not be more than 7 or 8? But before the cameraman could say a word, the boy ran down the hallway and disappeared among the shadows.

Perplexed, the cameraman called the office on his cell phone.

"Mary, I'm at Holy Family Orphanage and the oddest thing just happened. A little boy who claims he's your brother asked me to tell you he was fine and that he would wait for you here. Any idea what that's about?"

There was a long silence on the other end of the line. Then Mary Maguire spoke. "That was my brother Declan," she said. "He died in the orphanage 53 years ago."

The Sorcerer's Stones

Dealers in precious stones throughout Europe fell victim to an especially ingenious robber who had a unique way of getting the goods. Tapes from security cameras in a dozen jewelry stores showed the same well-dressed gentleman sitting across the counter from a jeweler's clerk. After a brief conversation, the stranger would lean forward and whisper something into the clerk's ear.

A moment later the clerk would enter the vault and emerge with a black velvet pouch filled with diamonds, rubies and emeralds. The clerk would hand the pouch to the stranger, who would slip it inside his coat and walk out of the shop. The clerks appeared dazed and robotic and remained so for a full 30 minutes after the thief had left the building.

When the clerks' viewed the tapes they claimed to have no recollection of the transaction or of ever setting eyes on the thief.

Several jewelry dealers pooled their resources and hired a film company that specialized in enhancing and studying tapes from security cameras. The film company technicians spent weeks magnifying each frame and amplifying the sound. At last they released their findings: The well-dressed stranger was a sorcerer who whispered a spell that overwhelmed the clerks' senses and forced them to turn over whatever jewels he demanded.

The Exploding Sauna

A well-to-do Park Avenue matron, famous among her acquaintances for her vanity, confessed to a close friend that she was beginning to have misgivings about her complexion.

"My pores aren't as tight as they once were," she complained. "I've had facial after facial, but nothing has worked."

The distraught woman's friend was sympathetic. "Poor dear. But I have to tell you you've wasted your money and your time going for facials. The best way to restore a youthful look to your skin is to take a nice long sauna at least three times a week."

The woman with loose pores was intrigued. "How long should I stay in the sauna?"

"At least an hour, my dear," her friend answered. "It will make you look and feel years younger."

"But surely I'll perspire a great deal during an hour in the sauna!"

"It's one of the sacrifices we must make for beauty," her friend replied.

The next day the woman rose early and went directly to her fitness salon. In the locker room she changed into a white terrycloth robe. Before she closed her locker door, she took a small spray vial of perfume from her bag and slipped it into the pocket of her robe.

For an hour she sat in the sauna waiting patiently for the heat to do its restorative work. It was intensely hot in the room, and none of the other women who entered the sauna could endure it for more than a few minutes. At the end of her hour, the matron was alone.

She had perspired a great deal. Rather than return to the dressing area trailing an unpleasant personal odor, she took out her little perfume vial and sprayed the nape of her neck.

A terrible explosion rocked the salon. The aerosol from the perfume bottle combined with the intense heat of the sauna to create a giant fireball that consumed the woman and destroyed the sauna.

A Mother's Plea

A couple taking a drive in the country came across a woman standing in the middle of the road waving her arms wildly. As they drew closer they could see that she was bruised and bleeding, and her clothes were torn.

The couple stopped the car and jumped out as the distraught woman ran toward them. "My family has been in a terrible car accident. We went off the road and into that ravine. My husband's dead, but my baby is still alive. Please, save my baby."

The man charged down the steep slope of the ravine. At the bottom, he found the battered car with two dead adults in the front seat and an infant, still strapped in her car seat, bawling but unharmed. He lifted the child out of the car and carried her carefully back to the road.

"Where's the mother?" the man asked his wife.

"She followed you down the ravine. Didn't you see her?"

The man handed the baby to his wife, and returned to the wrecked car. In the front seat were a dead man and a dead woman— the same woman who had flagged him down a few minutes earlier.

It's a Coffin and a Coffee Table

Lucy Green died after 30 years of marriage. Her husband Jeff couldn't bear the thought of never seeing his beloved wife again, so he hired the finest embalmer in the United States to preserve her body. He then contacted a manufacturer of glass display cases for museums and ordered a coffin made entirely of glass. The job cost $6,000, but Jeff didn't grudge the expense.

He had the coffin delivered to the mortuary, personally directed the placement of Lucy's body in the glass box, and watched as the work crew from the glass factory sealed the lid. Jeff then had the workmen carry the glass box to his house and place it in front of his and Lucy's matching recliners.

Not only does Jeff continue to enjoy Lucy's company, he also has a new coffee table. Lucy, meanwhile, lies perfectly preserved in the glass coffin.

Skinned Tom

Origins: A ghost who haunts the place where he or she died is a classic folklore motif. The story of Skinned Tom, however, combines the Old World lore with two elements from New World urban legends. In the world of urban legends, a betrayed spouse doesn't hire a divorce lawyer, he exacts a terrible vengeance personally. And as anyone who collects urban legends knows, the most dangerous place for two lovers is a deserted country road.

In the 1930s a young man named Tom lived in eastern Tennessee. Tom was a handsome, smooth-talking guy who had little trouble finding female companionship. One day he picked the wrong girl.

Tom had gone to the next town on a business errand when he saw a beautiful young woman going into one of the stores on Main Street. He followed her inside the shop, invented an excuse to talk to her and within five minutes had made a date for the following evening.

Tom didn't know—and his date didn't volunteer—that the young woman was married. Since her husband was away on business four nights out of every seven, the woman figured it would not be difficult to arrange things so neither man ever found out about the other.

On their first date, the woman made love to Tom in the backseat of his big, black De Soto. The car became their love nest because the woman would never let Tom into her house. "The neighbors will talk," she said.

Eventually the neighbors did catch on that the woman was running around with another man, and one of them told her husband.

The husband concealed his rage. A few days after learning of his wife's infidelity, he announced that he was going away on another business trip. He put his bags in the car, drove out of his driveway and down the street, but then doubled back, hid his car in the woods behind the house, and waited to see what would happen. An hour or so after dark, Tom arrived in the De Soto.

As the lovers pulled away from the curb, the husband followed at a distance. When he saw Tom's car pull into a deserted country

lane, the husband parked on the shoulder of the main road, took a big, nasty-looking hunting knife from under the front seat and headed into the woods. He walked parallel to the lane until he found the place where Tom had parked the De Soto. After ten or fifteen minutes, he crept over to Tom's car and yanked open the back door. There were Tom and the faithless wife, naked and in each other's arms.

"Don't hurt him!" the woman screamed to her husband. Then she said to Tom, "He's my husband."

"You cheating bitch!" the husband roared. He pulled his wife from the car, plunged the hunting knife into her stomach and tossed her aside. Then he reached into the car for Tom.

Tom scrambled to escape, but the husband grabbed him by one ankle and dragged him out.

"Please," Tom begged. "Don't hurt me. I didn't know she was married. Please! Don't kill me!"

The husband smiled. "I promise, I won't kill you." Then he seized Tom by the hair and half dragged, half carried him into the woods.

The husband kept his word. He didn't kill him, he skinned him, and he skinned Tom so carefully that Tom was still alive at the end of the ordeal. The husband draped Tom's hide over his arm, went back to his car, and drove to the police station where he turned himself in.

The cops rushed to the scene of the crime and found the wife still alive, but Tom had disappeared.

Ever since that night, couples who park on that deserted country lane run the risk of receiving a visit from Skinned Tom.

Some people say he appears to chase the young lovers away, but others insist Tom wants to avenge himself by skinning young men as handsome and reckless as he was.

The "Love Roller Coaster" Scream

Version One

In the mid-1970s, the Ohio Players had a string of funky, sexually suggestive hits. Their biggest single, which went to the top of the charts in 1975, was "Love Roller Coaster." When you pump up the volume, you can hear distinctly behind the twang of the guitars the sound of a woman screaming.

Most fans think the scream fits in with the roller coaster theme of the song, but in fact what they hear is a real death scream.

While recording their album, the band found a tape of a woman screaming as she fell to her death from the Blue Streak roller coaster at the Cedar Point Amusement Park. They incorporated it into their recording because they thought it was perfect for their single.

Version Two

Ohio Players' album Honey featured a naked woman dripping with honey as she knelt on a sheet of fiberglass. The album's producers—who were only looking for a sexy cover—didn't know that when honey hits fiberglass it forms an epoxy that is harder to dissolve than Super Glue. By the time the photo shoot was over, the poor girl's legs were permanently affixed to the fiberglass. The girl's skin

had to be sliced away from the fiberglass sheet, and she was left with such dreadful scars that her career as a model was over.

A few weeks later, while Ohio Players was recording "Love Roller Coaster," the maimed model broke into the recording studio, pulled a pistol out of her handbag and threatened to kill the band for ruining her life. The band's manager had a pocketknife; before the crazed woman could fire a shot, he stabbed her to death.

All this occurred while the tape was rolling. The sound of screaming on the final recording is the model's death scream.

Variations: The producer of the "Love Roller Coaster" single found the tape of a woman's death scream as she was being murdered. Without Ohio Players' knowledge, he had the engineers insert the scream behind the music. When the band got wind of the producer's trick, they vowed never to play "Love Roller Coaster" in concert or at any television appearance. Yet another version says that while the band was recording the song in guitarist/vocalist Jimmy Bonner's apartment, a woman was being murdered next door. The sound engineers at the recording studio heard the faint sound of screaming on the tape, so they enhanced it and made it part of the song.

The Haunted Shower

A kid in one of the dorms at the University of Florida kept to himself. He never invited friends to his room. He never hung out with anyone else in the dorm. And whenever there was a party in the dorm lounge, he would remain in his room.

Some of the rowdier guys on his floor started to play stupid practical jokes on the loner. But no matter what they did, the kid made no response. Soon, frustration turned the jokers mean.

The dorm bathrooms had never been updated. If a toilet was flushed while someone was taking a shower, the guy in the shower was hit by a sudden blast of hot water.

One night the quiet kid came back to the dorm late from studying, dropped his backpack on his desk and went down the hall to the bathroom for a shower. This was the opportunity the jokers had been waiting for. They waited until they heard the sound of running water in the shower stall, then they slipped into the bathroom, bolted the door, turned off all the lights so their victim wouldn't be able to identify them, and started flushing every toilet in the bathroom.

The kid screamed when the scalding water hit his naked body. He tried to open the shower door, but in his panic and with the lights off he couldn't find the handle. Meanwhile, the jokers kept flushing the toilets, laughing hysterically as their victim, trapped in the shower stall, shrieked in pain.

No one knows how long it went on, but when the kid stopped screaming, the jokers stopped flushing. The eerie silence in the

dark, steamy bathroom made the guys uncomfortable. "Let's take him back to his room," one of the guys suggested. He opened the shower door and there was the quiet kid, curled up in the corner of the stall, scalded to death.

The five jokers left the corpse where it was and ran from the bathroom. The police never discovered who perpetrated the prank. But over the following months, the five guys met with a series of accidents: One died when he slipped in the bathroom and fell out an open window. Another hanged himself in the shower stall where the quiet kid had died. A third broke a mirror in the bathroom and slit his throat with one of the shards of glass. A fourth drowned in the whirlpool. The fifth and last surviving member of the group refused to go anywhere near the bathroom. He stopped showering. He used his wastepaper basket as a toilet. Finally he locked himself in his dorm room and refused to come out. When campus security finally broke down his door, they found a filthy, stinking madman cowering in the corner. He is still in the state insane asylum.

The Trooper's Accident

A New Jersey state trooper accidentally shot and killed himself while trying to put his firearm back into its holster. A week after the tragedy, a 20-year veteran of the force showed a rookie how the mishap occurred.

"He had his weapon in his hand, see?" the senior trooper said. To demonstrate, he took his own firearm out of its holster. "And he was going to put the gun back in the holster when he fumbled."

The trooper pretended that the gun was about to slip out of his hand.

"So instead of sliding into the holster, the weapon wound up pointing against his side. Like this."

The veteran cop held his own firearm against his side, the barrel of the gun resting on his belt.

"And before he knew what happened, he accidentally pulled the trigger."

With that there was the sound of a gunshot. The veteran trooper dropped his weapon and clutched his side as blood poured out of the gaping wound. He collapsed and died before the paramedics could get him to a hospital.

"Bart Simpson Is Sleeping with Your Wives!"
and Other Military Misadventures

"Bart Simpson Is Sleeping with Your Wives!"

During the Gulf War, the Iraqi propaganda ministry was ordered to create radio programs in English designed to undermine the morale of American troops in the Gulf region. The official in charge of the agency had a foolproof plan: He would use American popular culture against the Americans. But since his staff was woefully underinformed about American society, he gave them magazines such as *People*, *Entertainment Weekly* and *Tiger Beat* to help them find contemporary references to use against the U.S. troops.

One staffer had a copy of *People* magazine with a photo of Brad Pitt on the cover but a subhead that read, "Bart Simpson is hot!"

The next day American troops heard a radio broadcast from the "Voice of Iraq's" English-speaking announcer, Baghdad Betty, in which she urged them to return home quickly because "Bart Simpson is sleeping with your wives!"

How Navy Fighter Pilots Spell Relief

Every man who signs up as a Navy fighter pilot knows the risks, but one hazard arose recently in the Arabian Sea that no recruit could have anticipated: The carrier *Theodore Roosevelt* ran out of piddle packs.

For the sake of civilians who aren't up on the latest military technology, a piddle pack is a resealable plastic bag with a sponge inside. Since fighter jets do not come equipped with toilets, the

piddle pack enables squadrons to relieve themselves in flight. In fall 2001, due to a bureaucratic snafu, no piddle packs were delivered to the *Theodore Roosevelt*. Suddenly the nine-hour flight to and from Afghanistan seemed more grim than usual.

When word of the shortage got out, members of the fighter squadron took emergency measures. A certain pilot embraced the idea that he was "a squadron of one," and began surreptitiously hoarding piddle packs in his footlocker. (During a routine inspection he was found to have concealed two dozen packs in his helmet bag.) Other members of the squadron adopted a personal dehydration program—they refused to drink any fluids for eight hours before their mission. More imaginative sorts put their trust in Emergency In-Flight Relief Vessels—empty Gatorade bottles.

While the piddle packs were on back order, officials at the main supply depot offered the men of *Theodore Roosevelt* an alternative: Depends. The commander of the carrier rejected the suggestion. "The last thing we need," he said, "is to have Al Qaeda take a downed U.S. pilot and parade him before television cameras in a diaper."

The Boy Who Wrote "Taps"

The Nelson family had a farm in Kentucky in the 1850s. Like so many of their neighbors, the Nelsons were torn by vehement arguments over slavery and states' rights. The father of the family upheld the old ways, while his youngest son argued just as passionately for the equality of all men. When the Civil War broke

out in 1861, the elder Nelson fought for the Confederacy, while his son enlisted in the Union army.

Two years passed without a single letter between father and son. Yet in spite of the silence, both men were enduring an agony of conscience. Neither could bear to be at odds with the other, but both were proud men and unwilling to be the first to back down. While the father tried to distract himself with visions of a glorious independent South, the son indulged in one of his favorite pastimes—writing music.

In July 1863, the two armies met amid the rich farmland of Pennsylvania at a little town called Gettysburg. Neither Nelson knew the other was there. On the third day of the battle, a Confederate major general named George Pickett led a suicidal charge across open country and up a steep hill toward the Union lines. Nelson Senior was among the few Southern fighting men to breach the Union defenses. As he climbed over the barricade he saw a young wounded soldier lying in the mud, near death. There was something familiar about the young man, so Nelson stepped closer. To his horror he recognized the dying soldier as his son.

As the battle raged on, father and son tried to say all the things they had yearned to say to each other during those two lost years, but the boy died a few minutes after his father found him.

As he clutched his dead son's body, Nelson heard the sound of crumpling paper. He reached inside his son's pocket and pulled out a sheet of music the boy had written.

The Southern troops were falling back. After placing a final kiss on his son's forehead, Nelson retreated to the Confederate lines.

At camp that night, Nelson found a bugler and asked him to

play the tune his son had written. The slow, sad air the bugler played that night is still played today. It is known as "Taps."

Where Have All the Flying Saucers Gone?

The English Society for the Encouragement of Sightings of Flying Saucers, the oldest organization to monitor UFO sightings, has disbanded.

The last president of the society, Edwin Treacle, explained that in recent years UFO sightings have virtually ceased. He attributed the abrupt end of UFO visitations to the end of the Cold War.

"We got their attention when the Americans set off two atomic bombs at the end of World War II," Treacle said. "That's why the flying saucers kept coming into Earth's airspace—to see how dangerous we were and if we posed a threat to other civilizations in the galaxy."

Now that the Cold War has ended and atomic-bomb testing is a thing of the past, visitors from other planets have lost interest in Earth.

Treacle said, "They've probably concluded that we are safe, but dull."

That's No Way to Ask for a Divorce

A soldier serving overseas received a video tape from his wife with a note that read, "Watch this when you are alone!" The soldier could hardly wait to see the video. He figured it had to be something really steamy.

That night, after everyone in his barracks was asleep, the soldier crept out of his bunk and took the tape to the mess tent where there was a television and VCR. He popped in the tape and made himself comfortable.

He immediately recognized his bedroom back home and saw that a man and woman were making love in his bed. The soldier couldn't believe that his wife had managed to secretly tape one of their nights together. And in spite of the fact that the picture was dark—the only light in the room came from a single candle—the video was more exciting than anything he had ever watched. He was proud of the fact that he could please his wife as much as the squeals she let out indicated.

Once the action was over, his wife switched on the bedside lamp. She pulled down the sheet, and the man beside her sat up and faced the camera. The soldier was stunned to see that the man who had made love to his wife was a stranger!

His smiling wife said sweetly into the camera, "I want a divorce!" and the screen went black.

The Rarest Fighting Aircraft of All

The Holy Grail for directors of military museums is the Lockheed Hudson bomber, one of the rarest fighting aircraft in the world. Only a handful were built during World War II, and only one survived the war intact—or so say the residents of southwest Nova Scotia, who claim that a pristine Lockheed Hudson lies beneath the surface of Lake Gaspereau.

In winter 1943, a Hudson bomber returning from bombing German U-boats off the coast of Canada ran out of fuel as it approached its base in Nova Scotia. The pilot landed the plane safely on the frozen surface of Lake Gaspereau and radioed the base to send out a tanker so they could refuel.

Once the fuel tank was full, the pilot started the twin engines and prepared for takeoff. The plane had not even begun to taxi when the crew heard the sound of ice breaking up. The vibrations from the plane engines had shattered the lake's frozen surface.

The crew scrambled out of the bomber and were running toward the shore when, with a tremendous roar, the ice around the plane gave way and the Lockheed Hudson sank to the bottom of the lake.

It is still there today, waiting to be salvaged.

Ollie North Tried to Warn Us

One of the most dramatic moments during the Iran– Contra scandal was Lt. Col. Oliver North's appearance before the Senate committee investigating the case.

At one point a senator asked North, "Did you not spend close to $60,000 for a home security system?"

North replied, "Yes, sir, I did."

The senator continued, "Don't you think that is a little much for a private citizen to spend on home security?"

"No, sir," North said.

"Indeed. And why not?" the senator asked.

"Because my life and the lives of every member of my family were threatened, sir."

The senator could not believe Colonel North's testimony.

"Threatened? Threatened by whom?" he said.

"By a terrorist, sir," North replied.

"A terrorist has threatened you? Who is this terrorist who threatens to attack an American family?"

"His name," said North, "is Osama bin Laden, sir."

At this point the senator tried to repeat the name, but couldn't pronounce it. A few people in the committee room laughed at the senator's feeble attempt. He blushed, but he kept talking.

"If this terrorist is so dangerous, what do you think should be done about him?"

"Well sir," North said, "if it were up to me, I would organize a special team to eliminate bin Laden and his men from the face of the earth."

"This is nonsense," the senator said. "The United States is not in the business of killing unknown individuals who pose no danger to the nation. I think you have an exaggerated sense of your own importance, Colonel North," the senator said.

The senator who interrogated Colonel North that day was from Tennessee and his name—Al Gore.

The Marines Send a Message

The next time you see President George W. Bush leaving his helicopter, watch the marine standing at the foot of the helicopter's stairs. He will give the commander in chief a sharp salute, then, as the president walks away, the marine will execute a right face and stand facing the president's back.

This tradition dates back to the 19th century. On U.S. Navy sailing ships, the captain used to be attended by a marine orderly. This marine always faced the captain, no matter where the officer stood, so he would be ready at a moment's notice to receive and perform the captain's orders.

The funny thing about this venerable sign of respect is that the marines never extended it to Bill Clinton when he was president. Throughout the eight years of the Clinton presidency, whenever the president descended the helicopter steps, the marine guard executed a sharp salute but never turned to face the commander in chief.

Standard Equipment

National Public Radio interviewed a U.S. Army general who had started a Boy Scout troop for the sons of officers. The interviewer asked the general if a Boy Scout troop on a military base learned things other Boy Scouts did not.

"No, we follow the standard program," the general said.

"We teach them about honor and responsibility, we teach them wilderness survival skills, and we give them instruction in canoeing, archery and how to shoot a rifle."

"Why are you teaching these boys how to shoot, General?" asked the interviewer.

"It's an outdoors skill," the general answered, "It's no different than learning how to pitch a tent in the dark or start a fire without matches."

"But isn't putting a rifle in the hands of children irresponsible?" the interviewer replied.

"No. We teach them that a rifle is dangerous and not to be played with. And they are closely supervised at all times while on the rifle range."

"But by teaching these boys how to shoot a rifle," the interviewer said, "don't you see that you are equipping them with the kind of skills that encourage them to become violent killers?"

The general was silent for a moment, then said, "Ma'am, you're taking this to an extreme. Just because a man has a gun doesn't mean that he's a murderer. One could say that you're equipped to be a prostitute, but I'll bet you aren't one."

The Senator Who Snubbed the Gold Star Mothers

The Gold Star Mothers was founded after World War I. It is an organization of women whose sons or daughters died in combat while serving in the United States armed forces. Recently a delegation of New York State Gold Star Mothers traveled to Washington, D.C., to meet their senators and representatives and discuss the group's concerns regarding benefits for the families of servicemen and women who were killed in the line of duty.

Everywhere they went in Washington, these women received a warm welcome. President George W. Bush invited the delegation to the White House for a private lunch with the president and the first lady, Laura Bush. They received the red-carpet treatment on Capitol Hill where Senate Majority Leader Tom Daschle and Vice-President Dick Cheney invited the women to their private offices to discuss the women's concerns.

If the top lawmakers in the land received the Gold Star Mothers so warmly, it stands to reason that the senators and representatives from the state of New York would also be generous with their time. And for the most part the New Yorkers in Congress did just that.

With one exception. Senator Hillary Clinton refused repeated requests to meet with the Gold Star Mothers. When the ladies asked to meet with members of her staff instead, Senator Clinton rejected that request, too.

The reason? Hillary Clinton's hatred of the U.S. military is so deeply rooted that she cannot even bear to be in the same room with mothers whose children gave their lives for America.

Every Hoof Tells a Story

Cities across the globe have monuments that show their fallen heroes riding horseback. Very few people who see these monuments realize the statues actually contain a secret code: The number of the horse's hooves lifted into the air tells how the rider died.

If a statue shows the horse with both front legs in the air, the person died in battle. If the horse is shown with only one leg lifted, the person died as a result of wounds received in combat. And if the horse has all four legs on the ground, the person died of natural causes.

Short Takes 8

• Air Force One, the U.S. president's plane, emits radio waves that neutralize automatic garage door openers.

• During wartime, a man or woman who is an only child is exempt from military service.

• During World War I, the sight of American GIs blowing bubbles with their chewing gum terrified French and German peasants. The country people thought Americans were freaks who could expel their lungs from their mouths and then suck them back in again.

• All branches of the United States armed forces put saltpeter in the food to curb the sexual appetites of their servicemen.

• All branches of the French armed forces put saltpeter in the wine to curb the sexual appetites of their servicemen.

• All branches of the Polish armed forces put saltpeter in the vodka to curb the sexual appetites of their servicemen.

Bronco Stadium's Smurf Turf
and Other Tales of the Great Outdoors

Bronco Stadium's Smurf Turf

There was never any question that Boise State University's Bronco Stadium would have artificial grass. It had been part of the stadium planners' design from the beginning. However, the planners and university administrators debated the color the artificial grass should be. Finally, they agreed on covering the field in royal blue and the end zones in orange, Boise's colors, rather than the standard grassy green.

The colors did make Bronco Stadium stand out from other sports arenas. And the university didn't mind that sports reporters christened their azure artificial grass "Smurf Turf" since the garish colors told visiting teams that they were definitely on somebody else's home turf.

Then one day a flock of Canadian geese winging its way over Boise spotted the stadium and, mistaking the blue turf for a lake, swooped in for a landing. Instead of gliding gently across a watery surface, the geese lurched and skidded and bounced on the plastic grass. Aside from some bruises and abrasions, the geese were unharmed by the rough landings.

Not wanting a similar incident to occur in the middle of a game, the coaches and school administration rethought the color scheme. Today the artificial grass of Bronco Stadium is striped instead of solid blue.

"You Killed Skippy!"

Microsoft offers its salespeople generous incentives. The top prize for the sales team that writes the most business is an all-expenses-paid golf outing to Australia where Microsoft sponsors a tournament.

One year, against all odds, the sales team from Microsoft beat the pros in the tournament and were awarded the prestigious green jackets. That night the Microsoft sales team partied like rock stars.

After downing way too many beers, the Americans piled into their rental car and headed back to the resort hotel where they were staying. Naturally, they got lost. As they careened down a dark deserted road, something large jumped in front of the car. The driver swerved, but even if his reflexes had not been severely beer-impaired, he would have hit the thing. Everyone in the car heard the loud "Thump!" and felt the car shake as the right fender glanced off the big object in their path.

The driver brought the car to a skidding stop, and the sales team stumbled out to see what the car had hit. Lying on the side of the road was a large adult kangaroo.

One of the drunks knelt down beside the animal, stroked its head, and said to the driver, "You killed Skippy!"

"Come on," one of the other drunks said. "Hitting kangaroos in Australia has got to be like hitting deer at home. We'll just roll him off the road and get out of here."

"Right," the driver said. "But first we need a picture."

While the drunks hauled the kangaroo to a standing position,

the driver pulled off his green golf tournament jacket and dressed the kangaroo in it. He mounted the camera on a tripod, set the timer, and squeezed himself into the group shot, right next to the kangaroo.

A heartbeat after the flash went off, the kangaroo began to stir. "Look!" one of the drunks cried. "Skippy's alive!"

Now fully conscious and not at all happy to be surrounded by drunken humans, the kangaroo drew itself up to its full height, jabbed with its right paw, and broke the driver's jaw. Then the animal bolted into the darkness, still wearing the driver's green golf jacket.

The driver collapsed to the ground, clutching his shattered face and moaning.

"We gotta get you to a hospital," one of his friends said. "Where are the car keys?"

The driver groaned. "They're in my jacket."

Variations: In other versions of the kangaroo story, the animal hops off wearing an expensive Gucci jacket, or wearing a jacket that holds the car keys, as well as the driver's wallet and passport.

Cobra in the Clothes Hamper

A woman shopping at Pier One asked a sales clerk if he had any wicker clothes hampers in stock.

"You're in luck," the clerk told her and led her to the back of the store. "We just got a shipment from India. Take your pick!"

The woman selected a large wicker hamper woven in a complicated pattern. At home, the woman placed the hamper in the corner of the bathroom, threw in some dirty laundry and replaced the lid.

A couple of days later, the hamper was full. The woman removed the lid and began sorting the laundry by color. When she was close to the bottom of the hamper, she heard a low hiss. It was July, so clearly the sound was not coming from the radiator. None of the spray cans were leaking and the pipes under the sink were securely tightened. She listened more closely and realized that the hissing sound was coming from the clothes hamper.

Using the handle of the toilet plunger, the woman carefully lifted out the laundry piece by piece. As she reached for the last item in the hamper, a towel, it began to move. The woman leaped back. The hissing grew louder, and the head of a cobra began to rise slowly over the rim of the hamper. The woman screamed and bolted out of the bathroom, slamming the door behind her.

She called the town's animal control department, which sent out a technician immediately. It took him less than five minutes to capture the cobra and lock it securely in a steel crate.

"Let me guess," the technician said to the woman. "You bought

the hamper at Pier One."

"Yes!" she said. "How did you know?"

"We get dozens of these calls every year. If it isn't cobras it's scorpions. You've got to be careful with these Indian imports. There's no telling what gets into them."

Variation: A related version of the story tells of a woman who shopped at a discount clothing outlet. She decided to try on a coat that had been made in India, unaware that a cobra lurked in one of the sleeves. When the woman slipped her arm into the sleeve, the snake bit her and she died.

The .22 Caliber Fuse

Two Arkansas men, Bobby Noseworthy and Sonny Campbell, went frog hunting up in the mountains. As they headed home, the headlights on Bobby's pickup truck went out. They pulled over and discovered that a fuse had burned out. Bobby didn't have a spare fuse in the truck, but Sonny realized that a bullet from his .22 caliber pistol was just the right size for the fuse box. They decided to try it.

The bullet worked! The headlights flickered on, and the boys were on their way. They had gone about ten miles and were following a winding mountain road when the heat from the truck's engine finally proved too much for the bullet. It fired itself from the fuse box and into the cabin of the truck, striking Bobby in the

right testicle. He lost control of the vehicle and crashed through the guardrail. The Arkansas State Police found the men's pickup suspended in the tree two hours later.

Sonny got away with just a few scratches and bruises, but Bobby lost the testicle. When two state troopers called on Bobby's wife to tell her the news, she hung her head and was quiet for a time. Then she asked, "Did they get many frogs?"

Swallowed by an Anaconda

In a village deep in the Amazon rainforest lived a husband and wife and their three sons. The family slept in the same part of the hut together, side by side.

One morning the family awoke to find that the youngest boy was missing. An enormous anaconda lay in his place, its belly grotesquely distended.

The family's screams brought the rest of the villagers to the hut. One villager had his machete with him and slit open the anaconda's belly. There was the missing boy, perfectly intact but dead.

There are now photos circulating on the Internet of the boy's body protruding from the snake's slit belly.

Variations: Doctored photos of the kid-swallowed-by-a-snake have been circulating on the Internet at least since 2000. Only the setting changes: Asia, Africa, the South Pacific–basically any tropical locale where huge serpents can be found.

The Stunted Trees of Turtle Bay

On the East Side of Manhattan in the 40s is a neighborhood known as Turtle Bay. The name dates from colonial times when an inlet on the East River was teeming with turtles. The original cove that gave the neighborhood its name was filled in when the United Nations complex was constructed there in the 1950s. In fact, this once bucolic area of New York is today a mass of soaring office towers and apartments. The tall buildings kept one street in particular in the East 40s in almost perpetual shade.

Years ago the merchants and residents of Turtle Bay planted saplings along the street, but the lack of sunlight stunted their growth; the trees never grew taller than seven or eight feet.

Then in the 1990s, a real estate developer purchased one of the old post–World War II white brick apartment houses. He tore it down and built a sleek modern apartment tower, its entire exterior covered with glass.

Then a strange thing occurred. The trees along East 47th Street began to grow. Their trunks thickened; they put out new branches; and within two years after the construction of the new apartment tower, the once-stunted trees soared to twenty feet high.

The perplexed residents of East 47th Street invited a botanist from the New York Botanical Gardens to come and inspect their trees and explain why, after years of being dormant, the trees were flourishing.

The botanist saw the reason within minutes of his arrival. "It's the new apartment building," he said. "The glass surface reflects the

sun and gives these trees the one thing they have needed and been lacking all those years—light."

"I Need a Bambulance!"

A man in rural Minnesota stopped at a roadside tavern for just one beer but wound up having several more than planned. As he was driving home on a dark country road, a deer jumped in front of his car. The drunk driver tried to swerve out of the way, but the beer had affected his reflexes. He clipped the deer with the car's right fender, sending the poor animal sprawling into a ditch.

The man was about to continue on, but decided he should take the perfectly good venison home to eat instead of leaving it in the ditch to rot.

He pulled over, dragged the animal out of the ditch and tied it to the hood of his car. It was then that he started feeling a little guilty.

"Poor little fella," he said as he stroked the deer's neck. "I didn't mean to hit you." Suddenly the drunk was sobbing, "I hate myself. I killed Bambi!"

At that moment, the deer stirred, started thrashing about and tried to get free of the rope that bound it.

"You're alive!" the drunk cried. "I didn't kill you! You must have just been stunned. Look, stay where you are. I'll get help."

The drunk staggered back to this car, took out his cell phone and dialed 911. "Hello! I'm on Route 6. I just hit a deer, and I need a Bambulance."

The Flying Deer Ticks

A Connecticut woman was driving home when a deer jumped over a stone wall and landed in the road directly in front of her car. She struck the animal head–on. The deer was propelled over the hood of the automobile and crashed through the windshield. From the force of the impact, hundreds of deer ticks flew off the deer and landed in the car and on the driver.

Local residents called an ambulance, which rushed the woman to a nearby hospital. After a thorough examination, the emergency room doctor gave the woman the results of the tests.

"The good news is you just have a few abrasions and bruises. No tissue damage, no broken bones, no internal bleeding," the doctor said. "The bad news is that the deer ticks gave you a fatal case of Lyme disease."

The Baby and the Bear

A family of nomads set up their tent in a remote corner of Iran. They had barely settled in when their herd of goats broke out of its pen and scattered across the countryside. The mother placed her six-month-old baby in its cradle and joined the rest of the family as it fanned out to recover the livestock.

After an hour, the family returned. While the rest of the clan drove the goats back into the pen, the mother went into the tent to check on the infant. The baby was gone!

The distraught family searched the area for some sign of what could have happened to the child. The grandfather spotted the first trace of trouble—bear tracks that led away from the camp and toward the mountains.

The men of the family, along with men recruited from nearby camps, set off in pursuit of the bear.

After six days of scouring the area, the hunters found a cave. The child's father lit a torch and crawled inside with two other men. It was a bear's den but, fortunately for the hunters, the bear was not there. And the baby didn't seem to be in the cave either.

As the men turned to leave, they heard the gurgling sound of a happy child. In a dark corner of the cave, lying on a bed of pine needles, they discovered the baby, unharmed, still wrapped in its blanket and obviously well fed. Beside the infant lay the body of a stillborn bear cub.

The mother bear had stolen the infant to replace her dead cub and had nursed the child as tenderly as if it were her own.

Short Takes 9

• Chickens are so dumb they'll look up at falling rain until the raindrops fill their beaks and nostrils, and the birds drown.

• To prevent overpopulation, chemical reactions occur in lemmings that cause the animals to stampede over a cliff to their deaths.

• Birds eat the rice thrown at weddings, but they can't digest it. Their stomachs swell as the grains enlarge, and the birds die in agony.

• Because of the insect's benefits to nature, it is a felony to kill a praying mantis.

• Opossums hang from tree limbs by their tails.

• The deadliest insect in the world is the daddy longlegs.

• Elephants are afraid of mice.

• If a human touches a baby bird, the bird's mother will reject it.

• The duck's quack is the only sound that does not echo.

• Rattlesnakes eat wild turkey eggs. When the wild turkey population in the woods of southern Ohio got out of control, the Department of Fish and Game attached baskets of rattlesnake eggs

to hot air balloons, gave each balloon a slow leak, and then released it. The baskets floated gently to earth in the wild turkey–infested forest, where the hungry snakes hatched and grew fat on wild turkey eggs.

• To frustrate deer hunters, animal rights activists captured 405 wild deer, dressed them in the bright orange vests hunters wear, and turned the animals loose in the woods. The vests functioned for the deer as they do for hunters–they kept the animals from being shot.

• In response to the rash of deer-and-auto collisions, a mail order company has been selling deer whistles to mount on automobiles. The sound is supposed to drive deer away. However, it actually causes obscure genetic coding in the deer to react, and the animals explode.

• If you cut off a cockroach's head, it will take nine days for the insect to die. The bug doesn't die because it's been beheaded; it starves to death.

THE CAT IN THE DRYER
AND OTHER PET-RELATED LEGENDS

The Cat in the Dryer

After ignoring the family laundry for a week and a half, a mother of five found herself facing a mountain of dirty clothes. Once her husband had left for work and the kids were off to school, the woman decided to devote an entire day to catching up on the laundry.

When the first load was dry, the woman removed the clean clothes and began folding them on the laundry-room table. Attracted by the warmth coming from the machine, the family cat slipped inside the dryer unnoticed by its owner. The washer finished its cycle and the woman transferred the soggy towels to the dryer, unaware that her pet was relaxing inside.

She returned to the laundry room a half hour later and removed the load, which seemed strangely heavy for a bunch of towels. When she placed the towels on the folding table, she noticed a tail sticking out from the pile. Frantically she pawed through the towels until she uncovered the cat. It was still breathing but unconscious.

Fifteen minutes later she came to a screeching halt in front of the veterinarian's office.

"As you'd expect," the vet told the woman, "she's pretty dehydrated. Leave her overnight, and she'll be herself again by morning.

The woman thanked the vet and as she turned to leave, he said, half joking, "You'd think I would have gotten a shock from a cat that had been in the dryer for so long."

"Oh no," replied the woman in all seriousness. "I use dryer sheets. They keep everything static free."

Caught Black-handed

A young man from a small dusty town in South Dakota had a rich uncle in California. The boy's parents wrote their wealthy relative asking him to help their son by giving him an entry level job at his firm. The uncle agreed on the condition that the young man could demonstrate that he was mature, responsible, and alert. To this end, the rich uncle invited his nephew to spend the weekend at his mansion in Beverly Hills.

The boy arrived at his uncle's house on Friday afternoon. He was polite and deferential to his aunt and uncle and even played with their prize toy poodle. As the kid was about to go to bed his uncle said, "You're off to a good start, boy. But tomorrow night's the real test. I'm giving a dinner party for my business partners and their wives. We'll see how you act in a crowd."

The boy from South Dakota could not sleep that night. What if he said the wrong thing to one of his uncle's partners? Or used the dessert fork when he should have used the shrimp fork?

All day Saturday, as the household staff prepared for the evening's party, the kid became more and more agitated.

When the hour for the party arrived at last, he came down from his room smartly dressed in a tuxedo his uncle had ordered for him. He went directly to the bar, "Just to take the edge off," he told himself. But as the guests arrived, the kid found it difficult to talk to any of them. He didn't play golf. He didn't like opera. And didn't understand a thing about the commodities market (except, perhaps, that he was more intimately familiar with pork bellies than

anyone else in the room). So the boy kept returning to the bar.

Once dinner was over the kid knew he was drunk so he slipped away to his uncle's office, sat down in the huge red leather desk chair, and fell asleep.

When he woke up the room was pitch black and the house was absolutely still. Although he was still half-drunk, the kid was able to figure out that the party must have ended. "The coast is clear!" he thought. He put both hands on the desk top and lifted himself out of the chair, but he felt something odd: one hand was dripping wet.

He grabbed for the desk lamp to see what he put his hand in, but he could not find the switch. "There's a light plate by the door," he thought. "I'll go turn that on." But as he tried to walk across the dark room, he tripped over a piece of furniture and fell flat on the antique Persian carpet. Holding on to a chair, he pulled himself up, managed to get to the door, and started patting the wall with his wet hand until at last he found the panel. The room suddenly blazed with light, and the kid was horrified by what he saw. He had put his hand in an open ink well, and now everything he had touched—the rare carpet, the antique furniture, the silk wall coverings—were stained with his black handprints.

He ran to his room and stayed in bed until eleven the next morning. When at last he came downstairs, he went straight to his uncle's office to apologize.

His uncle was seated at his desk. Most of the ink had been cleaned away, but the carpet was still stained, and so was the silk wallpaper. The boy's uncle did not look happy. Standing at the threshold the boy said, "Please uncle, I'd like to try to explain." His uncle beckoned him into the office and the kid walked across the

room. Just as he got to his uncle's desk he heard a crunching sound under one foot. "I don't know how to tell you this, sir," the boy said, "but I think I just crushed something."

"Yes," the uncle said. "That was my poodle."

Back from the Dead

A family from Chicago took their elderly black Labrador retriever with them on a trip to Yellowstone National Park. They had only been at the park for two days when the dog died. The children insisted their pet be buried in their yard in Chicago, but the parents couldn't imagine driving back home with the dead animal in their trunk.

After a long argument the father suggested they take the dog's body to a veterinarian, who would keep it on ice until the end of the family's vacation and then air ship it to their home for the backyard funeral.

A few days later the crate carrying the Lab's corpse arrived at O'Hare International Airport. One of the handlers peered inside the screen in the crate and was surprised to see a dead dog. He called his supervisor over.

"Jeez, Eddie, look at this," the baggage handler said. "The poor pooch died in transit."

"That's a damn shame," his boss said. "The family is going to be heartsick when the crate arrives. But there's nothing we can do about it."

As his supervisor walked away, the baggage handler decided

there was something he could do about it. During his lunch hour he drove to the dog pound, found a black Lab and adopted it. He drove back to the airport with the dog, took the corpse out of the crate and put the live Lab inside. Then he sent it on its way.

The children were ecstatic when they opened the crate and out bounded a live dog.

"God raised Blackie from the dead!" the little boy cried.

"And he made him a lot younger, too!" the little girl said.

"And this time God made Blackie a female," the mother whispered to her husband.

How Dogtown Got Its Name

After the St. Louis, Missouri World's Fair closed in 1904, members of the Igorot tribe from the Philippines, one of the "living exhibits" at the fair, decided to take up residence in the neighborhood.

Not long after the Igorots were settled, local residents noticed that all of the stray dogs had vanished. Then their pets began to disappear. At first, residents suspected professional dognappers, but that theory evaporated when none of the pet owners received a ransom note.

The police department received so many complaints that it launched a formal investigation. Eventually, the department discovered the source of the trouble. The Igorots had been stealing the dogs and cooking them for dinner.

The neighborhood on the western edge of St. Louis where the Igorot settled is now known as Dogtown.

The Price of Losing

One of the most popular attractions in New York's Chinatown is the chicken that plays ticktacktoe. For $5, anyone can step up to the stall and play against the smartest piece of poultry in Manhattan.

The astonishing thing about this attraction (aside from the fact that you are playing against a chicken) is that the bird almost never loses. The chicken has a powerful incentive to win and somehow knows her situation is precarious: If the human player loses, he or she is out $5, but if the chicken loses, she becomes that night's dinner.

Leave the Dog at Home

Ice fishermen in Minnesota tell the story of Blackie, a Labrador retriever that loved to play fetch. One frigid day in January, Blackie was sitting in his owner's fishing shack on Lake La Croix. Through the hole in the ice, Blackie saw a pike swim by and dove into the water after it.

Naturally the fish was faster than the dog and got away, but not before poor Blackie was trapped beneath the ice. He couldn't find his way back to his owner's fishing hole, and he was running out of air. Luckily, Blackie saw a glimmer of light from one of the shanties. He swam toward the light. When he was almost out of breath, the dog reached the hole and rocketed up out of the water and into the fishing hut.

The sight of a Labrador retriever leaping out of the frozen

lake frightened the fisherman whose hut Blackie had invaded. The poor man bolted out of the shack, raced across the ice, jumped into his pickup truck and headed for home where he promised his astonished wife that he would never drink whiskey again.

The Poop Bandits

A well-to-do, retired gentleman lived on New York's Upper East Side with his St. Bernard. Three times a day he took his dog for a walk. Because a St. Bernard produces a prodigious amount of poop, the gentleman always took a small garden shovel and a paper bag along on the walks to clean up after his dog.

One Saturday afternoon the man and the dog were at the tail end of their walk. In his right hand, the man carried a Saks Fifth Avenue shopping bag containing the St. Bernard's waste. While man and dog waited at a street corner for the light to change, three 13-year-old boys rushed up behind them, grabbed the shopping bag and ran away.

A doorman from a nearby apartment building hurried over and offered to call the police. The man with the dog told him not to bother. "They deserve what's in the bag," he said.

Variations: Thieves who don't get quite what they expected is a common strain in urban legends. One spin on this story has a female thief at a shopping mall run off with a package that contains a dead cat. Another version tells of carjackers who see a large bundle on the roof of a vacationing family's car and steal the automobile (the

bundle contains the corpse of the family's grandmother). From South Africa comes another story in which thieves carry off a large trunk that contains a live and very unhappy cheetah.

The Pampered Poodle

A woman had a poodle of whom she was inordinately fond. It slept on a toy bed in the woman's bedroom, ate from a silver bowl, wore a diamond-studded collar and went everywhere the woman went.

When the lady retired to Florida, she and the poodle had a fine time exploring all the wonderful sights. They toured the Everglades, visited Disney World and enjoyed the beaches at Miami. One day the lady decided to visit Sea World, and of course she took her darling poodle.

The woman timed her visit so she could see the Sea World staff feed the sharks. At one in the afternoon, a large crowd gathered around the shark tank. The woman elbowed her way to the front and perched her poodle on the railing.

The sharks circled the pool, anxiously waiting their feeding. Two Sea World employees carried a large steel tank of raw meat to the edge of the pool and began throwing chunks to the hungry sharks. The poodle smelled the raw meat and wiggled and squirmed each time a chunk was tossed into the pool. One throw went slightly astray and landed in the pool just below the lady and her pooch. The dog saw the chunk of meat splash into the water, and leaped in after it. One shark snagged the piece of beef, while another gobbled up the poodle—diamond-studded collar and all.

The Crushed Kitty

Origins: This story is thought to have originated in the late 1980s in Perth, Australia, although there are also versions set in London, England, and various cities and towns across the United States.

An elderly lady called the fire department to ask them to retrieve her cat from a tree. The captain sent a small crew over with a rescue truck and extension ladder to do the job, and everything went according to plan: The tree was large and sturdy enough to support the ladder. The cat did not climb out of reach when it saw the fireman who had come to rescue it. And the old lady was suitably sweet and grateful.

As the firemen got back into their truck, the lady stood on her front steps, the cat in her frail arms, waving good-bye. Just as the truck began to pull out of the driveway, the cat scratched her owner, leaped from her arms and ran straight into the path of the rescue truck. The firemen had to scrape the crushed kitty off the driveway with a shovel.

THE DEADLY LAUNDRY CHUTE
AND OTHER COLLEGE TRADITIONS

The Deadly Laundry Chute

Soon after construction had been completed at a building on the Vanderbilt University campus in Nashville, Tennessee, six drunken frat boys decided to inspect the new structure.

The elevators weren't operational yet, so the guys stumbled up the stairs, exploring each floor on the way. They wandered through the dark halls, whooped and raced up and down the corridors, and tried to scare each other. On the fourth floor, one of the guys found a closet with a large hole in the back wall. He stuck his head in the opening and discovered a gleaming steel shaft.

"Hey, look!" he yelled. "I found a slide."

His drunken friends crowded into the closet for a closer look.

"That's not a slide, you moron," one of them said. "It's a laundry chute."

"No," the boy who found the closet said. "It's a slide. I'll prove it."

Before anyone could stop him, the kid climbed into the opening and launched himself down the slide. His friends could hear him hooting with excitement as he slid down four floors. As he drew near the opening, he crossed through a laser tracking beam, but didn't pay any attention to it. The next thing he knew, he had shot out of the dark chute and landed with a hard thump on a mass of flattened garbage.

"Aw, crap!" he said. Then he yelled up the shaft to his friends, "This is the garbage chute."

The next sound his friends heard was the grinding of heavy

gears as the trash compactor went into operation and began crushing everything in the dumpster.

Variations: Although the name of the school where this story is said to have taken place changes depending on who is telling the story, the location is firmly rooted in Tennessee. One version of the legend has the poor student being cut to pieces by the trash compactor, but this is less a variant than an imprecise understanding of how a trash compactor operates.

The Fallen Woman

An average student from a rural Indiana town managed to get accepted at the state university. For his first English assignment, the student wrote a paper about an accident in a short story the class had read. While the paper was generally acceptable, the professor was shocked to read the line, "The girl tumbled down the stairs and lay prostitute at the bottom."

When the professor returned the graded papers, the student found this comment written in the margins: "You must learn to distinguish between a fallen woman and one who has merely slipped."

Can You Identify This Leg?

A University of Wisconsin freshman signed up for an ornithology course. Over 200 students crammed into the lecture hall; and the professor who taught the class never bothered to learn any of the students names.

On the morning of the final exam, the professor showed a slide of two dozen varieties of bird legs and asked the students to identify each bird by its legs.

The freshman was furious. The professor had never taught the class how to distinguish one bird from another simply by looking at their legs. The student stood up and shouted, "This is ridiculous!" Then he marched down to the stage, tore up his blue exam book and threw the bits of paper in the professor's face.

"That's it, Mister!" the professor shouted. "You just failed this class. What's your name?"

The student pulled off his shoes and socks, rolled up his pants and showed his legs and feet to the professor. "You tell me, Prof."

Fraternity and Sorority Secrets
at the Library of Congress

In the 1950s, Senator Joseph McCarthy was convinced that
Communists had infiltrated American college campuses. Because he
thought it would be easiest for the Reds to conceal their agenda in
such secretive organizations as fraternities and sororities, McCarthy
ordered all Greek organizations to submit a description of their
secret rituals and copies of their secret oaths to his committee for
review. After the senator's investigation, these documents were
deposited in the Library of Congress.

But not all fraternities were subjected to McCarthy's scrutiny.
Harry S. Truman, who was president at the time, insisted on an
exception for his fraternity, Lambda Chi Alpha. J. Edgar Hoover,
director of the FBI, also demanded an exemption for his fraternity,
Kappa Alpha.

In later years, other presidents, senators and movers and shakers
in Washington had the records of their fraternities and sororities
removed from the Library of Congress stacks. Among those who
restored the secret material to their Greek brothers and sisters were
Barry Goldwater, Ronald Reagan, George Bush, Geraldine Ferraro,
Elizabeth Dole and Hillary Clinton.

Stand, Then Flush

A college sophomore traveling to Sweden for a semester abroad left her seat to visit the rest room after the plane had been in the air for about an hour.

Once finished, and before she stood up, she hit the flush button beside the toilet. This proved to be a mistake. The high-pressure flush vacuum-sealed the woman's bare bottom to the toilet seat. She tried desperately to dislodge herself, but the seal was airtight; her butt would not budge.

The girl was humiliated by the thought of strangers seeing her in this predicament, but she had no other option but to push the alarm button.

She only had to wait a moment before she heard an attendant on the other side of the door ask, "Can you tell me what's wrong?"

"I'm stuck to the toilet," the poor student said.

"Oh, boy. Okay Miss, unlock the door and I'll see what I can do."

From her position, the young woman couldn't reach the lock.

"I can't," she said. "It's too far away. Don't you have a key?"

The flight attendant went off to search for the bathroom key and returned about ten minutes later.

"Miss, we can't find the key. But don't worry! The pilot will break down the door."

The embarrassed college girl hid her face in her hands as the pilot threw his shoulder against the door until the lock snapped. For the next hour, flight attendants and the pilot tried to break the

vacuum seal, but no amount of tugging or prying could lift the girl off the toilet seat. At last the crew admitted defeat.

"Miss," the pilot said, "I've radioed Stockholm. The ground crew said that once the plane's septic tank is opened, the vacuum seal will release. But we can't do that in midflight. It can only be done on the ground. I'm afraid you'll have to stay here until we land."

The Fan Who Knew What He Wanted

An alumnus of the University of Georgia and a fan of its Bulldogs football team made a special trip to Georgia Tech's ticket office to buy two tickets for the Tech-Georgia game.

The clerk at the window explained that Tech-Georgia was the hottest game of the year. The only way to get seats was to buy two sets of Tech season tickets. The cost? Four hundred dollars.

The Georgia alum didn't say a word, he just reached into his pocket, pulled out a wad of cash, and peeled off four $100 bills.

The clerk took the money and handed the fan two books of tickets for the entire season.

The Georgia fan tore off the tickets for the Tech-Georgia game, then crumpled the rest of the tickets into a ball and threw them into a nearby garbage can.

Holding up the Tech-Georgia tickets in front of the clerk's face, the Georgia alum said, "This is the only Tech game worth seeing. Them other tickets ain't worth the paper they're printed on." And he walked out of Tech's ticket office.

"Remember Pearl Harbor!"

Friday morning, December 5, 1941, students, faculty and staff of a high school in Missouri arrived at the building to find "Remember Pearl Harbor!" scribbled on walls in the corridors, scrawled in lipstick on bathroom mirrors and written in huge block letters on the blackboard in every classroom.

No one had any idea where Pearl Harbor was or why he or she should remember it. Even the geography teacher had to look up Pearl Harbor in an atlas. By lunchtime all the "Remember Pearl Harbor!" messages had been removed, but the school was still spooked.

Two days later, on December 7, 1941, the Japanese attacked and all but destroyed the U.S. Pacific Fleet at Pearl Harbor. To this day, no one knows who posted the prophetic message all over the high school.

The Professor's Ultimatum

Although cell phones and Palm Pilots have become commonplace on college campuses, many students don't understand when and where not to use them. One professor insisted his students turn off all such electronic devices while in his classroom, but one student ignored the ban. No reprimand from the professor could stop the kid from receiving messages on his Palm Pilot.

On one particular day the student was getting a lot of e-mail.

This proved especially irritating since he had programmed the Palm Pilot to play "The Yellow Rose of Texas" every time it received a new message.

At the first interruption, the professor asked the student to turn off the Palm Pilot.

At the second interruption, the professor insisted that the student turn off the device.

At the third interruption, the professor stormed out of the classroom and hurried to his office. He sat at his computer and sent the disruptive student an e-mail: "Either turn off the machine or flunk the course."

When the professor returned to the classroom a few moments later, the disruptive student was gone.

Variation: There is also a British version of this story in which the offending e-mailer is a party guest. An hour or so into the evening, the hostess sends her guest a message: "Turn it off or go home." When she returns to the party the blushing guest is still there, but his Palm Pilot (in England they are called Blackberries) is turned off and in his pocket.

How to Avoid Getting Points on Your Driver's License

A college kid was returning to school after a weekend at his parents' house. His roommate was throwing a party that night, and the kid didn't want to miss it, so his foot was a little heavier on the accelerator than it should have been. About 20 miles from campus, the kid heard a siren and saw the flashing red and blue lights of a police car in his rearview mirror. The cop had clocked him doing 85 in a 55-miles-per-hour zone.

By the time the speeder arrived at his dorm, his roommate's party was in full swing. He waded his way into the crowd, and had a few beers, but his heart wasn't in it.

The next morning he told his roommate his problem. "I'm screwed," he said. "I got a speeding ticket last night. My dad is gonna kill me."

"How will he know?" the roommate said.

"The car's in his name," the speeder said. "He'll know when he gets a notice that he has three points on his license, and his insurance rates go up."

"Okay," the roommate said. "Here's what you do. How much is the fine?"

The speeder dug the ticket out of his pocket. "It's $115," he said, and then he groaned.

"Cool. Send the motor vehicle people a check for $120."

"Why would I send those bloodsuckers extra money?" the speeder asked.

"Because then they'll have to send you a refund," his roommate said.

"And this helps me how?"

"You don't cash the refund check," the roommate said. "Until all financial transactions have been completed, no points can appear on a driver's record. And since the bastards already have your fine, they aren't going to chase after you to cash a check for five bucks. Believe me, it's foolproof."

Spray-on Calories

Young people in California take their physical appearance very seriously—young women especially. Dieting has become so commonplace that no one even comments on it anymore. But when there was an outbreak of anorexia at the University of California at Davis, the campus administration decided to do something about it.

The administration consulted a dietitian, who studied the problem and devised an ingenious solution. She instructed the cafeteria staff to spray the vegetables at the salad bar with a tasteless, high-calorie food additive. Its impact on the women's weight would be negligible, but it would provide them with the nutrients their bodies needed to avoid becoming anorexic.

The Power of Positive Reinforcement

Students in an introductory psychology class decided to test the behaviorist theory their professor had taught them by running a little experiment in the principles of positive reinforcement. They agreed that when the professor stood near the wastepaper basket in the front corner of the classroom, they would all pay close attention to what he was saying. If he strayed to any other part of the room, they would fidget and cough and talk among themselves.

The class followed the strategy faithfully, and after two weeks, the professor delivered his entire lecture standing in the corner of the room beside the trashcan.

A few of the more ambitious students in the class decided to bump the experiment up a notch. They began to arrive early to turn over the trashcan. Now, the class would only pay attention to their teacher if he stood in the corner with one foot on the can. As the semester progressed they trained him to teach standing on the basket. By the end of the term, the psychology professor was so well trained that he would walk into class, turn the wastepaper basket upside down, climb on top of it and begin to teach.

Variations: In another version, the class trains their psychology professor to write only on the right-hand side of the blackboard. They keep narrowing the field until, by the end of the semester, the class will only be attentive if he writes in a tiny upper corner of the board. Still another variant has the students training their teacher to lecture while standing on one leg.

The Guardian Angels

A series of muggings and campus rapes struck terror at a small, Midwest college. The campus police beefed up security, and the college fraternities began escorting female students to their dorms after dark, but the attacks continued.

One night, a sophomore named Sally fell asleep in the college library while studying for a history midterm. When she awoke sometime after one o'clock in the morning, she found herself alone in the dimly lit library.

It was too late to call for a fraternity escort, and she could not find any of the library's night custodians. Nervous but determined, Sally let herself out of the library and began the mile-long walk across the campus to her dorm. As she walked she prayed, "Lord, send your angels to protect me." Sally repeated this prayer over and over, and she began to feel less afraid.

The shortest route led down a narrow, tree-lined path. The path was dark, but Sally knew that if she hurried, she would be at the dorm in less than ten minutes. She quickened her pace; by the time she saw the residence hall, she was almost running. Just as she reached the steps, she heard terrible screams coming from the path. Sally ran into the dorm lobby and called 911.

Minutes later the police arrived. They searched the path Sally had taken and found the mutilated body of a young woman. Soon afterward they discovered the killer cowering in the woods nearby.

At the stationhouse, the cops asked the killer why he had attacked the other woman instead of Sally.

"I wanted to," said the murderer, "but she wasn't alone. There were these two huge guys walking on either side of her."

"What huge guys?" one of the cops said. She said she walked home alone.

"I'm telling you there were two guys with her," the killer said. "And they must have come from the same costume party because they were both dressed up like angels."

Dorm Room Décor

Editors at *New Jersey Monthly* decided to run a lengthy feature on students at Rutgers University in New Brunswick. A small battalion of reporters and photographers descended on the university to cover student activities on and off campus, academics, fashion, drinking, sex, and finally, a photo spread entitled, "How to Decorate Your Dorm Room."

In many respects, the photo essay seemed like the most innocuous part of the feature. The spread included photos of two guys who bragged about not having spent a dime to decorate their dorm room. Once the spread was published, it garnered a lot more attention than anyone ever expected.

A pawnbroker in Camden wrote Rutgers' president to say the sign hanging over the bed of one of the students had been stolen from outside his shop six months ago. He wanted it back, or he wanted $1,200 to purchase a new one.

A representative of The Circle Line, a company that operates cruises around the island of Manhattan, wrote the college to say

one of the company's life preservers was hanging on the dorm room wall. Since the life preserver was stenciled, "Peter Stuyvesant—The Circle Line," it would not be hard for the company to prove its case in court. The company demanded return of its property or a payment of $350.

Attorneys for Johnson & Johnson wanted the company banner off one of the students' bed and back on the flagpole outside corporate headquarters. A local steakhouse was glad to see its missing life-size gold-painted plastic steer was being well cared for in the dorm room, but wanted it back on the roof of the restaurant.

By the time the guys returned everything they had "borrowed," their dorm room was stripped down to two twin beds, two desks and a single Kid Rock poster.

"Every Morning at Breakfast I Spread Contraceptive Jelly on My Toast"

and Other Legends of Lust

Every Morning at Breakfast I Spread Contraceptive Jelly on My Toast

After three weeks had passed and she still had not had her period, a young college student visited the campus health clinic.

"Young lady," the doctor said, "you're pregnant."

At first the woman was shocked. Then shock gave way to confusion—after all, she had been using contraceptive jelly. Finally, her confusion was replaced by outrage. Clearly the manufacturer of the contraceptive jelly was selling a defective product.

She hurried back to her dorm room, sat down at her desk and wrote this letter:

"Dear Sir,

"For the past six months, I have been using your contraceptive jelly faithfully. Yet, today I learned from the doctor at my college's health clinic that I am pregnant. Obviously your product does not work. I demand compensation from your company or I will contact every television, radio station and newspaper in the country to let them know that your product is defective."

A week later, the young woman received a call from a customer service representative at the pharmaceutical company.

"When I read your letter I was very distressed," the customer service rep said. "Can you tell me how long you have been using our product?"

"Six months," the college woman said.

"And the package you have has not reached the expiration date?"

"No," answered the pregnant woman. "The date on the package

says it won't expire for another 18 months."

"I see," said the customer rep. "And you are certain you use the jelly every day?"

"Of course!" the girl said. "I've been spreading it on my toast every morning since I got it."

Another Reason to be Afraid in Public Rest Rooms

A radical activist group broke away from the Zero Population Movement to start a new faction known as No More! The goal of No More! is to reduce the population explosion by any means necessary, including involuntary castration.

Posing as plumbers or cleaning crews, members of the splinter group infiltrated several corporate headquarters in Detroit. Once inside, the radicals installed a nasty device under the seats in men's room toilet stalls. Within seconds after the victim sits on the toilet, the mechanism releases a razor that swings forward and slices off the man's testicles.

Several dozen of the devices have been found and removed from the men's rooms in office buildings, but the panic among male employees has compelled companies in Detroit to install security guards in the men's rooms round-the-clock.

Origins: This legend seems to be a direct (and more gruesome) outgrowth of the late 1990's tale of poisonous tropical spiders lurking under toilet seats in airport rest rooms.

Just What the Doctor Ordered

A recent article in the *New England Journal of Medicine* reported that men can improve their health and extend their lives just by doing what comes naturally. According to Dr. Francis Cabot Lowell of Boston, ten minutes of ogling women's breasts delivers the same health benefits as thirty minutes of aerobic exercise.

"The purpose of aerobic exercise is to increase the circulation of the blood," Dr. Lowell said. "And nothing gets a man's blood pumping like contemplating a woman's breasts."

Clinical research conducted by Dr. Lowell and his colleagues has proved that men who spend ten minutes a day throwing appreciative glances at the female anatomy enjoy lower blood pressure and fewer instances of stroke and heart disease.

"Ogling has many advantages over aerobics," Dr. Lowell said. "You can do it anywhere. You don't need special clothes. And there is no monthly membership fee. Although afterwards you still may have to hit the showers."

Damning Evidence

A prospective bride did not want her husband-to-be to have a bachelor party. "You can't be trusted," she told him. "You'll be with all your stupid friends, you'll have too many drinks, and the next thing you know you'll be doing the horizontal mambo with the stripper."

The guy begged and pleaded with his fiancée to let him have a party. "I'll be good," he said. "I promise. Nothing will happen."

In the end, the woman relented. But at the party things went along exactly as the bride-to-be had predicted. The guest of honor had way too many drinks, and before the night was over he had sex with the stripper.

Later that night, the drunken groom stumbled into his apartment. He made his way to the bedroom where his fiancée was sitting up in bed waiting for him.

She took one look at him and said, "You bastard. I knew this would happen. I should call off the wedding."

"No, really, honey," the man said as he got undressed for bed. "Nothing happened. I got drunk, that's all. Really, I didn't cheat on you. Why won't you trust me?"

He answered his own question when he removed his boxers and they both saw a full condom hanging from his penis.

Framed!

A wife in Paris was emptying the pockets of her husband's clothes before taking them to the dry cleaner when she found a letter tucked into the inside pocket of his overcoat. The letter was written on expensive, well-made paper, the kind one uses for special correspondence. The woman read the letter and was shocked to discover that her husband was having a torrid love affair with another woman.

The wife was crushed, but she could think only of plotting revenge. Her husband's birthday was in three weeks, and she began planning a large, elaborate party. She invited their entire family, all their friends and neighbors, and her husband's most important business colleagues.

On the day of the party, the wife called all the guests together so they could see the special gift she had for her husband. The crowd buzzed with excitement and anticipation. As the husband opened the box, the eager guests crowded around, each wanting to be the first to see the marvelous gift.

Inside the box, professionally mounted and framed, was the love letter from her husband's mistress.

"Fornicating Under Consent of the King"

The word "f——" is one of the few words to come into modern English intact from Old English. But it didn't begin as a word: It was originally an abbreviation.

Just 1500 years ago in England, the king's power was absolute. Anyone who wished to start a business applied to him for permission. Likewise, any two people who wanted to marry asked for the king's blessing. And when a couple was ready to have children, they asked the king for his consent.

If the king agreed, the happy couple received a license that they were to post on the door of their house. The license read: "Fornicating Under Consent of the King." Eventually this was abbreviated.

What a Burn!

A car dealer in Columbus, Ohio, started cheating on his wife with a new saleswoman at the dealership. The lady's tastes ran to the dangerous, and one afternoon she persuaded the man to make love to her in his own home, in the bed he shared with his wife.

Once they were undressed, the woman dug around in her bag and pulled out some silk ropes. She had just finished tying the cheating husband to the bed when they heard the front door open. The mistress grabbed her clothes and ran. But the husband, tied as he was to the bed, couldn't move. A moment later, his wife walked

into the bedroom.

The betrayed woman didn't say a word. Instead, she went into the bathroom. Several minutes later she emerged with a hot curling iron in her hand.

Later that afternoon a team of paramedics were called to the house.

"I came home a while ago and found my husband in bed with his girlfriend," said the wife to the paramedic. "Apparently she is a little kinky because my husband has some serious burns around his rectum."

The husband never contradicted his wife's story.

Origins: This story of the wife's revenge first cropped up in the early 1990s in Columbus, Ohio, but its roots are much older. In Geoffrey Chaucer's "The Miller's Tale," a philanderer is punished by having his butt burned with a red-hot poker. And there is a centuries-old rumor that in 1327 Queen Isabella of England had her gay husband, King Edward II, slowly put to death by having hot irons shoved repeatedly up his anus.

Short Takes 10

• Humans and dolphins are the only mammals that have sex purely for pleasure.

• The month with the highest number of conceptions is December.

• Not long after the 2001 winner of the Miss France contest had been crowned, the judges were stunned to discover that the beauty queen had been born a man.

• Aspirin dissolved in Coca-Cola is an aphrodisiac.

• The cover of *Playboy* always bears a certain number of stars: It is code for how many times *Playboy*'s publisher, Hugh Hefner, slept with that month's Playmate.

• The sexually voracious silent-movie star, Clara Bow, once invited the entire University of Southern California football team to her house for an orgy during which she serviced them all.

• Elton John collapsed at a Hollywood party and was rushed to a hospital emergency room. The medical team pumped the singer's stomach and removed a pint of semen.

• Rod Stewart collapsed at a Hollywood party and was rushed to a hospital emergency room. The medical team pumped the singer's stomach and removed several pints of semen.

THE SURPRISE URINE TEST
AND OTHER JOB-RELATED ODDITIES

The Surprise Urine Test

A 19-year-old machinist landed a job at a large auto manufacturer. The day he accepted the offer, the shop manager warned him, "Stay clean, kid, because the company does random, unannounced drug testing."

The new kid wasn't too worried because he was only an occasional user.

Five weeks after the machinist was hired, the shop manager tapped the kid on the shoulder and said, "There's a drug test today and your number came up. You need to report to the nurse's office for a urine test."

Immediately, the kid broke out in a sweat. The night before he had smoked marijuana with his friends. He was sure he would fail the urinalysis and lose his job.

By the time he reached the nurse's office, the kid was on the verge of panic. The nurse didn't seem to notice. She handed him a plastic cup, pointed to a door and said, "You can fill it up in there."

Inside the tiny examination room the kid thought he might as well just quit and save himself the embarrassment of being fired. Then he noticed several little plastic cups, just like his, all containing yellow liquid. He lifted the lid of one of them and took a whiff: It was definitely urine.

And it was worth a gamble.

He poured some of the urine into his specimen cup, waited a few minutes and then took the cup to the nurse.

The next morning the shop foreman met the kid in the parking lot. "The results of urine test came in last night," the foreman said.

"You were clean."

"That's great," the kid said.

"And there's something else you might not think is great," the foreman said. "You're pregnant."

Milk Doesn't Count

Father Huber, a Catholic priest, was named bishop of a Midwestern diocese. After the consecration ceremony, the new bishop, his family, friends, and a small army of clergy repaired to a fine restaurant for a reception.

After dinner, the new bishop's mother walked to the podium and told the assembled guests a story about her son.

"When my baby was just two days old he had a terrible seizure. We had not taken him to church yet to be christened, and I was afraid he would die any moment. So I took the baby bottle, poured the milk over his forehead, and performed an emergency baptism. The seizure passed, and my baby grew up to be the strong healthy man you see today."

The lay people in the audience were delighted by the story. To the sound of warm applause, the mother returned to her seat. But the priests and bishops in the hall—especially Bishop Huber—seemed uneasy. As the woman sat down, a monsignor seated beside her leaned over and said, "What a charming story, Mrs. Huber.

By the way, did you ever take your son to church for a formal christening?"

"Oh no, Monsignor," the woman said. "I know my catechism. I had baptized my boy, and baptism cannot be repeated."

"You're absolutely right," the monsignor said. But he still looked nervous—and the monsignor and every cleric in the room had every reason to be upset. By Church law baptism, even an emergency baptism, must be performed with water. No other liquid counts. So the monsignor rose from his chair, walked over to the new bishop and whispered in his ear, "We can set this right after the reception. We'll wait until everyone has gone home."

At the end of the evening, after everyone had left the hall, the monsignor drove Bishop Huber back to the cathedral. Inside the church all the priests and bishops from the reception were waiting. First they baptized the bishop, then they ordained him a priest, and finally they consecrated him a bishop. And this time, all the ceremonies were official.

The Auto Industry vs. the Computer Industry

In an offhand remark at a computer trade show in Detroit, Bill Gates said, "If auto makers had pursued new technologies as aggressively as the computer industry has, we would all be driving twenty-five dollar cars that get a thousand miles to the gallon."

A few days later, in response to Gate's comment, General Motors issued this press release:

"If the auto industry had taken the computer industry as its model, we would all be driving cars with the following characteristics:

1. For no reason whatsoever your car would crash twice a day.

2. If you tried to execute a maneuver your car didn't like, it would shut down and refuse to restart until you reinstalled the engine.

3. Only one person at a time could use the car unless you bought "CarNT."

4. Macintosh would make a car that was powered by the sun, was reliable, five times as fast, and twice as easy to drive—but it would only run on 5 percent of the roads.

5. The airbag system would ask, "Are you sure?" before deploying.

6. Occasionally, for no apparent reason, your car would lock you out and refuse to let you in until you simultaneously lifted the door handle, turned the key and grabbed hold of the antenna.

7. GM would require all car buyers to also purchase a deluxe set of Rand McNally road maps (now a GM subsidiary), even

though drivers neither needed nor wanted them. Any attempt on the driver's part to delete this option would immediately cause the car's performance to diminish by 50 percent or more. Moreover, GM would become a target for investigation by the Justice Department.

8. Every time GM introduced a new model, car buyers would have to learn to drive all over again because none of the controls would operate in the same manner as the old car.

9. You'd have to press the "start" button to turn off the engine.

Better Than FedEx

Many Filipino women leave their homes to take well-paying jobs as "amahs," that is, housekeepers, cooks and nannies in Hong Kong. Every payday, these women throng the markets and stores of the city shopping for clothes, small appliances and toys to send home to their families in the Philippines. The cost of mailing these packages—some of which can be very large—is expensive, so the ladies are always on the watch for someone returning to the islands who can carry the packages home for them.

One day a prominent Filipino businessman in Hong Kong died. The parish priest was touched by the large number of amahs who came to the wake. The priest took it as a demonstration of national solidarity.

After the funeral, the casket was shipped to the Philippines so the businessman could be buried in his family's vault. When the coffin arrived, the family lifted the lid so they could see their relative one last time. There he lay on satin pillows, wearing a handsome

dark suit and surrounded by pairs of Nike sneakers, bundles of padded bras and electric toaster ovens, each carefully labeled with the name and the address of the could-be recipient.

Sharing the Wealth

If an animal contracts hoof-and-mouth disease, it must be destroyed and the carcass burned to prevent the disease from spreading. When the disease broke out among cattle in Britain, dozens of farmers were suddenly in danger of financial ruin. To prevent an epidemic of bankruptcies in the agricultural community, the British government awarded a hefty compensation to the farmers whose livestock had become infected.

The compensation was so generous that some farmers regretted that their herds were healthy. The farmers with stricken animals came up with an imaginative solution that allowed their fellow herdsmen to share in the wealth. After the sick cattle were slaughtered, the farmers cut out the animals' tongues and sold them to farmers with healthy herds. These farmers could infect their herd by rubbing the cattle's mouths with the contaminated tongues. Once their herd had contracted hoof-and-mouth disease, the farmers could file a claim with the government and receive compensation for their losses.

It Loses Something in Translation

The Sumitomo Corporation of Japan developed an extremely strong, rust-resistant steel pipe. The company executives felt certain it was ideal for bathroom plumbing and hired a Tokyo advertising agency to market the pipe in the United States.

The agency suggested the company give their pipe a name that would inspire confidence. The name they suggested was "Sumitomo: Highest Integrity and Toughness." And since Americans like to use abbreviations, the agency assured the Sumitomo executives that they would promote their pipe in the United States using the acronym.

Within weeks the first full-page ads appeared in American interior design magazines. One headline asked, "Do you have S—— in your bathroom?" Another announced: "Japan is proud to send S—— to America." A third urged consumers: "Trust Sumitomo. We produce S—— everyday."

The Death of George Turklebaum

For over 30 years George Turklebaum worked at a large New York corporation. He was always the first one in the office each morning and the last one to leave each night. He never went to lunch with co-workers, visited them in their offices or chatted with them around the water cooler. The only contact his colleagues had with him was saying, "Morning, George," and "Night, George," as they passed his office door each day.

One morning the entire staff found a memo waiting for them from the CEO of the firm. It read: "I regret to inform you that George Turklebaum has died. Last night a member of the office cleaning crew found George slumped over his desk. The coroner's report says that at the time he was discovered, George had been dead for five days."

The Deadly Traffic Circle

In the 1930s, as the automobile became increasingly popular in California, the Department of Transportation hired engineers to improve the condition of the roads, especially at heavily trafficked intersections.

In Long Beach, the busiest and most dangerous intersection was where the Pacific Coast Highway crossed Lakewood Boulevard and Los Coyotes diagonally. The planners recommended a staggered system of traffic lights to control the flow of cars, but the

chief engineer disagreed. He felt the lights would be too slow and would only frustrate drivers. Against the advice of the planners, the engineer insisted that a simple traffic circle would solve the problem. And since he was in charge of the project, his will was law. When the traffic circle was completed, it created such a confused, even terrifying, traffic pattern that the planners made one last appeal to the chief engineer to scrap the project and install traffic lights instead.

The engineer lost his temper. "You're a bunch of idiots!" he screamed. "I'll show you how easy it is to drive around a circle."

He got into his car and drove to the circle where he waited patiently to merge into the dense traffic.

Brakes squealed and horns blared as the drivers tried to figure out how to get around the circle and back on the road they wanted. The driver of a large truck became especially frustrated as he waited for an opening in the traffic. At last he saw a small break in the crowd of cars and floored the accelerator and roared into traffic. Another car, whose driver also wanted to take advantage of the opening, pulled into the circle just in front of the truck. Before the trucker could react, his truck slammed into the car and smashed it against a concrete barrier.

The car was crushed, and the engineer who had designed the traffic circle was dead.

Short Takes 11

• If a baby is born in flight, it gets free air travel on that airline for the rest of its life.

• When read by Arab speakers right to left, the Coca-Cola logo expresses an anti-Islamic message, which explains why the beverage never caught on in the Muslim world.

• In the Middle Ages, the Pope forbade Catholics to eat meat on Fridays in hopes of stimulating the sagging fish industry.

• The Big Mac was originally sold in France under the name Gros Mec, an expression that means "big pimp" in French.

• If you want to rent a Ford Caliente in Mexico, ask for an S-22. Ford changed the model's name when the company learned that "caliente" is slang for "hooker" in Mexico.

• The Jotter, a pen made by Parker, became a favorite joke in Latin America where "jotter" is slang for "jockstrap".

• Colgate-Palmolive's marketing executives could not understand why the company's popular Cue toothpaste didn't sell in France—until they found out that Cue is the title of a notorious French pornographic magazine.

• Clairol renamed its Mist Stick curling iron for the German market when the company discovered that in German "mist" means "human waste."

• The name Air France always gets a laugh in Syria where "air" is slang for male genitals.

Bananas Can Eat Your Flesh!
Your Flesh!
and Other Gruesome Happenings

Bananas Can Eat Your Flesh!

The U.S. Centers for Disease Control and Prevention (CDC) issued a warning to the American public that bananas from Costa Rica are infected with bacteria that can cause necrotizing fasciitis, a recently discovered infection that eats human and animal flesh.

Scientists discovered the bacterial infection when they observed that monkeys in the jungles of Costa Rica were dying by the thousands. Research led the scientists to conclude that the bacteria that killed the monkeys came from fruit and was especially virulent in bananas—Costa Rica's main export.

The symptoms of necrotizing fasciitis appear within three days of eating a banana. The victim develops a painful skin rash and runs a high fever. The bacteria begin eating the victim's flesh at a rate of about one to two inches per hour. If a victim can't get to a hospital quickly, he should treat himself by burning his flesh just ahead of the bacteria. The burn will slow the infection down and give the victim more time to reach a medical facility. The only effective treatment for necrotizing fasciitis is amputation of the infected limb or body part.

Lethal Pay Phones

The gangs of Los Angeles have developed a new initiation rite for incoming members. The recruits visit as many pay phones as they can in a single night and brush a mixture of LSD and strychnine onto the buttons.

LSD, of course, is an illegal hallucinogenic narcotic, and strychnine is a deadly chemical used in rat poison. When combined, the LSD and strychnine form a lethal substance that is absorbed through the pores of human skin on contact, and then attacks the central nervous system, killing the victim within minutes.

On gang initiation nights, 911 operators are overwhelmed by calls from passersby who have found corpses in or near pay phones.

Shortly after the deadly initiation rite began, the Los Angeles Police Department urged the payphone-using public to wipe the buttons before placing a call.

Lethal ATM Envelopes

One Thursday evening a woman stopped by her bank's automated teller machine to make a deposit. She took a deposit envelope from the rack beside the machine, placed her check and deposit slip inside, licked the adhesive strip to seal the envelope and slid it into the ATM.

A short time later, the next ATM customer found the woman dead beside her car.

An autopsy revealed a lethal dose of cyanide in the woman's bloodstream and traces of the poison, mixed with a common adhesive used on envelopes, in the woman's mouth. After learning the autopsy results, the police returned to the bank where the woman had died and collected all the envelopes from the ATM.

Tests of the ATM envelopes found that of the 200 that had been collected by the police, six were contaminated with cyanide.

Police investigated every bank in town for more tainted envelopes, but none was found. They also staked out the ATM for months, but the killer never returned.

Lethal Shampoo

The American Cancer Society issued a warning that sodium laureth sulfate, or SLS, causes cancer. Though it was developed as an industrial cleanser for heavy machinery, the chemical is commonly used in shampoo because it forms a rich, thick, soapy foam when it comes in contact with water.

A representative of the Cancer Society contacted a vice president at one of the leading shampoo manufacturers about SLS. The executive admitted that his company used the chemical and that they knew it was dangerous, but claimed that there wasn't a cheaper or foamier alternative.

Researchers at the American Cancer Society recently discovered that SLS is also used in toothpaste.

The Dangers of Waterproof Sunscreen

On a hot Saturday morning in July, a New Jersey family drove to the shore. The mother gave her three children waterproof sunscreen and told them to rub it all over their bodies.

The youngest, a 4-year-old boy, accidentally rubbed some of the cream into his eyes. The boy complained that his eyes burned, and he began to cry. His mother tried to flush his eyes out with bottled water, but it had no effect. The sunscreen was waterproof!

She held her son and hoped his salt tears would wash out the cream, but the little boy became more and more hysterical.

Desperate, she pulled out her cell phone and called 911. When she explained to the operator that the child had sunscreen in his eyes, the operator urged the mother to go to a hospital emergency room immediately.

The family left their belongings on the beach and raced to the emergency room. By the time they arrived, the little boy was screaming in agony.

An ER doctor gave the child a sedative, and then an entire team of doctors and nurses tried one solvent after another to flush out the sunscreen, but nothing worked.

In the end, they had to tell the unfortunate parents that their child was permanently blind.

How to Get Rid of a Tapeworm

A young woman returned from a trip to Southeast Asia to find that while overseas she had contracted a tapeworm. She was allergic to all the medications her doctor prescribed, and out of desperation turned to an old remedy suggested by a friend.

"This is disgusting," the woman's friend said, "but my grandmother swears that it works. For three days, don't eat anything and drink only water. At the end of the third day, fill a large bowl full of sour milk, and hold it up to your mouth. The tapeworm will be starving by this point, and the smell of the sour milk will draw it out."

The sick woman did exactly as her friend suggested. For three

days, she lived on nothing but plain water. At the end of the third day, she sat down at her kitchen table with a huge bowl of sour milk. She bent low over the bowl and opened her mouth as wide as she could. She inhaled deeply through her mouth, hoping the fumes from the rancid milk would make their way down her throat to her stomach.

For the first couple of minutes, nothing happened. Then she felt a queer stirring in her stomach. Slowly she could feel something creeping up her esophagus. She wanted to gag, but she resisted the urge. Then she felt the worm at the back of her throat, crawling over her tongue. It was the most disgusting thing the woman had ever experienced, but she braced herself.

The slimy creature then brushed against the teeth of her lower jaw. When the tapeworm poked its head out of the woman's mouth, she grabbed it, yanked the worm from her body, and threw it across the room. A tapeworm, five feet long, struck the kitchen wall and fell dead to the floor.

Origins: This Old World remedy for getting rid of a tapeworm has been around for centuries, but has no factual basis. The roundworm, however, is another story. If the roundworm is starved, it will crawl out of the stomach and into the host's esophagus, at which point the gag reflex will cause the victim to vomit up the worm.

The Finicky Restaurant Patron

A woman stopped at a steak restaurant with her husband. She ordered a sirloin and told the waiter emphatically, "I want the steak well done. I don't want to see any trace of pink in the meat."

When the waiter brought the couple their meals, the woman asked him to wait while she inspected the steak. She sliced off a piece of meat and saw a small patch of pink in the center.

"Please take it back and tell the chef to cook it well done," said the woman.

The waiter apologized, took up the plate and headed for the kitchen. He returned a few minutes later with the steak. The surface of the meat was deeply charred, but again the woman asked him to wait while she inspected her meal.

She sliced off a bit of the darkened meat and put it in her mouth. She swallowed, then sighed heavily. "This is still too rare. Please tell the chef to leave it on the grill until the juice is completely cooked out."

Again, the waiter apologized and carried the woman's meal back to the kitchen. Ten minutes later he returned. The steak was black—absolutely carbonized. Yet again the woman made the poor man stand by as she tested her food. She cut off a small piece, chewed and swallowed and then threw her silverware on the table. "This is hopeless! Wrap it up and I'll take it to my dog."

That night the woman began to feel ill. The next day she had severe stomach cramps and was vomiting. She went to her doctor, who ran tests, including a blood analysis. The next day he called the

woman with the results. "I'm sorry to tell you that you have a rare and virulent strain of venereal disease. You should get in touch with all of your sexual partners of the last couple of weeks so they can be tested."

"That's absurd," the woman said. "I haven't slept with anyone but my husband in ten years."

"Well, I can't imagine how you could have been infected then," said the doctor. "The disease is only transmitted through body fluids."

The woman was silent for a moment. "Maybe you can't imagine it, but I can. If I bring something over for analysis, could I get the results tomorrow?"

"Yes, of course," the doctor said, somewhat puzzled.

The woman hung up the phone, took the leftover steak from her refrigerator and drove to the doctor's office.

The next day he called with the test results. "We found five different kinds of human saliva on the meat," the doctor said. "One of them is infected with venereal disease."

The woman sued the kitchen staff, her waiter and the restaurant for contaminating her food. A jury awarded her $2.5 million in damages.

Variation: In a raunchier version, members of the restaurant staff masturbate on the woman's steak.

Meat Is Meat

During World War I, millions of young Australian men answered the call and joined the Allies in the fight against Germany. Of course all those hungry soldiers had to be fed, so Australia's canned-goods manufacturers felt enormous pressure to produce record quantities of canned meats, fruits and vegetables. The factories went on 24-hour shifts and stopped production for nothing.

One day in 1917, a worker at the Fray Bentos meat-canning plant fell into the chopping machine. The poor man was cut to bits, and his diced body parts carried by conveyor belt into the immense processing tank. The cannery's management was notified of the tragedy at once. There wasn't much debate among the managers as to what they should do. They decided meat was meat, and a little human flesh wouldn't hurt anyone.

A month later the canned meat, some of it containing bits of the unlucky factory worker, arrived at the front. If there were any complaints from the troops, the Australian manufacturer never heard them.

The Rat and the Ring

On a hot summer day in Houston, a woman stopped to buy an ice cream. As she walked along, the heat melted the ice cream faster than she could eat it. In a matter of minutes, her hand was covered with melted chocolate-chip mint. Disgusted with the mess, she threw the cone into a garbage can, and fished a tissue from her purse. As she wiped her hand, her wedding ring slipped off her finger, fell into the gutter and rolled through a sewer grate.

On her hands and knees in the gutter, the woman watched as a large rat sniffed the ice-cream-covered ring and then carried it off into the sewer.

The woman was heartbroken, of course. Her husband bought her another wedding band, identical to the one she had lost. He even had the inside of the ring engraved with their wedding date, just like the original. The woman wore the replacement, but she mourned the loss of the original.

A few months later the woman ordered lunch at a fast-food restaurant. She chose a corner table and sat down to eat. As she bit into a piece of breast meat, her teeth struck something hard. The woman covered her mouth with her napkin, removed the meat, and set it on her plate to see what the hard object could be.

Something glittered in the half-chewed, white meat of the chicken breast. The woman dug it out and held it up to the light. It was her lost wedding ring.

Short Takes 12

• Italians were unwilling to give up the lire for the euro because unnamed sources revealed the new currency was radioactive.

• In Britain, shoppers who bought pirated DVDs of first-run movies got a nasty surprise when they got the bootleg copies home. The DVD played the movie beautifully the first time, but with each subsequent viewing the picture faded more and more until by the fifth playing the screen was completely blank.

• Pot scrubbers manufactured by Proctor & Gamble contain a soapy product that is actually made from Agent Orange, the deadly chemical the U.S. military dropped on the Viet Cong during the Vietnam War.

• Mountain Dew is bad for teenage boys: It shrinks the penis.

• Mountain Dew is bad for teenage boys: It makes the testicles shrivel up.

• Don't eat shrimp the same day you take a Vitamin C tablet! The iodine in the shrimp combines with the Vitamin C to produce arsenic.

• Don't cook with canola oil! It may be low in saturated fats, but it is derived from rapeseed oil, which is used to grease heavy machinery and is extremely poisonous to humans.

• Don't pump your own gas in Florida! Someone is embedding AIDS-infected needles in the handles of gas pumps at self-service stations throughout the Sunshine State.

In New Orleans It Is Illegal to Tie an Alligator to a Fire Hydrant and Leave It Unattended

and Other Criminal Mischief

Weird Laws

State and local law books are filled with ordinances that are outdated, quaint or just plain weird. Some examples. . .

• Alabamans may not drive any vehicle while blindfolded.

• In Alaska, one may not awaken a sleeping bear in order to take its picture.

• It's illegal to hunt camels in Arizona.

• It's legal for a man to beat his wife in Arkansas, but only once a month.

• Animals risk jail time in California if they mate within 1,500 feet of a school or a house of worship.

• It's illegal for dandelions to grow within the city limits of Pueblo, Colorado.

• In Connecticut, a husband and wife must live together or face imprisonment.

• In Florida, if an elephant is left tied to a parking meter, the parking fee has to be paid just as it would for a vehicle.

- A chicken may not cross the road in Quitman, Georgia.

- Chicagoans may not take a French poodle to the opera.

- By law, Kansans may not shoot jackrabbits from a motorboat.

- In New Orleans, Louisiana, it is illegal to tie an alligator to a fire hydrant and leave it unattended.

- Maryland bans mistreatment of oysters.

- Detroit residents can make love in their cars, but only if the vehicle is parked on their own property.

- A Minnesota man who has eaten onions, garlic or sardines is required by law to brush his teeth before making love to his wife.

- Nebraska outlaws sleeping in the nude, even if the couple is married.

- Pickles that have gone bad may not be tossed into the street in New Jersey.

- In New York, the penalty for jumping off a building is death.

- Massage parlors are banned in Hornytown, North Carolina.

• In North Dakota, it is illegal to lie down and fall asleep with your shoes on.

• Ohio forbids its citizens to fish for whales on Sunday.

• Pennsylvania, in an effort to stamp out brothels, made it illegal for five unrelated women to live in the same house together. As a result, both sorority houses and convents are illegal in the state.

• Tennesseeans may not use a lasso to catch fish.

• Texans may not shoot a buffalo from the second-story window of a hotel.

• On Utah highways, birds have the right of way.

• Men in Lebanon, Virginia, may not kick their wives out of bed.

• In West Virginia, it is illegal for a member of the clergy to tell jokes from the pulpit during a church service.

• Wyoming outlaws men and women from making love standing up in a walk-in meat freezer.

The Missing Gonads

On a business trip to Atlanta, an executive met an exotic, beautiful woman in a hotel bar. She had thick, lustrous black hair, dark eyes and a beautiful bronze complexion. After a couple of drinks, the woman leaned over and whispered into the man's ear, "Why don't we go up to your room?"

Although the executive was married, this opportunity was too good to pass up. He signed for the bar tab and led the woman to his room.

She was a skillful lover, and after two or three hours, the exhausted man fell into a deep sleep. He awoke several hours later to the sensation of a terrible pain in his groin. He turned on the bedside light and threw back the covers. What he saw made him scream in terror. His legs and scrotum were encrusted with dried blood, and his testicles were gone.

At the hospital, two Atlanta police detectives explained to the man that he had fallen victim to a ring of gypsy testicle smugglers. Gypsy women were known to seduce American men, drug their drinks, and once the men had passed out, castrate their victims. The reason? In China, American testicles are regarded as a powerful aphrodisiac: Chinese men will pay thousands of dollars for just one.

Variations: This is a new spin on two older stories: the seductress who steals a man's kidneys, and the AIDS-infected woman who gets her revenge by seducing strangers and leaving a message scrawled on their bathroom mirror that reads, "Welcome to the wonderful world of AIDS!"

No Time for Burglars

Late one night a man heard strange sounds coming from his garage. He went to a window and saw two men with crowbars prying open the garage's locked side door. He called the police.

The dispatch officer asked him, "What do you have in the garage?"

"My car and my power tools," the man answered.

"This doesn't sound too urgent, and we don't have the manpower to send anyone over right now. We'll send someone as soon as we can."

"Fine. If you're too busy, I'll get my shotgun and shoot the burglars myself," the man said and slammed down the phone.

He turned on all the outside lights, which startled the burglars. They ran off before they could break into the garage.

A minute or two later three squad cars roared into the driveway. Six police officers ran into the garage, where they found the homeowner alone.

One of the cops said, "I thought you had shot two burglars."

The man answered, "I thought you didn't have any men available to come out here."

Variation: This story is also popular in England where the burglars break into a potting shed rather than a garage.

The Foiled Kidnapping

A mother took her 4-year-old daughter, Katie, with her to a discount warehouse supermarket. The woman held the little girl's hand firmly as they made their way through the crowded store, but in the meat department she let go so she could examine some of the cuts of beef. A few minutes later, after she had made her selection, the mother reached for her daughter's hand. The little girl was gone.

At first she walked up and down the aisles searching for the child. Then, still maintaining her composure, she began asking other shoppers if they had seen a 4-year-old girl. None of them had. Finally the distraught mother raced frantically around the store calling her baby's name, "Katie! Katie!"

Several store employees, including the manager, hurried over to find out what was wrong. "My little girl's disappeared!" the mother cried.

The manager ordered all of the exit doors closed and locked, had an employee call 911, and then announced over the loudspeaker system that a child was missing and no one would be permitted to leave the store until the police arrived.

Within minutes, three police cars pulled up in front of the building. Assisted by the store's employees, the police officers began a systematic search. After half an hour, they found the little girl in the ladies' room. She was unharmed, but her hair had been cut short and she had been undressed down to her underwear. Lying on the floor next to her was a shopping bag that contained a wig and a change of clothes to disguise the child's appearance. The kidnapper

had disappeared into the crowd of shoppers when she realized the police were on their way.

Since that day, a sign has been posted at the main entrance of every store: "Please keep your children with you at all times while shopping in our store."

Variations: In another version of this story, the missing child is a little boy lost in a Toys R Us. When he is found, his hair has been cut and his shirt has been removed. Yet another rendition of this legend takes place in a department store, but this time when the child is discovered in the ladies' room, the two women who attempted to kidnap the little girl are caught in the act of cutting her hair and changing her clothes.

The Missing Car Keys

Late one Saturday night a young woman and her boyfriend were on their way home from a date when the boy's car ran out of gas on a dark, country road.

"There was a farmhouse about two miles back," the boy said. "I'll walk to it and get help. Just stay here and keep the doors locked. You'll be okay."

The girl was afraid to be left alone on a deserted road late at night, but she agreed to do as her boyfriend said and locked the doors as soon as he got out of the car.

After thirty minutes, the boy had not returned, and the girl began to worry. Another half hour went by, and still there was no

sign of her boyfriend. The girl considered walking to the farmhouse in search of him, but the thought of being alone in the dark terrified her. She checked the locks on all four doors then scrunched down in the seat and waited.

Suddenly she heard a bump against the car. She sat up and saw a man staring in the window at her. He slowly raised his right hand and pressed a large object against the glass. It was the boyfriend's head, an expression of shock and pain frozen on his face. The girl screamed and frantically hit all the locks with the palm of her hands to make certain the madman could not get in.

Then, slowly, the killer raised his left hand and swung something before the frightened girl's eyes: It was her boyfriend's car keys.

Variations: There are many versions of the young couple and the broken-down car. In one, the boyfriend leaves to find help, and sometime later the girl hears scratching sounds on the roof of the car. In panic, she drives away to escape whatever is on the roof. As she pulls away, in the rear view mirror she sees her boyfriend hanging from a tree branch. The scratching sounds were his shoes scraping the top of the car, and by pulling away the girl hanged her own boyfriend. In another version the girl falls asleep in the car. When she awakens in the morning she finds her boyfriend's head impaled on the antenna.

The Knife in the Briefcase

A woman vacationing in Southampton on Long Island was driving to see her parents at their summerhouse on Shelter Island. As she drove to the ferry, she noticed that she was nearly out of gas. The woman pulled into a gas station and told the attendant, "Fill her up. I have to catch the next ferry to Shelter Island, so please hurry."

Meanwhile, a well-dressed, young man carrying a briefcase approached the woman. "I'm sorry to trouble you," he said, "but my car broke down and I couldn't help overhearing that you are going to Shelter Island. Would you mind giving me a lift? I have an important appointment there."

The woman agreed, and the stranger put his briefcase on the backseat, saying, "I'll just tell the repairman that I'll come back for my car in the morning."

As the young man walked toward the garage, the woman called out, "Hurry! The ferry leaves in ten minutes."

While the stranger was in the garage, the woman paid for the gas, started the engine and waited impatiently for him to return. After five minutes, he still had not returned. Afraid that she would miss the ferry and have to wait an hour and a half for the next one, she drove away.

The woman caught the boat and arrived at her parents' summerhouse on time. Later that day she remembered the stranger's briefcase. She went to the car and opened the case to look for some identification so she could return it to the man. Inside she found a roll of duct tape, several lengths of heavy rope and a large butcher knife.

Variation: In another version, the woman returns to her car in a shopping mall parking lot and finds that she has a flat tire. The stranger with the briefcase offers to help her change the tire. When the woman arrives home, she finds the duct tape, the rope, the butcher knife, and an icepick that the stranger used to puncture her tire.

Origins: The earliest printed version of this legend has a gentleman in a rig stop to give a lone woman a ride. Once the trucker notices the "woman's" hairy forearms, the hitchhiker runs off, leaving behind an overnight bag. Inside, the gentleman finds a pair of loaded pistols.

Up in Smoke

A man in Charlotte, North Carolina, managed to get hold of two-dozen extremely rare, pre-Castro Cuban cigars. He wanted to smoke the cigars, but if he did he would essentially be burning the tens of thousands of dollars he had paid for them. Finally it occurred to him how he could smoke the cigars but not lose the money.

The cigar aficionado called insurance companies until he found one that agreed to insure his collection of fine cigars—against fire. After he had signed the insurance documents, but before he had paid the first premium, the aficionado began smoking the cigars. When they were gone, he filed a claim with the insurance company that the cigars had been destroyed in what he described as "a succession of small fires."

The insurance company sued the man for fraud, but was surprised in court when the judge said the insurance company

was obligated to honor the claim because it had agreed to insure the cigars against fire without going into the specifics of what the company would consider an acceptable fire or an unacceptable fire.

But the story doesn't end there. After paying the settlement, the insurance company had the man arrested for 24 counts of arson. Since the man could not deny that he had personally "set" all 24 fires, he was found guilty and sentenced to 24 months in prison.

No Body? No Problem

A man was charged with murdering his wife. Although many witnesses came forward to testify that the man had often threatened to kill the woman, no one had actually seen him do it. The trial was complicated by the fact that the missing wife's body had not been found.

In the final summation, the accused killer's defense attorney stood before the jury and argued that the evidence against his client was flimsy at best. "We don't know that this woman is dead. She may have simply left her husband. For all we know, she might walk into this courtroom in the next moment!"

The attorney was such an eloquent speaker, and the idea that the accused man's wife was about to make a dramatic entrance into the courtroom was so compelling, that the judge, the jury, the bailiffs and all the spectators turned to stare at the courtroom doors to see if the missing woman would indeed appear.

It was a brilliant ploy and would probably save the accused man from life in prison.

Next, it was the prosecutor's turn to speak. He walked slowly to the jury box. "Ladies and gentlemen," he said, "the defense's argument was the finest I have heard in all my years of practicing law. He suggested to us that the missing woman might at the very next moment walk into this courtroom. And the power of this suggestion was so strong that every one of us turned toward the door. All of us that is, except one man. The defendant did not look toward the courtroom door. Why should he? He knew his wife would not step across that threshold because she is dead. And he killed her!"

Short Takes 13

• Veterinarians use Progesterex to sterilize large animals such as horses. Recently, it has become known as the "date-rape drug" because guys slip it into a woman's drink. The victim passes out, and the guy has his way with her. As if date rape weren't enough, the drug also causes sterility in women.

• In the United States, state and federal authorities get only one shot at executing a prisoner. If the hangman's rope snaps or the electric chair malfunctions, the prisoner's life must be spared.

• By federal law, U.S. citizens are prohibited from having any contact with extraterrestrials.

• A prank caller caused mayhem at McDonald's restaurants across the upper Midwest. In Milwaukee, Minneapolis, Bismarck and Billings, the caller got the restaurant manager on the phone, told her he was a police officer and that one of her male employees was a thief. The caller then convinced the manager to perform a strip search on the hapless employee.

• It is impossible for hijackers or terrorists to reach the cockpit on an El Al jet, the national airline of Israel. To reach the pilot's cabin one has to pass through a set of double doors separated by a tiny chamber. If anyone who does not have the proper access code manages to get through the first door and into the entrance chamber, the pilot can seal the chamber and release a poison gas that kills the intruder in seconds.

INDEX